TUSKS

BY

GENE HALE

Order this book online at www.trafford.com
or email orders@trafford.com

Most Trafford titles are also available at major online book retailers.

Printed in the United States of America.

ISBN: 978-1-4669-6814-1 (sc)
ISBN: 978-1-4669-6815-8 (e)

Library of Congress Control Number: 2012921271

Trafford rev. 12/03/2012

www.trafford.com

North America & international
toll-free: 1 888 232 4444 (USA & Canada)
phone: 250 383 6864 • fax: 812 355 4082

Chapter One

A cloud of dust twisted wildly through the wind as a black and white jeep came barreling down the road. The brutal African sun bore down on the two occupants as their laughter rang out above the vehicle's noisy engine. Winston, the driver, was a gaunt Englishman with a sharp, craggy face and piercing blue eyes. Named after his mother's favorite statesman, he bore no resemblance to his famous namesake. Thinning sandy hair flopped over his freckled face as he crinkled his pale blue eyes against the sun's glare. His companion, a tall muscular Black man by the name of Maso, jostled against him as the jeep swerved and bumped along the rocky road. Winston, the big game hunter and Maso, his African guide, were headed for Gabon in search of elephants.

A former French colony, Gabon is located on the Equator, in central Africa. Sharing borders with Equatorial Guinea, Cameroon, Republic of Congo and the Gulf of Guinea, it is one of the most prosperous countries in the region, with an extensive system of rain forests covering 85% of the country.

As they approached the Gabonese border, Winston patted his top pocket and checked to make sure his passport was still there.

"How many more times are you going to check that?" asked Maso.

Winston laughed nervously. "Nervous habit, I'm afraid, just making sure." And he patted his pocket once more.

Maso laughed to himself, and then turned to survey the passing landscape.

"I say, old chap," Winston continued in his clipped English accent, "I do hope they let us through."

"Well, *old chap,* replied Maso, mimicking Winston's upper class accent, "I'm Gabonese, so I'll have no problem; they'll definitely let me through." He smiled brightly, revealing perfect white teeth. "Not so sure about your lily white English ass, though," he added with a wink.

"Money talks," replied Winston. "At least it did in Equatorial Guinea. I've never known such a corrupt bunch of criminals in all my life!" The two men had spent the last couple of weeks in that country and had found that bribery and corruption were a way of life.

"Everyone's on the take there, from the top down, including the police, government officials, customs and immigration, you name it," said Winston. "They would have kept my passport if I hadn't handed over a couple of hundred dollars."

Maso nodded. "You got that right, man."

"And that president, Obiang, is the worst of all," said Winston. "I'm glad to be leaving there."

"Me too," replied Maso. "Glad to be going home to Gabon."

"Well, it's probably just the same in Gabon. I'll just grease their palms and we'll be on our way," chuckled Winston. He slowed the jeep briefly and placed two one-hundred dollar bills between the pages of his passport. "There, that should do it."

Now at the border crossing in Mongamo, Winston slowed to a stop and took a deep breath.

"Here goes," he whispered to Maso.

Two armed guards in full uniform stood on either side of the jeep and glared at the two passengers. "Passports!" demanded the taller of the two guards, whose face sported a large jagged scar running from brow to chin.

Maso passed over his first. The guard gave it a cursory glance, then returned it to Maso without a word.

"Yours," sneered the other guard, pointing at Winston, his dark face mean and angry.

Winston smiled nervously and tried to make conversation. "Certainly, old chap," he said, handing over his British passport. "Nice day, isn't it?"

The guard ignored him and snatched the passport from his hand. Winston held his breath. *Would they accept the bribe or would they arrest him and throw him in jail for attempting to bribe an officer in the employ of the Gabonese government.*

The smaller guard studied the passport for several minutes, then stared at Winston long and hard.

"Another two hundred dollars for my friend here," he said, holding out his sweaty hand.

Winston gulped and searched his inside pocket. Pulling out two additional crisp one-hundred dollar bills, he passed them to the surly guard. "There you go, old chap. Happy hunting!"

The guard snatched the bills from his hand and passed them to his colleague.

"What do you mean, happy hunting?" demanded the guard with the scarred face.

Sweat gathered on Winston's forehead. *Damn! Why did I have to go and say that? We were almost free and clear.* "Just a turn of phrase, old chap," he said cheerfully, trying hard to mask his nervousness. "It's like saying *Have a nice day.*"

The two guards looked puzzled. They weren't familiar with that particular phrase, nor did they understand why the strange white Englishman kept calling them *old chap.* Neither of them was old; far from it. They eyed Winston suspiciously.

"You better not be thinking of hunting here, Englishman," said the smaller guard. "Hunting and poaching are illegal in Gabon."

"Yes," sneered the other guard, "we'll sling your ass in jail and throw away the key if we catch you hunting and poaching our animals."

"Especially our precious elephants," added the other.

Central Africa is a killing ground for elephants under relentless pressure from the illegal ivory trade. Elephant numbers have fallen dramatically. In Gabon alone, poachers kill between 500 and 1,000 elephants a year out of a population of 20,000. The trade comes mainly from China where the demand for ivory is extremely high, with collectors paying top dollar for exquisite ivory pieces.

Winston gulped again and wiped the sweat from his brow. He was still chastising himself for using the word hunting. Maso came to his rescue. Pointing at Winston, he addressed the two guards. "Not a problem, my friends, he's just a tourist and I'm his guide. He wants to see all the wildlife in Gabon, visit all our National Parks." Mao smiled at the two guards, and then continued. "In fact, we're on our way to Lope now. Lots of wildlife there."

Lope National Park, located in the center of Gabon, became the first protected area in Gabon, and is part of a network of 13 parks in the country. Although the terrain is mostly rain forest, in the north the park contains the last remnants of grass savannahs created in Central Africa during the last Ice Age, 15,000 years ago. Teeming with wildlife, including the forest elephant, gorilla, chimpanzee, mandrill, forest buffalo, leopard, sitatunga, and thousands of exotic birds, the Lope area has been inhabited almost continuously as of 400,000 years ago.

The guards exchanged glances. They did not look convinced. They had taken the bribe money, but would it be enough? Would they let them through?

Maso tried again. A sudden idea had popped into his head. "The Englishman is also a photographer," he said, pointing to a camera which was sitting on the seat between him and Winston. "He's here to take photos of the wildlife for a well-known magazine in London."

"What's this magazine called?" asked Scarface.

"National Geographic," chirped in Winston before Maso could reply. He was amazed at how easily the lie came to his lips.

The small guard looked impressed. "I've heard of that," he said. "It's a famous magazine."

Winston nodded. "Oh yes, old chap, very famous."

A look of annoyance crossed the guard's face. Maso caught Winston's eye and glared at him as if to say, *Stop calling him old chap!* Quickly, he turned to the guards and said, "Yep, we're going to shoot us some photos of the sitatunga, the Dja river warbler, the yellow-backed duiker, the gorilla, the mandrill… ,"and Maso proceeded to list as many animals and birds as he could remember. "He's especially interested in the mandrill, aren't you, Winston? And Lope has the largest mandrill troupes in the world."

The guards seemed impressed by Maso's knowledge of Gabon's wildlife. Winston, too. They all stared at Maso in amazement.

"Aren't you, Winston, interested in the mandrill?" asked Maso again, nudging him in the ribs.

"Oh, yes, absolutely," he said, nodding his head emphatically, but having no idea what a mandrill was.

Still the guards remained unconvinced. Staring at their sullen faces, an idea suddenly came to Winston. "I can take a photo of you two, if you like," he said with a smile. "For my magazine, National Geographic. You'll be famous." He looked over at Maso and winked, making sure that the guards didn't see him. How easily the lies slipped off his tongue.

The guards' sullen expressions changed abruptly. Now they were both grinning broadly, revealing two identical sets of pearly white teeth.

"We'll be in a magazine, in London?" asked Scarface.

"Yes, yes, old…oops, sorry." Winston stopped himself just in time. "Yes," he continued, "and they may put you on the front cover if we get a good shot."

The two guards beamed. They were going to be famous! Dusting off their uniforms, they primped and preened, and straightened their tight curly black hair.

Winston grabbed the camera, which contained no film, and pretended to study the two men carefully from different angles. Impatient to get started, the smaller guard shouted, "Okay, man, let's do it. We're going to be famous."

"Just checking the light," said Winston. "Have to make sure that it's just right."

Maso smiled to himself. *What a con, he's really getting into this.*

For the next twenty minutes, Winston pretended to shoot photos of the two men in every conceivable pose and from every possible angle. Maso watched in amusement. *Time to go,* he thought, *while the going's good.* Winston caught his glance.

"Okay, that's a wrap," he said, getting into the lingo. "I think I have all I need."

The two guards nodded and smiled. Quite a change from their sour expressions of an hour ago.

"Jolly good," said Winston, placing the filmless camera back on the seat. "As soon as the magazine comes out, I'll send you both a copy, care of the border crossing at Mongomo."

Now grinning from ear to ear, Scarface and Shorty, as Winston had aptly named them to himself, shook hands with Winston and Maso. They were now the best of friends. After all, they were going to be famous.

"You are free to cross into Gabon now," said Scarface, waving them through. "Good luck."

"Thanks," said Winston. "Cheerio."

Maso nodded and waved at them.

"Good luck," shouted Shorty, "And Happy Hunting!"

Safely out of sight, Winston and Maso looked at each other and burst out laughing.

Happy Hunting! Little did they know that was exactly what they were going to do!

Chapter Two

"Wow! that was a close one," Winston exclaimed. "Good job you thought of the photographer angle, old chap."

"Just happened to see the camera and it came to me," said Maso.

"So, now it's down to Happy Hunting – I can't believe we're actually here."

Winston's excitement increased with each mile. He had never shot an elephant before and his nervous energy filled the jeep. He turned to Maso, digging him sharply in the ribs. "Hand me that bloody whiskey bottle, old chap," he yelled. "I need a drink after all that excitement at the border. Seems that the guards here are just as corrupt as those in Equatorial Guinea."

Maso frowned but said nothing. He did not like Winston casting aspersions on his fellow countrymen. But the Englishman did have a point. Bribery was rife, both here and in the rest of Central Africa. He sighed to himself. What could he do? He was just a simple guide. But at least he made his money honestly. Time to have that drink and forget about it. Reaching under the seat, Maso pulled out a quart of Johnny Walker Red and handed it to Winston.

"Damn it, man, open up the top!" exclaimed Winston. "I can't drive and open up the bottle at the same time." Maso frowned again, his liquid brown eyes revealing a hint of annoyance as he screwed off the top. "That's it," said Winston. "Now, you take the first drink, then give it to me."

Maso smiled as the burning whiskey slid down his throat. "Damn, that good whiskey," he said, handing the bottle to Winston.

Winston grabbed the bottle and took a long hard drink. The fiery liquid stung his throat and he started coughing. "By God," he spluttered, laughing and coughing at the same time. "That's bloody good." He handed the bottle back to Maso. "Here, take another drink."

As they passed the bottle back and forth, they both started laughing. Then Winston burst into song. "I'm going to shoot me an elephant today – a big, bad, bloody elephant."

The jeep trundled along, spewing out dirt and stones and covering the two men in a grimy film of dust. Maso pointed out a group of warthog gathered by the side of the road, then a large herd of water buffalo emerged from the nearby trees. He knew they were getting closer to the elephants.

"We're almost there," he said. "Make a right turn."

They drove in silence for about two miles. The bush was getting thicker and thicker. Finally, Maso told Winston to stop the jeep. "This is the spot," he whispered. "This is where the elephants were spotted this morning."

Winston pushed down on the brake pedal, bringing the jeep to a silent halt.

"Get your elephant gun and follow me," said Maso, "and try to be very quiet."

Rivulets of sweat streamed down their faces as they crept through the towering trees and the thick underbrush. A large vulture startled them as it took flight, flapping its voluminous wings and upsetting the quietude of the forest. Winston raised his rifle and took aim.

Maso yanked the gun from his hand. "No," he said sharply, shaking his head. "If you fire that gun, we might as well go back to the jeep and finish off that bottle."

Winston nodded. "Sorry, Maso. You know how I hate those vultures. They remind me of the devil."

They scrambled through the forest trying hard not to step on anything that would make a noise. Maso pulled back a tree branch and motioned to Winston to be quiet. He pointed to a clearing surrounded by a scattering of large trees, then bent down to one knee.

"Look at the third tree to your right and be very, very quiet," he whispered to Winston.

Winston reached back for the binoculars slung across his shoulder. Placing them to his eyes, he focused on the trees. Settling on the third three, his eyes grew as wide as saucers – there, rubbing its side on the grainy bark was the largest elephant he had ever seen!

"Bloody hell," he exclaimed, his hands shaking. "That's a big one." The blood had drained from his face and his hands felt clammy. "And just look at those tusks," he said, racking up the dollars in his mind. "I am going to be rich." He turned to Maso to say something. His lips moved but nothing came out.

Maso grabbed the binoculars and took a quick look. "Whoa, you're right, that's a big one," he whispered. "We have to get closer so you can get a good shot." Winston nodded.

Suddenly, the massive elephant turned its head and looked straight at them. The two men froze. They stood like statues amidst the magnificence of the verdant forest. The elephant held their gaze, then slowly lowered its head and started munching on the tree, unconcerned. Winston and Maso shook off their fear and edged closer to their quarry. Maso's only weapon was a long wooden stick; he knew his fate hung in Winston's hands. They locked eyes as they crept closer and closer.

As they approached a small tree, Maso signaled that they were close enough for Winston to take a shot. Winston raised the rifle to his shoulder. Sweat trickled down his forehead, clouding his eyes. Lowering the rifle, he wiped away the sweat with his left hand and took a deep breath. Maso watched him nervously. Again, Winston raised the rifle to his shoulder, waiting for the right moment to take a shot.

As if it had a sixth sense, the elephant turned and faced them. Its trunk shot up in the air and its ears started flopping back and forth. Then it let out a loud bellow, sending shivers down both men's spines. Now the elephant was up on its hind legs, its ears still flapping furiously back and forth. Winston steadied his nerves and took aim. As his finger started to squeeze off the shot, his back leg stepped into a hole and the shot flew high just grazing the elephant's giant head. The elephant fell down on one knee and stayed there for a few seconds. Meanwhile, Winston had fallen forward, jamming the rifle in the dirt and rendering it useless.

Maso reacted immediately. He had never been in a situation like this before, but instinctively, he knew what to do. Helping Winston to his feet, he watched as the great elephant struggled to get back on its feet. "Run like you've never run before," he yelled at Winston. "And pray that he stays down."

Winston could see the fear in Maso's eyes and knew he had to run.

"Quick, we have to get to the jeep before he gets to us," urged Maso, tugging on Winston's arm. "We have no protection out in the open like this; we have to make it to the jeep."

Winston scrambled to his feet, huffing and puffing. He was not in as good a shape as Maso. In the distance, they could see the elephant moving rapidly toward them. It was gaining strength with every step. Maso urged Winston to move faster. "Hurry, hurry," he yelled. "We still have a long way to go before we reach the jeep."

Winston stopped. "Maso, Maso, I can't go on," he panted.

"We must go on or we will both die," said Maso. Grabbing the water bottle that was strapped around his waist, he poured water over Winston's head to cool him down. Then he passed him the bottle. "Here, take a swig and then run for your life."

Winston grabbed the bottle and took a quick gulp. In the background, they could hear the elephant roaring and bellowing. "I do believe it's angry," said Winston with characteristic understatement, typical of the English. He stumbled forward, trying to save his life. He knew that the elephant would make short work of both of them. "Thank God, we're going to make it." Maso shook his head. "Don't be too sure, that elephant can move about 25 miles an hour." He turned sharply to see the great elephant charging toward them at a rapid pace. "He's coming...he's coming, and he's gaining on us," yelled Maso. He grabbed Winston's arm and propelled him forward. "Run, Winston! Run like you've never run before!"

Winston didn't need to be told twice. Adrenalin kicked in and the two men made a mad dash for the jeep. Reaching the vehicle at the same time, they both leapt into their seats.

"Let's get the hell out of here," Maso yelled at Winston.

Winston fumbled to get his key in the ignition. He was breathing heavily and his hands were shaking. The keys slipped from his hand and dropped to the floor. He searched in vain to find them, his hands still shaking. "I can't find them," he cried. The roars of the elephant echoed in his ears. "We're done for."

Without missing a beat, Maso reached down quickly, found the key and slotted it in the ignition. He turned his head and looked back. The elephant was almost upon them, blood streaming down its head from the impact of the bullet. A few more strides and they would be crushed to death.

"Start the engine!" Maso screamed at Winston. "Start the engine; he's going to kill us both."

Winston turned the key and the engine spluttered. "The bloody thing won't start," he barked.

"Pump the gas, pump the gas," said Maso. "He's going to ram us."

Winston jiggled the key, stepping on the gas at the same time. Nothing. Struggling to control his trembling body, he tried again. The engine kicked in furiously, spinning the jeep's wheels and sending up a cloud of dust. Both men sighed in relief and then turned in unison to face a charging elephant. Its bellows were now deafening, its eyes wild with fury.

"God save us," cried Maso as the elephant's tusks rammed the side of the jeep, rocking the vehicle and almost ejecting its two occupants. "Get us out of here," screamed Maso.

Instinctively, Winston rammed his foot hard on the accelerator and the jeep shot forward, dust and debris flying in its wake. Temporarily blinded by the swirling cloud of dirt, the elephant stopped in mid-charge and stood on its hind legs bellowing loudly.

The jeep screeched ahead. "Hand me that bloody bottle," said Winston after they had covered several miles and were safely out of reach of the elephant, "I need a drink. That was a close shave, old chap."

Maso passed him the bottle, with trembling hands. "Well, we tried to kill him, so now he wants a piece of our ass," said Maso.

Winston handed the bottle back to him and he took a quick swig, wiping his mouth on his bare arm. "Elephants never forget your face or your smell," continued Maso. "Let's hope we never run into him again or we're dead meat."

Winston shuddered. "I'll drink to that," he said.

They traveled along in silence for several miles, each man lost in thought. Their close brush with death had rendered them temporarily mute. But both men were thinking the same thought: *An elephant never forgets...*

Chapter Three

Cheyenne, Wyoming. Cheyenne Cole was packing his luggage for a flight to Central Africa. Still in mourning for his beloved father Robert, who had died six months earlier, Cheyenne was on a mission to save the elephants of Africa. Ever since Cheyenne was a small child, his father had instilled in him a love of the elephant. Robert had told him many stories of this big intelligent animal; its sensitivity and mild, gentle manner. He told of one elephant that preferred beer to water, and of another that was electrocuted for crushing somebody. The unfortunate animal was prodded and mistreated, then placed on wet iron plates and hooked up to electric wires.

Every time Cheyenne's father told this story, his voice would break and tears would fill his eyes. Robert Cole had always wanted to go to Africa to save his beloved elephants from death and mistreatment, but with a family to raise, he never seemed to have the time. Then it was too late. Now the mantle had passed to his son.

Fortunately for Cheyenne, his father had amassed considerable wealth over his lifetime, setting up trust funds for each of his children. Cheyenne had left his trust untouched and joined the Army, where he had trained as a sniper and joined the Special Forces. A crack shot, with a steady hand and a focused eye, Cheyenne could pick off a target at a thousand yards. He never, ever missed.

Twenty years earlier Robert Cole had taken Cheyenne to the local county fair in Laramie. The featured attraction was a trio of African elephants. Robert was fascinated by the magnificent animals. He had told Cheyenne how the great elephants roamed the plains of Africa and how their numbers were dwindling because of the hunt for their ivory tusks.

"Let me tell you the story of Molly," said Robert, pulling Cheyenne to one side as they watched the performing elephants.

Cheyenne nodded eagerly. He loved listening to his father's stories of the elephants.

"Old Molly had been in captivity for most of her life," began Robert, "passed from circus to circus, from owner to owner. Some of her owners had treated her cruelly, beating her bloody on numerous occasions if she hadn't performed to their liking. During one particularly savage beating, she had accidentally crushed her owner against a wall and killed him."

Cheyenne's widened as Robert continued his story.

"Well," sighed Robert, "old Molly was condemned to death, and now the circus owners would decide how she would die. Some said she should be shot, others said she should be poisoned, and some said she should be allowed to live."

"I would have voted to let her live," said young Cheyenne. "After all, it was an accident and they had been beating her."

"You got that right, son," said Robert. "But these were mean fellas – real mean." His eyes watered. "Anyway," he continued, wiping his eyes, "one man stood up and said that old Molly should be electrocuted just like the murderers on death row. They took a vote and old Molly's fate was sealed – she would be electrocuted at the waterfront docks in New York City."

Cheyenne cried out. "Oh no, Dad, did they really fry her? What happened next?"

"Let me tell you," said Robert. "Three days later, a huge crowd, including newspaper reporters from all over the States, gathered at the docks to watch poor old Molly die. The crowd grew so large that police had to put up barricades to contain all the people.

"At eleven o'clock old Molly came lumbering around the corner. Three heavy chains were draped around her thick neck and she was pulled along by three men on each side. The crowd let out a huge roar. 'Old Molly, old Molly,' they yelled. When she heard her name, she stopped and turned her head toward the crowd." Robert sighed and wiped his eyes again, remembering. He had been in that crowd, and old Molly had looked straight at him with her kind gentle eyes. "She probably thought she was just going for a long walk," he said, blinking back the tears. "She had such a look of serenity on her face – I'll never forget it as long as I live."

Cheyenne touched his father's arm. "It's okay, Dad."

"I know, son, I know." He paused then continued on. "Well, all the yelling and shouting didn't seem to bother her – she was used to raucous circus crowds. After all, she'd performed in front of them, all her life. She trundled down the street, turning her giant head back and forth and finally came to a stop in front of her executioner who pointed to four large iron plates, connected by electric wire to a black box fitted with a brass handle. This handle would turn the electricity on and off. 'Bring her over,' said the executioner to Molly's six handlers."

Robert paused again and smiled wryly. "Old Molly probably thought she was just going to perform another circus trick. Poor old girl." He continued with his story. "The men tried to drag her forward, but old Molly refused to move. They tugged and tugged on the heavy chains, but still she refused to budge. As a last resort, they jabbed her with pointed sticks from behind and old Molly had no choice but to step onto the iron plates. "As she felt the chains slacken from around her neck, she stood up on her back legs and trumpeted a bellow of defiance. The noise was deafening, sending shivers down the spines of the spectators. Many of them scattered, fearing that old Molly would break loose and crush them. As she came down on her front legs, the whole dock shook.

"Her handlers stood there in shock, loosening their grip on the chains. Old Molly let out another bellow and again rose up on her back legs, knocking three men off the dock, into the water. More people fled in fright as she thundered back to her feet." Robert smiled. "Old Molly's eyes were no longer kind. She was mad – real mad." He chuckled to himself, picturing that day. "They didn't know what the old girl was going to do next."

Cheyenne's eyes widened. "What did she do next, Dad?"

"Well, now the man in charge had twelve men holding onto the chains, and old Molly was getting tired. She shook her head, raised her trunk in the air a few times, and flapped her ears. All the fight had gone out of her." Tears filled Robert's eyes as he remembered that fateful day. He could see old Molly standing on the plates, silently accepting her fate. "They pulled the handle and old Molly was no more," finished Robert, blinking away the tears.

Cheyenne sobbed into his sleeve, the story of old Molly etched in his mind forever. Just like the elephant, he would never, ever forget.

Robert and Cheyenne left the elephant ring and wandered around the fair. It was a hot, sunny day, so they stopped to buy an ice cream at one of the nearby stalls. They were cooling off, enjoying their treat, when Cheyenne noticed a sign that read, 'Don't miss Black Bart, the fastest draw in the West.'

"Dad, can we go see him," said Cheyenne, tugging on his father's arm.

Mr. Cole hesitated for a second and then nodded. "Okay, son, that's what fairs are for."

They arrived at the show just in time, taking their seats near the front of the stage. The announcer was showing the audience a target. "Okay, people, here is the target." He held it aloft, front and back. "See, it's perfectly clean, no holes, no tricks," he said.

The audience murmured in anticipation.

And now," he continued, "it is my honor to introduce the one and only Black Bart, the fastest draw in the West."

Loud applause greeted this announcement. Cheyenne clapped his hands together enthusiastically. He was eager to see the infamous Black Bart.

Black Bart strode onto the stage. Dressed all in black, from head to toe, sweat glistened on his coal black skin as he marched forward, silver spurs clicking, and stood perfectly still like a soldier. Tall and thin, with dark deep set eyes and a square jaw, he glared at the audience as if to say, "Don't mess with me or else..."

A convicted felon, Bart had spent twenty years in prison for murder. Whilst in jail, he had practiced his draw hour after hour, day after day, with a makeshift toy gun. His fellow prisoners claimed he was faster than Billy the Kid. After his release, Black Bart had perfected his skill in the outside world, and soon became a dead shot. The circus snapped him up immediately – he was their star attraction.

The announcer continued with his introduction. "Now, ladies and gentlemen," he said, handing a shiny Colt 45 with six bullets to Black Bart, "keep your eyes on the gun because the hand is quicker than the eyes."

Black Bart took the gun, gently cradling it in his hands as if it were his firstborn child, and placed it in his holster. Meanwhile, the announcer took the target and placed it on a rack approximately 30 yards from Black Bart. It would take an expert to hit the tiny bull's eye in the middle of the target.

Cheyenne and his father had their eyes glued on Black Bart. They didn't want to miss one second of this show.

All of a sudden, the announcer walked down to the target, picked it up and showed it to the audience. There in the center of the target was a gaping hole. Black Bart had hit bull's-eye.

Robert Cole turned to his son, a look of astonishment on his face. "Did you see him draw?"

Cheyenne shook his head. "Dad, I didn't see him move."

"Amazing," said Robert, "truly amazing."

On the way home, Cheyenne couldn't stop talking about Black Bart. "Dad, I'm gonna be faster than Black Bart. I'm gonna practice and practice and practice, and I'm gonna be the fastest draw in the West."

Mr. Cole just smiled. Once Cheyenne set his mind on something, there was no stopping him.

"We'll see, son," he said, patting his son on the shoulder. "We'll see..."

Chapter Four

As Winston and Maso rounded the edge of the forest, they spotted the straw roofs of a small town, nestled by the side of a glistening lake. Dozens and dozens of huts and makeshift wooden buildings lined both sides of a dusty main street bustling with activity. Drawing closer to the town, they passed several women walking down the side of the road, carrying baskets on the top of their heads. Dressed in long, multi-colored gowns, their arms jangling with bracelets and other adornments, the women smiled at the two men, revealing white pearly teeth. Winston and Maso waved their hands in greeting, and smiled.

"Let's stop here for a while," said Winston. "See if we can get a drink somewhere." He pointed at the women and grinned. "It looks as if the natives are friendly."

Maso smiled broadly. "Yessir." It felt good to smile again after their recent brush with death.

They pulled up in front of a small bar-restaurant, alongside a few other jeeps. Emblazoned in bright gold letters across the front of the building were the words *The African Queen.*

"Appropriate name, old chap," observed Winston, pointing to the sign as they jumped out of the jeep and headed toward the restaurant. He clapped Maso on the back. "Let's have a drink in here," he said, tossing the empty whiskey bottle in a nearby basket. "The drinks are on me!"

Maso grabbed Winston by the arm. "Be careful what you say inside," he warned. "What you did was illegal. You could get into serious trouble if you say something to the wrong person."

"I know," he said as they entered the bar. "Don't worry, old chap, I'll be the soul of discretion."

The two men took a table by the side of the bar. Animal heads – lion, zebra, black rhino to name but a few - adorned the walls. And in the middle of the bar hung a huge pair of water buffalo horns. Bright yellow tablecloths covered the tables and the wooden walls were varnished dark brown. Winston and Maso looked around, surveying their surroundings. They could smell the delicious aroma of food, and hear the rattling of pots and pans in the kitchen. A waitress bustled back and forth, carrying trays of food. The bar was packed. A mix of the local African populace sprinkled with a few Europeans and Americans here and there.

Winston gazed around the bar, soaking up the sights and sounds. At the far end of the bar, he noticed a man whose dress was different than that of the rest of the patrons. Tall and lean, with a solid sturdy build, the man was wearing a broad cowboy hat with one side turned up. He had very distinct features: a strong firm jaw with high chiseled cheekbones and piercing blue eyes topped with long dark lashes and dark eyebrows. He stood straight and erect, and Winston knew from his posture that he was a military man. Wisps of dark black hair stuck out from under his hat and when he smiled his perfect white teeth sparkled.

Winston recognized his companion, an American by the name of Geigy DeBrown, whom he had met briefly during his travels around Central Africa. DeBrown had left his wife and children and come to Africa for a new start. Heavyset and balding, DeBrown was fond of the bottle. He had been thrown out of the bar on numerous occasions and had built up a reputation as a happy-go-lucky drunk. The two men were now deep in conversation.

In the far corner of the bar sat Python, a mean-looking African whose black eyes glittered with hatred. He had crushed a man to death, hence his nickname. He had served no time for the crime, his defense being that it was a fair fight; he just didn't know his own strength. Greedy and cruel, Python lived to make money, selling tusks, weapons and drugs. It was all he thought about.

Sitting with Python was a Russian arms dealer who had connections to the Russian Mafia. His name, quite aptly, was the Russian. Heavyset and stocky, he stood about five foot seven, with a shaved head and cold gray eyes. A sadist, who loved torturing people and hearing them scream, he was notorious for extracting information.

Also seated with Python was a Pygmy who never left his side. Answering to the name of Ego, he would do anything that Python asked of him. According to Python, a hostile tribe had attacked Ego's village and murdered all the inhabitants. Ego had been left for dead. As he trekked through the jungle on one of his many drug runs, Python had found Ego, hidden under a blanket by the side of his slain parents whose throats had been slashed. Python had saved his life, and he never let Ego forget it.

Ego rarely smiled. His lips were curled in a perpetual sneer and his eyes were cold and hard. Although he was only four feet tall, his defiant swagger made him appear much taller. Like the Russian, he enjoyed inflicting pain. It was his way at getting back at people who were taller than he.

Cheyenne Cole stood at the bar talking to Geigy DeBrown. He had just flown in from Wyoming on a mission to save the elephants. A mission that his father had always wanted to undertake but never had the chance. Now it was up to his son. Cheyenne was waiting for a ship to bring his two six-shooters and his long range rifle. He was also looking to hire a jeep to take him around the rough terrain. He figured that the bar was the best place to meet the local people to glean information and learn about the surrounding area.

He was surprised, and happy, to meet a fellow American. Like Cheyenne, Geigy was an ex-Marine so the two men had much in common. Geigy was also an explosives expert who had specialized in blowing up bridges and other structures. At five foot eight, he was strong and rugged, his only weakness being a fondness for the booze.

During their conversation, Geigy had pointed to Python and told Cheyenne how Python had crushed a man to death because of some girl. Cheyenne's eyes widened in surprise.

"No kidding," he said, looking over at Python. "He doesn't look that strong."

"You better believe it," replied Geigy. "He's one mean son-of-a-bitch. Stay clear of him."

Cheyenne nodded. "What happened? Why did he crush the guy?"

Geigy took a long swig of beer and wiped his mouth with the back of his hand. "Well, the way the story goes, this guy was playing the jukebox, and Python's girlfriend wandered over and asked if he would play one of her favorite songs. Python saw them talking together and thought the guy was flirting with her. A fight broke out and Python got a bear hug on the man and that was it," said Geigy, shrugging his shoulders. "Crushed the poor bastard to death."

"Didn't anyone try to stop him?" asked Cheyenne.

"Ebony, she's Python's girl…Ebony tried to stop him, but as I said before he's one mean son-of-a-bitch with an explosive temper." Geigy glanced over at Python, making sure the guy hadn't heard him, then continued. "He wouldn't stop until he'd crushed the guy's ribs so hard they pierced the poor bastard's heart."

Cheyenne swallowed hard. "That's a helluva story. I'll remember not to get on his bad side."

"Yes, steer clear," warned Geigy. "He's bad news. Kills elephants and sells their tusks. He's also a drug runner, and an arms dealer – sends weapons to Somali and Afghanistan – wherever there's trouble." Geigy took another drink. "And he's tight with the local constable and the military that control the town. They turn a blind eye to his dealings."

Geigy also warned Cheyenne about Ego and the Russian. "And watch out for those two – cold-blooded killers, both of them."

Cheyenne looked over at the menacing trio and shook his head in astonishment. He was beginning to wonder what kind of place he had come to. He just wanted to help to save the elephants. Now here he was, mixing with drug runners, arms dealers, and killers!

Chapter Five

Since his conversation with Geigy, Cheyenne was even more interested in finding out about the elephants being slaughtered for their tusks, not to mention the arms shipments to Somali and Afghanistan. So, the next day, he decided to drop by *The African Queen* again to see if Geigy was there. He stepped into the bar and sure enough, there was Geigy sitting by himself in the corner, a bottle of beer clutched in his hand. He motioned for Cheyenne to join him.

"Hey there, buddy," he said with a grin. "Come grab a beer with me."

Cheyenne turned to the bartender. "Hello, Harold, good to see you again. I'll take a beer and one for my friend over there."

"Yessir, coming right up," said Harold, passing two bottles to Cheyenne.

Cheyenne strolled over to his friend and sat down. "Cheers," he said, handing one of the beers to Geigy.

"Cheers," said Geigy with a smile.

Just then, the door swung open and in walked Winston and Maso, followed closely by Python, the Russian and Ego. Winston and Maso took seats at the bar and ordered a couple of whiskeys. Python and the Russian surveyed the bar, then headed for the far corner of the restaurant. Ego lagged behind, grimacing at Cheyenne and Geigy as he passed by, and baring his rotten yellow teeth.

"What's his problem?" asked Cheyenne.

"Oh, don't worry about him," replied Geigy, "even though he's a little squirt, he thinks he's a big shot. Thinks he's scaring us."

"Oh, yeah, I'm shaking in my boots," said Cheyenne sarcastically.

Geigy leaned in closer. "Don't underestimate any of them," he whispered. "All three are evil – pure evil."

A few moments later, Harold wandered over and asked if they'd like another drink.

"My round, I think," said Geigy. "We'll have two more beers, Harold, please." He looked over at the bar. "Hey, is that Winston and Maso?" He was acquainted with the two men, but hadn't spoken to them for a while.

"Yeah," replied Harold, "they've just been telling me about this crazy elephant that's roaming around the Gabon region. They call it "Monsoon."

Cheyenne's eyes widened.

"Is that right?" said Geigy.

"Yeah, that's the rumor," continued Harold. "According to Winston, people are claiming that it has enormous tusks about twelve foot long."

"My God," exclaimed Geigy, "that must be one bad elephant."

Cheyenne shook his head in disbelief. "A crazy elephant, that's pretty hard to believe," he said. "Most elephants are very kind and intelligent, gentle even."

Geigy agreed. "I've been here for years and I've never seen a crazy elephant. You do have to be careful if they're in musk season, or if they have a small baby. Other than that they leave people alone."

"Well, they claim that this Monsoon has killed a few people," Harold explained.

Cheyenne jumped up from his seat and headed over to Winston and Maso. Without introducing himself, he said, "Where did you get this information about a crazy elephant? I came all the way from Wyoming to save the elephants. Now you're saying that there's a crazy elephant out there with twelve foot tusks, killing people."

Winston and Maso looked at Cheyenne in surprise. They had noticed him at the bar yesterday, but they had no idea who he was. "I'm sorry but I don't think we've been formally introduced, old chap," said Winston, in his clipped British accent. He held out his hand. "I'm Winston Holmes and this is my friend Maso."

Cheyenne shook hands with both men and gave them an apologetic smile. "Sorry, guys, I'm Cheyenne Cole. I apologize for my outburst, but I'm really concerned about the elephants. I've come here to save them."

"No problem, old chap," said Winston, patting Cheyenne on the back. "We heard about the elephant from some natives in the bush. Apparently, some of the natives were carrying firewood back to their village, when Monsoon came up behind them. He impaled one of them with his tusks, and he crushed the other two."

Cheyenne shook his head again. He still found this hard to believe. "Something must have happened to him. Most elephants are gentle creatures – not killers."

Meanwhile from the far corner of bar, Python was watching the three men curiously. He had seen Cheyenne jump up out of his chair and charge toward Winston and Maso. *Something's in the air,* he thought to himself. He motioned to Ego to find out what was going on. Ego strolled over to the bar and stood unobserved behind Cheyenne. His eyes widened as he heard about the crazy elephant.

Cheyenne chatted with Winston and Maso for a few more minutes, then turned to go back to his seat. As he did so, he bumped into Ego who was standing there with a sly grin on his face.

"Huh, sorry…," said Cheyenne as he tried to sidestep the pygmy.

Ego would not budge. "Excuse me," said Cheyenne, brushing past him and returning to his seat.

Geigy and Harold had been watching the exchange from their seats. "I warned you about that little bastard," said Geigy as Cheyenne flopped into his seat and took a long gulp of beer. "You're lucky that he didn't grab you by the balls – that's his trademark, and he's just the right height." He looked over at Ego, who was now back in the corner with his cohorts. "I think he was more interested in getting information for Python."

Geigy had guessed correctly. Ego was telling Python and the Russian what he had learned about Monsoon and the killings in the bush. "That American is here to save the elephants," he said. Python and the Russian raised their glasses and laughed.

Once again, the door swung open and in walked the most beautiful black woman Cheyenne had ever laid eyes on. Spotting Harold, she smiled and said, "Where is he?"

Harold motioned with his head toward the far corner of the restaurant. "He's over there in the back," he replied, "with Ego and the Russian."

She flashed him another dazzling smile, revealing perfect white teeth. "Thanks," she said softly. "I guess that's the darkest corner in the place. That's where the black rat likes to hide." She had a deep sultry voice. "He is a black rat, you know," she whispered.

Harold just shrugged his shoulders and nodded.

Cheyenne couldn't take his eyes off her – her beauty was mesmerizing. Lustrous black hair framed her ebony face and hung down to her slender waist. Her opal eyes fringed by thick black lashes sparkled as she sauntered past the table where Cheyenne and Geigy were sitting. She wore a slinky satin dress that clung to the contours of her muscular body and showed off her long, shapely legs. On a scale of one to ten, she was an eleven.

Cheyenne's eyes followed her as she sashayed across the dance floor, her six-inch high heels click-clacking against the wooden floor. She held her head proudly, knowing that all eyes were on her. She knew she was beautiful. And with beauty came power.

"That's Ebony," Geigy whispered to Cheyenne, tugging on his arm and breaking the spell that Ebony had cast over him. "Python's girl. She's the girl I was telling you about – Python killed that poor guy just for talking to her. "Poor bastard," finished Geigy, "he was in the wrong place at the wrong time."

"She is absolutely gorgeous," said Cheyenne. "I wonder what she's doing with a slug like Python?"

"Beats me," said Geigy. "What do you think, Harold?"

Harold shrugged his shoulders again. "Who knows, man…money, power? He sure don't treat her very well. If I had a woman like that, I'd be her slave."

Cheyenne and Geigy nodded their heads in agreement.

Python and the others were laughing and joking as Ebony approached the table. Python rose to his feet to greet her, but she jabbed him in the chest.

"If you ever touch my mother again and call her a fat old water buffalo, I'll stick a knife in you," she shouted at Python.

The Russian threw his head back and guffawed. Ebony pushed by him and slapped Python hard across the face, leaving a red mark on his cheek. Python rubbed his sore face, incensed. He couldn't believe that Ebony had actually hit him. Hesitating for a second, he slapped her across the face, knocking her to her knees. Another hard slap sent her sprawling to the floor by the side of the Russian's feet. Dazed and disoriented, she stumbled to her feet, tears streaming down her face, and dashed out the door.

Python shook his fist angrily and yelled after her. "Your mother is a fat old water buffalo, and I'll push her around any time I want."

When Python had slapped Ebony the first time, Cheyenne had sprung to his feet in anger, ready to go to her aid. Geigy had placed his hand on Cheyenne's shoulder and pushed him down.

"Hold your horses," said Geigy firmly. "This happens all the time. Ebony's mother and Python hate each other. She knows that Python is bad news, but Ebony can't see above the clouds yet."

"He shouldn't have hit her," said Cheyenne. "If it happens again, I'll definitely step in."

"Don't say I didn't warn you," said Geigy. "Python is bad news – it's best not to mess with him."

After things had settled down, Cheyenne told Geigy that he had purchased a Land Rover.

"It's in pretty good shape," he said. "And my guns and rifle will be arriving soon – I'm having them shipped over."

"What do you plan on doing then?" asked Geigy.

"I'm going deep into the bush to try to save as many elephants as I can from these evil people who only kill them for their tusks."

Geigy took a long draw on his beer and looked straight at Cheyenne. "That can become a very dangerous mission," he said, wiping his mouth on his sleeve. "As I told you before, Python and the Russian are two of those evil people," he whispered.

"Yeah, that figures," said Cheyenne, looking over at the two shadowy forms. *Um, I wonder where the little guy went,* he thought, turning to his right. And there stood Ego, baring his rotten yellow teeth, a wicked smile etched on his face. Cheyenne covered his mouth and nose to ward off the stench of Ego's breath. The smell was nauseating.

"Whaddya want, Ego?" asked Harold. "Why don't you go back to your *friends*."

Ego wouldn't budge. He just stood there, glaring at Cheyenne.

Harold tried again. "Don't be bothering my customers, Ego, otherwise I'll get the boss," he warned.

Ego continued to ignore him. He stood like a statue, his crooked yellow smile fixed pointedly on Cheyenne. Furious, Harold stomped into the backroom of the bar to fetch his boss. The owner, a big jolly black man, with a bright smile, emerged from the room and strode over to Ego. Harold followed closely on his heels.

The big man bent down to Ego and smiled. "Now then, Ego, what's going on here?" He glanced over at Cheyenne and Geigy apologetically, and then patted Ego on the shoulder. "Come on, you've had your fun, now go and sit yourself down with your friends. Let's not have any trouble," he said in a kind but stern voice.

Ego glared at the owner then turned on his heel and shuffled back to the table on his short legs.

"Sorry about that, gentlemen," said the owner, addressing Cheyenne and Geigy. He extended his hand. "My name is Jackal Jarvis, and I would like to apologize for Ego's behavior. He's harmless, you know, unless he gets a hold of your balls."

"No problem," said Cheyenne, shaking his hand. "I'm Cheyenne, and I guess you already know Geigy here."

"Sure do," he said, nodding at Geigy. "Pleased to meet you, Cheyenne."

"Likewise."

"Yeah, don't worry about it," said Geigy. "That little squirt don't bother us."

Jackal smiled brightly. "Harold, get these two gentlemen a drink, on the house."

"Yessir." He scurried back to the bar to prepare the drinks.

"That fight earlier, with Python and Ebony, it's a regular occurrence," said Jackal. "See that big stuffed leopard over there, with that extra long tail." He pointed to the wall in the far corner. "Well, after one of their fights, Python bought that for her. She left it here because she doesn't want her mother to see it. She always forgives Python after their fights," he finished.

Harold came over with the drinks and placed them in front of Cheyenne and Geigy.

"Well, gentlemen, if you'll excuse me, I have work to do," said Jackal. Enjoy your drinks."

"Cheers," said Cheyenne and Geigy in unison.

"Anytime," said Jackal. And with that he took his leave and disappeared into the backroom.

Ego sat down at the table with a grunt. Python grilled him. "What did you hear? What were they talking about?" he demanded.

"I didn't hear nothin'," he said sullenly. "They were talking too softly."

"You ain't good for nothin'," said Python, slapping him up the side of the head.

Ego winced. "Ouch, what was that for?"

"For coming back with nothin'."

The Russian roared with laughter.

"What's so funny," asked Python angrily.

"Nothin'," said the Russian.

Cheyenne and Geigy continued chatting, enjoying their beers. Cheyenne was worried about Ego. "I hope that Pygmy didn't overhear our conversation," he said.

Geigy glanced over at their table. "By look on Python's face," he said, "the little squirt heard nothin'."

Chapter Six

A few days after the incident in the bar, Cheyenne's six-shooters and long range rifle arrived. Cheyenne filled in the necessary paperwork, and the weapons were released to him. A couple of officials, cronies of Python, eyed him suspiciously, but he had proved to be the rightful owner and all the paperwork was in order. Still Python might be interested in the American with the six-shooters and long range rifle.

Cheyenne had rented a small room in the center of town. Nothing fancy – just big enough to hold all his belongings. He didn't plan on staying long. Arriving back at his room, he laid the weapons on his bed, and then went to take a shower. After showering and changing, he put the rifle in the tiny closet, next to his clothes, and placed his six-shooters on the desk by the side of the bed. Feeling relieved that his weapons had finally arrived, he decided to take a short nap. He slept soundlessly for a couple of hours, then awoke with a start. He had dreamt that he was running for his life, through the jungle. Monsoon, the crazy elephant with the twelve-foot tusks, was chasing him. And just as Monsoon was about to stick a huge tusk in his guts, he woke up. Sweat streamed down Cheyenne's face and his heart was beating like a drum. *I came here to save the elephant not to be chased by one.*

He took several deep breaths to calm his nerves and then decided to go and look for Geigy. He needed a friend right now. Strapping on his two six-shooters underneath his jacket, he headed to *The African Queen* in search of his friend.

As he entered the bar, Geigy called out his name. "Hey, Cheyenne, over here. There's a chair next to me with your name on it." As usual, Geigy was seated at the bar.

Cheyenne smiled and walked over to his friend. "So, how are you doing today, Geigy?" he asked, sliding onto a seat next to him.

"Oh, I'm doing just fine, my friend, just fine." He smiled happily and took a swig of beer. "How about a beer? Hey, Harold, get my buddy here an ice-cold beer."

"Coming right up," said Harold, placing the cold beer in front of Cheyenne. "Say what's that you have strapped around your waist?" Harold had noticed the bulge under Cheyenne's jacket.

"That's my two six-shooters. I've been waiting for them to arrive from the States."

"Damn, they're really nice-looking. Can you hit anything with them?" Harold laughed.

"Well, once in a while I hit something," joked Cheyenne. "One day, back in Wyoming, I took first prize in a contest for being the most accurate shot and the fastest draw."

"Damn, man, you're starting to scare me a little?" said Harold.

"You have nothing to worry about," Cheyenne told him, patting his guns gently. Just then, he noticed something, or rather someone, out of the corner of his eye. There stood Ego, looking up at him and smiling his sickly yellow smile. *That little runt is everywhere,* he thought to himself. Ego scurried back to Python and the Russian, who were seated at their usual table in the shadowy corner of the bar, and told them what he had heard.

"Perhaps he's just bragging," said the Russian.

"Yeah, who knows if he's telling the truth," said Python. "He don't look like no crack shot to me." Grimacing, he got up from his chair and strode across the dance floor toward Cheyenne. As Python approached, Harold said, "Hey, Python, I want you to meet Cheyenne. He came all the way from Wyoming…that's in the United States of America…to be here."

Python made no offer to shake hands, nor did Cheyenne. The two men just glared at each other.

"So, I hear you're pretty good with the six-shooter," said Python.

"I do all right," Cheyenne replied.

The Russian and Ego had now positioned themselves on either side of Python.

"Well, the Russian here thinks you might be bragging." Python smirked at his two sidekicks. "In other words," he continued, "maybe you can just about hit the broadside of a shithouse."

Geigy rushed to his friend's defense. "Maybe you'd like to see a little demonstration."

The Russian asked if he could see one of the six-shooters. Cheyenne drew one of the guns out of its holster and slowly turned the cylinder to make sure all six bullets were removed.

"Here," he said, passing it to the Russian. "Make sure you handle it carefully."

The Russian examined the gun. "That's a pretty heavy gun for its size, but between both guns, you only have twelve bullets!"

Geigy piped in. "Yeah, that means twelve dead men!"

The Russian chuckled, his fat stomach heaving up and down.

"That six-shooter wouldn't stand much of a chance against an automatic weapon," said Python.

"Well, as I said before, Cheyenne can give you a little show if you want," said Geigy.

Cheyenne was thinking. *What is this, the Honeymooners? Geigy is Norton and I'm Ralph.*

Geigy continued. "In fact, we'll put this demonstration on tomorrow, about six."

"Sounds good to me," said Python, looking over at the Russian and Ego.

The Russian handed the six-shooter to Python so he could feel its weight. Python took the gun and suddenly pointed it right between Cheyenne's eyes and pulled the trigger. *Click.* All three villains burst out laughing.

Cheyenne sprang from his seat and grabbed the gun out of Python's hand. His face suffused with anger, he pressed himself up against Python, nose to nose, and looked him directly in the eye. "Don't you ever a point a gun at anybody," he snarled, "unless you mean to kill them." The Russian started to pump up, ready to throw a punch, but Cheyenne hit him hard and fast. The Russian hit the floor. Python stepped back, and Ego tried to grab Cheyenne by the balls, but Geigy grabbed his arm.

"Get back to the table, Ego," Python ordered as he helped the Russian to his feet. "And you, you damn American," he yelled, shaking his fist angrily, "and your damn freedom. Communism is the only way!"

Cheyenne ignored him. He had moved back to the bar and was busy putting the bullets back in his gun.

Python continued to yell at him from across the room. "Make sure you're here at six o'clock sharp tomorrow night for that demonstration."

Cheyenne yelled back. "I'll make damn sure I'm here. Just make sure you show up."

Just then, Harold came rushing over. "Damn, I was in the back, what happened out here?"

Geigy told him. "Everything's all right," he said, "just make sure you're here at 6 o'clock tomorrow. Cheyenne's putting on a demonstration to prove how fast and accurate he is with those guns strapped around his waist."

"I'll be here," replied Harold. "Wouldn't miss it for the world."

Geigy slapped him on the back and started laughing. Harold looked at him, perplexed. "What's so funny, Geigy? I've known you for years and I've never heard you laugh."

"Well, Cheyenne here is making me forget all about my ex-wife."

"Glad to be of help," said Cheyenne, and the three men burst into laughter.

Chapter Seven

The next day Cheyenne awoke at the crack of dawn. He had passed a restless night, and was eager for the confrontation with Python. *I'll show 'em,* he thought as he cleaned and polished his prized six-shooters. *Roll on six o'clock, I'm ready!*

The hours seemed to drag, but eventually the sun started to sink. *There'll be enough light for a couple more hours,* mused Cheyenne as he gazed out of the window of his rented room. The sky was a rainbow of colors, as if someone had upturned dozens of paint cans, and splashed them across the heavens. Cheyenne stared in wonder. He was not particularly religious, but looking at the array of colors sprayed across the sky, he could only marvel that such beauty lay at the hand of God.

Time to get moving. He strapped the six-shooters around his waist and headed for the door.

Geigy was waiting for him outside. He greeted Cheyenne with a smile. "How are ya doing?" he said, slapping his friend on the shoulder. "Ready for the demonstration?"

"You bet," replied Cheyenne, patting his trusty guns.

The two men strolled down the street which was practically deserted except for a few stray dogs and a couple of children playing football.

"I wonder where everybody is?" said Geigy. His question was answered as they rounded the corner to *The African Queen.* "Well, would you look at that!" he exclaimed.

The two men stared in astonishment at the crowd of people gathered in front of the restaurant.

A beaming Jackal greeted them. He had not known about the shooting demonstration until last night. And now his business had never been so good. "Maybe we could do this every year," he said. "Business is booming."

"No, Jackal, this is a one-time only deal," said Geigy firmly.

Drinking and betting abounded. People were yelling and shouting, and betting on the twelve bottles that stood on a two by four arranged at the back of the bar. They even brought in another bartender so that Harold could collect all the bets. Some people were betting that Cheyenne would hit six bottles; others that he would hit four, and a few were betting on all twelve.

"Where's your rifle for long distance?" asked Jackal. They are also betting on that."

Cheyenne stared at him in surprise. *How did they know about his long range sniper rifle?* Then he realized that when he picked up the rifle from the shipper's some of Python's men had seen him. So now he had to go back to his lodgings and collect the weapon.

He pulled Geigy aside and told him to bet fifty dollars that he would hit all twelve bottles.

"I just happen to have a fifty on me," said Geigy with a wink.

"Good man," said Cheyenne. "You won't be sorry." And with a quick nod, he turned on his heel and hurried back to his lodgings to pick up the rifle. He was a little nervous with all the people betting on him. He knew that Python had gotten everyone together to make a fool out of him. *With my cowboy hat and six-shooters slung around my waist, I certainly stand out in a crowd.*

A sudden gust of wind kicked up some dust, blowing it into his eyes and temporarily blinding him. Before he knew it, he had bumped into someone and the two of them were now sprawled in the middle of the road. He had fallen right on top of Ebony!

"Damn it, watch where you're going!" cried Ebony as she pushed him off her and tried to struggle to her feet. Grimy streaks of dust clung to her face and clothes. "Just look at me, I'm covered in dirt."

"I'm so sorry," murmured Cheyenne. "I got some dust in my eyes. Did I hurt you in any way?"

"No, you didn't hurt me, but could you please get off me."

Their eyes met and all Cheyenne could see was her beautiful smile. For him, time stopped.

Ebony broke his reverie. "Could you please get off me," she repeated.

"Oh, sorry," said Cheyenne, rolling off her and helping her to her feet. "Are you okay."

"I'll live," said Ebony as she dusted herself off. "But look at my clothes. They're ruined!"

"Sorry…," he said sheepishly.

One of Cheyenne's six-shooters had ended up between her legs.

"Wow, that's a big gun! I was wondering what was pressing against me," said Ebony. She stared into his eyes again. "You're the cowboy that's getting this town all worked up."

Cheyenne returned her gaze. "And you're Ebony. I saw you at *The African Queen* the other day."

She stared at him more intently. "Oh, yes, you were standing with Geigy." She licked her fingers and rubbed her smudged face. "I was really mad that day, but I'm fine now."

Cheyenne held out his hand. "My name is Cheyenne Cole, and I'm here to save the elephants."

She shook his hand and once again their eyes locked. "Pleased to meet you Cheyenne Cole."

She smiled coyly and brushed the hair from her face. "Saving the elephants could be a little dangerous, especially as their tusks are so valuable."

Cheyenne changed the subject. "Are you coming down to *The African Queen* to see me shoot?"

Ebony grinned at him. "So that's what all the commotion is about. They're all taking bets."

"Yep, some will win and some will lose. Don't think I'm gonna be too popular with the losers."

"They'll get over it," she said. "I'm on my way back home to talk to my mother, but I'll try to make it." She gave Cheyenne another sly smile and hurried down the dusty street.

Cheyenne returned to the shouting crowd. The noise had reached a crescendo. He could hardly hear himself think, let alone handle a six-shooter. People were patting him on the back, others were just getting out of the way as Geigy and Jackal rushed up to greet him.

Harold was yelling out, "The more glasses you bet, the more money you make."

People clamored around him, thrusting money into his hands. Some of them were poor, so they could not afford too much. Others had plenty of cash. Harold continued to yell out above the buzz of the crowd. "It's almost showtime. You have fifteen more minutes to place your bets."

Meanwhile, out in the bush, Monsoon was eating off a luscious green tree. As he munched on the succulent leaves, his mind dwelled on the two men who had hurt him. An elephant never forgets and Monsoon's mind was telling him to get even with these two men. They had given him pain and now he must give them pain – he must kill them. The bullet had ripped off some flesh from his gigantic head, and although it had healed, it had affected his brain. Now all he wanted to do was to kill anything that got in his way.

Monsoon heard a sudden crash. He stopped munching and lifted his head. A big rhino came hurtling through the brush destroying leaves and foliage in its wake. Monsoon gave chase.

The rhino stopped in its tracks and turned to face Monsoon who was now trumpeting loudly and flapping his huge ears. This was the rhino's territory and Monsoon was invading his territory. He was not going to let the intruder get away with this.

Monsoon rose up on his back legs and let out a terrifying sound, a sound that would petrify most animals, but not this rhino. On the contrary, he was emboldened. This would be a fight to the death. Grunting and blowing air through his nostrils, the rhino stomped his feet like a bull and moved in a slow trot toward Monsoon. His eyes blazed with anger.

Monsoon stood his ground and met the rhino head on. The rhino being low to the ground managed to get under Monsoon's huge tusks. He brushed across Monsoon's left leg but did no damage. Monsoon bellowed loudly.

The rhino turned away quickly and rushed toward Monsoon again. This time he was not so lucky -- one of Monsoon's razor-sharp tusks penetrated his tough hide. Monsoon raised his powerful neck and lifted the rhino off his hind legs. The rhino stumbled and fell on his side, sending up a cloud of dust.

Monsoon moved in for the kill. Sensing victory, he hurtled toward the downed animal and plunged his lethal tusks into the soft belly of his victim. The rhino gasped in agony, then drew his last breath. To make sure that his foe was dead, Monsoon bent his front legs and lowered himself onto the rhino's limp body, crushing him with all his weight.

Back at *The African Queen,* the demonstration was about to start. All the bettors were chattering excitedly, anxious for the show to start. Serious money could exchange hands in the next few minutes. Cheyenne would determine the winners, and the losers.

Standing on a tall stool, Harold towered over the crowd and proceeded to count down to showtime, just like the space shuttle take-off.

"Okay, my friends, take your places and let the games begin. Five, four..."

Cheyenne stood alone as the frenzied crowd milled round, drinking and shouting. Shutting them out of his mind, he closed his eyes and transported himself back to Wyoming. *I'm just a simple cowboy, but I'm one of the fastest draws in the West and I'm gonna show 'em what I can do.*

Harold continued the countdown. "Three, two…"

Cheyenne stood like a stone. He surveyed the twelve bottles standing like silent sentries on a wooden plank overlooking a verdant green savannah. The sun blazed fiercely as the clouds skittered slowly across the sky. Cheyenne gripped his pistols as the countdown hit zero.

Like a flash of lightning, Cheyenne pulled out both guns and started firing. And like lightning, he jammed both guns back in his holster. The crowd fell silent, not knowing what they had just witnessed. All one could hear was the soft murmur of the wind mingling with the pungent aroma of gun smoke. Then an exultant cry from Harold sent the crowd into a frenzy.

"My God!" he yelled. "My God, he got all twelve bottles!"

People shook their heads in disbelief as they stared at the shattered bottles. They hadn't seen the guns leave Cheyenne's holster – it was as if an alien force had smashed the bottles. They stared in wonder, amazed at Cheyenne's lightning fast speed. Never in their lives had they seen anyone as fast on the draw as Cheyenne. Not to mention his accuracy. All twelve bottles had been hit.

They gathered round him, shaking his hand and patting him on the back. Even the losers joined in the congratulations.

"How did you do that, man?" said one.

"You're faster than the speed of light," said another.

"I can't believe my eyes," remarked another.

"Amazing…" "Remarkable…" "Unbelievable…" "Incredible…"

And on and on. All were in awe of Cheyenne and his marksmanship. All except for one.

Python stood in the shadows, glowering. Anger suffused his dark face and his lips curled in a menacing grimace. He had willed the cowboy to fail, but the cowboy had triumphed beyond anyone's wildest dreams. By his side stood Ego and the Russian. They too had been awed by the cowboy's prowess, but they would never let Python know. They'd be dead meat in a second.

"He just got lucky," said Ego, his trademark leer creasing his dirty face.

"Yeah, boss," offered the Russian. "It was a fluke. Let's see how he does with the sniper rifle."

Python nodded. "Yeah, you're right. Let's go and see the cowboy."

"We're right behind you, boss," said Ego as he picked at his rotten teeth with a twig. In his other hand, he carried an empty beer can.

The three thugs trudged over to Cheyenne, who was still engulfed by a sea of cheering fans. He was their new hero – the fastest shot they had ever seen – and they weren't about to let him go. The crowd parted like the Red Sea as Python approached. Hero or no hero, they were all afraid of Python and his henchmen.

Python had to say something. "Nice shooting," he said through gritted teeth. "Now, let's see how good you are with that rifle." He motioned to Ego. "Okay, Ego, you know what to do."

Ego took off across the field, clutching the empty beer can to his chest. As he scurried across the brush, Harold opened up the betting once again. "Okay, place your bets. Hit or miss."

"What are we betting on this time?" asked one man.

Harold pointed to Ego, who was now climbing a distant tree. "See the Pygmy, over there in the far distance. Well, he's going to the place the target on the tree branch."

"What target?" replied the man. "I can barely see the Pygmy, let alone the target!"

"Exactly!" said Harold with a chuckle. "So, what's your bet – hit or miss?" Harold asked him.

"Definitely miss – ten francs says he misses."

Ego was now climbing along the limb of a sturdy branch, extending himself as far as his small stature would allow, to place the beer can firmly in place. Giving a thumbs-up, which no one could see, he scuttled down the tree and moved himself well away from the target.

Python turned to Cheyenne and pointed to the beer can which was barely visible.

"That empty beer can is your target," he sneered. "Let's see how good you really are."

Cheyenne met his gaze with a defiant stare. The two men locked eyes for several seconds until Cheyenne finally broke the silence. "No problem," he said simply, and started unwrapping his rifle from the soft protective cloth.

Once again, the crowd was working itself into a frenzy, the excitement building by the second. Harold was busy taking the bets, while another bartender took over at the drinks counter.

"Hit or miss?" yelled Harold. He knew how to work the crowd. "Come on, place your bets. Can the cowboy hit the can? Roll up, place your bets - it's almost show time - place your bets."

Jackal's face glowed like a candle as the money kept pouring in. This was going to be his biggest money day ever! He blessed the day the cowboy walked into town. *Thank you, Lord.*

Cheyenne was now positioning his rifle. A hush fell over the crowd – all eyes were on the cowboy. Unfazed by all the attention, Cheyenne picked up some sand and threw it in the air to see how the wind was blowing. It was as if he were all alone on the plains of Wyoming, practicing his draw. Target practice as usual.

Taking a long bullet from his pocket, Cheyenne adjusted the sights on the rifle and placed the bullet in the chamber. The crowd heaved a collective sigh.

"No more bets," cried Harold. "The time has come."

The people tensed. They watched in awe as Cheyenne raised the rifle to his shoulder and took aim at the target. His body was rigid. He knew this was a difficult shot. As he set the sight on the beer can, a gust of wind rippled through the crowd. Cheyenne fired.

Everyone stood in silence as Ego ran toward the tree. Then the spell was broken as several spectators cried out. *Did he hit it? Did he miss? Did that gust of wind blow the can over?*

Python and the Russian watched from the shadows as Ego clambered up the tree to retrieve the can. Grabbing the target with both hands, Ego let out a scream as he tumbled through the air, still clutching the can. He hit the ground with a thud.

"What is that crazy Pygmy doing now?" muttered the Russian.

"Maybe he's knocked some sense into his thick head, after that fall," replied Python.

Ego rose up on his short legs and dusted himself off. Then he started running toward *The African Queen* as fast as those stubby legs would carry him. He stumbled several times, but the beer can never left his hand. The crowd could hear him yelling and screaming in the distance.

"What the hell is he yelling about?" asked Harold.

"Don't ask me," said Jackal.

"The little runt sure is excited," observed Geigy.

The crowd joined in. "Did he hit it? Did he hit?"

Ego staggered toward them, drawing closer and closer with each faltering step. His head was bobbing from side to side and his face looked as if it was about to explode. Rivulets of sweat ran down his cheeks and perspiration soaked his wiry hair. He was still screaming loudly.

Python turned to the Russian. "What the hell is wrong with that little bastard?"

The Russian shrugged and shook his head.

Geigy was standing beside Cheyenne as Ego finally burst through into the crowd.

"He hit the can! He hit the can!" he yelled, waving the beer can high so that everyone could see the hole. People stared in amazement. The cowboy had hit the target – a perfect round hole in the center of the can. They couldn't believe their eyes.

Geigy slapped Cheyenne on the shoulder. "What a shot! Unbelievable! Unfucking believable!"

Cheyenne shrugged modestly. He had made similar shots many times before, back in his beloved Wyoming, and in the service.

"Let me shake your hand, my friend," said Geigy, grabbing Cheyenne's hand and pumping it up and down. "I take my hat off to you. That was one helluva shot. I've never seen anything like it."

Others also gathered round Cheyenne, clamoring to shake his hand and pat him on the back. The tall cowboy was now the local hero.

Python was not happy. He and the Russian had both bet against the shot. He watched from the shadows, his dark face clouded with anger. The Russian was so furious, he could hardly speak. He finally found his voice. "Just look at those stupid people, falling over themselves to shake the cowboy's hand. He just got lucky," he sneered.

Harold stood on an overturned wooden crate and covered all the bets. Some people had won; some had lost. But win or lose, most of them went away happy. On this day, they had witnessed an amazing show of sharpshooting. The cowboy had done them proud.

The sky was darkening as the crowd slowly dispersed. They would be talking about this day for years. A story to pass on to their grandchildren. Cheyenne waved his goodbyes, then cleaned his rifle and packed it neatly in its cloth.

Geigy tapped him on the shoulder. "Care to join me at the bar for a small celebration? The drinks are on me," he winked.

"You bet. I was mighty tense back there for a moment. Wasn't sure if I'd hit it."

"Never doubted you for a second," said Geigy, dragging him toward the front entrance of *The African Queen.* "Not for a second."

The first drink was on Jackal. He was ecstatic over the amount of money he had made in the last couple of hours. Rushing over to Cheyenne, he shook his hand vigorously.

"Whatever you want, it's on the house," he gushed. "In all my life, I never saw shooting like that before." He stared at Cheyenne in wide-eyed wonder. "You have the hands of lightning."

Cheyenne tipped his cowboy hat. "Thank you, sir."

Jackal smiled. "Remember, anything you want, it's on the house." Then he turned on his heel and scurried back to the kitchen to help Harold count the money and to pay off the winners. Most of the losers had already left. The winners were still drinking. *So I may have lost some of the bets, but I'll get it back on the drinks. They're gonna drink themselves silly tonight.*

Cheyenne and Geigy stood by the side of the bar, relaxing and enjoying their drinks. About an hour later, Jackal joined them once more and handed Geigy a cool three hundred dollars.

"Your winnings, I believe," he said with a grin.

"Thanks, Jackal," he said, pocketing the money. "Hope you don't mind, Cheyenne, but I had a little bet on you." He raised his glass. "Cheers, I knew you wouldn't let me down."

Jackal turned to Willie, the new bartender. "Willie, look after Cheyenne and Geigy here. Anything they want, it's on the house." Willie nodded.

As the night wore on, people started to drift away and soon only Cheyenne and Geigy and a few others were left at the bar. Willie came down to join them. Wafer thin, with a big friendly smile that lit up his crinkled dark face, he told them that he was half-Pigmy, and related to Ego.

Geigy started laughing. "I don't believe you, Willie. Just look at the size of you." He looked him up and down. "You're as tall as me, and I'm five foot ten."

"It's the truth," said Willie. "By all that's holy, I swear it." He leaned in close and whispered very slowly. "I have a dark secret, and if I told Ego, it would probably cost me my life."

Willie jerked upright as an empty glass thudded against the bar. He excused himself and hurried down to the other end of the bar to fill the empty glass.

Geigy turned to Cheyenne. "What do you make of that? Willy related to that little runt, Ego?"

"Very strange," said Cheyenne. "I'd have to hear more."

Geigy looked around the deserted bar. He nudged Cheyenne. "Well, well, well, look who's sitting at the table in the far corner. I didn't notice them before with all the people celebrating."

Cheyenne started to turn around but Geigy stopped him. "No, don't turn around, they're looking this way. It's Python, the Russian and Ego, with three sleazy looking men."

"Oh, yeah," said Cheyenne. "Wonder what they're cooking up now."

"Nothing good, I can tell you that," said Geigy as he took another slurp of beer.

Jackal emerged from the kitchen and walked over to Cheyenne and Geigy.

"How about another drink?" he offered.

"No, thanks," said Cheyenne, "I've had enough for one night!"

Geigy never refused a drink. "Yep, I'll have one more, Jackal, especially as you're paying." Smiling, he drained the last of his beer and passed the empty glass to Jackal.

"Hey, Willie, another beer over here for my friend," called Jackal. He turned to Cheyenne. "Hey, we're having a party and barbeque on Friday night. Come on down. You, too, Geigy."

The two men nodded. "We'll be here," they said in unison.

It was past midnight now, and Cheyenne was feeling tired. The shoot-out had drained his energy. It was time for him to hit the sack.

"Well, guys, if you don't mind, I'm gonna turn in now. It's been an exhausting night, to say the least," he said with a grin. As he headed toward the door, he turned and waved. "Goodnight, all, see you Friday night."

Geigy returned the wave. "See ya, Cowboy, sleep well. You've earned it."

"Hear, hear," said Jackal, grinning from ear to ear. He had made more money tonight than he'd made in the last year.

Cheyenne stepped out into the warm, balmy night. A soft breeze caressed his face as he stared up at the shimmering moon. *Africa is one beautiful and exciting country. I love Wyoming, but this place takes some beating.*

As he wandered along the street, he couldn't stop thinking about Willie and his dark secret. *What possible secret could cost Willie his life?* he wondered.

Chapter Eight

On Friday night Cheyenne headed for *The African Queen.* He had been looking forward to the party all week. Approaching the restaurant, he could hear the blare of the juke box and the noisy buzz of chatter and laughter. *Sounds as if they're having a good time. The party's in full swing.* The first person he spotted as he strode in through the door was Geigy, propped up in his usual place at the bar, a cold beer set before him. Cheyenne walked over to him.

"Hi, Geigy, thanks for saving me a seat," he said as he settled in next to him.

"My pleasure," said Geigy, shaking Cheyenne's hand. "Glad you could make it." He surveyed the crowded bar. "Looks like a fun night."

Cheyenne nodded and ordered a beer. Harold and Willie were both working the bar.

"Beer here, please, Harold," said Cheyenne. "And another cold one for my friend."

"Coming right up," said Harold, smiling.

Cheyenne checked out the bar and spotted Ebony in the shadowy corner, fighting with Python. She was wearing a short, black mini-skirt and a low-cut satin blouse that showed off her ample cleavage. Bright red lipstick outlined her luscious lips and her long, glossy hair was pulled back in dreadlocks. Cheyenne couldn't take his eyes off her – she looked stunning.

The Russian and Ego sat on either side of Python, and both seemed to be enjoying the fight. Smiling smugly, they watched with relish as Python and Ebony argued back and forth.

Cheyenne dragged his eyes away and looked around the rest of the bar. Single women in tight mini-skirts and stacked high heels mingled with the usual patrons. He turned to Geigy. "Yeah, you're right, it looks like a fun night!"

As the evening progressed, the bar became more and more crowded. Music blared. Young women danced with each other, or alone. There weren't too many couples. At the back table, Python was deep in conversation with the Russian. He and Ebony had finally stopped fighting.

"That cowboy is here to save the elephants, and he's going to be a thorn in your side," said the Russian. "We have to get rid of him somehow."

Python took a long draw on his drink. "The night is young, let's have a few more drinks and then I'll think about it."

Ebony walked over to the table and sat down.

"Where have you been, bitch?" demanded Python, slamming his glass on the table.

Ebony's dark eyes blazing with anger. "None of your business, you Black Devil," she shouted.

Furious, Python jumped to his feet, ready to backhand her, but he decided against it. There were too many people around. He didn't want them to think that he was a woman beater. Instead, he turned to Ego. "Go up and get us a round of drinks."

Ego gestured to the waitresses, busy taking orders from the crowded tables. "But, boss..."

Python cut him off. "I need a drink now!" He prodded Ego sharply in the ribs. "Go, go!"

Ego rubbed his sore ribs and stumbled toward the bar. "Okay, okay, I'm going."

Cheyenne was telling Geigy about his new Range Rover. "It has four-wheel drive and it runs real good," he said. "I also bought ten cans of gas. I don't want to run out of gas in the bush."

"You're right on that," said Geigy. "The bush can be dangerous, especially if you're on foot."

Before Cheyenne could respond, Harold's voice rang out. "The barbeque is ready. Everybody grab a plate and get something to eat. It's going to be delicious."

Many people rushed outside immediately, hoping to grab a place at the front of the line.

"Let's wait until the line goes down," said Geigy. Cheyenne nodded.

Fifteen minutes later, the two friends finished their drinks and headed for the chow line.

Meanwhile, Python, Ego and the Russian had been joined at their table by the three sleazy-looking men from the other night. Ebony was absent once again. All six had full plates of food and were eating hungrily. No one was talking. The sleazy men chomped noisily, mouths open, their tongues slurping the food, like three big dogs lapping water.

Python looked over at them. "So, what are your names?" he asked, trying to ignore their eating habits. No response. The three men were too busy gobbling down their food. Python repeated the question, louder this time.

Finally, the leader of the group looked up, his mouth crammed with food. "My name is Hi, and that's Ho and Cracker." Then without missing a beat, he continued chomping, beans and meat spilling from his mouth, gravy dribbling down his chin. .

Python could stand it no longer. "Did any of you have a mother?" he asked them.

The three men stopped chomping and started laughing. "We all have the same mother," said Ho.

"Did she teach you how to eat without smashing your lips? You sound like hogs at a trough."

Ho slammed his fist on the table, sending food and cutlery flying. "You can call us hogs, but don't be saying anything about our mother," he said angrily. "We come from the bush and we don't like to hear anything bad about our mother."

Python stood his ground. "Well, I don't think your mother did a very good job bringing you up."

The bush men jumped to their feet, knocking over their chairs. "Don't say anything about our mother," they shouted in unison.

Python sprang to his feet and faced the angry trio. Ho stepped forward, fists raised, but Cracker pulled him back. "Steady on, Ho, he ain't worth it."

"Ho, Ho, Ho, why the hell don't you sit down," taunted Python.

Ho charged. He was about to slam his fist into Python's face when Ebony stepped between them. She had heard the commotion from the other end of bar and had come rushing over.

"What are you fighting over now?" she shouted. "Can't you men talk about anything but Ho, Ho, Ho."

"We're not talking about any Ho, Ho, Ho. His name is Ho," said Python, pointing at Ho.

Ebony burst out laughing. "I heard those lip smacking sounds from these bush people and then I heard Ho, Ho, Ho. Now you're trying to cover this up by saying his name is Ho." She shook her head in disbelief. "I've heard everything now!"

She started to walk away, but Python grabbed her arm and pulled her back.

"Where the hell have you been?" he shouted. "I was looking for you, so we could eat together."

"I went to see my mother," she replied.

"You spend too much time with your damn mother. You know she hates me."

Ebony shoved him away. "She has reasons for hating you, and you know what they are."

Her response seemed to rub Python the wrong way. He couldn't let her embarrass him in front of his friends and the three bush men. Without warning, he backhanded Ebony across the face twice. She stumbled slightly then came right back at him with a hard smack across his face. Caught by surprise, Python rubbed at his sore cheek, his mouth wide open in astonishment.

"Why, you little bitch…" he began, but before he could grab her again, Ebony had raced across the room, tears streaming down her face, and stumbled out of the door.

Cheyenne and Geigy had watched the scene unfold from their seats at the bar. Both were angry and upset. "Did you see that?" said Cheyenne in disgust. "What a bastard! Beating up on that poor girl. She's half the size of him. I've a good mind to go over and punch his lights out."

"Take it easy, Cheyenne," said Geigy. "There's six of them and one of you. But you're right, Python is a bastard, and a first-class asshole."

Cheyenne frowned. "I'm puzzled, what's a beautiful girl like Ebony doing with scum like that?"

Geigy shrugged. "You got me! God knows why she stays with him. They've been together for a long time. Perhaps she's afraid that he'd kill her if she tried to break off with him."

"He'd probably get away with it too – more than likely bury her body in the jungle or bush."

Geigy nodded. "Women! Who knows why they fall for such lousy bastards who beat them up."

"Well, at least she smacked him back," said Cheyenne with a grin. "She sure is spunky."

"That she is," agreed Geigy. "I'll drink to that."

"Me, too," said Cheyenne, and two men clinked glasses. "Cheers."

Back in the corner, Python called over one of the bartenders who happened to be his cousin, and handed him a small plastic bag containing some white powder. "Here, Sinto, put this powder in the cowboy's glass," he said, "and don't get caught." He squeezed Sinto's arm hard.

Sinto nodded. "Do you want me to put some in Geigy's glass also?"

"No, he's like immune to this stuff. We tried it on him before and nothing happened."

"Okay, I'll take care of it," said Sinto as he turned on his heel and walked back to the bar.

Python rubbed his hands together. "This should make the night a little more exciting."

The Russian laughed. "Very good, very good. Let's have some fun."

Sinto worked his way down the bar, casually clearing glasses and wiping down the counter top. Soon he was close enough to Cheyenne, to be able to get the next drink for him.

"Two more beers here, please," said Cheyenne, pushing his glass forward along with Geigy's.

Sinto pushed past Harold. "Coming right up, sir," said Sinto, with a smile. He grabbed the glasses and placed them under the bar. After filling Geigy's glass, he slipped the package out of his pocket and opened it. Looking up to make sure that Harold was busy with other customers, he poured the powder into Cheyenne's beer and stirred it up.

Perfect. The powder blends well with the frothy beer. He'll never notice.

Grabbing the two beers, he sauntered over to Cheyenne and Geigy and placed the two glasses on the counter in front of them. "Here you go, sir, two ice-cold beers. Enjoy." He smiled brightly.

"Thanks," said Cheyenne, pushing one of the beers toward Geigy.

As Cheyenne was about to take his first sip, Ebony came strolling into the bar. Passing by Cheyenne, she touched him on the shoulder and winked, then joined a gaggle of girls at the far end of the bar. Cheyenne nodded his head in greeting.

Ignoring Python and the Russian, who were seated nearby, Ebony joked with her girlfriends.

Python glared at her. *I'll make the bitch pay for embarrassing me in front of my friends.*

The Russian watched as Cheyenne sipped his beer. This drug affected people in different ways. To his surprise, Cheyenne finished the beer and ordered another. The Russian nudged Python. "Look, the cowboy is ordering another beer. The drug hasn't affected him at all."

Sinto looked over at Python to see if he should put some more powder in Cheyenne's next beer. Python nodded. Unnoticed again, Sinto repeated the process and passed the spiked beer to Cheyenne. Cheyenne finished about half of his drink and then turned to Geigy and said, "I can hear every beat of the music and I feel really warm inside." He stood up from his seat and looked down at his feet. "These feet were made for dancing. I want to dance, dance, dance."

Geigy looked at him in amazement. "Go for it," he said.

Cheyenne spun round and round, his whole body swaying in time to the music. Flinging his arms in the air, he whirled faster and faster, oblivious to everything but the beat of the music.

Geigy couldn't believe his eyes. *I must have had more to drink than I thought,* he muttered as he watched the whirling dervish before him.

Suddenly, Cheyenne stopped in mid-twirl and turned to Geigy. "Would you like to dance?"

"Hell, no," cried Geigy, almost spilling his drink. "I don't want to dance. Are you all right, Cheyenne? You're acting kinda crazy."

"I'm fine, I just want to dance, dance, dance."

Without missing a beat, Cheyenne danced across the room toward the far corner of the restaurant. There he spotted the stuffed leopard with the extra long tail: Ebony's gift to Python.

Cheyenne asked the leopard if she would like to dance and she must have said yes, because Cheyenne grabbed her by the tail and started dancing across the floor. Ebony was standing with her girlfriends at the corner of the bar as Cheyenne and the leopard glided past.

"Boy, he can really dance," she said.

"Yeah, he's hot," said Raquel, one of Ebony's girlfriends.

Unfortunately for Cheyenne, he kept tripping over the panther's tail.

"Think I'll go and help him," said Raquel, licking her lips.

In the meantime, Python and his cronies were laughing up a storm. "Just look at that crazy cowboy," said Python, pointing at Cheyenne. "He's fucking loco." Everyone laughed.

Several girls, including Ebony, had joined Cheyenne and the leopard on the dance floor. Gyrating and writhing bodies now enveloped Cheyenne – everyone was caught up in the music. Ebony pulled the leopard's tail between her legs, dancing around with frenzied abandon. Python wasn't laughing now. His face like thunder, he watched as his woman cavorted with the crazy cowboy, the leopard's tail sticking out from her ass. His cronies fell silent. They knew his explosive temper could not be controlled.

"Just look at that bitch," he yelled. "She's just asking for it."

No one said a word. They would wait and see how this played out. Suddenly the music stopped and the dancers returned to their seats. Python rose from his chair and approached Ebony. His dark eyes were clouded with anger, his jaw set in a tight grimace.

"What the hell do you think you're doing, dancing and wiggling your ass like a common ho?"

Ebony pushed him away. "Go away and don't ruin a fun evening. I'm having a wild time."

Surprisingly, Python backed off and let her be for the time being. His cronies stared in astonishment as Python walked back to their table. They had expected him to whack her hard. He sat down and grunted. "Bitch," he muttered into his drink.

The music had started again, and more people crowded onto the dance floor. Ebony sashayed over to Cheyenne, her shapely ass swaying back and forth. "How about it, Cowboy, care to trip the light fantastic one more time?" She smiled seductively, her opal eyes flashing.

Cheyenne stood. His head was still spinning from the effect of the drugs. Ebony took his hand and led him onto the dance floor. A slow ballad began. Cheyenne took her in his arms and with their bodies pressed together, they swayed to the gentle rhythm of the music. Python watched from the shadows. His eyes blazed with anger. Turning to the Russian, he said, "Look at those two assholes. His fucking hand is on her fucking ass!" He pushed the Russian forward. "Go out there and cut in," he ordered.

Reluctantly, the Russian marched over to the swaying couple and tapped Cheyenne on the shoulder. "My turn to dance with the *lady* I believe," he said with a growl.

Before Cheyenne could respond, Ebony piped up, "I asked him to dance, so if you want to dance with somebody, you have to dance with Cheyenne."

The Russian shrugged and ambled back to Python.

"What happened?" demanded Python. "Why ain't you dancing with my woman?"

"She told me I have to dance with the cowboy," he said sheepishly.

Python's face turned purple under his black skin. "She's being a real bitch tonight. I'm gonna fix her ass." Grabbing one of the girls who was standing nearby, he headed for the dance floor, dragging her behind him. The startled girl, fearful of Python's explosive temper, did not protest. Whirling her round, he purposely bumped into Cheyenne. "Oh, I'm so sorry," he said.

"Oh, I just bet you are," said Ebony.

Python bumped into them again; so hard this time that he broke them apart. Cheyenne went down on one knee. Ebony slapped and kicked Python.

"What the hell do you think you're doing, you bastard!" she yelled.

"Crazy bitch," cried Python. He shoved her hard, sending her sprawling over two tables. She crashed to the floor with a thud. Then Python turned and attacked Cheyenne, knocking him to the floor. Dazed and confused, Cheyenne didn't know what was happening. The drugs held him in their grip. He didn't want to fight, he just wanted to dance.

As Cheyenne tried to struggle to his feet, Python cold cocked him, knocking him flat on his back. Python dove on top of him, fists flying. Raising his legs under Python's body, Cheyenne managed to push him off. Python fell back, knocking over a table and two chairs. He shouted to his cronies who were still seated in the corner. "Get over here, now!"

They scrambled to their feet and rushed over. Cheyenne now found himself surrounded by six burly men. Two men held his arms, while the others punched him hard in the stomach and the head. Cheyenne fell to the ground, unconscious. The men kicked him in the ribs a few times, then picked up his limp body and threw him out the back door, by the garbage.

Willie the bartender was taking a smoke break when the back door slammed open with a bang and three men emerged carrying Cheyenne. He watched as the men tossed him into the black bags of garbage. Fortunately for Willie, the men didn't see him standing in the shadows, otherwise he may have joined Cheyenne in the garbage bags. He heard one of the men say, "Do you think he might be dead?"

"Yes, I think he's dead," replied another.

Willie held his breath and waited until the door closed behind the three thugs. He was about to rush over to see who the person was, when the door flew open again and a cowboy hat came sailing out. He gasped in horror. *My God, it's the cowboy!* He surveyed Cheyenne's bruised and battered body. *It's Cheyenne, the brave man who came here to save the elephants!*

Meanwhile, back in the bar Ebony confronted the three men who had just tossed Cheyenne into the garbage. "You dirty rotten cowards!" she screamed as she tried to kick and claw at them. Python rushed over and grabbed her arm. She tried to shake free, but he slapped her hard in the face. "You're my woman," he yelled in her ear, "and you will only be dancing with me from now on. Do you hear?"

"Like hell I will," screamed Ebony, kicking him hard in shins. "My mother was right about you, you're nothing but a black devil."

She broke free and ran out of the bar, sobbing bitterly. She had really liked Cheyenne.

Out in the back, Willie checked to see if Cheyenne was still alive. Detecting a faint pulse, he tried to make Cheyenne as comfortable as possible, too afraid of Python to call for help. Placing his jacket under Cheyenne's head, he wiped away the blood on Cheyenne's face with his handkerchief. Startled, he heard the click-clack of high heels against the stone ground, then silence. He looked round to see Ebony taking off her shoes and walking toward him in the dark.

"Ebony," he whispered, "it's me, Willie. I have Cheyenne. He's still breathing…he's alive."

"Thank God for that," said Ebony. "How bad is he?"

"Pretty bad," said Willie. "We have to get him to a doctor – he needs help."

Ebony bent down and touched Cheyenne gently on forehead. She gasped when she saw his beaten and bloodied face. "Willie, we have to get him to my mother's house. If we take him to the hospital, Python's men will kill him – he has spies everywhere, even in the hospital."

Willie nodded. They tried to lift him, but at six foot two, and weighing about 220 pounds, Cheyenne was too heavy for them.

"We have to hurry in case they come out again," said Ebony. "What are we going to do?"

Willie wrinkled his brow, thinking hard. His face lit up. "The wheelbarrow!" he exclaimed.

Ebony eyed him quizzically. "What wheelbarrow?"

"The wheelbarrow we use for carrying all the beer and liquor. We keep it out here at the back. Let me try and find it." He grinned, pleased that the idea had come to him.

"Hurry, Willie! Hurry!" urged Ebony as she stroked Cheyenne's face.

Willie dashed off and within seconds he was back, pushing the wheelbarrow. "I've found it!"

"Okay, you grab his arms and I'll take his feet," said Ebony. "Gently now, he may have some broken bones or ribs."

Together, she and Willie lifted Cheyenne into the wheelbarrow. They both sighed with relief.

"Good, let's get out of here," said Ebony.

Inside the *African Queen,* Python was buying drinks for everyone.

"Here's to Python and Africa," the patrons of the bar shouted as they raised their glasses high.

Python's reputation was well-known – they were all afraid of him.

Python smiled and strode across the dance floor to his table. Around the table sat the Russian, and Ego, and the three bush men, who had helped to beat up Cheyenne. Cracker's knuckles were bleeding, blood streamed from Ho's cut lip, and Hi was rubbing his sore knee.

"Damn, I must have twisted it in all the commotion," he said.

The Russian had had a ringside view of the fight. "That was a wonderful beating, if ever I saw one," he said, his Russian accent more pronounced than usual. "The cowboy is dead, is he not?"

"If he's not dead now, he will be by morning," replied Cracker.

The Russian slammed his fist on the table, knocking glasses and bottles flying. "He's still alive!"

He turned to Python. "The cowboy is a menace to our business. He must be killed *now!*"

Python looked over at Ego and smiled. "Do you have your knife, Ego?" he asked.

Ego nodded and patted his pocket. "Yes, I have my very *sharp* knife."

"Make sure he's dead," commanded Python.

Ego smiled his sick smile. "You got it, boss, leave it to me," he said as he rose from his chair.

The Russian grabbed his arm. "Make sure you cut his throat."

"From ear to ear," assured Ego, touching one ear and then the other.

The Russian laughed and slugged down another shot of whiskey. "Nostravia."

Chapter Nine

Ebony and Willie were moving Cheyenne as fast as they could in the wheelbarrow. They raced down the dusty street, which was practically deserted except for a few stray dogs and a couple of drunken revelers. Finally, they pulled up in front of a small shack, well kept but shabby. Ebony banged on the faded red door.

"Mother, " she called softly, anxious not to disturb the neighbors. "Wake up, it's me, Ebony."

Her mother's head poked out through the window. "What's going on?" she asked, rubbing her eyes. "What's all the commotion?"

"Mother, we have an injured man who needs help desperately!"

"I'll be right there," said her mother. "Who is that with you?" she asked, staring through the darkness at Willie.

"It's Willie, the bartender from *The African Queen.* He's helping me."

A few moments later, the door opened and Ebony's mother appeared on the doorstep in her nightgown. An older version of Ebony, her opal eyes glittered in the darkness like cat's eyes. The years had taken their toll, but she had once been a great beauty just like her daughter.

"Okay, bring him in, let me take a look," said Emerald.

Emerald was a retired nurse. She had worked for years in the emergency room of the local hospital, and had dealt with the complete gamut of injuries from nose bleeds to heart attacks.

"Lay him on the sofa."

Ebony and Willie pushed the wheelbarrow through the door and into the small living room. Carefully, they lifted Cheyenne and lay him gently on the sofa. He was still unconscious. The room was simply decorated: wooden walls painted brown with white trim. A faded picture of Nelson Mandela hung over the fireplace. Sparsely furnished, it contained little more than a table with two chairs and a worn blue sofa.

"What happened to this man?" asked Emerald as she checked Cheyenne's pulse and examined his battered body.

"It's all my fault, Mother. I was dancing with him and Python didn't like it." Her eyes filled with tears. "He ordered his cronies to beat him up," she sobbed.

"Python!" exclaimed Emerald, anger clouding her face. "You know how much I despise that animal." She shook her head. "Why in God's name are you still with him? He's evil!"

Ebony hung her head meekly. She knew her mother was right.

Emerald finished her examination. "Well, I don't think he has any broken bones... a few broken ribs perhaps. Not much we can do about that – they'll heal on their own."

She stared at Cheyenne's bloody face. His left eye had now swollen to the size of a golf ball. "He's badly concussed, but I think he'll come around soon. He's going to have one heck of a headache, not to mention the pain from his broken ribs." She turned to Ebony. "Let's get him cleaned up. Start heating up some water and grab some towels from the linen cupboard. Hurry!"

Ebony did as her mother ordered. She felt guilty. *If it wasn't for me, none of this would have happened.*

"What can I do?" asked Willie.

"You have to get the wheelbarrow back fast," said Ebony. "And make sure you go in the front door." She walked over and hugged him. "Thank you so much for helping me, Willie. I couldn't have done it without you."

Willie smiled sheepishly. "Cheyenne is a good man. I hope he'll be all right." He took her hand and squeezed it. "Don't worry, I'll take care of the wheelbarrow. You just take care of Cheyenne." And with a quick wave, he and the wheelbarrow disappeared into the darkness.

After putting the wheelbarrow back in place, Willie hurried to the front of *The African Queen.* Flipping a cigarette out onto the street to make it look as if he had just come in from a smoke break, he strode in through the door. No one suspected anything.

Harold was busy wiping down the counter. "Hey, man," he whispered, "you just missed a fight."

"What fight?" Willie asked innocently.

Harold leaned in close. "Well, you know that cowboy, the tall guy who can shoot fast?"

"You mean Cheyenne," said Willie.

"Yeah, that's him," said Harold. "Well, he was messing with Python's woman and Python's boys worked him over bad."

Willie looked shocked. "I hope they didn't kill him," he whispered.

Harold picked up a beer glass and inspected it for stains. "I don't know for sure, but he wouldn't be the first one," he replied.

They both looked over at Python's table and saw the Russian grab Ego by the arm and whisper in his ear. "I wonder what they're up to now," said Harold.

They watched as Ego pulled a knife from his pocket and slid his finger along the edge. Then, smiling his sick smile, he walked toward the back door and out into the night. The door slammed behind him.

My God, thought Willie, *me and Ebony have saved Cheyenne's life. No thanks to Geigy there.*

He glanced down the bar to see that Geigy was still sound asleep. Dead drunk, he had passed out and slept through the entire fight.

"Must have really tied one on," said Willie, listening to Geigy's loud snores.

"You got that right," replied Harold. "You know Geigy."

Ego sauntered out of the back door intent on finishing off the cowboy. He was like an animal looking for a kill. His beady eyes searched the darkness. "Where are you, Cowboy, I'm comin' to get you?" He smiled in anticipation, revealing his rotten yellow teeth. "Where are you, Cowboy?" he called again. "Come out, come out, wherever you!"

His eyes finally came to rest on the black garbage bags. "Aha, I do believe my prey is close." He fingered the sharp knife and waddled over to the bags as fast as his stumpy legs could carry him. *Where the hell is the bastard,* he muttered, frantically tossing the bags aside. *He must have crawled off into a corner somewhere.*

He continued searching wildly, stabbing the bags with his knife and flinging them in the air. Cheyenne was nowhere to be found. And Ego was beginning to get nervous. *The bastard has to be here somewhere.* Flailing around, he bumped into the wheelbarrow which was parked near the back door. "Ouch," he yelled, rubbing his side. Angrily, he kicked the wheelbarrow, slamming it hard against the door.

Inside, Python and his cronies heard the loud crash. "That's what we call overkill," said the Russian, and they all burst into laughter.

"Let's have another shot to celebrate," said Python.

As they raised their glasses, the door flung open and in stormed Ego, knife in hand. "He's gone!" he screamed. "The dirty bastard cowboy is gone!"

Python and the Russian leapt to their feet. Drinks spilled, glasses shattered. Hi, Ho and Cracker were stomping over one another, scrambling to reach the back door. All of them ended up in the back, tearing apart garbage bags like rats in an alley. Nothing! Nano! Zilch! They searched every nook, every cranny, and finally came to the grim conclusion that the *cowboy had gone.*

"The bastard can't have disappeared into thin air," said Python.

"Someone must have helped him," said the Russian. The others agreed.

"He must be close by. Let's check the street," said Ho.

They ran down the now deserted street, searching alleys and checking doorways, but there was no sign of Cheyenne.

"We should have made sure he was dead when they threw him into the garbage bags," yelled Python.

"We could have dropped his body off in the desert and let the animals do the rest," said the Russian.

"All right, all right, *should have, could have,* it's too late now," muttered Python. "We'll continue searching when the sun comes up. Maybe someone will find his body in the morning.

"Let's go inside and have another drink," said Python, leading the way to *The African Queen.* "I need one badly." He wiped the sweat from his forehead. "Tomorrow we find him or someone's going to pay…"

Chapter Ten

Cheyenne was still unconscious. Emerald tended to his wounds, cleaning and the dressing the cuts, and bandaging his cracked ribs.

"Let's hope he wakes up soon," she said, wiping the last of the blood from his face. "All we can do is keep the wounds clean and wet his lips with water. Thank God, he has no other serious injuries." She turned to Ebony. "Now, my girl, who is this man and what is he doing in Gabon?"

"Mother, this is the man who came all the way from America to save the elephants. He's the one I was telling you about, remember? The man who is so good with a gun."

"Ah, I remember now," said Emerald. "Cheyenne, the cowboy. No wonder that black devil, Python, doesn't like him," she said, wiping her hands on a towel. "He was probably just waiting for an excuse to try and kill him."

"Mother, I'm afraid that Python and his hoodlums will be looking for him, to finish him off!"

Emerald patted her arm. "Don't worry, honey," she said, looking over at the double-barreled shot gun resting against the far corner wall. "You told me that you and Python weren't seeing eye to eye, so that's going to be our excuse not to let him in the house." And, raising her hands in the air, Emerald looked toward the ceiling and cried, "It's over, thank God, it's over. Hallelujah!"

Meanwhile, back at *The African Queen* Python was forming his posse. They had been drinking all night, plotting and formulating a plan. Bleary-eyed, he addressed his henchmen. "If you find the cowboy and he's still alive, make it look like he died from the fight with Cracker."

"Let me be the one to find him," spouted Ego. "Let me be the one to find him!"

"Settle down, Ego. Whoever finds him, finds him. Now get outta here. Get me that cowboy!"

They took off in different vehicles, and searched high and low for Cheyenne. Ho and Cracker drove into the bush and spent all day scouring the jungle and surrounding area. Hi and Ego covered the town. Nothing. No one had seen hide nor hair of the cowboy. Later that night, they met up at *The African Queen.* Python stood in the center of the bar and addressed the patrons. "Does anyone here have any idea what happened to the cowboy?"

Geigy was sitting in his usual place at the bar, drinking a beer. He got up and marched over to Python. "I would like to know the same thing," he said. "The last time I saw him, he was dancing with that damn long-tailed leopard!!" He scratched his head in puzzlement. "That's all I can remember, I must have passed out after that."

Everyone started laughing. Geigy was famous for passing out at the bar. He threw his hands up in the air. "Well, if you see him, tell him the first drink's on me," he said, returning to the bar. Python joined his friends at their usual table in the corner.

"I have a feeling that Ebony has something to do with his disappearance," barked the Russian.

"I saw her running out the front door crying," said Cracker.

There was complete silence as Python looked straight ahead, then he spoke. "Let's go down and pay Ebony and her bitch mother a little visit," he sneered. "We'll walk, it's not that far."

He sprang to his feet and headed for the back door. The others fell in line behind him like rats following the Pied Piper.

Ebony and her mother were taking care of Cheyenne as best they could. The swelling had gone down in his face, but he was still unconscious.

"If he doesn't come out of this coma soon," said Emerald, "we'll have to take him to the hospital. He needs nutrients, an intravenous drip, otherwise he'll starve."

Before Ebony could respond, Cheyenne suddenly shouted out, "Black Bart. Black Bart."

The two women stared at him in surprise. Ebony grabbed a damp washcloth and wiped his forehead. "You're all right, baby," she soothed, "you're all right."

"He must have had a nightmare," said Emerald. "Who is Black Bart? Do you know?"

"I have no idea," replied Ebony as she continued to wipe his forehead.

A loud crashing noise followed by a stream of curses made them both jump in alarm.

"What's all that commotion outside," said Emerald as she walked to the window and looked out. "Oh, God," she cried, "it's that black devil Python and his gang, and they're headed this way!"

Ebony dropped the washcloth. She was trembling from head to toe. "God help us, Mother, what are we going to do? If they find Cheyenne, they'll kill him."

Emerald rushed over and hugged her close. "Don't you worry, my darling girl. I'll handle this."

A loud bang thudded against the front door. Ebony jumped. Emerald marched over to the far corner of the room and grabbed the shotgun. "Who's there?" she cried, a fierce look of determination on her face.

"It's Python, and I want to talk to Ebony."

"Well, she doesn't want to talk to you," Emerald shouted. "It's all over between you and her."

"Open the fucking door, you old bitch," demanded Python, "or I'll kick it in."

"Don't open it, Mother," cried Ebony. She was still shaking with fear.

"Don't worry, honey," soothed Emerald. "Mama's gonna take care of you."

Emerald opened the door slowly and raised the shotgun. Python stood there staring down the barrel of the gun. He took a step back, stumbling into his cronies who were standing behind him. He raised his hands. "Whoa, hold on there, you crazy old bitch, that gun could go off."

"Damn right," said Emerald, "and a few of you will be going down if I pull the trigger."

"Take it easy, old woman, we ain't here to fight with you."

Emerald kept the shotgun steady, still aiming between Python's eyes. "What do you want, you black devil? Ebony wants no part of you. Why don't you get going. Go on! Get out of here!"

Python struggled to control his anger. *That crazy bitch could pull the trigger any time.*

"You tell your precious daughter she can go to hell as far as I'm concerned. We're looking for the cowboy and you'd better not be hiding him," Python warned as he took a step forward.

Emerald leveled the rifle. "You come across that doorway and you're a dead man," she shouted.

Python hesitated. "Come on, come on, take that step and I'll rid Africa of a tyrant!"

They glared at each other with hatred. "I'm warning you," said Emerald, "one more step forward and you're a goner." Python stepped back. "We haven't seen the person you're looking for, and besides, it's none of your business," she yelled.

"You better be telling the truth, old woman, otherwise…" he ran his finger across his throat.

"Tell Ebony I'll be seeing her later." He motioned to his posse, and they took off down the road.

Emerald closed the door and locked it. Ebony was still trembling like a leaf. Emerald placed the shotgun back in the corner, then cradled her daughter in her arms.

"Don't worry, baby, you have nothing to worry about as long as I'm around." She stroked Ebony's long lustrous hair. "Don't worry, honey," she consoled. "I'll take care of you."

Fortunately, Cheyenne had been silent during the confrontation at the door. Now, once again, he blurted out, "Black Bart. Black Bart."

Ebony caressed his brow. "It's okay, Cheyenne. Mama's gonna take care of both of us."

Ebony tossed and turned all night, thinking about the cowboy in the next room.

It's all my fault that he's in a coma. Dear God, I pray that he wakes up soon.

Emerald too passed a restless night, dreaming about Cheyenne.

I hope that boy wakes up soon, for all our sakes, she prayed.

To their surprise, the very next day their prayers were answered. They awoke to hear a voice calling, "Hello, hello, is anybody there?"

Rushing into the room, they found Cheyenne sitting up in bed, asking, "What am I doing here?"

He rubbed his sore head. "Ouch, my head hurts."

The two women stared at him, temporarily lost for words. Cheyenne looked straight at Ebony. "I remember you, you're from *The African Queen,*" he said. Ebony nodded.

Cheyenne pointed at Emerald. "But I don't know you," he said.

Ebony finally found her voice. "Yes, I'm Ebony, and this is my mother, Emerald. She's a retired nurse, and she's been taking care of your wounds."

Cheyenne looked at the bandages around his middle and at the cuts and bruises on his body. "What happened? How did I get all these cuts and bruises?" He stroked his sides. "And my ribs ache like hell."

"Don't you remember anything?" asked Ebony.

"The last thing I remember was having a drink at the bar with Geigy."

"I think they put something in both your drinks," Ebony told him.

"*They* meaning Python and the Russian, I take it," said Cheyenne.

"Yes," she replied. "You started dancing, and you got into trouble when you started dancing with me. Python got jealous. His cronies took you out back and beat you up." She looked at her mother and then continued. "They left you for dead, but Willie found you, and he and I brought you here to my mother's house. You've been in a coma for the last couple of days."

Cheyenne stared at her, still trying to comprehend what had happened. "You saved my life and I don't know how to thank you," he said finally. "I have to get out of here as soon as possible."

"They're looking for you," said Emerald. "That black devil Python came here with his so-called posse last night, but I saw them off with my trusty shotgun."

Cheyenne looked puzzled.

That's right," said Ebony, laughing. "Mama here showed them who's boss. They took one look at her gun and soon turned tail down the road."

"Ain't no black devil gonna scare me," said Emerald, her eyes blazing.

It hurt to laugh, but Cheyenne couldn't help himself. He laughed in spite of the pain.

"Remind me not to mess with you, Emerald," he grinned. "I am in your debt, ladies. Thank you for saving my hide." They smiled. "If they're still looking for me, I better get going quickly. I don't want to put you in any more danger. You've done enough already." He tried to struggle out of bed, but the pain was too much. He lay back against the pillow, panting hard.

"You need a couple more days in bed so your ribs can heal properly," said Emerald. "You took quite a beating, you know. It's lucky you don't have any broken bones."

"I'm supposed to be leaving for the bush with Geigy and Willie. We're going to look for poachers who are killing elephants for their tusks."

Ebony touched his arm gently. "I'll get in touch with Geigy and Willie, and we'll figure something out. Willie already knows you're hurt, and he may have told Geigy by now. He knows that you're good friends."

Cheyenne sighed. "Thank you, Ebony," he said softly as he slipped back into a deep sleep.

Ebony was as good as her word. The next day, she bumped into Geigy in the street and told him everything – from the spiked drinks to the fight – to finding Cheyenne left for dead amongst the garbage bags and his rescue by her and Willie.

Geigy listened in astonishment. "I was wondering what had happened to him," he said.

"Well, he's at my mother's house now. She's a retired nurse, so she's been taking good care of him. He was in a coma, but he's conscious now. He's in a lot of pain because of the broken ribs, but he's getting better every day."

Geigy nodded. "Thank God, he's okay."

Ebony told him about the visit from Python and his posse.

"We have to get him out of town before they kill him," she continued. "I'm coming with you."

"Willie and me are all set to go," said Geigy. "Just let us know when he's fit to travel."

"Be ready to roll in a couple of days," she replied. "His ribs should be better by then."

"You got it," said Geigy.

Ebony placed her hand on his arm. "Be careful around Python and the Russian," she warned.

"Don't worry, I'll be okay. Just take care of the cowboy."

"You got it," smiled Ebony as she turned and hurried away.

The next day, while Emerald was out shopping, Ebony passed by Cheyenne's room and peeked in. She smiled brightly. "How's the patient feeling today?" She was wearing a short nightgown that showed off her long, brown legs.

"I'm feeling pretty good this morning," he replied, noticing her shapely limbs. "Could you come here a second, please."

"Yes, of course," said Ebony. "What seems to be the problem?"

"I think I'd like to get up and try to walk around a bit," Cheyenne told her.

Her opal eyes sparkled. "Oh, great, let me help you."

She helped him to his feet. "How's that?" she asked as Cheyenne stood up and started walking slowly around the room. He leaned on Ebony for support.

"Just a little pain, but not too much," he said.

Ebony let him walk around for a few more minutes, then she said, "I think that's enough for now. You don't want to overdo it."

"I think you're right," he agreed.

She helped him back to the bed. Cheyenne took a misstep and they both fell in a huddle on top of the bed. Ebony looked worried. "I hope you're not hurt," she said.

Cheyenne looked into her clear opal eyes. "You're so beautiful, you take my breath away." Their lips met and Ebony sighed. His deep blue eyes held her gaze. She was mesmerized. His hand crept slowly up her leg. She held her breath in anticipation. Reaching the top of her thigh, he explored the dark area between her legs. She wasn't wearing any panties. He gasped as his fingers touched her moist vagina. Ebony sighed deeply and opened her legs wider.

"Oh, Cheyenne," she panted, "that feels so good."

"Feels good to me, too," Cheyenne whispered in her ear.

He probed deeper and gently suckled on her nipples. Ebony cried out in delight and pulled him closer, wrapping her legs around his lean supple body.

"Take me now," she panted, her hot breath caressing his ear. "Take me now."

Cheyenne sighed and plunged deep inside her, his throbbing penis thrusting in and out. Ebony squealed in ecstasy and gripped him tighter with her legs, pulling him deeper and deeper inside her. "I want to feel all of you," she breathed, "every inch."

Cheyenne continued pumping vigorously as she met his every thrust.

"I hope I'm not hurting your ribs," she whispered.

"I can't feel anything but you," he said softly in her ear.

"Oh, Cheyenne," she whispered back. "I've wanted you since the day we danced together. I wanted you to…to…"

She broke off in mid-sentence as her body shuddered violently, her nerve endings on fire.

"Ebony, Ebony," cried out Cheyenne. "Come with me, now!"

"Yes, now…now!" she yelled as they both reached a shattering climax.

Limp and breathless, their bodies soaked in sweat, they collapsed on the bed exhausted. For about five minutes neither of them spoke as they basked in the afterglow. Finally, Ebony turned to him and said, "Oh, my God, that was incredible, you literally took my breath away."

Cheyenne pulled her close and kissed her gently on the lips. "Likewise," he said softly.

They held each tightly, neither wanting to break the spell. Ebony gazed into his eyes.

"We'll be leaving in a few days," she told him.

He stroked her breasts. "I'm ready any time, I'm feeling much better now."

She smiled at the double entendre as she grasped his hardening cock.

"Yes, you certainly are!"

Chapter Eleven

In the dark of night, the four adventurers took off into the wild. As their land rover sped down the dirt road, further and further from the clutches of Python, they all breathed a sigh of relief.

Hours later, dawn broke, revealing a spectacular blue sky. The sun blazed down ruthlessly.

"It's gonna be a hot one," observed Geigy, wiping his brow. "It's still very early and I'm already sweating up a storm."

They all gazed up, shielding their eyes from the sun's brutal glare. Dozens of buzzards circled overhead, watching, waiting…

"There must be something dead or dying," Ebony said, pointing to the deadly formation.

Cheyenne turned to Geigy and Willie, who were sitting in the backseat. "Let's check it out."

They nodded and stared out of the window, looking for the source of buzzards' attention. As they came over a small rise, they saw the form of a large animal, lying on its side by a clump of trees. Nearby a huge elephant was trumpeting loudly.

"Look! Over there!" shouted Willie, almost jumping out of the jeep.

Geigy pulled out his binoculars and scanned the area. "Holy shit!" he cried. "Look at the size of that elephant." As they drew closer, the elephant's trumpeting grew louder. "And he sure is pissed at something," added Geigy.

Cheyenne stopped the land rover. "I want to see. Let me have those binoculars, Geigy."

Geigy passed them over. "Wow, you're right!" exclaimed Cheyenne, focusing on the large animal. "What a beautiful elephant that is!"

They took turns looking at the magnificent animal, which was now running wildly, flapping its ears and raising its trunk in the air. Little did they know that they had just clapped eyes on the killer elephant, Monsoon. As they watched the great elephant disappear into the bushes, Cheyenne turned to them.

"Don't get out of the vehicle yet," he warned. "Geigy, hand me the long range rifle. I don't want to take any chances with that animal," he said, pointing to the still form lying by the trees. Geigy handed him the rifle. They all jumped out of the land rover and walked cautiously toward the downed animal.

"My God, it's a big rhino," exclaimed Ebony as they drew closer. "Is it dead?"

Cheyenne nodded. "I think so," he said, pointing to all the animal tracks surrounding the carcass. "Look at all the elephant and rhino tracks around this area."

"I think we just missed a great battle between the rhino and that huge elephant," Geigy told them. "This was more than likely a battle over territory. I imagine that the elephant came into the rhino's territory, and that's what the fight was about."

"Why not the rhino coming into the elephant's territory?" asked Cheyenne.

"Well, I've been in Africa a long time," replied Geigy, "and elephants tend to move around a lot more, searching for food."

Ebony pointed to the sky again. "Look! Those buzzards are circling lower and lower. Let's get out of here before they start feasting."

"Good idea," agreed Cheyenne. "Let's go."

They all jumped back into the safety of the land rover and sped away down the dusty dirt road.

I wonder what other things I'll be running into in this vast continent, Cheyenne thought.

As they drove deeper and deeper into the wild, they saw more and more animals: zebras, rhinos, water buffalo, lions, and a myriad other species dotted the vast landscape.

"I'm very lucky to be alive," Willie suddenly told them. Seeing all the wildlife had evoked painful memories. "I just happened to be out looking at different animals, deep in the bush. I'd been out for some time, so I started back. As I got closer to my village, I could hear gun shots and people yelling and screaming." He paused.

"Go on, Willie," said Geigy. He had their attention.

"Well," he continued, "I hid behind some bushes and a large rock. I knew my life was in danger, so I just watched as my family and everyone in the village was killed." His eyes welled with tears. Ebony reached back and patted his hand.

"I was very young and very scared, so I just watched," he said, brushing away the tears. "I saw Python kill my parents and then pick up my half-brother who was only a year old. I'll never forget his face as he looked around, making sure that everyone was dead." Willie shuddered at the memory. "Ego is that half-brother and he has no idea. He's been with Python ever since."

The others looked shocked. "Why have you never told him," asked Geigy.

Willie shook his head. "Python would kill me if he knew – after all, I witnessed the whole thing. And Ego would never believe me. All he knows is that Python saved his life, and Python never lets him forget it. Ego doesn't know that Python was responsible for the massacre in the first place. Python tells everyone that a hostile tribe attacked the village, but it was him and the Russian and their gang of thugs. I saw them with my own eyes."

"Why would they do such a thing?" asked Cheyenne.

"It was because the Pygmies, my people - we belong to a certain religion."

"They also call that genocide, which can happen quite often in Africa," said Geigy.

"Will you ever tell Ego that you're his half-brother?" asked Ebony.

"Perhaps one day when the time is right," said Willie. "When I no longer have to fear Python. But even then Ego might not believe me – he would lay down his life for Python."

"So that's your dark secret," said Cheyenne.

"Yes," said Willie simply.

"Well, your secret's safe with us," replied Cheyenne. "Right, guys?"

Before Ebony and Geigy could respond, Cheyenne suddenly slammed on the brakes and looked down the road. "What the hell is that coming at us?" he said.

Four pairs of eyes widened in horror as they watched a giant elephant charging down the road toward them. Dust and debris flew everywhere as its huge feet thundered along the dirt road.

Ebony screamed. "Turn round! Turn round! He's going to ram us!"

Cheyenne put the Land Rover in reverse and slammed his foot on the accelerator, sending the rover spinning around in a cloud of dust.

"Hurry! Hurry!" yelled the others, "he's gaining on us."

"All right, all right," cried Cheyenne, "I'm trying to turn round." He stomped on the accelerator again, but the rear wheels were now stuck in the sand. "Shit," he yelled as the wheels spun deeper and deeper into the sand. "We're stuck."

"Oh my God," screamed Ebony as she watched the thundering elephant. "He's almost upon us."

Cheyenne took charge. "Quickly, you three get out and push the Rover as hard as you can. We don't have much time."

One hears of people who have superhuman strength when they are afraid or in a crisis. Well, on this particular day, these three people were frightened for their lives and they literally lifted the vehicle out of the sand.

Ebony was still screaming. "Hurry! Hurry! You men move your asses fast or we're dead meat." She stared at the galloping beast in horror. "He's gonna hit on my side."

Cheyenne yelled at Geigy and Willie. "Get in, get in quickly. We're back on the road."

He didn't have to ask them twice. They literally threw themselves into the Land Rover and slammed the doors.

"Move, move," shouted Geigy, "that mad beast is out to kill us!"

"Hit the gas," screamed Willie.

"I'm hitting the gas," shouted Cheyenne.

The rear wheels started spinning again and it seemed like an eternity before they began to move.

Geigy cursed. "He's right on top of us."

Cheyenne stomped on the gas again. The Rover sputtered, then lurched forward and screeched away from the crazed animal, scattering dust and stones in its wake. Dazed and disoriented, they sat in silence for the next few miles. Finally, Geigy spoke up. "That crazy elephant is taller than this truck, and I saw a mark across his head." His voice was weak and scared. "People, we just crossed paths with none other than the legendary elephant they call Monsoon!"

Cheyenne stopped the truck and sighed deeply. "Holy shit! Are you okay, Ebony?"

She put her arms around him and he could feel her body trembling. "I'm okay now," she said softly. "But it was a close call."

"Did you see Monsoon standing on his hind legs, and his trunk way up in the air?" Willie asked.

"How about his bloodshot eyes and the noise he made after we got away?" added Geigy.

"Yes, that sent chills through my whole body," shuddered Ebony as she grabbed Cheyenne's hand and pulled him close.

Cheyenne folded her in his arms. She was still shaking. "I think we've put enough miles between us and Monsoon," he said. "And it's starting to get dark. There's a bunch of trees and bush up ahead. Let's camp there for the night."

They cut a few branches from a tree, and the three men covered up the tire tracks so that no one could see them. They also cut some brush to cover up the Land Rover. The sun was sinking slowly into the night as they finished their preparations, leaving a myriad of brilliant colors.

"Just look at the sky," said Ebony. "It's a rainbow of colors – orange, red, blue, purple…I can't begin to count them all."

"Everything is more colorful out here in the wild, including that crazy Monsoon," said Geigy dryly. He and Willie had bunked down for the night in their sleeping bags.

Cheyenne was practicing his draw. Ebony watched him for a few seconds and said, "Your hands are so fast, it's just like a blur and then your gun is out. Why do you have to be so fast?"

He looked up and held her gaze. "My father took me to a circus one day to see the elephants. We happened to see a sign that said 'Black Bart - Fastest Gun in the West.'

Ebony's eyes widened. "Black Bart? You said that name when you had your concussion."

A look of surprise crossed his face. "I did?" he said. "Well, I always wanted to be faster than Black Bart, but I guess I'll never know."

"You are faster than Black Bart, and you never miss," she replied. "I saw you shoot when Python put you in that contest." She smiled at him, a mischievous glint in her eyes. "If you want to practice on something, why don't you practice on me?"

He grinned and grabbed her by the hand. “Sounds good to me.” And with a laugh, they walked off into the bush.

They had agreed to take turns standing guard throughout the night. Sooner or later Python would figure things out and come after them. They needed to be alert at all times. Willie gazed up at the starry sky. He had been on watch for over an hour and was beginning to feel drowsy. The sound of trucks approaching jerked him wide awake. He raced over to Geigy who was snoring loudly.

“Geigy, it’s me, Willie. Wake up,” he said, shaking him gently.

Geigy rolled over and rubbed his eyes. “What’s up?” he asked. “What’s all the fuss about?”

“Trucks approaching. You were snoring so loudly, I thought they’d hear you.”

“Very funny,” said Geigy, rising to his feet.

Willie scurried over to Cheyenne and Ebony who were curled up together in a single sleeping bag. *Now, how the hell do they fit in there?* He shook them awake. “Trucks coming down the road,” he whispered urgently.

Cheyenne jumped up instantly as a blaze of headlights came into sight. He extended his hand and helped a sleepy Ebony to her feet.

“What’s happening?” she asked.

“Sssh,” he cautioned, pointing at the headlights, “I think we have visitors.”

Geigy grabbed the binoculars and took a look. It was still dark, but the headlights illuminated the area.

“What do you see, Geigy?” whispered Cheyenne.

"Not too much, it's pretty dark. The headlights are providing some light. There's a jeep in front with a driver and two men. I can't really make them out, but it looks like Python and the Russian." Geigy continued to scan the area. "God, I wish it wasn't so dark," he muttered. "The jeep behind them has a machine gun, with three people." His jaw dropped.

"What is it?" asked Cheyenne. "What's wrong?"

"There are two trucks behind loaded with men - can't tell how many – with rifles and machetes."

Cheyenne rubbed his jaw. "I wonder where they're going?"

"I've no idea, but I think the three men with the machine gun were Hi, Ho and Cracker."

"Let's lie low. Make sure they don't see us," said Cheyenne. "You guys get some shuteye, and I'll keep watch until sun-up. I think we'll be staying here until we know they're out of this territory. I don't want to meet them on the road with that machine gun."

The others settled down again for the night and Cheyenne kept watch until dawn. There was no sign of the 'visitors.' As they were eating breakfast, Cheyenne came up with an idea.

"Look, Geigy, you've been in the Service, so you know how to shoot, but Willie and Ebony should learn a little bit about shooting."

Geigy opened his mouth in surprise. "You're going to give Ebony a gun with live bullets," he said. "In that case, I'm digging a foxhole!"

Cheyenne shook his head. "No, I'm taking the bullets out and they can get some idea how to shoot. I'll teach them."

"What for?" asked Geigy, not understanding.

"You saw all those men with Python. We need all the help we can get."

Geigy nodded. Realization had finally dawned.

"What's a foxhole?" asked Ebony.

“I hope I never have to show you one, I mean, dig you one,” laughed Geigy.

While Cheyenne was teaching Ebony and Willie how to shoot, Geigy stood guard.

“Hey, everybody,” he called. “I hear some trucks or something coming.” He crouched behind a tree and some low bushes. Moments later, the others joined him and looked down the road.

They heard the sudden blast of a machine gun followed by Python yelling at his underlings.

“Damn it, Cracker, stop shooting at those water bucks. I won’t tell you again.”

Cheyenne was ready for them. He had his long range rifle loaded and aimed at Cracker if they were spotted. He knew they were no match against that machine gun.

Ebony put her hand on Cheyenne’s shoulder and whispered in his ear. “Thank God, they didn’t spot us,” she said as the convoy of vehicles continued down the road.

After the convoy was long gone, Cheyenne said, “We’ll move out now. Let’s pack up and hit the road.”

They had just started out when Geigy said, “Hold on just a minute. I think I see what we’re going to have for supper.”

Ebony looked at him, puzzled. “What do you mean?” she asked.

Geigy jumped out of the truck. “Follow me,” he told them.

They did as he asked and followed him down the dirt road. About fifty yards away Geigy stopped and grabbed a big water buck by its horns.

“See what I’m telling you,” he said. “Cracker got him with that machine gun blast.”

Ebony smiled. “I’ll cook up some of that meat tonight, just like Geigy said.”

Chapter Twelve

Another beautiful day dawned in Africa as they continued on their quest. Last night they had enjoyed a feast fit for kings, thanks to Geigy's keen eye and Ebony's superb culinary skills. Now rested and replete, they looked forward to their next adventure. As they passed by a hill, Cheyenne pulled over sharply.

"Do you hear that noise?" he asked. The others strained their ears.

"Yes," said Willie. "I can hear yelling and it's coming from the other side of that hill."

Cheyenne jumped out of the Rover. "I'll be right back," he told them.

"Be careful," called Ebony.

"Don't worry, I won't be long."

He scrambled to the top of the hill and looked over. Down in the valley below, he could see five African children throwing stones at a baby elephant stuck in the mud. Furious, he shook his fist and started down the hill toward the children. "Leave that baby elephant alone," he shouted, anger suffusing his face.

"Let's get out of here," said one of the boys, and they ran off into the bush.

Willie had now climbed to the top of the hill. Cheyenne called to him. "Tell Geigy to get the rope out of the truck. We need to rescue this little guy."

Well, he's not exactly little, thought Cheyenne as he approached the stranded animal. The baby elephant trumpeted as Cheyenne drew closer. Fear clouded its eyes. "It's okay, little fella," soothed Cheyenne. "We're gonna get you out of there. We're not gonna hurt you."

Geigy and Ebony ran over with the rope, while Willie stood watch on top of the hill.

"Oh, he's adorable," said Ebony when she saw the baby elephant.

"Okay, let's not frighten him. Those kids really scared him, so we have to tread carefully."

"Poor creature," said Ebony. "How could anyone want to harm him."

"There are a lot of cruel people in this world, Ebony," said Cheyenne, "as you well know."

"Yes," she said softly.

"Now, we have to put a rope around him and pull him out," said Cheyenne. "And we have to do it quickly. He's scared and he has a mother that's not too far away." Ebony and Geigy nodded.

"Mother elephants are very protective of their babies," continued Cheyenne. "This baby elephant must have wandered off and got lost."

He edged closer to the elephant, all the time talking to the frightened animal in a soothing voice.

"That's right, little guy, I'm just going to wrap this rope around you," he coaxed. "I'm not going to hurt you."

Geigy nudged Ebony. "I've heard of the horse whisperer," he said, "but never the elephant whisperer. Now I've seen and heard it all!"

Ebony smiled. "Yes, Cheyenne definitely has a way about him, doesn't he? Look how the elephant is responding to his voice. It doesn't look frightened anymore."

Cheyenne looped the rope around the elephant's thick neck.

"There you go," he said gently. "Now we're going to try to pull you out of that mud."

He beckoned to Geigy and Ebony and they all took hold of the rope and pulled with all their might. But to no avail. The elephant didn't budge an inch. It was still stuck firmly in the mud.

Cheyenne scratched his head. "Let me think," he said.

Geigy turned to him. "You know, Cheyenne, at the horse races when a horse doesn't want to go into the starting gate, the men get behind it and lock their arms."

"Let's do it," said Cheyenne.

He and Geigy took off their boots, rolled up their trouser legs and stepped into the slimy mud. Positioning themselves behind the baby elephant, they locked arms and pushed as Ebony pulled on the rope.

"Okay, Ebony, on the count of three pull as hard as you can, and we'll push. Are you ready?"

"Ready when you are," she said, grasping the rope tightly.

"Okay, one, two, three, go," cried Cheyenne as they pushed and pulled together.

There was a loud squelching sound and suddenly the elephant was free. He bleated loudly and galloped off.

"I think he's calling for his mother," said Cheyenne. He grinned like a Cheshire cat. "Thanks, guys, we finally did it. We set the little guy free."

"He wasn't so little," said Geigy. "Did you see the size of his legs, they were like tree trunks."

Cheyenne nodded. "Yeah, not so little, but still a baby." He couldn't stop smiling. "I came to Africa to save the elephants and guess what, I just saved one."

Geigy coughed. "Ahem…," he started.

Ebony cut him off. "Excuse me…," she began.

Cheyenne looked at them sheepishly. "Sorry," he said, "I meant to say, *we* just saved one!"

"Apology accepted," said Ebony, laughing

The three friends embraced and then clambered back up the hill to join Willie.

"Well done, guys," said Willie, patting them on the back. "I saw what you did down there, rescuing that little elephant. Way to go!" he grinned.

"Let's sit down for a while and dry off," said Cheyenne, looking down at his muddy feet.

"Good idea," said Geigy.

They sat down on the crest of the hill and watched the baby elephant galloping off in the valley below.

"What a magnificent animal," said Cheyenne, overcome with emotion. No sooner had he uttered the words than they heard the loud trumpets of an elephant crashing through the nearby brush.

Ebony jumped to her feet and screamed. "Let's get out of here before we get crushed."

Cheyenne and Geigy grabbed their boots and started running barefoot. Willie followed behind.

"Oh my God," he cried. "Oh, my God, look at the size of that elephant."

The four friends ran for their lives.

"Look," cried Ebony, "she's putting herself between us and the baby."

The three men stopped and turned. The massive elephant, ears and trunk raised, charged at them and then stopped.

"She's just letting us know that we have to get by her to get to the baby," Cheyenne told them.

They raced toward the Land Rover.

"Damn, that got my heart beating fast," panted Willie as they jumped inside the Rover and slammed the doors. Cheyenne pumped the gas and they sped off in a cloud of dust.

"That was close," said Ebony, sighing in relief.

"Damn close," said Geigy.

"She was just doing what any mother would do," said Cheyenne. "Protecting her baby."

"Amen to that," said Willie.

Chapter Thirteen

They traveled along for several miles, taking their time, until they spotted a narrow lane leading off to the right. Cheyenne stopped the Rover and they all jumped out.

“Look at the turn,” said Cheyenne, pointing to the dirt road. “All the dirt is dug up. This is where Python’s trucks went. “Should we find out where the road leads?”

They were all a little hesitant but finally agreed to follow the road.

“Let’s do it,” said Geigy, grabbing the long range rifle and holding it at the ready.

Cheyenne turned to Ebony. “I want you to drive,” he said as he deftly loaded his two pistols.

From the deep grooves in the road, they could see where the big truck had driven off the road making turns. “Take it slow, Ebony,” said Cheyenne as they drove along the twisting lane.

She nodded nervously in response, her hands tightly gripping the steering wheel. About a mile further on, she suddenly jammed on the brakes and the Rover came to an abrupt stop, its occupants lurching forward in their seats.

“What’s wrong, Ebony?” asked Cheyenne, grabbing the dashboard to steady himself.

“I can see a house coming into view.” She pointed up ahead and the others swiveled their eyes forward. “Look, up there!”

“We’re getting a little low on gas, so we can use that as an excuse to stop,” said Cheyenne.

Slowly, they drove on in silence, and pulled up in front of the house. Built of white wood and different colored stones, the house was large and well-kept, with several polished windows and a sturdy front door surrounded by brightly speckled flowers.

Ebony looked around. "It's so quiet here," she whispered.

"Yes, eerily quiet," agreed Cheyenne as he noticed a dead dog lying in front of the house. Jumping out of the Land Rover, he patted the trusty pistols at his side. "Ebony, you stay here with Willie. Geigy, come with me and bring your rifle."

Geigy rubbed his fingers along the barrel of the rifle and leapt out of the Rover. "I'm right behind you," he said.

Cheyenne surveyed their surroundings. "I have a bad feeling about this place," he said. "There are bullet holes all over the place."

The two men inched forward cautiously. Cheyenne noticed a flattened-out cigar lying near the door. Picking it up, he studied the still-smoldering butt. "Looks like one of the Russian's. I'd say Python and his henchmen have paid this house a visit…and not too long ago, judging by this filthy butt-end." He flung the cigar to the ground in disgust and wiped his hands on his shirt, in an effort to remove all trace of the Russian.

"Be careful!" said Ebony. "They might still be here."

As they moved slowly to the front door of the house, they noticed that the dog had been shot numerous times and its throat cut.

"Oh my god, poor thing," said Cheyenne. "Damn that bastard Python to hell."

"Be careful, the door is wide open," warned Geigy as Cheyenne stepped forward with pistols drawn and almost fell over a body sprawled near the door. "Cheyenne!" yelled Geigy.

"I see him." Cheyenne knelt down to touch the dead man whose throat had also been slashed.

"Is he dead?" asked Geigy.

"Yep, looks worse than the dog. His throat has been slashed from ear to ear. Pretty gruesome sight." He stood up and clenched his fists. "This is Python's work. Murdering bastard."

"Cheyenne, you have blood dripping from your knee," Geigy whispered. "To me, that means they haven't been dead that long. Blood hasn't had time to clot."

"You're right. If only we'd got here earlier, we might have been able to save them," he said, shaking his head sadly as he gazed down at the bloody corpse. "I can't make out what race he is, there's too much blood."

Geigy inched forward and stared at the dead man. Bile rose in his throat as he cast his eyes over the bloody carnage. "He's a white farmer," he said at last, wiping his brow. He sighed deeply. "What a mess. Poor guy didn't stand a chance; they almost decapitated him." He, too, clenched his fists. "Bastards, may they rot in hell."

"Yeah, poor guy," said Cheyenne softly as he knelt down again and closed the man's eyes which had been frozen open when death struck. "Keep your eyes open, Geigy, they may have left someone behind to bury him. Let's check out the rest of the house."

The two friends slowly entered the house, both hoping that no one was hiding inside, lying in wait for them. Gripping their weapons tightly, they looked around the house.

"This looks like the kitchen," said Cheyenne, entering a large spacious room off to the right. "I see a table with dishes and an oven in the far corner. Looks like they were getting ready to have breakfast."

Geigy nodded in agreement as he stepped into the room.

"My God!" exclaimed Cheyenne, "there's another body here in the corner to my left. A woman..." He knelt down to inspect the body, feeling for a pulse.

"Is she alive?" asked Geigy.

Cheyenne stood up and shook his head. "No, she's definitely dead. Slaughtered just like the man." He turned to Geigy who was clutching his rifle even tighter. "Let's check the stairs – see if there's anyone else around. Let's hope we don't run into any more dead bodies."

Geigy patted his rifle. "Lead on, I'm right behind you."

The wooden stairs creaked and groaned under their weight as they slowly made their way up to the next floor. They were about to reach the landing when a screaming and yelling Ebony charged through the front door and raced up the stairs. Pushing past Geigy, she flung her arms around Cheyenne's neck, tears streaming down her face. Her body trembled violently.

"There are bodies all over the place," she sobbed. "And they're all hacked up." Instead of staying in the Rover, she and Willie had been exploring around the outside of the house and had discovered the bloody massacre.

Cheyenne drew her close and held her shaking body. "It's okay, baby, take it easy, you're in shock," he said, looking into her opal eyes. "You should have stayed in the Rover."

She gazed up at him defiantly, her body still trembling with fear. "Well, I'm not leaving your side until this is over."

He kissed her gently on the forehead. "Okay, okay, we're just going to check up here. Is Willie still downstairs in the Rover?"

She nodded. "Yes, I think so, he's scared too. When I saw all the bodies, I just ran to you."

He kissed her again. "It's okay, baby, you're safe now. I won't let anything happen to you."

Ebony held on tightly to his hand as they came to a hallway leading to the bathroom. Bullet holes peppered the door. Cheyenne stopped. "Stay back with Geigy until I check this out."

With both guns drawn, he stepped into the bathroom and looked around. More bloody carnage met his eyes. In the bath tub lay a naked woman covered in blood. Her body had been hacked and slashed, her throat almost decapitated. Cheyenne gagged. He had never before seen such a gruesome sight. He held onto the sink to steady himself. Behind him, Geigy recoiled at the sight, then turned and threw up in the toilet.

"What's wrong?" asked Ebony anxiously. "What have you found?"

Cheyenne struggled for control. "Stay back, Ebony, don't come in here," he warned. "We've found another body…another woman. Her throat's been cut."

Ebony cried out in horror. "Oh no…"

"Looks like she was taking a shower. Probably never heard them until it was too late." He looked at the dripping faucet. "At least they turned the shower off. *How decent of them.*"

Geigy stood at the sink and splashed his face with cold water. "My God, Cheyenne," he finally said, "Python and his thugs are savages, cold-blooded butchers…"

Ebony cut him off mid-sentence. "I can't take this anymore," she cried, racing down the stairs. Willie was standing at the bottom. Pushing past him, she rushed out of the front door.

"What's going on?" shouted Willie.

"We found another body," said Geigy. "Willie, go with Ebony and try to calm her down. There are a couple more rooms at the end of the hallway that we need to search."

"Okay, I'll take care of her." Fear etched his face. "Be careful, looks like there's been one helluva massacre here," he said as he turned and exited the house, in search of Ebony.

"Stay there," Cheyenne told Geigy, "I'll check this first room at the end of the hallway.

"Okay, be careful. I'll cover you from behind."

Cheyenne opened the door cautiously and peered inside. "There's another body – a boy about fourteen or fifteen. He's the same as the others."

He closed the door gently and continued on to the next room. Steeling himself, he pushed open the door and froze midstep. Tied and spread-eagled on the bed, lay the bloody and battered body of a young woman. Cheyenne could tell that she had been raped repeatedly. "And then the bastard cut her throat," he muttered to himself. "Geigy, come here fast," he shouted, steadying himself against the door jamb. The savagery was overwhelming.

Geigy charged through the door, rifle raised, then stopped in his tracks when he saw the slaughtered girl. "Those dirty cowardly bastards," he cried, barely believing his eyes, "we have to kill them all!" He stared at the brutalized girl, his eyes filling with tears. "Filthy, murdering bastards…" his voice trailed off.

Cheyenne put his arm around him. "We'll get Python and those bastards sooner or later," he said. "But, Geigy, this young lady can't be humiliated like this. This is between you and me."

Geigy nodded and wiped his eyes. "Let's untie her, place her legs together, and cover her with a blanket."

"Yes," replied Cheyenne, "she died a horrific death – let us honor her by giving her dignity and respect."

Slowly and solemnly they completed their task, then headed outside for some fresh air. Neither man spoke, both of them lost in thought. Ebony walked over to them and broke the silence. Her tear-stained face was creased with sadness. "How many bodies are there inside," she asked.

Cheyenne stirred from his reverie. "Six, including the dog. Ebony, why don't you pick out a beautiful spot for the victims. We have to give them a proper burial."

She patted his arm. "Of course. I'll be right back."

"If you want me, I'll be sitting in that chair, under the tree."

Geigy and Willie walked over and sat down beside him. Not a word was spoken. The bloody carnage had rendered them speechless. Fifteen minutes later, Ebony returned to find the three men still sitting in silence.

"I've found the perfect spot for them," she said, pointing. "Under that big tree over there, where they can see the whole farm. Something tells me that they would approve of this as their last resting place," she added, blinking back tears.

"It's perfect, Ebony," said Cheyenne. "You did good, real good."

It took them most of the day to bury the six bodies. They worked in silence. When the last body was finally interred, they placed crosses on the graves and bowed their heads in prayer.

Overhead the sky was a blaze of iridescent colors as the African sun sank slowly in the west.

Geigy crossed himself. "Okay, let's go. I've filled the gas tank with fuel from the spare gas containers. It's time to hit the road."

"Yes, let's get out of here," said Ebony, gently tugging on Cheyenne's arm. He was still lost in thought. "Come on, Cheyenne, we've done all we can do here."

He nodded, and turned toward her. "Yes, let's go," he said softly.

Glancing once more at the six newly dug graves, they turned and walked toward the Rover.

As they drove back down the twisting lane, Willie said, "I feel like I just came from a funeral."

"You did, Willie," said Cheyenne. "We all did." He clenched his fist and looked to the heavens. "Python will pay for this. As God is my witness, Python will pay for this!"

Chapter Fourteen

They drove on in silence for several miles, until Ebony suddenly yelled, "Look! elephant tracks."

Cheyenne stopped the Rover and jumped out to inspect the tracks. "You're right, Ebony, these are definitely elephant tracks, and they look quite fresh. Looks like the elephants came through here some time yesterday."

"Let's follow the tracks," said Geigy.

Ebony grabbed Cheyenne's arm. "Look!" she said, pointing to some fresh tire tracks alongside the elephant tracks, "someone else is also following them."

"Let's speed it up a bit," said Cheyenne, pushing down hard on the accelerator. "I hope the elephants are safe."

They traveled along for another twenty miles, when Ebony pointed to the skies and exclaimed, "Buzzards circling."

"Oh, no, I hope it's not what I think it is," said Cheyenne, "or I'm gonna be really pissed." He had been thinking all along that the tire tracks might be those of poachers. "Let's pull up here and walk the rest of the way. Geigy, grab the long rifle and my two forty-fives."

"Yessir," said Geigy, handing him the forty-fives as the Rover drew to a halt. Cheyenne strapped on his guns and tied them down around his leg.

"Looks like some of the buzzards have something in their beaks," observed Willie as he watched the buzzards circling overhead.

Cheyenne looked up at the buzzards, and then down at the road ahead. In the distance, he could make out the shapes of three slain animals. He edged closer. "There are three dead elephants here," he shouted, "and they've all been shot." He shook his head in disgust. "And their tusks are missing." His eyes filled with tears. "How could anyone shoot these big, beautiful animals, just for their tusks. And one of them didn't even have tusks – they just kill them for no reason."

Ebony ran over and touched his arm. "I know how much you love elephants, but there's nothing you can do now," she said gently.

"They're not getting away with this," said Cheyenne. "I'm gonna find the guys who did this."

"Looks like they used a power saw to cut off the tusks," said Geigy. He pointed to the tracks.

"And look, the tracks are headed that way – see how deep they are from the weight of the tusks."

"Get in the Rover," ordered Cheyenne. "We're gonna follow those tracks and make them pay."

Anger suffused his face. "Hang on," he told them as he stepped on the gas. The tires spun wildly, spraying dust over everyone.

"Take it easy, Cheyenne," said Geigy, wiping the dirt from his face and clothes.

"Sorry about that," said Cheyenne sheepishly, "but I'm in a hurry."

"Yeah, a man on a mission," said Geigy. "Ain't nothing stands between a man and his mission."

Cheyenne laughed. "You got that right, Geigy."

They drove on in silence. Finally, Ebony asked, "How far have we driven so far?"

"About twenty-five miles or so," Cheyenne told her. "I have a feeling we'll be seeing those poachers soon." He patted his two forty-fives, and then turned to Geigy. "Get your rifle ready, my friend, I think we'll be seeing some action soon."

"What's that?" said Ebony. "I can hear some yelling."

Cheyenne stopped the Rover. "Let's check it out," he said, leaping from the truck. "Geigy, bring your binoculars and come with me. Ebony, you and Willie stay in the Rover." He passed one of his guns to her. "Here, just in case something happens."

She took the gun and shuddered. "I don't know how to use it."

"Don't worry, you probably won't have to. I just want you and Willie to have it for protection."

"Okay," she said weakly.

Cheyenne turned to Geigy. "Let's crawl up and see what's on the other side of the hill."

"Good luck!" cried Ebony.

The two friends scrambled to the top of the hill.

"Pass me the binoculars, Geigy, I'm gonna take a look." He scanned the valley below, in a sweeping arc from left to right.

"What do you see?" whispered Geigy.

Cheyenne lowered the binoculars. "Three men, and they have rifles. I'm betting these are our poachers."

"We have to be careful, Cheyenne," said Geigy. "These three could be very dangerous."

Cheyenne nodded. "You're right, Geigy, let's go back to the Rover and talk this out."

They slithered back down the hill and told Ebony and Willie about the three men on the other side. Cheyenne took charge. From the outset, he had been their undisputed leader.

"Geigy, I want you to circle in behind them. I'm going up the hill again to get as close to them as I can."

"You got it," said Geigy, patting his rifle.

Cheyenne turned to Ebony and Willie. "When things are under control, I'll call for you both."

"Be careful," said Ebony.

"Don't worry, honey, we'll be okay. Just keep that gun at the ready. Okay, Geigy, let's go."

Ebony and Willie watched as Geigy started circling, and Cheyenne crawled back up the hill and disappeared over the brow. Creeping closer to the men, he patted his gun. He was now close enough to take a clear shot.

Sprawled against a circle of small trees, the three men were passing a whiskey bottle back and forth. Cheyenne watched them warily, then crawled closer, hidden by a cluster of scraggly bushes. Oblivious to the intruder in their midst, the men laughed and guffawed, bragging about shooting the elephants.

"I shot that big old bull right between the eyes."

"Sweet. Did you see that little one crying for its mother?"

"I soon put it out of its misery."

"We're sitting pretty. Python's gonna be pleased – these tusks should fetch a hefty price on the black market."

Python! They worked for Python! Cheyenne couldn't stand to listen to their drunken rants any longer. *They were monsters!* He sprang to his feet, gun drawn.

"What the hell…"slurred one of the men.

"Don't move, or try to go for your weapons," he warned. "You're covered from both sides."

Geigy had circled the hill and come up behind them.

"Nicely done, Geigy, we make a good team." And then turning, he called for Ebony and Willie.

The leader of the group, a stocky black man, with dark beady eyes and a long shaggy beard, stepped forward. "Who the hell are you, cowboy," he sneered, "with your damn cowboy hat? You're in the wrong country for that bullshit." He brandished the whiskey bottle, and then went for his gun.

Quick as lightning, Cheyenne shot him through the hand, shattering the whiskey bottle. The injured man held his bleeding hand, a look of astonishment on his face.

"You damn cowboy, you shot me," he said. "I'm bleeding all over the place." He looked at his two cohorts who were cowering behind him.

"I told you not to go for your weapon," said Cheyenne. "Now you know better."

Ebony and Willie came running over. "Oh, Cheyenne, thank God you're safe," she said, flinging her arms around him. "I heard a shot and thought you might be hurt."

"I'm okay, but that guy's not doing too good," he said, pointing to the bearded thug who was still cradling his injured arm. "I'm placing them all under citizen's arrest."

"For what?" said the leader.

"For the brutal slaughter of those poor elephants. You are monsters who deserve to burn in hell."

"Prove it," challenged the leader defiantly. "We didn't slaughter nobody, did we, boys?"

The other men shook their heads but said nothing.

"Geigy, check out their truck over there. See what's in it."

Geigy walked over and rifled through the back of the truck and returned carrying a power saw and a bloody elephant tusk. "The back of the truck is full of tusks," he said, passing the tusk to Cheyenne.

"Well, well, well, what do we have here," said Cheyenne, holding the tusk aloft. "Do you know that killing elephants for their tusks is against the law?"

The bearded man glared at Cheyenne. "What the hell," he snarled. "You're not the law. It's none of your business what we do." He spat on the ground as if to add weight to his argument.

Cheyenne looked at him in disgust.

"I am placing all of you under citizen's arrest for the slaughter and illegal poaching of elephant tusks. We have all the evidence we need right here," he said, pointing to the power saw and the bloody elephant tusks. And the rest of the evidence is right there in the back of your truck."

Before Cheyenne could stop her, Ebony darted forward and confronted the men, shaking her fists in their faces. "I hope you all burn in hell," she cried. "You are savages…evil, cruel savages. And you shot that beautiful elephant that had no tusks, for no reason."

Cheyenne dragged her back. "Easy, Ebony, easy," he soothed.

"That damn elephant was trying to kill us," the leader replied. "We had no choice but to shoot her."

Ebony rubbed the tears from her eyes and pointed the gun at the leader. "Those gentle, defenseless elephants didn't stand a chance. You killed them, so now I'm going to make things even." Her eyes blazed with anger. "I'm going to shoot the three of you right in the balls and then I'm going to blow your heads off."

Cheyenne looked at her in amazement. *What a woman.*

Ebony approached the three thugs, brandishing the gun in their faces. They shrank back in fear. "May you burn in hell," she spat, taking aim.

"Don't shoot! Don't shoot!" cried the leader. "Okay, we did it, we did it! We killed them for their tusks." He looked over at Cheyenne and pleaded, "Take us to jail, please, cowboy. We're guilty. Just call off that crazy black bitch."

Cheyenne shrugged. "That depends. If I call her off, will you do what I ask from now on?"

"We'll do anything you want," he screamed. "Just call off that bitch."

"And if you call her a bitch one more time," said Cheyenne, "I'll shoot off your balls myself and feed them to the buzzards."

"Sorry, sorry, we'll do what you ask, just call her off."

Ebony continued to walk up and down, pointing the gun at each man's scrotum in turn. They cowered in fear, trying to shield their manhood.

"Okay," said Cheyenne, "the first thing I want you to do is untie your boots. I don't like chasing murdering poachers through the jungle."

The three men looked at him questioningly, then bent down and untied their boots.

Cheyenne turned to Willie. "I see some rope in the back of their truck. Could you bring it over here?"

"Sure thing, Cheyenne." He darted over to the truck and grabbed the coil of rope.

Cheyenne addressed the men again. "Now turn around and put your hands behind your back."

They did as commanded, keeping an eye on Ebony who was still brandishing the gun.

"Geigy, tie their bootlaces together. This way, they can't run."

Geigy laughed. "Good idea. It will be my pleasure," he said, bending down to tie the laces.

"Willie, take the rope and tie them up. Make sure the knots are nice and tight."

Willie nodded. "You got it, boss," he grinned.

After they were tied up, Cheyenne walked over to Ebony. "Okay, honey, you can put down that unloaded revolver now."

"What a tricky b.... she is," the leader blurted out, stopping himself just in time.

Ebony brought her face close to his and stared into his cruel eyes. "Consider this your lucky day," she spat. "The next time, I will have a real bullet in that gun, and you will meet your maker." Then with a flick of her hair, she turned and walked over to Cheyenne.

Yep, she's quite a woman, Cheyenne murmured. *Quite a woman.*

Chapter Fifteen

The sound of an approaching vehicle startled them, and moments later a dark colored jeep barreled over the hill, spewing dust and debris in its wake. Spinning sideways, it slid to a stop behind the poachers' truck. A tall, wiry black man dressed in a smart khaki uniform emerged from the vehicle and paused to look inside the back of the truck. He grimaced and walked stiffly toward the waiting group.

"It's a park ranger," Willie whispered to Cheyenne.

The ranger looked at each person in turn, his eyes finally coming to rest on the bound and shackled trio. "What's going on here? Why are those men tied up, and what are those bloody tusks doing in the back of that truck?" He spoke with authority, in a deep sonorous voice.

Silence. No one spoke.

The ranger stared at Cheyenne who was still holding the gun. "What is this, some Hollywood movie? I don't see any cameras," he said sarcastically, looking around. "Let's put the gun down – it looks like the bad guys are pretty secure."

Cheyenne lowered the gun. He told the ranger how they'd stumbled upon the massacre at the farm, and how they'd surprised the poachers and discovered the tusks in their truck.

"We had just finished tying them up when you arrived on the scene," finished Cheyenne.

The ranger nodded in approval and ran his fingers through his thick black hair. At six foot two, he had a commanding presence. "Good work," he said, extending his hand to Cheyenne. "My name is Jocko, and this is my territory."

"Cheyenne Cole," said Cheyenne, shaking the ranger's hand. "Pleased to meet you." Then he turned to introduce his friends.

"I can see that I'm talking to someone who's been in the military service by the way you have these poachers tied up," said Jocko, looking over at the tethered trio who were staring down at their feet. "I like the idea of their boots being tied together. They can only take small steps." He laughed heartily, his white teeth gleaming in the sunlight.

Cheyenne laughed with him. "They aren't going anywhere fast."

"I've been following you from the farmhouse," said Jocko, "and I saw the six graves." He shook his head sadly. "The drums told me that a gang of men had done something bad at the house. The owner of that farm was going to testify against some big shot in Gabon."

"It was a bloody massacre," said Cheyenne. "I've never seen such carnage…" his voice trailed off as his mind flashed back to the bloody scene. "But I don't believe these men were the killers."

"Oh, what makes you think that?" asked Jocko.

"That bloody slaughter has all the hallmarks of a vicious thug called Python and his cowardly henchmen. I'm sure that he's the 'big shot' in Gabon that you just referred to, and as proof, I found one of his sidekick's trademark cigars at the scene."

"Is that so," said Jocko.

"I'll bet my life on it," said Cheyenne. "There's only one big shot in Gabon, and that's Python. If the farmer was going to testify against him, he would make sure he'd silence him forever."

"Well, I know all about this Python – his reputation precedes him. Crushed a man to death, I hear, and got away with it. Don't worry, we'll find him and his gang, and they'll be punished to the fullest extent of the law," said Jocko, "and that's a promise." He turned to the three poachers. "And so will these butchers," he added, shaking his head in disgust at the three men.

"I came here to save the elephants from scum like them," said Cheyenne. "And my friends here are with me all the way."

"Well, I'll be damned, this is my lucky day," said Jocko as he headed for his jeep. "I have something for all four of you." He returned clutching four shiny badges.

"I've been working this whole area all by myself for a month," he said. "One park ranger got shot, another quit and another had an accident. And I had to fire one because he was in cahoots with the poachers." He shook his head. "Damn bad luck, but now my luck seems to have changed." He smiled broadly, once again revealing those gleaming white teeth.

"Now, stand in a row and face me and raise your right hand," he ordered. They did as he asked.

"Do you solemnly swear to protect this great continent of Africa with all your strength and knowledge?"

"Yes, we do," they replied in unison.

Jocko pinned the badges on their shirts, and then pulled out a notepad. "I will need your full names. You will be paid every thirty days. Not much, and since you're in the bush, your pay will be held for you. When you need money, go to any park station and give them your names."

"This is an honor, Jocko," said Cheyenne proudly. He looked over at his friends. "I think I speak for all of us when I say we will honor this badge, and everything it stands for."

"This is a proud day for all of us," said Geigy.

"One we'll always remember," offered Ebony.

"I can't believe it," said Willie, "me, a park ranger!" He patted the badge and beamed proudly.

"To Africa," said Cheyenne, raising his arm.

"To Africa," they all repeated.

Jocko smiled and walked back to his jeep. Reaching into the glove box, he pulled out a cell phone. "I almost forgot about this," he said, handing the phone to Cheyenne. "You can charge this from your cigarette lighter, or you can take out this handle and crank it. Any questions?"

"Yes," said Cheyenne. "My father had a dear friend whose name is Dr. Gift, and he has a daughter called Tara. He started with the Peace Corps here in Gabon. Do you know him by any chance? Or perhaps you could tell me where I can find him?"

Jocko thought for a moment and rubbed his chin. "I have heard the drums telling me about a doctor and teacher helping the poor people in this region. I'm sure this must be the man you're looking for, but he moves from village to village. He doesn't have a fixed abode. I will make enquiries at the other ranger stations – perhaps someone there knows his whereabouts."

"Thank you, Jocko," said Cheyenne. "In the meantime, I'll keep looking for him."

"Oh, I almost forgot to give each of you the equalizer," said Jocko. He walked over to his jeep again and retrieved a bag from under the front seat.

"What's the equalizer?" asked Willie.

"Here you go," said Jocko, handing Willie a loaded forty-five and a shoulder holster. "Now, they're loaded, so be careful," he added, passing the same to the other three.

"Don't give that crazy woman a loaded gun, she's nuts!" shouted the leader of the poachers.

"Well, she doesn't look crazy to me, so quiet down," said Jocko.

Ebony smiled slyly and strapped the forty-five over her shoulder.

Jocko walked over to the three poachers. "Let's get these three guys in the jeep." He turned to Geigy and Willie. "Could you give me a hand here?"

Geigy and Willie rushed over and between them they secured the three felons in the back of the jeep, along with the power saw and the bloody tusks.

"Thanks, fellas, I'm going to take this lot to jail now," said Jocko. He pointed to the poachers' truck. "I guess you could take their truck. Take all your weapons, and here's some extra ammunition," he said, handing them a small case, "you may need it."

"Thanks, Jocko," said Cheyenne.

Jocko smiled. "Teach Willie and that gal how to shoot. I trust you will find your doctor and his daughter, but be careful out there." And with a quick wave of his hand, he jumped in the jeep and sped off in a cloud of dust.

They watched as the jeep became a distant speck on the horizon. Cheyenne was the first to speak. "Well, now that we have all these guns and ammunition, it's a perfect day to learn how to shoot and protect ourselves. You first, Ebony. See that lonely bush straight ahead?" She followed the direction of his finger, and nodded. "That will be our target. Geigy, you know how to shoot, so you help Willie, and I'll help Ebony. We'll practice without bullets first and then we'll have a little contest between Ebony and Willie with real ammunition."

They spent the next hour teaching them how to hold the gun, how to take aim, and how to squeeze the trigger just so. Squeeze the trigger, don't pull it…Keep your arm steady and take aim…Gently now, gently…Get the feel of the gun in your hand…Let it become an extension of your arm…Focus on the target…Feel the gun, feel it…

"Okay, now we're ready for some real bullets," said Cheyenne. "And remember the golden rule, never point a loaded gun or an empty gun at anyone, unless you plan to shoot them."

He walked over to the poachers' truck and pulled out an empty whiskey bottle. Then striding over to the solitary bush, he placed the bottle in the dirt beside it. "Now let's see who can hit the bottle first," he called. "Geigy, give each of them six bullets."

Geigy handed them the bullets, and they slid them into their gun's chamber.

"Good, we taught you well," said Geigy as he watched them both expertly load their guns.

"Ebony, you take the first shot, and remember to squeeze the trigger slowly," said Cheyenne.

She looked over at him and nodded. "Let the games begin," he said with a smile.

To Cheyenne's surprise, Ebony hit the target with her fifth shot, knocking off the head of the bottle. Willie finished it off with his sixth shot.

Cheyenne placed his hands on their shoulders. "I'm proud of you both. That was fine shooting."

"Hear! Hear!" said Geigy, clapping his hands in appreciation.

"We had some good teachers," said Ebony.

Cheyenne kissed her gently. "Let's have some supper and call it a day."

They made camp for the night under the shelter of several tall Banyan trees. Ebony cooked beans and rice over a small fire, and basking in the fire's glow, they recounted the day's events.

"It's been one helluva day," said Cheyenne. "One I will never forget. The massacre at the farmhouse will stay with me forever."

"Me too," said Geigy.

Ebony stared into the flames of the fire. "Me too," she said softly.

Willie broke the spell. "But on the bright side, we did meet Jocko, and now we've been deputized as park rangers."

"And we did catch three of the bad guys," said Geigy.

"And we did learn how to shoot, Ebony," said Willie.

Ebony looked up and nodded. "True," she said. "The day wasn't all bad."

Now that they had two vehicles, they were able to settle down comfortably for the night, stretched across the seats. Cheyenne and Ebony took the Land Rover, while Geigy and Willie stayed in the poachers' truck. As they lay there in the dark, listening to the sounds of the jungle, Cheyenne said, "Isn't Africa truly amazing, with its great size, its sounds and smells?"

"And its danger," added Ebony.

A loud roar jolted both of them. "Talking of sounds and danger, I think that's the roar of a lion," said Cheyenne.

They clutched each other tightly and looked up at the vast African sky, ablaze with millions of twinkling stars. "It's a perfect night for making love," whispered Cheyenne as his hand caressed her breast.

Ebony sighed. "Yes, a perfect night…"

Chapter Sixteen

The next morning they all awoke at dawn. Even at such an early hour, the brutal African sun blazed fiercely, scorching the dusty earth around them. After a quick breakfast of fruit and rolls, they packed up their supplies and hit the road.

"Let's follow the elephant tracks," said Cheyenne. "Ebony and I will take the Rover. Geigy, you and Willie follow in the truck."

"We're right behind you," said Geigy. "Let's go…

Meanwhile, back at *The African Queen,* Python was fuming. "Sonofabitch, that bitch and her devil mother were hiding that damned cowboy all the time." He thumped the table furiously, sending bottles and glasses crashing to the floor. "That no-good Geigy and that shithead Willie were both in on this," he thundered. "I want them all dead!"

His eyes bulged and the veins on his neck and forehead looked ready to burst. Anger spewed forth from his every pore. "I want them dead!" he repeated. "I want everyone out in the bush looking for them."

He continued to rant and rave, his rage building by the second. Ego and the Russian and the three bush men stared at him but said nothing – they knew better than to interrupt *the boss* when he was in the middle of one of his rages.

"I have many men working for me in Gabon, they cannot hide forever," he said, banging the table again for emphasis. "The drums tell me that they're going after the elephant poachers – I don't want them messing up my tusk provider. The Chinese and Japanese want more tusks. Business is booming! I don't want anyone standing in my way. Does everyone understand?"

"Yes, boss," they all replied.

Just then Jackal came bursting through the door, carrying the limp body of a young boy about twelve years old. "Python, Python, I found this boy on a dirt road outside of town," Jackal panted, struggling to catch his breath. "He has a message for you."

"What's wrong with him?" asked Python.

"He's badly dehydrated, must have been walking for days," replied Jackal. "He needs rest and water."

"Bring him over here and lay him on that table," ordered Python, pointing to a nearby table.

Jackal rushed over and gently laid the young boy on the table. Python continued to issue orders. "Get some water and a towel and wash him off, he's covered in dust and dirt."

Jackal scurried off and within seconds he was back with fresh water and a towel.

Python turned to Ego. "Give him some water, Ego, but slowly, otherwise he might choke."

The Russian stood by Python's side as they stared at the young boy. "Is he going to make it?"

"Look! Look!" cried Ego, wetting the boy's lips with water, "his eyes are starting to flutter."

He administered a few more drops of water. "Look, his eyes are opening now."

The boy's eyelids fluttered open to reveal deep brown eyes fringed by long black lashes. He looked around in a daze and said weakly, "Where am I? Where am I?"

Jackal patted his arm. "It's okay, you're safe now. You're in *The African Queen,* in the town of Gardon."

The boy struggled to raise his head, but the effort was too much. He flopped back on the table.

"I'm looking for a man by the name of Python," he said faintly, still trying to gather his wits. "I'm so tired…been walking for days…need food…water…" His voice trailed off as his eyelids closed.

"Is he dead?" asked Ego.

"Nah, he's just tired and beat," said Python. "Jackal, get this boy some food before he dies on us. And make it quick."

Jackal rushed off to the kitchen and returned with a steaming plate of rice and a hunk of bread.

"Give him the bread first, not too much, otherwise he'll be sick," said Python.

Jackal looked up, amazed at Python's concern for the boy's health and well-being. Then it clicked. *Python doesn't want him to die before he gets the message.*

The boy devoured the bread like a starved animal.

"Easy now, slow down," said Jackal, "otherwise that food's gonna come right back up. Here, take a little rice," and he spooned the food into the boy's mouth and watched him slowly chew.

Gradually, the color started returning to the boy's face. He took a few more sips of water and sat up. "I feel stronger now," he said.

Python stared at him. "My name is Python. What do you have to tell me?"

The boy looked into Python's cruel eyes and gulped. "One of the guards at the prison gave me some money to deliver this message, and he's going to give me some more after I return."

"Okay, get on with it, what's the message?" said Python impatiently.

"He told me to tell you that three of your tusk hunters were arrested by three men and a crazy black woman."

Python's eyes blazed with anger. "Go on," he said.

"The leader was wearing a brown cowboy hat. He's faster than lightning with his guns."

"That bastard cowboy," yelled Python.

The boy trembled. "Your men had some tusks for you," he continued, "but Jocko, the park ranger, showed up and confiscated them."

Python lost control. Flinging his arms in the air, he shouted, "Those four bastards are costing me money. I want them dead, dead, dead."

"Yes, Python, we must kill them all, because our money is at risk," blurted out the Russian.

Python pounded the table, shattering more glasses. "Start packing the gear, we're moving deep into the bush. Hi, Ho, and Cracker, start looking for more recruits and find us a village."

He upturned the table and sent a bottle crashing against the wall. "We'll crush them all, just like that bottle. Just like we crushed that squealer farmer and his family. We'll crush them into a million pieces. No one messes with Python and lives to tell about it. *No one!*

The young boy cowered in fear as he watched this outburst. Python was a madman.

"Don't worry, son," whispered Jackal, "it ain't your fault, you're just the messenger. He ain't got no quarrel with you."

Then under his breath, he muttered, *Yeah, Python, don't shoot the messenger.*

Chapter Seventeen

Deep in the jungle, Winston, the suave Englishman turned big game hunter, was driving along a dusty trail, savoring his surroundings. *It's good to be alive.* He loved Africa. The sights, the sounds, the smells – the incredible sunsets and the wide open spaces – filled him with joy. Compared with wet, rainy England, it was a magical land filled with exotic animals of every size and shape. To him, the animals were just like humans – trying to survive in an unpredictable world, and fighting to protect their young.

He lay back in his seat and shielded his eyes against the sun's fiery glare. *Why did I have to shoot that magnificent elephant?* He tried desperately to banish the thought from his head. *Why?* Tumbleweeds, stirred by the gentle wind, swirled by the open jeep, gathering dust with every turn. A herd of zebras raced across the vast plain like a long black and white streak piercing the horizon. Antelope and gazelles stood shoulder to shoulder with hippos and water buffalo at a nearby watering hole. Winston looked on in wonder.

"God, I love this country," he cried out. "You never know what you're going to see next."

He clutched a half-empty bottle of whiskey, occasionally raising it to his lips to take a sip.

"Yes, it's bloody good to be alive," he said, reducing his speed as the jeep hit a rocky patch of terrain.

As the jeep slowed to a steady crawl, he glanced to his left to see a huge elephant charging straight towards him. Before he could react, the massive beast slammed against the vehicle with such force that the jeep flipped over on its side. Temporarily stunned by the impact, Winston lay pressed against the jeep's door, shards of the shattered whiskey bottle clinging to his face and hair. *Bloody hell,* he moaned.

A high-pitched scream jolted him to his senses. He would recognize that shrill cry anywhere. Monsoon! The elephant he had taken a shot at, and missed. The old adage rolled through his head with piercing clarity. *An elephant never forgets!* And this elephant certainly remembered him. *Monsoon wanted to kill him!*

The realization galvanized him into action. *Bloody hell, I've got to get out of here, and quick.*

As he struggled to free himself from the jeep, Monsoon rammed his razor-sharp tusks inside the truck, missing Winston by inches "Oh, my God," he shrieked, "that was bloody close!"

Monsoon continued to ram the jeep with his tusks, bellowing loudly. His giant head was now level with Winston's. Their eyes met. Recognition. Monsoon let out another menacing bellow, then rose up on his hind legs and crashed down on the jeep with all his might. Winston curled himself into a tight ball and realized that the spectacular sunrise he had witnessed that morning might have been his last. Although not a religious man, he now prayed fervently. Only a few moments ago, he had been relishing life, and now he was facing death. *The fickleness of life* he mused.

Monsoon pounded the jeep, still trumpeting loudly. Winston cowered in fear, still praying to whichever deity he hoped was listening. As if in answer to his prayers, the pounding stopped and Monsoon circled the jeep. Winston watched the elephant with bated breath. He could see the ragged scar where the bullet had grazed Monsoon's massive head, missing its mark by inches.

That massive head now smashed into the jeep, rolling it over and over until it crashed sideways against a tree. Although battered and bruised by the jolting and bashing of the jeep, Winston was not seriously hurt. He felt his arms and legs for injury and breathed a sigh of relief. *Thank you, God,* he muttered silently.

Fortunately for Winston, Monsoon was now struggling to maneuver around the tree. Winston watched the elephant warily. Dusk was falling, and there was no way he was getting out of the jeep. He would stay put for the night. Hopefully, the elephant would tire of the hunt and leave him alone. If he stayed very still, perhaps Monsoon would think he was dead.

That night he prayed as he'd never prayed before, eventually falling into a fitful sleep. He awoke at dawn to a sunrise so exquisite that he thought he must be in heaven. Set against the backcloth of the bluest African sky he had ever seen hovered a sun so brilliant, so luminous, he had to shield his eyes from its penetrating glare. The vast sky was ablaze with an array of vivid colors.

"Oh, my God," said Winston. "That is truly amazing. If I didn't believe in God before, I do now. Perhaps this is his way of telling me how close I came to dying yesterday." Squinting his eyes, he looked up at the blazing sun, and pressed his hands together in prayer. "Today I am looking at the face of God."

He looked around him. No sign of Monsoon. Winston was pretty sure that the huge animal had left the territory, but he wasn't taking any chances. Looking through every crack and cranny of his crushed vehicle, he scanned the area for any sign of the crazed elephant. *He may be gone for now, but an elephant never forgets.*

Taking one last look to make sure it was safe, he hesitated momentarily, then slowly dug his way out of the overturned jeep. Stiff and sore from lying in a cramped position all night, he shook his arms and legs and massaged the joints. After a few knee bends and a couple of twists of his body, he felt much better. *I guess I'll live.*

He surveyed the surrounding terrain once more, shading his eyes from the sun's ruthless glare. Scattered far and wide on the dusty plain lay most of Winston's belongings from the jeep: a water canteen, boxes of ammunition, bullets strewn here and there, the broken whiskey bottle, and another bottle miraculously intact, a wide brimmed hat, and assorted pieces of clothing. He spotted his revolver half-buried in the dirt but saw no sign of his rifle.

Turning on his heel, he returned to the jeep and searched under the vehicle. There, buried under a pile of debris, sat his trusty rifle. He patted it reassuringly. "I think I'm going to need you, old friend," he said.

Studying the dusty ground, he noticed that the large elephant tracks swerved off to the west, so he decided to set off in the opposite direction. He had no wish to meet up with crazy Monsoon again! Gathering his belongings together and slinging his rifle over his shoulder, he marched down the narrow dirt trail, heading to wherever the road would take him.

"It's good to be alive," he chanted. "Bloody good to be alive!"

Chapter Eighteen

Meanwhile, Cheyenne and his group were following the tracks of a large herd of elephants as they continued on their hazardous journey to find water. At the head, the Monarch elephant bellowed loudly reinforcing his superiority as the rightful leader. The herd was his responsibility, and he would lead them to water. The others, including females and baby elephants, followed meekly behind, trusting in their leader. Cheyenne surveyed the herd through his binoculars.

"See all those baby elephants," he said to Ebony, pointing to his left. "Soon the females will be ready to mate and the bull elephants will soon come into musth."

"How do you know that?" queried Ebony.

"Well, ever since I was a little boy, I've read everything there is to read about elephants," replied Cheyenne. "When the female is ready to mate she sounds loud mating calls to the males to let them know that she is ready. The males elephants go into musth, which means their testosterone levels are very high, for a couple of months every year. They also sound loud mating calls and actively seek out the females. And this is when they come together and mate."

"Fascinating," said Ebony with a smile. "Just like humans in a way – we sound each other out."

"True," said Cheyenne, winking, "but not just for two months a year, thank God!"

Ebony punched him playfully. "Men!"

"Women!"

Ebony turned and called out to Geigy and Willie who were following behind in the poachers' truck. "Let's pull off the tracks and have some lunch under that big shade tree, over there." She pointed to a sturdy tree that looked as if it were standing guard over the entire terrain.

"Good idea," shouted Willie, rubbing his stomach. "I'm starved."

"Me too," said Geigy.

They settled down under the shade of the tree and stretched their legs. Ebony dug through the supplies and spread out a simple picnic lunch of salted meat, bread, and berries. As they relaxed in the afternoon sun, enjoying their meal, they suddenly heard the distant but unmistakable sound of an approaching vehicle.

"I think we have visitors," said Cheyenne, fingering his gun. "Let's be ready for them."

As the vehicle drew closer, they could make out the silhouettes of two Africans who were studying the elephant tracks intently, unaware of the four friends.

Cheyenne whispered to the others. "Just let them go on their way, and we'll check them out."

Willie pulled out the binoculars and raised them to his eyes. "I'm already checking them out," he said, surveying the back of the men's truck, "and it looks like they have killed an elephant already." He lowered the binoculars and passed them to Cheyenne. "Here, take a look."

Cheyenne dropped the binoculars and let out a deep sigh. "They kill them just for their tusks and the money they will get for them." His eyes watered. "What a damn shame!" Taking out his phone, he angrily punched in a series of numbers. "I'm going to call Jocko to see what he wants us to do."

Jocko picked up after a couple of rings. "Hello, this is Jocko, how may I help you?"

"Hi Jocko, this is Cheyenne. Remember me and my friends, your newly hired park rangers?"

Jocko grinned. "Hey, of course I remember you. How are the four of you doing out there?"

"We're doing fine, but we have a problem," replied Cheyenne.

Jocko's smile was quickly replaced by a deep frown. "What kind of problem?"

"We just spotted two poachers with two large elephant tusks in the back of their truck." Cheyenne paused for effect. "And they're looking for more."

Jocko could feel his anger rising. As a dedicated park ranger for over thirty years, he had devoted his life to protecting and saving the wildlife of Gabon, especially his beloved elephants. And now, another one of his flock had been slaughtered for its tusks. If he had his way, these damned poachers would be locked up, and he would personally throw away the key. Cheyenne's voice broke through, shaking Jocko from his reverie.

"Jocko, are you there? Did you hear what I said?"

"Sorry, Cheyenne, I get so damned mad when I hear about another slaughter. Those poor defenseless animals don't stand a chance against a rifle. And for what? So that some rich scumbag can add another piece of ivory to his precious collection."

Cheyenne nodded. "I hear you, I hear you," he repeated sadly.

Jocko jumped to attention. "Okay, enough of that, time's a wasting. I want you to arrest those two *murderers* before they kill another elephant," he shouted.

"It will be our pleasure," said Cheyenne. "I can't wait to get my hands on them."

"I want the four of you to be very careful," Jocko warned.

"Oh, don't worry about us," said Cheyenne, looking over at his three friends, "we'll be fine. We..."

"No, you don't understand," interrupted Jocko, "you four have a price on your heads."

"What are you talking about?" cried Cheyenne, a deep frown creasing his weathered face.

"Well, it may be just a rumor and I don't want to alarm you, but I heard through the drums that *someone* is offering $25,000 for each one of you, *dead or alive.*"

Cheyenne stood in shocked silence, his mind in overdrive. *And I can guess who that someone is. Python!*

Jocko continued speaking on the other end of the phone. "From what I hear you would be better off dead rather than let this person get hold of you."

Cheyenne patted his trusty guns. "Don't worry, we can take care of ourselves."

"Okay, but don't take any unnecessary risks," said Jocko. "I have a man in that area, so let me know what happens."

"Will do," replied Cheyenne.

"Good luck. *You're going to need it,* muttered Jocko as he put down the phone.

Cheyenne looked over at the others who were staring at him expectantly. They had heard bits and pieces of the conversation; Cheyenne filled them in on the rest.

"Well, here we go again," blurted out Geigy.

Ebony trembled slightly, while Willie stared off in the distance, chewing nervously on his fingernails. Cheyenne called them together and they all gathered round waiting for him to speak. He took a deep breath and began. "Look, this could be very dangerous. It was my idea to save the elephants, and I don't want to get anyone hurt." He looked at each of them in turn. "So, I want each of you to think very carefully and decide what you want to do." No one spoke.

Cheyenne sighed. "I got you all in a real mess. One helluva mess," he said, smiling wryly.

"And now we've got a price on our heads. $25,000 each, dead or alive!

"Yeah, how about that?" chuckled Geigy. "I thought we'd be worth more than that."

Cheyenne smiled, appreciating Geigy's attempt to lighten the mood, if only for a few seconds.

"Seriously though," Cheyenne continued, "I landed you all in this mess, so you don't have to come with me on this one." He patted his guns again. "I can go it alone with the help of these two buddies."

Ebony was the first to speak. "Damn it, Cheyenne, it took me long enough to nurse you back to health." She shook her head, lustrous hair flying back and forth, her green eyes blazing. "I'm going to make damn sure I don't have to go through that again."

Cheyenne stared at her in wonder. *What a woman! She's truly amazing.* Reluctantly tearing his eyes away from her, he turned to Geigy. "What about you, Geigy?"

Geigy drew himself to his full height. "Hell, this is more exciting than sitting in a bar all day," he exclaimed. "Count me in, I'm with you every step of the way." He rubbed his mouth ruefully. "But I sure could go for an ice-cold beer and a shot of whiskey right now."

They all laughed. Once again, Geigy had lightened the somber mood with his special brand of humor. As the laughter subsided, Cheyenne turned to Willie who was still chewing on his nails. "What about you, Willie? We have an extra jeep, maybe you'd like to go back to the village?"

Willie stopped biting his nails and jumped to attention. "I don't even know if my village still exists," he said sadly, "and I hate each and every poacher. I'm with you."

Cheyenne's eyes watered. He was truly moved by their loyalty and support. Once again, Ebony broke the silence. "Well, what are we waiting for?" she yelled, jumping into the Land Rover. "Let's hit the road."

Cheyenne turned to Geigy and Willie. "You heard the lady," he said with a wink, "let's go."

"We're right behind you," grinned Geigy, grabbing Willie by the arm and steering him toward the other vehicle.

Ebony smiled. "Okay, let's go round up those bad guys!"

Chapter Nineteen

They fired up the engines and drove slowly along the rough dirt track, but fast enough to keep pace with the poachers. Unaware that they were being followed, the two poachers had turned off the track, leaving their jeep partially hidden under a clump of bushes. Cheyenne and the others pulled up alongside it.

"They're out there in the bush staking out their next kill," Cheyenne whispered. "Now, remember how we do this so all of us don't shoot at the same person." They nodded.

"I hope it doesn't come to that," he added. "Okay, let's go."

With Cheyenne leading, in single file they followed the footprints along the dusty track.

"Let's be extra careful here," cautioned Cheyenne, stopping abruptly. "We're coming into some heavy brush and trees. Try to avoid stepping on any sticks or branches. We don't want them to hear us."

They walked on for several yards, treading carefully so as not to alert the poachers to their presence. As they rounded a clump of trees, Cheyenne raised his hand for them to stop. He pointed to a tall burly man who was holding a rifle aloft.

"Where's the other one?" whispered Geigy.

"I don't know," said Cheyenne, scanning the area in a wide arc. "He's got to be here somewhere. Keep your eyes peeled."

Willie touched Cheyenne on the shoulder. "Look, over there!" he said, pointing to a nearby bush where the other poacher was crouched down, rifle in hand. His gun was aimed at a large male elephant that had been following the herd, and he was about to pull the trigger.

"He's going to kill that big male," cried Cheyenne, and before the others could stop him, he charged toward the poacher who had now been joined by his friend. Cheyenne's mind was racing. *I could get killed, but I have to stop these men before they kill this beautiful animal.* Breathing heavily, his heart pumping, he crept up behind them and raised his rifle.

"Drop those guns," he yelled. "This is the park ranger." The poachers whirled around in surprise, still clutching their rifles.

"Don't do anything stupid," shouted Geigy, coming up alongside Cheyenne. "There are four of us and our guns are pointed right at you."

Ebony and Willie stepped from the shadow of the trees, their guns aimed at the two startled men.

"Drop those guns," cried Ebony, "otherwise you're dead meat."

"Do it NOW!" yelled Cheyenne.

The two poachers looked at each other. "It's the cowboy and his group," said the tall burly one, raising his rifle. "Let's get them."

A volley of shots rang out, shattering the serenity of the rainforest. Birds and animals scattered in every direction. Then silence. The poachers lay dead, their blood staining the dusty ground a crimson red. The four friends looked at each other in amazement. No one had been hurt.

Ebony ran to Cheyenne and threw her arms around him, burying her face in his chest.

"Why did they try to kill us?" she asked. Her voice trembled and her hands were shaking.

"Maybe it had something to do with the $100,000 that's on our heads," said Geigy. "Remember what the guy yelled: '*It's the cowboy and his group.*'"

Ebony held on to Cheyenne, still shaking uncontrollably. Cheyenne held her close and stroked her hair. "It's okay, honey, you're safe now," he soothed. "We had no choice, it was them or us."

She looked up at him with tear filled eyes. "I guess you're right," she said. "It was them or us."

Cheyenne nodded. "And by the way, everyone, nice shooting. We just saved an elephant."

"He took off running after all the shooting," said Willie. "He wanted no part of that, and I can't say I blame him."

"Let me give Jocko a call," said Cheyenne, gently freeing himself from Ebony's embrace and grabbing his phone. Once again, Jocko picked up after a couple of rings.

"Hello, Jocko here."

"Jocko, it's Cheyenne."

"Well, hello, I didn't expect to hear from you so soon. What's up?"

"We had to kill both of them, Jocko; both poachers."

"You killed both of them," Jocko repeated.

"That's right. We had no choice – it was them or us. They wouldn't put down their guns, and they tried to shoot us."

Jocko shook his head. "Unfortunately, most of them won't surrender, because if the people they're working for find out that they didn't try to kill you, they will kill them or their family."

"I see," said Cheyenne.

Jocko continued. "I have a man in your area who will pick up the bodies for identification. He should be there in about three hours."

"Okay, we'll wait for him."

"Watch your backs," said Jocko, "others may be close by, gunning for you."

"Will do," promised Cheyenne.

"Okay, talk to you later."

In the back of the poachers' truck, a heavy green canvas covered the two heavy tusks.

"Let's cover up the bodies with that canvas while we wait for Jocko's man," said Geigy.

"Good idea," replied Cheyenne.

After covering the bodies, they lifted the tusks out of the truck and laid them on the ground. Cheyenne stroked them gently. "You poor animals," he murmured. "Just so you can end up on someone's mantelpiece. Or be added to someone's collection. I'm going to fight for you. As God is my witness, I'm going to fight for your existence."

The others watched him and nodded silently to one another. They too would fight for the elephants. Geigy broke the silence. "Damn, I'm hungry," he said, rubbing his stomach.

"Me too," said Ebony, taking out some cans of beans and soup from their supplies. "I'll have this ready shortly."

After eating their fill, they relaxed in the shade of the trees and tried to snatch a few minutes of sleep. The noise of a fast moving vehicle jerked them awake. Dust billowed in the air as they watched its rapid approach.

"Get your weapons ready just in case this isn't a friendly visitor," Cheyenne told them.

"Willie, take a look with your binoculars," said Ebony.

Willie raised the binoculars to his eyes and scanned the horizon. "I can't tell for sure who it is until the truck comes over that small hill." He looked again. "Yes, it's the park ranger – I can make out the markings of his jeep now."

"Hold your weapons until we're sure," said Cheyenne.

The ranger pulled up in a cloud of dust and jumped out of his jeep. All the guns were pointed at the ground. "Hi, my name is Fritz," said the ranger, striding toward them with his arm outstretched. Tall and blond, with high chiseled cheekbones and piercing blue eyes, Fritz looked like a Viking warrior. One would have placed him in the Nordic environs not in the heart of the African continent. He spoke with a slight German accent. "I'm here to pick up the two bodies," he said, flashing a dazzling smile.

Cheyenne took his hand and shook it heartily. "Nice to meet you, Fritz. My name is Cheyenne and these are my friends, Ebony, Geigy and Willie."

They all smiled and shook hands. Fritz pointed to the green canvas. "Are they under that canvas?" Cheyenne nodded.

"I can't understand these poachers," said Fritz in his clipped German accent. "This is how most of them end up. Well, let's take a look at them." Bending down he pulled back the canvas. "Well, I'll be damned, I can see why these two put up a fight." The others looked at him quizzically. "We've been looking for these two escaped convicts for over two years," he said, smiling at the four friends. "You've done Africa a big favor by shooting these two criminals."

"Why is that?" asked Ebony.

"Between them, these two thugs have killed at least fifty people, including women and children and several judges."

Shocked, Ebony looked from Fritz to the two bodies. "Oh, my God," she cried, mouth agape.

"They were going to spend the rest of their lives in jail, which is not a very pleasant place," said Fritz, looking more closely at the bodies and noticing the two head shots. "See those two head shots, that's what killed them instantly."

"That's my boy Cheyenne," said Geigy, patting his friend on the back.

Fritz looked at Cheyenne. "So you're the cowboy that all the drums are talking about all over Africa. They're spreading the message everywhere."

Cheyenne smiled. "I guess that's me."

"Damn, let me shake your hand again," said Fritz. "It's an honor and a pleasure to meet you."

Cheyenne grinned and held out his hand again. "The pleasure's all mine, Fritz."

"Wait until Jocko finds out about the identity of these two poachers. He'll be thrilled."

Together, they placed the two bodies in body bags and led by Cheyenne, they bowed their heads and recited the Lord's Prayer.

"It's not for us to judge them," said Cheyenne. "May God have mercy on their souls."

"Amen," said the others in unison.

"Well, there's nothing more I can do here," said Fritz. "I'd better get these two back to base."

Cheyenne, Willie and Geigy helped him to load the two bodies into the back of his jeep.

"Thanks, it's been a pleasure meeting you all," said Fritz as he jumped in the driver's seat. And with another dazzling smile and a quick wave, he spun the jeep round and sped off down the dirt road.

"Shit, you forgot to give him the tusks," said Geigy, tripping over one of them and falling flat on his face. He sat up and wiped off the dust and grime. "I'll put them in the back of our truck."

"Okay," said Cheyenne. "Let's spend the night here and then we'll head off in the morning."

They all nodded. It had been a long, stressful day, and they were ready to snatch a few hours' sleep.

Chapter Twenty

They awoke at dawn to a sizzling hot sun. Although still very early, the heat was brutal.

"I feel as if I'm being fried like bacon in a frying pan," said Geigy, rubbing his head. "This heat is too much."

"I hear you," said Cheyenne. "What I wouldn't give for a cool breeze."

A herd of water buffalo sauntered past about a quarter of a mile from them.

"Look how beautiful and free and proud they are with their young calves," said Ebony.

"But look what's following the herd," yelled Geigy. "A bunch of painted wolves!"

"What on earth are painted wolves?" asked Cheyenne. "I've never heard of them."

"They are also called African wild dogs," Geigy explained. "They have four toes instead of five like domesticated dogs."

"You know lots of things about Africa, Geigy. Now if I saw their tracks, I would think they were missing a toe," laughed Cheyenne.

Ebony smiled and held his hand. "You have much to learn about Africa, my American cowboy."

"Yes, ma'am, that I do," he said, tipping his hat to her. "Now let's hit the road."

Cheyenne and Ebony drove on in silence for the next few miles, followed closely by Geigy and Willie in the other truck. The dirt road was rough and bumpy like most of the roads traversing the rainforests.

"Not exactly a smooth ride, is it?" observed Cheyenne as they hit yet another pothole and bounced up on their seats.

Ebony laughed. "That's Gabon for you. All rainforests and savannah, but no good roads!"

"Well, at least we won't get a speeding ticket," said Cheyenne, grinning.

Ebony punched him in the ribs playfully. "Very funny, cowboy."

A few moments later, they moved slowly across a well-traveled road, still engaged in idle banter. Flirting and teasing each other like two young lovers in the birth of their relationship.

Unbeknownst to them, Geigy and Willie had stopped in the middle of the road, and were looking up and down in both directions. Geigy put his foot on the gas, ready to cross the road, when Willie suddenly grabbed his arm. "Hold it, Geigy, I think I see someone or something walking up the road. From this distance, I can't make out what it is."

Geigy slammed on the brakes and tooted his horn at Cheyenne and Ebony. They turned in alarm, and Cheyenne stopped the truck.

"What's the matter? You scared the hell out of us," cried Ebony.

"Yeah, what's going on?" asked Cheyenne.

"We see something coming down the road," shouted Willie.

"Something or someone?" asked Cheyenne.

Willie grabbed his binoculars and took a closer look.

"Well, what do you see?" asked Geigy impatiently.

Willie lowered the binoculars. "It's a man dressed in khaki shorts and shirt, and wearing a wide brimmed hat. He's carrying a rifle and a pack on his back."

They all scrambled out of their vehicles and looked down the road.

"Willie, let me take a look," said Ebony, grabbing the binoculars and taking a long sweeping look. "My God!" she exclaimed, "it's that English hunter who came in the *African Queen*. I've forgotten his name – Johnston, Winsome or something." She handed the binoculars to Cheyenne.

"You're right, Ebony, it's Winston, the English game hunter," said Cheyenne, surveying the approaching figure. "Let's go and get him. He looks exhausted, and from the way he's walking, I think he might be hurt."

The four friends jumped back in their trucks and screeched down the road toward Winston.

"Look, he's collapsed in the middle of the road," cried Ebony as they pulled up beside him.

Cheyenne leapt out of the truck and knelt beside the fallen man. "Winston, Winston, are you all right?" he said, cradling Winston's head in his arms.

No response. Cheyenne shook his head in dismay. Then like music to his ears, he heard that unmistakable British accent. "I say, old fellow, I'm bloody glad to see you chaps."

"What happened to you?" asked Cheyenne. "You're a mess of cuts and bruises."

Winston looked up at him and smiled faintly. "Well, old chap, I had a bit of a run-in with that bloody elephant Monsoon. He attacked me on the road, and really did a number on my jeep. I thought he was going to kill me and he damn near bloody well achieved his mission. I thought I was a goner."

Geigy knelt down by the injured man. "Winston, let me take your backpack off, so you can be more comfortable."

"Thanks, old chap," said Winston, pulling out a bottle of whiskey from his jacket. "Anyone care for a drink?"

Geigy laughed. "Damn, I don't mind if I do," and taking a hefty swig, he passed the bottle to Cheyenne. "That really hit the spot. Good stuff. Thanks, Winston."

"My pleasure, Geigy, old chap," said Winston, trying to hold his head up. They all took a hit and sighed in appreciation. "I have more whiskey in my bloody jeep. I knew I might be in for a long walk, so I just took one bottle."

"You have more whiskey in your jeep!" exclaimed Geigy.

"That's right, old chap. I have a whole case and I don't think Monsoon broke a single bottle."

Geigy's eyes glistened. *A whole case of whiskey!* He licked his lips in anticipation. "How far down the road are you?"

"About thirty-five miles or so, maybe more. It's hard to gauge." He sighed and let his head fall back on Cheyenne's arm.

Geigy pulled frantically on Cheyenne's other arm. "Let's go! Let's go and get the whiskey."

Cheyenne shrugged him off. "Hold on a second, Geigy. All in good time." He turned to Winston. "What else do you have in your jeep that we could use?"

Winston closed his eyes and thought for a while. Finally, his eyelids fluttered open. "Well, now, I have some food, five canisters of gas, a few guns and some ammunition. I think that's it."

"Good, that should do it," said Cheyenne. "Are you all right to travel?"

Winston answered with a cheery grin. "My dear chap, I've bloody well walked this far, so I will definitely enjoy the ride back."

The others laughed heartily. And the smile on Geigy's face was so delightful, so bright, it could have lit up the whole of Manhattan! *Whiskey! A whole case of whiskey!*

When they arrived at the site of the encounter between man, elephant and jeep, they stared in disbelief at the damage and destruction.

"My God, Winston, you were lucky to come out of this alive," said Cheyenne.

Winston nodded. "It's a bloody miracle, old chap."

"A bloody miracle," repeated Geigy.

"Yes, a miracle indeed," said Ebony.

"What's a miracle?" asked Willie. And they all burst into laughter.

"Seriously, though," continued Winston, "if it wasn't for that bloody tree, I would be dead. The tree stopped his charge." He shuddered imperceptibly. "Otherwise he would have bloody well crushed me."

"Look at those deep prints he left in the dirt," Ebony said as she measured the foot marks with the side of her hand. "Look at the difference between my hand and Monsoon's foot."

Monsoon's foot was about three times the size of Ebony's hand.

"He's one big mean elephant, and that's an understatement," said Cheyenne, turning to the others. "Let's grab everything we can use: food, gas, ammunition…"

Geigy interrupted. "And the whiskey, don't forget the whiskey."

Cheyenne laughed loudly. "That's right, Geigy, let's not forget the whiskey!"

As Geigy was pulling out the precious case of whiskey, he found that one bottle was broken. *Damn!* He also found something else. "Hey, look what I found – a harmonica!" he exclaimed. "I used to play one of these pretty well."

Winston looked at each of them in turn. "I just had that with me on lonely nights to break the silence."

"Let's have a party," cried Ebony. "After we build a fire, eat and drink some whiskey."

"Yes, yes," they all agreed. "Sounds like a great idea."

"Let's gather some wood and whatever we can burn, before it gets dark," suggested Willie.

"Good idea, old chap," said Winston, patting Willie on the shoulder. Willie beamed.

Cheyenne pulled Ebony toward him in an embrace. "What's for supper tonight?" he asked her. And then under his breath, he whispered, "I think I know what's for dessert."

She pushed him away, feigning annoyance, but secretly, she couldn't wait for dessert.

"Oh, a can of this and a can of that," she said nonchalantly. "Thank God for you, Winston, we were getting a little short on food supplies," she added, batting her eyelids at him.

Cheyenne felt a twinge of jealousy. *My God, she's flirting with him. And she's doing it on purpose, just to annoy me.* Pretending not to notice, he said, "Yes, we have to find a village that has supplies and gas."

Winston raised his right hand and pointed. "There's a dead tree not too far from here that we can use for firewood."

"Perfect," said Ebony, still batting her eyelids.

Winston pointed again, in the opposite direction. "And see that big tree over there, let's have the party underneath that."

"Hey, that's the perfect place," they all agreed.

Just bloody perfect, old chap, muttered Cheyenne to himself, mimicking the Englishman *perfectly.*

Chapter Twenty-One

So later that night, they had their party. Geigy started things off with a snappy little tune on the harmonica. Cheyenne approached Ebony and bowed his head. "May I have the pleasure of this dance, my lady?" he said, proffering his hand.

Ebony played along. "With pleasure, my lord," she said saucily, taking his hand. Buoyed by the whiskey, the others broke into gales of laughter.

Cheyenne and Ebony stepped forward and danced in a circle as the rest of the merry group clapped their hands in rhythm with the music. Then they all took turns dancing with Ebony.

"I think I need to take a break now," said Ebony, rubbing her aching feet. She had been dancing for hours.

Winston handed them all a bottle of whiskey from the case. "Let's drink to the bottle that got broken," he cried.

They all took a sip from their individual bottles. "To the broken bottle," they toasted in unison.

Geigy stopped playing the harmonica and started dancing around the fire, Indian style. Then, grabbing two teaspoons from the back of the truck, he started banging them together.

"I used to call square dancing back in upstate New York, so grab your partners," he cried, stamping his foot on the ground and banging the spoons together. The others stared at him in amazement.

"Don't just stand there like a bunch of stuffed puppets," he yelled. "Follow my words, and all four of you get out here." Cheyenne and Ebony paired off, along with Willie and Winston.

"Okay, old chap," said Winston to his partner, "let's trip the bloody light fantastic."

"You got it," said Willie.

Geigy called out commands, still stamping his foot and banging the spoons together.

"Now, swing your partner, turn him or her around, now all join hands, now circle to the right, now circle to the left, now doce do, now all change partners and swing them around." On and on he went as they all kept drinking and spinning around in a frenzy.

Willie was the first to stop. "Damn, I'm exhausted. I think I'll lie down for minute or two." And taking another slug of whiskey, he collapsed in a deep sleep. Between them, Cheyenne and Winston lifted Willie and gently lay him in the back of the Rover.

"I think my partner's out for the count," said Winston, stumbling around, barely keeping his balance. Cheyenne led him to the Rover and helped him into the back, alongside Willie. He fell asleep immediately.

"Another one out for the count," said Cheyenne.

"These men have no stamina," said Ebony who was still whirling around, her long black hair flowing behind her.

Geigy was a veteran drinker – it would take more than a few drinks to knock him out. But eventually, Cheyenne found him propped against a large Banyan tree, snoring loudly.

"One more out for the count," chuckled Cheyenne.

"Yeah, another one hits the dust *literally,*" said Ebony. "They're going down like flies. I guess it's just you and me, cowboy."

Cheyenne grinned. "I guess so."

Together he and Ebony managed to lift Geigy into the other truck. "He weighs more than I thought," said Cheyenne.

"A dead weight," Ebony agreed. "I'm exhausted."

"Me too. How about we have that dessert now," he said, winking at her.

Ebony rolled her eyes. "I noticed that you weren't drinking that much."

Cheyenne smiled. "I could say the same about you."

"Are we thinking the same thing?" she said, batting her eyelids flirtatiously.

"Yes, I think we are," said Cheyenne, touching her cheek. "Now, how about that dessert?"

Ebony drew close and he folded her in his arms, sighing deeply. Their lips met and they joined together in a long kiss. When they finally broke apart, Cheyenne took her hand and said softly, "Follow me." Grabbing a couple of blankets and his six-shooters from the Rover, he led her to a clump of bushes. Slivers of moonlight illuminated their path and a warm breeze caressed their faces. They looked into each other's eyes and kissed deeply again. A sudden noise jolted their embrace.

"Did you hear that?" said Cheyenne, startled.

"Yes, that's a leopard looking for something to eat," said Ebony, her luminous eyes glinting mischievously.

"Damn, he didn't sound that far away to me," said Cheyenne. "And I'm on a mission."

Ebony drew him close, and giggled. "Oh, I like this mission stuff," she said, gazing up at him.

Cheyenne held her gaze. "Did you ever have sex in a tree?"

"Are you serious?"

"Yep, deadly serious."

"Well, the answer is no, but who am I to stop a man on a mission," she laughed.

Cheyenne looked around, his eyes scanning the darkness. “I’m sorry, Ebony, but we can’t stay on the ground with that leopard prowling around. We could be his next meal.”

Ebony nodded. “You’re right, cowboy. Hand me those blankets and give me a boost up,” she commanded as she sauntered over to a nearby tree.

“Aye, aye, captain,” said Cheyenne, giving her a quick salute.

“Very funny,” said Ebony as Cheyenne hoisted her up into the tree and passed her the blankets. “Now give me your hand and I’ll help you up.”

“No problem, I think I can manage,” said Cheyenne as he scooted up the tree.

Ebony watched in amazement. “Wow, that was quick. You look as if you’ve been climbing trees all your life.”

Cheyenne grinned at her. “Tree climbing is one of my specialties. In a past life, I think I might have been a monkey!”

Ebony burst out laughing. “Cowboy, you are one funny guy.”

They climbed up higher and higher into the tree, guided by the shimmering moonlight.

“Thank God for the moon,” said Ebony as she clambered from limb to limb. “At least we can see where we’re going.”

Cheyenne followed behind her, nimble and surefooted. *Perhaps I was a monkey, after all.*

Finally Ebony spotted the perfect place: a sturdy tree limb with three wide branches. “This will do nicely,” she said, spreading the blanket over the limb. Stepping back, she admired her work. “Look, a bed in the trees, it’s perfect,” she said, clapping her hands together.

Cheyenne smiled. “Just perfect,” he agreed, taking her in his arms once more. They kissed again. Cheyenne could feel his guns digging into his side. “Let me get rid of these guns,” he said, draping the holster around a tree limb. “That’s better, now I can get closer to you.”

She smiled at him seductively.

"Now where were we," he said, drawing her close and undoing the buttons of her blouse. Ebony sighed as he slowly removed her blouse and in one deft movement unhooked the fastenings of her bra. Her luscious breasts sprang free, the full rosy nipples glistening in the moonlight. Now it was Cheyenne's turn to sigh. "My God, you are so beautiful, I could eat you up," he gasped.

"Then why don't you," she purred.

He caressed her breasts and felt himself harden. Ebony moaned in delight. "Don't stop," she whispered. "Don't stop."

Cheyenne lowered his head and suckled each breast in turn, running his tongue and lips over the soft nipples and bringing them to erection. "I told you I could eat you," he said, now rubbing her erect nipples between his thumb and forefinger.

Ebony cried out. "Oh, cowboy, that feels so good. Just keep doing what you're doing."

"You have such beautiful breasts," he murmured as he reached down to stroke the curly hair between her legs. Ebony could stand it no longer. She wanted him, and she wanted him right now. In one swift movement, she tore off his shirt and unbuttoned his pants. Her fingers grasped his rock hard cock. Cheyenne gasped. She fondled him, one hand rubbing his cock up and down, and the other caressing his nipples. They were both locked in the world of lust. Cheyenne thrust his fingers inside her and felt her moistness. "I love it when you're wet with passion," he whispered.

Ebony sighed a long deep sigh. "And I love you, Cheyenne," she panted, lowering herself onto his hardened cock. Her legs buckled as he entered her, burying himself deep inside.

"It's time to begin your mission," she said huskily.

Cheyenne gasped in ecstasy as he felt her hotness close around his throbbing cock. It took all his control not to explode inside her right there and then. "God, that feels so good," he moaned. "I want to stay like this forever."

Ebony laughed between her moans of delight. "Yes, my cowboy lover, let's stay entwined like this forever – locked together as one for all eternity." She spread her legs wider then clamped down on him tighter than before, her legs now wrapped around his waist. "Fuck me, Cheyenne," she panted. "I want to feel every single inch of you. Fuck me hard."

Cheyenne didn't need any urging. He rammed his cock up to the hilt in her warm moistness, pumping hard and harder with every thrust. She groaned with pleasure, opening herself to him as he fucked her with long hard strokes.

"I'm going to fuck you until you beg me to stop," he whispered in her ear.

"I never want you to stop," she cried. "Never, never."

Cheyenne felt himself about to explode. He was nearing the brink and he wanted her to come with him. "Are you ready? Ready to fall over the edge with me?"

"Yes, yes, my loving cowboy, I'm ready," she practically screamed. And together they fell over the edge into the arms of ecstasy. In fact, they almost fell over the edge *literally!* Locked in the throes of passion, they had forgotten that they were making love in a tree and almost toppled from the tree limb. Hearts pumping hard, their passion now ebbing, they managed to catch their balance and now lay back against the tree branches.

"Now that's what I call a fantastic *dessert*!" exclaimed Cheyenne. He closed his eyes, luxuriating in the afterglow of their lovemaking.

"Yes, my red hot cowboy," she purred, licking her lips. "That was the best dessert I've ever tasted!"

Chapter Twenty-Two

The two lovers awoke early in their lofty perch, still entwined in each other's arms.

"It's a wonder we didn't fall out of this tree in the night," said Cheyenne.

Ebony laughed. "I slept like a babe. Don't think I moved a muscle after our night of passion."

Cheyenne winked at her. "Me neither. Want to try it again?" And once again they moved together and christened the tree limb amidst the squawking and chirping of several small birds displeased at the invasion of their territory.

"That was wonderful, Cheyenne," said Ebony, after their second bout of lovemaking. "Let's stay in this tree forever, looking out at the world below and making love every day."

Cheyenne laughed and planted a wet kiss on her lips. "I would love to, but I don't think the birds and monkeys would be too happy with us." He pointed to the squawking birds and a couple of chattering monkey who were perched on a nearby tree limb. "They're already mad at us for invading their territory. They're saying: *You humans belong on the ground, not in our trees.*"

Ebony returned his kiss. "Yes, you're right, let's get out of here. I'm starving."

"Me too," said Cheyenne. "I'm so hungry I could eat a..." He stopped mid-sentence, and they both laughed together, remembering.

Grabbing the blankets and Cheyenne's guns, they climbed down the tree and headed back to camp. The others were still fast asleep in the trucks, snoring loudly.

"Rise and shine, everybody," yelled Ebony, "it's time for breakfast." She went from truck to truck, nudging the sleeping occupants. "Come on, you sleepyheads, it's time to get up. Cheyenne and I have been up for hours, haven't we, cowboy?" she said, giving him a saucy wink.

"Yes, I've been *up* for quite a while," said Cheyenne, leering at Ebony, "and I can definitely recommend it."

Ebony flashed him a brilliant smile. "Me too," she said.

Geigy was the first to wake. He staggered from the truck, rubbing his sleepy eyes. "Why are you two so chirpy this morning?" he asked, looking from one to the other. "It's bad enough having to listen to those squawking birds without you two adding to the chatter."

The lovers exchanged glances. No words were necessary. They each knew what the other was thinking. Cheyenne felt himself harden again. *My God, I've just had her twice, and I'm ready to take her again, here and now.* Reading his thoughts, Ebony blushed and felt the wetness between her legs.

Cheyenne turned to Geigy. "Well, old chap, as Winston would say, it's a beautiful day; the sun is shining, the birds are chirping, and we don't want to miss a single second." He inhaled the crisp morning air and looked around, his eyes resting on Ebony. "It feels good to be alive."

"Yeah, yeah," said Geigy grumpily, "well, beautiful day or not, I'm hungry. What's for breakfast?"

Ebony smiled. "Well, thanks to Winston, we now have some more supplies. How would powdered eggs and beans suit you?"

"Sounds good to me," said Geigy, still rubbing his eyes.

Winston and Willie now stumbled from the trucks, both holding their heads.

"Good morning, sleepyheads," said Ebony cheerily as she busied herself preparing breakfast for everyone. "Breakfast is almost ready."

"Morning," said Winston weakly. "My bloody head is killing me, but I'm hungry as hell."

Cheyenne stared at him. "I'm not surprised, after all the whiskey you drank last night."

"Well, it was a party, old chap, and you bloody well drink at parties." He looked closely at Cheyenne. "And why are you so hale and hearty this morning, my good man?"

"Well…" Cheyenne started to answer, but Geigy cut him off.

"Don't ask, he'll give you a long spiel about a beautiful sunny morning and chirping birds. Just forget it."

Winston nodded. "Rightio, old chap." He rubbed his head. "God, my bloody head is splitting."

"Here, Winston, sit down, breakfast is ready," said Ebony. "You'll feel much better after you've eaten."

"Why, thank you, my dear, most kind."

Ebony smiled at him. "My pleasure." She turned to Willie. "You too, Willie, take a seat. Eggs and beans coming right up."

Willie gagged. "Sorry, Ebony, but I may have to pass on breakfast. I'm not feeling so good." He patted his stomach. "Must be something I ate yesterday."

They all laughed. "More like something you drank, you mean," said Geigy.

"Come on, Willie," urged Cheyenne, "wash up and you'll feel a lot better. And you should have a little something to eat. Those eggs and beans sure smell good, Ebony."

At the mention of food, Willie gagged again. "Excuse me a second," he said as he ran behind a clump of bushes and promptly threw up. The others watched as he emerged from the bushes, wiping his mouth on his sleeve. "Ah, that feels much better. I'm ready for those eggs and beans now, Ebony."

They all burst out laughing. "Good man, Willie," said Winston, patting him on the back.

After breakfast Cheyenne pulled Winston aside. "Winston, could I have a word with you?"

"Of course, old chap, I'm all yours. What do you want to talk about?"

"Well, when we met you, you were going in that direction," Cheyenne said, pointing up the road.

"That's right, old chap."

"And we were going the other way."

"Right again, old chap."

Cheyenne hesitated, then continued. "Well, as you're on foot, I could give you one of our vehicles, if you wish." He cleared his throat. "But I like having two vehicles."

"Spit it out, dear chap, I won't bite you. What are you trying to say?"

Cheyenne grinned. "Well, I know this might sound strange, you being a big game hunter and all, but I was wondering if you might want to join us in our quest to save the elephants. There, I've said it."

Winston patted him on the back. "Put your mind at rest, laddie. In the last few weeks, I have found out how smart and beautiful elephants really are, and they are definitely worth saving. So, old chap, I'm coming with the four of you on your quest."

Cheyenne beamed. "Glad to have you aboard, Winston. The more the merrier." He turned to the others, still grinning widely. "Winston is going to join us, so now there are five of us."

"Hurrah!" The others let out a yell and welcomed their newest recruit.

Chapter Twenty-Three

The next morning they checked out Winston's vehicle one last time.

"Look what I found, a busted up camera and a map," Willie told them.

Cheyenne turned to Winston. "What's the camera for?"

Winston rubbed his head. "Well, I used to take pictures of Africa and sell them to magazine companies like *National Geographic*, to make money."

Cheyenne nodded. "I see."

"What's with this map?" asked Geigy, studying the crumpled guide.

Winston reached for the map. "This is a map of a cave I have to show you."

"Okay, let's hit the road then," said Cheyenne as Geigy gave him a thumbs up.

It was another blistering hot day with scarcely a breeze to soften the sun's brutal glare. Fortunately, they had plentiful supplies of food and water and fuel, as well as several bottles of whiskey, thanks to Winston. They traveled in silence for the next few miles, gazing thoughtfully at the verdant rainforests and vast grasslands.

"Look!" exclaimed Ebony, "a herd of water buffalos." She pointed to the shaggy herd quenching their thirst at a nearby waterhole. The others swiveled their heads in their direction.

"That's a sizeable herd," observed Geigy.

Winston pointed to the sky. "And look at those vultures circling overhead."

Cheyenne looked up. "Yes, something must have been killed recently. Let's check it out," he said, motioning to Willie and Geigy as they pulled off the main road.

As they approached the herd, Willie called out, "Look, it's the carcass of a large water buffalo."

"Look at the lion tracks," said Geigy. "Unfortunately, water buffalos can't climb trees, otherwise he may have made it."

Ebony grabbed Cheyenne's hand. "You're fair game if you get separated from the main herd."

"I hate those damn vultures," said Winston, grabbing his rifle and taking aim at the circling group. He fired off a shot killing one instantly as the others flew off squawking and fluttering in the burnished sky.

"They'll be back as soon as we drive away," said Geigy.

"Yeah, no way they're gonna leave their night's dinner," said Willie.

Retracing their steps, they drove back to where they had first met up with Winston. As they were about to start following the elephant tracks, a chilling noise stopped them dead in their tracks. It was Monsoon!

"No mistaking that sound," said Winston, his heart pounding rapidly. "I'd know that animal anywhere." He shuddered, thinking of his near-death brush with the large beast.

Monsoon had been trailing a herd of elephants, looking for a female partner. The main herd was made up of related females and their young, directed by the matriarch, the eldest female. As a male, Monsoon had left the pack when reaching adolescence, to form herds with other elephants of the same age. Later, the herds spread out, the male elephants like Monsoon leading a lonely life, approaching the female herds only during mating season. Monsoon had not ventured too far from his family and recognized the herd immediately when re-encountered.

Cheyenne looked through his binoculars, studying the magnificent animal. "My God!" he exclaimed, "that lad has a fine pair of tusks on him."

"That he does," agreed Winston, nodding his head. "And I should know, I almost got impaled on them." He shuddered again, thinking how lucky he was to be alive.

"I can see the scar above his eye, it is definitely Monsoon," Cheyenne told them.

"Give me those," said Winston, grabbing the binoculars from Cheyenne and raising them to his eyes. "I have to be sure." He swiveled to and fro, studying the animal from all angles. Finally, he said simply, "You're right, it's Monsoon."

"Hand me my sniper rifle, Winston," said Cheyenne, nudging him from his reverie.

Winston stared at him, a puzzled look on his face. "What for?"

"Look, we're upwind from Monsoon," explained Cheyenne, grabbing the rifle and pointing it in the direction of Monsoon. "He doesn't even know we're here."

Ebony stomped towards him, her face like thunder. "What the hell do you think you're doing," she demanded.

"I'm going to kill Monsoon," he replied. His finger flirted with the trigger and he took aim.

Ebony stamped her feet angrily. "Like hell you are," she shouted, knocking the rifle from his hand.

Cheyenne stood in shock. "What the hell are you doing?" he cried.

She glared at him, her opal eyes blazing. "You came here to save the elephants not to kill them," she thundered. "The person to blame for Monsoon's rampage is the person who tried to kill him in the first place!"

Winston's face reddened. "It was me! It was me!" he cried. "I'm the one who shot Monsoon and missed." The others gasped. Shock registered on their faces.

"I'm the brave white hunter who did this terrible thing," continued Winston, "and I'm so sorry." He hung his head in shame. Silence. No one said a word. Winston looked at each of them in turn, his eyes pleading for forgiveness. "I wanted to be a big brave hunter and bring home those magnificent tusks," he said. "I imagined that people would greet me as a hero, but now I feel like a coward." He shook his head sadly. "A big white coward."

Cheyenne stepped forward and patted Winston on the shoulder. "Don't worry about it, we all make mistakes. It takes a brave man to admit he's wrong."

"Thanks, Cheyenne, but I still feel like a coward."

Ebony approached and took his hand in hers. "You're not a coward, Winston, you're just human. We'd all like to be hailed as heroes."

"Hear! Hear!" said Geigy.

"Ain't that the truth," added Willie.

Winston looked at them, his face filled with gratitude. "Thanks, chaps," he said. "Thanks for understanding."

Suddenly, Cheyenne yelled out, "Oh, no, here we go again," as he motioned for Geigy to turn around. Geigy spun around to see Monsoon bearing down upon them at lightning speed.

"Let's get out of here," cried Ebony, "he's out to kill us!"

They didn't need telling twice. Bumping into one another in their haste to beat a quick retreat, they ran to the nearby jeeps. Monsoon thundered down the road, his roaring bellows sending chills down their spines.

"Move out! Move out!" shouted Winston, remembering his recent ordeal with the huge elephant.

Stumbling and scrambling, they fell into the jeeps and screeched down the potholed road, tires burning. A cloud of dust and debris followed in their wake partially blinding Monsoon as he hit his top stride.

"My God, that was close," said Cheyenne, turning in his seat to look at Monsoon.

Ebony sighed in relief. "I thought we were goners. I had no idea that elephants could move so quickly."

"About 30 miles an hour," said Cheyenne. "Some can even reach a top speed of 35."

Ebony looked at him in amazement. All she could utter was a simple "Wow!"

Monsoon was shaking his massive head back and forth, trying to clear the dust from his eyes. Rising up on his back legs, he trumpeted loudly as if to say *I'll get you later* as he watched the distant vehicles disappear from view.

The two jeeps roared down the road, still kicking up clouds of dust so heavy that they lost sight of Monsoon. After a few miles, Cheyenne motioned for Geigy and the others to pull over.

"How many more times are we going to run into Monsoon?" asked Willie as they finally slowed to a stop at the side of the road.

"Well, no more today," replied Cheyenne. "I think we've lost him for the time being. He's lost all sense of direction in that cloud of dust. In my last glimpse of him, he was headed in the other direction." Hearing this, the others visibly relaxed and let out a collective sigh of relief.

"Praise the lord," said Willie.

"Hear! Hear!" said Geigy.

"I'll drink to that," added Winston, pulling a bottle of whiskey from his jacket. After taking a quick swig, he passed the bottle around and they all took a drink to steady their nerves.

"Thanks, Winston, I needed that," said Geigy gratefully.

Winston grinned and wiped his mouth on his sleeve. “Any time, old chap,” he said with a wink.

Geigy took another hearty swig. “Cheers, *old chap.*”

“Well, since we’ve come back this way, I might as well show you all this,” said Winston, pulling out his self-drawn map. “About two miles down the road there’s a path we have to follow.”

Ebony looked at him quizzically. “What are you going to show us?”

Winston turned and shot her a crooked grin. “I have to make this a surprise for all of you because it is quite depressing, but I have no choice but to show you.”

They looked at him expectantly. “Lead the way,” said Cheyenne.

“Okay, let’s go.” Winston slid the map back into his pocket. “I don’t want anyone else seeing this.”

They leapt back into the jeeps, Cheyenne, Ebony and Winston leading the way followed closely by Geigy and Willie.

“My God, it’s hot,” said Winston, wiping his brow. “As an Englishman, I’m not used to this heat.” He smiled wryly. “It’s not good for my delicate English skin,” he said, pointing to the myriad freckles that dotted his body.

Cheyenne and Ebony laughed. “We’ll make a native out of you yet,” said Ebony, her burnished black skin contrasting sharply against his pale form.

They drove on in silence for the next few miles surveying the dusty savannah and the vast sprawl of dense rain forest. Winston finally broke the silence. “Do you know that three-quarters of this country is covered with rain forest,” he observed.

“I didn’t realize that,” said Cheyenne, shading his eyes from the blazing sun.

“I’ve lived here all my life and I didn’t know that,” said Ebony, embarrassed by her lack of knowledge of her own country.

"It's true. I read up on Gabon before I came here…" He stopped mid-sentence and pointed to a mountain that suddenly emerged through the clouds. "That's where we're going," he said, his voice taking on a sad tone. Noting the sadness in his voice, Cheyenne and Ebony exchanged glances as if to say *What's going on?* But Winston fell silent again. They would have to wait.

After traveling for several more hours, they finally arrived at the foot of the mountain. Winston stared at the darkening sky. "It's going to be dark in an hour or so," he told them as they emerged from their respective jeeps. "Let's call it a day."

The others nodded in agreement – it had been a long, exhausting day.

"Make sure you get some rest tonight," continued Winston, looking at each of them in turn, "because we'll be doing a lot of walking come sun-up."

Geigy yawned. "I'll be out for the count as soon as my head hits the pillow, or should I say, ground," he said with a smile. "I'm tired after all that driving."

"Me, too," said Cheyenne. "Let's hit the sack." He winked at Ebony and they shared a secret smile.

Winston looked at them and grinned. *I don't think those two will be getting much sleep tonight,* he mused. *Lucky Cheyenne.*

Chapter Twenty-Four

They arose bright and early the next morning. Ebony prepared a light breakfast of fruit, cheese and rolls, washed down with hot coffee. As they started to head out, Cheyenne tapped Winston on the shoulder. "Should we leave someone behind to watch the vehicles?" he asked.

Winston looked around. "No, this is quite a desolate area, I don't think we have anything to worry about."

Cheyenne nodded, but he didn't seem convinced. Noticing his concern, Winston added, "But we should camouflage them with some brush."

Cheyenne brightened. "Good idea, Winston." He turned to Geigy and Willie. "Okay, guys, let's gather some brush and hide those vehicles as best we can."

The men jumped into action and soon the two vehicles were hidden from view.

"Okay, that's great, but there's just one more thing," said Winston. "Ebony, could you make sure that we have enough food and water for a couple of days."

"A couple of days!" exclaimed Cheyenne. "Just how far are we walking?"

Winston grinned at him. "You'll see," he said, "you'll see."

Ebony scurried around, gathering supplies for their long hike.

"Okay, are we all ready?" asked Winston. They nodded. "Then let's go," he cried, and marched off up the mountain like a drill sergeant leading his troops into battle.

"Where the hell are we going?" Geigy whispered to Cheyenne.

"Beats me," said Cheyenne. "Let's follow our leader."

The brutal African sun beat down on them as they trudged wearily up the mountain. Although still very early, its heat was merciless. Winston continued to march ahead at a rapid pace. For a pale, gaunt Englishman unused to such heat, he showed remarkable stamina.

"What did he have for breakfast? Wheaties?" said Cheyenne.

Ebony looked at him questioningly. "What are wheaties?"

"Oh, forget it," said Cheyenne, "you have to be American to know what I'm talking about. Right, Geigy?"

Geigy smiled. "Right."

On and on they climbed, stopping at intervals to rest and quench their thirst. Winston continued to force the pace. He was like the Duracell bunny on speed. Turning back to the others, he pointed to the left side of the mountain. "The cave is on this side," he said, "and it's not too high up now. I hope we can find it without too much difficulty."

"How much longer?" asked Cheyenne, panting.

"Oh, about another hour's climbing," said Winston brightly as if he were taking a leisurely stroll in the park. The others moaned. The relentless heat had taken its toll on them, sapping their energy.

"Another hour," said Willie. "My legs feel like lead."

"And my body feels as if it's on fire," said Geigy. "Let's rest in the shade for a while."

"Good idea," said Cheyenne as they plunked down under some nearby brush.

Winston wanted to continue. "But we're almost there, chaps."

"You go ahead, Winston, we're stopping here for a while," said Ebony.

Reluctantly, Winston joined them. "Okay, okay, you win. But I must say, old chaps, I'm surprised at your lack of stamina." They glared at him. Winston backed off. "Sorry, no offence."

After resting for an hour, they resumed their climb. Winston clambered ahead searching the scraggly brush and stray vegetation for telltale signs of the cave.

"How much longer, Winston?" asked a weary Cheyenne.

Winston beat back the brush with his arm. "It's here somewhere," he said, exasperated. "I know we're close."

Cheyenne sighed. "That's what you said an hour ago."

"Yes, I know, but I can sense that we're really close now," he replied. "Just be patient a little while longer."

So on and on they climbed, their weary bodies drenched in sweat. They were about to take another rest, when Winston suddenly let out a loud yelp. "Alleluia!" he cried as he pulled back a huge bush and dove into its center. "Here's the opening, I told you it was close."

The others rushed forward, forgetting the tiredness in their aching limbs. Pure adrenalin propelled them forward. Winston stood erect, a look of triumph on his freckled face.

"By golly, old chaps, we have found the cave," he whispered as if he didn't want anyone to hear.

Ebony stared at him. "You're giving me the chills. What's inside the cave?"

"Yes, what's the big surprise?" asked Geigy.

Winston touched his finger to his lips. "All in good time, my dear chaps, all in good time. You'll find out soon enough," he said as he took a flashlight from his pocket and squeezed through the small opening. "I'll need my trusty torch with me because it's bloody dark in there."

Cheyenne shuddered. "I have the chills, too," he whispered. "I hope this is not catacombs with underground passageways and tombs and bodies lying all over the place."

"Me, too," whispered Geigy.

"And me," whispered Willie as they watched Winston disappear through the hole, flashlight in hand.

Ebony punched Cheyenne on the arm. "Will you all please stop whispering," she told them. "I'm about ready to scream!"

"Sorry…" began Cheyenne. He stopped mid-sentence as they heard Winston's muffled cry from inside the cave.

"Come on, you lot, stop squabbling out there," he admonished. "You sound like a bunch of bratty school kids." They looked at one another and blushed. "Follow me," shouted Winston.

"After you," said Ebony to the others. "I'm not going in there first." She hesitated for a second. "But I'm not going last either. I'll go third."

Cheyenne led the way and the three friends followed in single file behind him: Geigy, Ebony, and then Willie bringing up the rear.

"Hey, why am I last?" said Willie, a finger of fear prickling his skin as they pushed their way through the small entrance to the cave. Total darkness and icy dank air greeted them. They shivered.

"Oh, it's cold and damp in here," said Ebony. After the intense heat outside, the cave felt like a refrigerator.

"I'm freezing and I can't see a darned thing," moaned Geigy, his teeth chattering in the icy cold.

"Hey, Winston," called Cheyenne, "shine a light this way. We can't see a damn thing, and you have the only flashlight."

Winston spun around and shone the light in their direction. "Oops, dreadfully sorry, old chaps, I forgot," he said as he edged back to them. "Come on, I'll lead the way. Just watch your step."

Cheyenne nodded. "We're right behind you."

A narrow pathway led down to a vast chamber below. They inched along slowly, straining their eyes to see. "I wish we had another flashlight," said Cheyenne.

"Yeah," agreed Geigy, coming to a stop behind him, "I can hardly see a thing."

"Well, we'll have to make do with this little torch," said Winston. "Just follow me carefully and watch your step. There are a lot of loose stones around." He flashed the light on the walls of the dank cave. Still trembling from the cold, they surveyed the grimy walls.

"See all these big wooden sticks with the bark on the end," said Winston, pointing at several sticks that jutted from the wall. "Does anyone have a match, and I'll light one."

Cheyenne fished around in his top pocket and found a small pack of matches. "It's lucky I have these on me," he said, passing the book of matches to Winston.

"Thanks, old chap," said Winston, striking the match and lighting one of the wooden torches. It sputtered at first in the damp air, then finally burst into flame, illuminating the shadowy cave.

"Ah, that's better," said Winston. "It gives off much more light than this tiny battery torch. I'll light the other torches as we continue on."

"Please do that, and be quick about it," cried Ebony. "This place is really creepy." She shivered again and drew in her breath. "It gives me the chills."

Cheyenne placed his arm around her and drew her close. "Come here, honey, I'll keep you warm," he said, smiling.

She nuzzled in the crook of his arm, feeling the warmth of his body. "Thanks, Cheyenne, I feel safer now. This place is so scary."

"Don't worry, you're safe with me." He kissed her tenderly. "I won't let anything happen to you." She sighed and he felt her body relax against his as he stroked the top of her head. Winston had now lit all the torches along the cave walls. "Look, there's a path that goes all round the cave, and another path that leads to the bottom," he said. They nodded and looked around the vast cavern. "Follow me, old chaps," urged Winston, leading the way. They fell in line behind him, grateful for the light from the blazing torches.

"Cheyenne, I have one room that happens to be for you," said Winston, "and it's coming up."

Cheyenne looked puzzled. "What do you mean, you have a room for me? What are you talking about?"

"You'll see. All in good time, dear chap. All in good time."

"What's he up to?" asked Geigy.

Cheyenne shrugged. "Search me. He's a crazy eccentric Englishman," he said. "They are known for their eccentricity."

"What does eccentricity mean?" asked Willie.

"Oh, forget it," said Geigy, "it's hard to explain. Let's just call him crazy and leave it at that."

They followed Winston down to the bottom of the cave and came to another opening about six feet wide. Winston stopped in his tracks and raised his hand to signal them to a halt. "Stay here until I light up this cave so that you can see," he ordered.

"Aye, aye, captain," joked Geigy, raising his hand in a mock salute.

Ebony grabbed Cheyenne by his waist and held on tightly. She was trembling from head to toe. "I'm really frightened about what's waiting inside for us," she whispered.

"It's okay, honey," soothed Cheyenne, stroking her hair. "I told you before, I won't let anything happen to you."

"Okay," she said falteringly, not entirely convinced.

"Look! Winston has lit up the room," he said, giving her hand a gentle squeeze.

"Come on in," shouted Winston. "It's all lit up now. Don't be surprised at what you see."

They hesitated at first, and then Cheyenne stepped forward, pulling Ebony behind him. "I'll lead the way," he said. "Come on, there's nothing to be afraid of."

The others fell in line behind him and he stepped into the room. The chamber was ablaze with dozens of flaming torches and at first he was temporarily blinded by the dazzling light. Rubbing his eyes, he surveyed the illuminated chamber, his eyes glued to hundreds of glistening objects at the far end of the cave. He rubbed his eyes again, unable to identify what he was looking at.

"What the hell," he said, his eyes assaulted by the gleaming light.

"What is it, Cheyenne?" asked Ebony, standing close behind him. "What are you looking at?" She shaded her eyes from the dazzling light.

"I've no idea," said Cheyenne. "I can't make...," he stopped and then his voice rose several octaves. "Just a minute!" he exclaimed, "I've just realized what I'm looking at!"

"What?" repeated Ebony, tugging on his arm. "What is it? This light is too bright for me."

"My god, they're tusks! Hundreds and hundreds of tusks!" said Cheyenne, dropping to his knees as the tears flowed down his cheeks.

"Oh, dear lord," cried Ebony as she too was overcome with emotion. "Those poor, poor elephants."

Geigy and Willie stared at the tusks in amazement, too shocked to speak.

Winston shook his head sadly. "I'm so sorry, so very sorry. I knew it would be a great shock to you." He paused, then continued. "I did try to prepare you – to warn you that the surprise was depressing." He hung his head in shame. "I had no choice but to show you."

No one spoke – they were still in a state of shock. Cheyenne wept silently. He could barely comprehend what he was seeing. *Can this be real? Are my eyes playing tricks on me?* He wiped away the salty tears. *Am I really looking at hundreds of elephant tusks?* In his mind's eye, he could see all of these elephants walking one by one, in the impenetrable rain forests, on the vast savannahs, in the dense lowland jungles, on the dusty plains. These gentle creatures that had no known enemies, other than man.

He could see the roaming herds with the matriarch at the head. Mothers caressing their young with their trunks; others using their trunks to pick up fruit the size of a marble, or a branch a foot thick. Young males frolicking in the river or wallowing in mud baths; hosing themselves off, or spraying one another with the cool water.

He could see them calling to one another, using calls too low for humans to hear, the sounds traveling for several miles, even through thick vegetation. The females calling to the males during mating season, and the males responding. In his mind's eyes, he saw them all.

Cheyenne raised his head and stared at the glistening tusks. They seemed to cry out to him.

They killed us for our tusks. They shot us so that some collector could add us to his ivory collection, or hang our tusks on his wall. They took our tusks and left us to die all alone in the blistering sun.

Their voices screamed louder and louder in his head. *Don't let us die in vain! Save our brothers and sisters, our mothers and fathers, our sons and daughters. Don't let us die in vain!* The voices grew louder. Bile rose in his throat and he could feel the anger spilling over. *I have to stop the slaughter. I have to stop the slaughter of these magnificent animals.*

His thoughts drifted to his childhood days: his beloved father and his overwhelming love for the elephant – a love that he had passed on to his only son. He thought of the circus and the story of Old Molly and her brutal electrocution. *No more, no more. I have to stop the slaughter.*

The others watched him in silence. No one dared to speak. Finally, Cheyenne rose to his feet, a look of fierce determination on his face. "In the name of my beloved father, Robert Cole, and in memory of Old Molly, I swear to you, they will not die in vain," he said through gritted teeth. Then turning on his heel, he bowed deferentially and addressed the array of gleaming tusks.

"I, Cheyenne Cole, swear to you this day that as long as there is breath in my body and blood in my veins, I will fight to save your brothers, your sisters, your mothers, your fathers, your sons and your daughters. You will not die in vain."

An eerie silence filled the cavern, and then Cheyenne felt a soft breeze caress his face. He touched his cheek and he knew…he knew that the elephants had heard him. He would not let them down.

Ebony rushed over to him and threw her arms around him. "You're right, Cheyenne, they will not die in vain," she cried.

The others gathered around and together they made a pact. From this day forward, they would do everything in their power to save the elephants.

Chapter Twenty-Five

"Winston, you sure gave me a shock," said Cheyenne, finally finding his voice again. "The sight of those tusks totally overwhelmed me."

Winston placed his hand on Cheyenne's shoulder and patted it gently. "I felt the same way you did, my dear chap, when I first laid eyes on them. Rendered me totally speechless!"

"Well, since we're here, why don't we spread out and see what else we can find," said Cheyenne.

"Good idea, old chap."

"What do you think happened here, Winston?" asked Geigy.

Winston frowned and scratched his head. "Well, whoever got all these tusks was probably hiding them to get the best possible price."

"Must have been a gang or something," said Cheyenne. "There's no way that one person could haul all these tusks up the mountain."

"I wonder if they're coming back?" said Willie, looking around nervously.

"They might be watching us now," said Ebony.

"No, these tusks have been here for quite a while," said Winston. "I think that whoever brought them here is either dead or in jail."

"I hope you're right," Cheyenne said, placing his arm around Ebony. "They'd be pretty upset to find us here."

"They certainly would, old chap."

"It was very fortunate to have found that cave. Those tusks could have been there for many years without anyone even knowing," said Cheyenne, shaking his head. A sudden shout rang out, causing him to stumble slightly. It was Geigy yelling at the top of his lungs.

"What the hell…," said Cheyenne, struggling to regain his balance.

"Come quick! Come quick! Look what I found," screamed Geigy. "Hurry! Hurry!"

"Okay, hold your horses," shouted Cheyenne, "we're coming."

"Sounds like he really hit the jackpot," said Winston as they all rushed to the sound of Geigy's voice. They found him sitting on a rusty old chest inscribed with the skull and crossbones.

"Pirate treasure!" exclaimed Winston.

"No," replied Geigy, "look closely at the side of the chest."

They all leaned forward and scrutinized the rusty chest. It was tough to see in the dim light of the cave. Emblazoned in faded red letters were the words DANGEROUS, HIGH EXPLOSIVES.

"And look at all these," said Geigy, pointing to a stack of similar boxes, also inscribed with the skull and crossbones.

"What the hell…," began Cheyenne.

"What are all these boxes?" said Ebony, cutting him off in mid-sentence.

Geigy stood erect. "Well, being an ex-Marine and an explosives expert," he said, "I would say we have a shitload of dynamite here. He grinned sheepishly. "Excuse the French, Ebony."

"No problem."

"And I mean *dynamite!*" he said, smiling that smile that told everyone he was in his glory. This was his specialty, his territory. "I can blow this whole damn place up and hide those tusks so that nobody will ever find them," he finished triumphantly. The others stared at him in silence as he turned and faced Cheyenne. "Just give me the word, Cheyenne, and I will do that for you."

"No, we are not going to blow up this cave until every single tusk is taken out of here," he said.

"Good idea, old chap," said Winston.

"You got it," said Geigy.

Cheyenne continued. "Listen, everybody, we'll never make it back before dark, so we'll have to spend the night in this cave."

Ebony shuddered and huddled close to him. "Cheyenne, you'd better be right next to me all night. It's scary with all these tusks and dynamite, and Geigy with his wild eyes."

They all turned to look at Geigy who kept repeating, "I'll blow it all up for you, just say the word. I really think we should." His eyes glittered in the darkness. "Just say the word."

Cheyenne laughed and patted him on the shoulder. "Okay, Geigy, calm down, we're not blowing anything up yet. Let's sleep on it and decide what to do in the morning."

"I'm not sleeping on no dynamite," said Willie.

The others laughed heartily, their laughter echoing through the gloomy cave.

"It's just figure of speech, old chap," said Winston, patting Willie's arm.

Willie was not convinced. "Figure of speech or not, I still ain't sleeping on no dynamite!"

That night Cheyenne had a nightmare, waking the others with his cries of anguish.

"No, no," he screamed, "stop shooting!"

Ebony leaned over to comfort him. "It's okay, Cheyenne baby, it was just a nightmare," she said softly, wiping the sweat from his brow. "Are you all right now?"

"Yes, I'm fine. Sorry I woke you all. Go back to sleep, guys. You, too, babe, I'm okay now."

Ebony stroked his hair. "Do you want to tell me all about your nightmare?" she asked softly.

"No, not really, it was terrible," he said with a grimace.

"I think it would be best if you told me," she pressed. "It would make you feel better."

The others had fallen asleep again, the sound of their snores echoing through the cave.

"Okay, here goes," said Cheyenne. "It was a beautiful day; the sun was shining brightly. Then over this rise came a line of magnificent elephants. Down at the bottom of the hill stood ten poachers with their rifles at the ready. And they just started killing these elephants one by one. And the elephants just kept on coming." Cheyenne paused and wiped his brow.

"Keep on going, baby," said Ebony gently, "I'm listening. What happened next?"

Cheyenne took a deep breath and continued his story. "I tried running up the hill to stop them. I had to climb over all the dead elephants and the pile of bodies kept getting higher and higher. As I reached the top, the pile was so high that I was going to fall to my death." He shuddered. "That's when I woke up."

Ebony held him close. "I'm so glad you told me. Remember, it was only a dream. She nestled up closer. "Now let's get some sleep."

Meanwhile, Python was gathering a posse of men to hunt down, *the cowboy and his group of no-good do-gooders.* His efforts had paid off, and now about 100 men stood before him. As he opened his mouth to address them, he heard the sound of drums beating across the land. "What are the drums saying, Ego?" he asked.

Ego cocked his ear and listened carefully. "*Hands of Lightning* has killed some of your poachers."

Python stamped his feet and cursed loudly. "Sonofabitch!" he yelled.

"We have to get rid of that bastard American," said the Russian.

Python turned to face his volunteers. "Men, I'm going to pay you well, every month."

The men cheered wildly. Ego and the Russian exchanged glances and smiled. They knew that by the end of the month most of these volunteers would probably be dead.

"Money talks," said the Russian, puffing on a fat cigar.

"And money kills," grinned Ego, revealing his broken yellow teeth.

Python continued. "You will hunt down and kill the cowboy and his bunch of cut-throats."

Python expected the men to cheer, but instead they whispered amongst each other, and shuffled their feet. "He wants us to hunt down and kill the *Hands of Lightning!*" shouted one man.

Several men broke from the rabble and ran back into the jungle, crying, "*Hands of Lightning!*

Python shook his fists. "Come back here you bunch of lily-livered cowards!" But his words fell on deaf ears; the men had disappeared into the depths of the jungle. They were long gone.

The leader of the remaining group approached Python, who was still shouting. "We want half of our month's pay now," he demanded.

True to his brutal nature, Python reacted instinctively, striking the man in the head and knocking him to the ground. He was about to kick the prone man again, when the Russian grabbed him from behind, and the other men surrounded both of them. All hell was about to break loose, when a jeep screeched to a halt in front of the angry mob. A machine gun, mounted in the back, was pointed right at them. At the helm stood Hi, Ho and Cracker.

"Hold it right there, my friends," shouted Cracker, his finger on the trigger. "You touch Python and I'll blow you to smithereens."

"Stand clear or we'll blow your heads off," yelled Hi.

"Back off or you won't know your back from your front," screamed Ho.

The angry mob parted and the Russian hustled Python inside his hut and set him down in a chair. Ego stood by his side, smiling his broken yellow smile.

"Look, Python, I know you're pissed off, but we need these men," said the Russian.

"So what do you need me to do?" said Python, looking up at the Russian who was still puffing on his cigar. Spirals of smoke circled his head. Ego waved them away and rubbed his eyes.

"The smoke is making my eyes water," he said.

"Shut up, crybaby," snarled the Russian. "We have a crisis on our hands and all you care about is your stupid eyes! Quit moaning!" And he blew a cloud of smoke directly into Ego's eyes.

Ego shrank back. The Russian had made his point. Taking another drag on his cigar, he turned to Python. "Now where was I? Ah yes, first I want you to apologize to the man you hit, and then tell them that they will get a full month's pay if they sign up today."

Python sprang to his feet. "A whole month's pay," he screamed. "To hell with that."

The Russian took another slow drag on his cigar and pushed Python back down in his chair.

"Take it easy. Don't forget, you don't have to pay those men who ran off into the jungle."

Python shook his head stubbornly. "I ain't paying any of 'em squat," he said.

The cool Russian finally lost his cool and thumped the table in front of Python, sending glasses flying. Shards of glass scattered everywhere, one of them finding its way into Ego's hand.

"Ouch," Ego cried, pulling the shard from his bloody hand.

"I told you to shut up, crybaby, and I won't tell you again," shouted the Russian. Turning to Python, he pounded the table. "Come to your senses," he growled, his face as black as thunder.

Python looked at the Russian and knew he was right. "All right, all right," he said, throwing his hands up in the air, "I'll do what you say. We do need those men."

"Finally," said the Russian, blowing another stream of smoke in Ego's direction. Ego coughed and spluttered but knew better than to complain. There was no messing with the Russian today. Python stood and walked outside to the man whom he had knocked to the ground. The gaggle of men watched nervously, keeping one eye on the machine gun which was still trained on them. Python motioned to Hi, Ho and Cracker to put down the gun. "Okay, fellas, stand easy and put down the gun. We're gonna settle this amicably. No need for any more violence. We're all friends here, right?" he said, putting his arms around the injured man. The leader shied away at first, thinking this was just another one of Python's tricks. An ugly red gash ran from his forehead to chin, where Python had struck him.

"No tricks, I come in peace," said Python, shaking the leader's hand. "Sorry about the blow to your head, I don't know what came over me." The leader took a step back – he wasn't taking any chances. Python tried again. "Okay, you win. Tell your men that they will be getting a full month's pay today, when they sign up."

Still the leader hesitated. "How can I trust you?" he said.

Python looked him in the eye and said, "You have my word. Let's shake on it."

The two men shook hands.

"That's good enough for me," said the leader finally. Little did he know that Python's word was like a speck of dust in the wind, blown away with the slightest gust.

So now Python had his small *army* to hunt down the *Hands of Lightning!* Turning to Ego, he said, "After the men are trained, I'm going to send you out on patrol to hunt down this so-called *Hands of Lightning.*" Ego nodded. "And I want you to bring him back to me, *dead or alive!*"

Ego smiled, revealing his broken yellow teeth. "Yes, Python, I will do that for you.

Dead or alive!"

Chapter Twenty-Six

Cheyenne and his group had scrambled back down the mountain and returned to their jeeps.

"Cheyenne, I know you didn't like what you saw in the cave, so I'm going to show you something positive," Winston told him.

"Okay, lead the way, partner," he said, jumping in the jeep.

Winston jumped in alongside him. "It's about half a day's drive from here, old chap. Let's go!"

The sun beat down relentlessly as they trundled across the vast plain. Progress was slow. Dust spewed up from the bumpy, pot-holed road, covering the windscreen in a grimy film of dirt.

"It's another hot one," said Cheyenne, wiping the sweat from his brow. "And this road is little more than a dirt track. I can hardly see through the windscreen. How much longer, Winston?"

"Not too far now, old chap," said Winston, surveying the surrounding terrain. "I see some familiar landmarks." He pointed to a nearby watering hole shaded by a clump of towering trees. "Popular meeting place, huh! Look at all the animals. We have our favorite bars and they have their favorite watering holes!!"

Cheyenne looked over at the watering hole and laughed. "I see what you mean."

The watering hole was teeming with wildlife. Forest buffalo looked on as a group of hippopotamuses wallowed and bathed in the refreshing water. Dozens of elephants lined the edge, dipping their trunks in the water, spraying themselves and each other. A myriad of colorful birds circled overhead, swooping down occasionally to cool off.

"Now if only we humans could live in such peaceful harmony," said Winston with a grin.

"Yeah, just wait until the lions arrive!" deadpanned Cheyenne.

Ebony, who had been sleeping for the past three hours, suddenly awoke with a start.

"What lions? Where are they?" she asked nervously, rubbing the sleep from her eyes.

Cheyenne stroked her hair. "Just a joke, honey, nothing to worry about."

"We're very close now," said Winston, espying several native Gabonese walking in the distance.

As they drew level with a man and woman and two small children, Winston gestured for Cheyenne to stop. Geigy and Willie, following behind in the other truck, also slowed to a halt.

In a language that none of the others could understand, Winston conversed with the man.

He shook the man's hand and then turned back to the others. "The big guy is in their village."

"Who is the big guy?" asked Cheyenne.

"The chief, the head honcho, old chap," he replied.

"You can speak their language?" asked Ebony, answering her own question.

Winston beamed. "Yes, and quite well too, although I do say so myself," he said.

"You are full of surprises," said Geigy

"Quite so, old chap," said Winston.

"Where is this village?" asked Cheyenne, anxious to move on.

"A few miles from here, old chap. Let's go!"

They jumped back in the jeeps and headed along the dusty trail for a few more miles.

"Stop, we're here," said Winston, pointing to a huge cluster of mud huts nestled by the edge of the rain forest.

"Are the natives friendly, or will we end up being their main course for supper?" asked Cheyenne, half-jokingly.

Ebony gasped. "Oh, my God, are they cannibals? I don't want to end up in their cooking pot."

"Me neither," said Geigy.

"Nor me," said Willie. "I ain't gonna be anybody's dinner. Besides I'm too skinny. Not too much meat on these bones."

"No, no, they are very friendly," Winston reassured them. "But don't let that fool you, they are also known for their hunting and killing skills. All the other tribes stay away from the Ji-Hi tribe, with their bright fighting colors."

"Okay, lead the way, *old chap,*" said Geigy, mimicking Winston's accent.

Winston led the group down a narrow path leading to a clearing at the edge of the rain forest. Approaching the clearing, they were met by a gaggle of sun-bronzed, scantily clad children, with bright smiling faces and gleaming white teeth, all trying to get closer to the white strangers with their funny clothes and pale faces. The drums beat out a solemn dirge as they entered the village.

"Look at all those huts," exclaimed Ebony, "there must be hundreds of them."

For as far as the eye could see, clusters of straw covered mud huts, set in circles, met their gaze. As they drew closer, dozens of semi-naked women emerged from the huts and stared at the five intruders. The group inched forward slowly, surrounded by the children who were singing and dancing to the beat of the drums.

"I don't know about you guys," said Ebony, looking at the women's sullen faces, "but I'm feeling a little nervous right now. Are they eyeing up tonight's main course?"

"Me too," said Willie, "they sure don't look too friendly."

Winston tried once again to reassure them. "Don't worry, they're not hostile, just curious. Some of them have never seen a white person before."

"The children seem to like us," said Geigy, looking at the laughing children who continued to sing and dance.

"Where are the men?" asked Cheyenne.

"Oh, they're here," said Winston, "most likely watching us right now. We just can't see them. They'll reveal themselves when they'r ready." He paused…"They're sizing us up right now."

"Not for the cooking pot, I hope!" said Geigy.

"I assure you, chaps, you have nothing to fear," said Winston. I know these people, they're friendly." The others laughed nervously.

"Hope you're right," said Cheyenne. "We'll find out soon enough."

Ebony pointed to the huts, many of them brightly colored. "Look, they are all the colors of the rainbow: Red, blue, orange, red, yellow, purple, pink. How did they manage that?" she asked.

"A large cargo plane, filled with paint, crashed in the jungle," said Winston. "No survivors. The tribe took the spoils and painted their homes. Makes a change from mud-colored."

"Look at that big white one," said Ebony, pointing to a beautiful white hut, set apart from the others. "Who lives there?" she asked.

"That's where the big guy lives," said Winston.

"Is this where I'm supposed to say *Take me to your leader*?" Cheyenne deadpanned.

"Very funny, old chap," said Winston.

Now as they moved closer to the big white hut, they were suddenly surrounded by hundreds of unsmiling dark men. "Where the hell did they come from?" cried Geigy.

"They just seemed to appear from nowhere," said Ebony.

"I told you they would reveal themselves when they were good and ready," said Winston. "They've been watching us this whole time."

"This is scary," said Ebony, inching closer to Cheyenne. "There are hundreds of them and they seem to be swallowing us up. I can hardly breathe."

Cheyenne hugged her close. "Do something, Winston. Talk to them. Otherwise we're gonna get crushed to death."

"Don't worry, old chap, I'll handle it." Turning to the milling crowd, he held up his hand and shouted STOP! STOP! in their language. After a few minutes, they settled down and looked at Winston expectantly, respect evident in their faces.

"Look at that," Cheyenne whispered to Ebony, "they seem to honor him. They act like he is one of them."

Ebony nodded. "Yes, Winston is quite the dark horse," she replied.

A hush fell over the crowd as Winston pointed to the big white hut. All eyes turned to see a huge figure emerge from the hut. "Look at the size of that man!" exclaimed Geigy. "He's at least six foot six, and he has to weigh over 350 pounds."

"He's a giant compared to the rest of them," remarked Cheyenne.

"No wonder he's the chief," said Geigy.

"Now, we know why they call him the big guy," said Ebony.

"How did he get to be so tall?" said Willie. "The rest of them are just average."

"Look!" said Geigy, "the men are backing away from Winston, leaving him by himself."

Winston walked toward the huge man. "I don't like this," said Cheyenne.

The men met halfway and embraced.

"Would you look at that," said Geigy, "they're like bosom buddies."

"That crazy Englishman never ceases to amaze me," said Cheyenne as they watched the huge giant of a man hug their pale, scrawny friend.

"My God, they're walking towards us," said Willie.

"I'm scared," said Ebony, grabbing Cheyenne by the hand.

"Don't worry, honey, Winston knows what he's doing," said Cheyenne, patting her hand. "He'll make sure nothing happens to us."

Winston strode forward with his huge friend. "I say, old chaps, I want you all to meet my good friend Ho Goo," he said with a flourish.

Ho Goo looked down at the small group and bowed his head politely. Naked, except for a robelike loin cloth tied around his middle, Ho Goo's massive hairy chest was adorned with row upon row of beads. Animal bones pierced his nose and hung from his ears. A bold and fearless warrior, his body bore the scars from many battles. He smiled widely, revealing several missing teeth. Thrusting out his large gnarled hand, he shook hands with all the men, and bowed again to Ebony. Then, raising both his arms, he turned and yelled out something to his tribesmen. In response, they all cheered wildly and waved their arms back and forth.

"What did he say?" Cheyenne asked Winston.

Winston smiled. "He told them that tomorrow night we'll be having a party in honor of our guests. That means us, old chap."

"Just as long as we're not the main course, and…," said Cheyenne. He stopped mid-sentence and pointed. "Look, there's a small elephant."

They all turned and looked at the baby elephant which was tearing the leaves from a nearby tree.

"That's one of the reasons why I brought you all here," said Winston. "This tribe takes care of elephants that have been orphaned or abandoned by their mothers. As you know, very often they are killed for their tusks and these small elephants would perish without help."

Cheyenne's face lit up. "That's wonderful," he said, and for a while he forgot all about the tusks in the cave.

"I told you they were good people," said Winston, patting him on the back.

Ho Goo gestured for them to follow him, and as they approached a large clearing, he gave out a shrill whistle.

"What's that noise?" asked Geigy. Before anyone could reply, a huge elephant with a boy on its back came charging towards them.

"Don't worry," Winston told them as they took a step backwards, "this is a trained elephant. He won't hurt you."

"Look at the size of those tusks," said Cheyenne. "They're enormous."

As the elephant drew close to Ho Goo, it stopped and knelt down, letting the small native boy slide to the ground. Running to Ho Goo, the slender boy flung his arms around Ho Goo's giant waist.

"This is Goo, Ho Goo's young son," Winston told the group. "And the elephant's name is Kia. Go over and say hello to him."

The four friends walked over to the docile animal which was watching them with his big soulful eyes. "He's very gentle," said Cheyenne, stroking his tough hide.

"He's beautiful," said Ebony.

Winston nodded. "Goo and Kia grew up together," he said. "Kia's mother was shot by poachers and so the tribe took care of him."

Cheyenne could not take his eyes off this magnificent kind-eyed elephant. "Winston, would you tell Goo that I can see how much the elephant loves him," said Cheyenne with a kind of envy in his voice. "How he watches over him."

Before Winston could respond, Goo said, "Yes, I know, and I love him, too," in perfect English as he smiled fondly at Kia.

The others were taken aback to hear the young boy speaking English. Turning to Winston, Cheyenne asked, "How did he learn to speak English?"

"A doctor and his young daughter lived in the village for two years, and the daughter taught a few of the tribe how to speak English," said Winston. "I will tell you the rest of the story tonight."

Chapter Twenty-Seven

After wandering around the village for the rest of the day, they were each given a bucket of water so they could clean themselves off. And after a light supper of fish and berries, they settled down for the night in the same hut. Ebony, Geigy and Willie fell asleep immediately, while Cheyenne and Winston sat up talking.

"So, tell me, Winston, how did you become so friendly with the Ji-Hi tribe?"

"Well, old chap," replied Winston, "one night I pulled my jeep over to get some sleep. The next morning I woke up to see six Ji-Hi, dressed in their battle colors, bending over me." He shuddered, recalling that first encounter. "Scared me half to death, they did, with their garishly painted faces and their bows and arrows and long spears." He shuddered again. "Thought I was a goner, old chap, I don't mind telling you."

"Go on," said Cheyenne.

"Well," he continued, "they made me follow them to the village, thinking I might be one of their enemies. Thank God, the good doctor and his daughter were there because they may have saved my life."

"What happened next?" asked Cheyenne, eager for Winston to continue his story.

"Well, after things got peaceful again, the Ji-Hi tribe came down with this flu and a few of the older ones died. Doctor Gift - that's the name of the good doctor, I just remembered it - told me that there was a vaccination for this flu, but he had lost all his connections with the United States. I had plenty of connections to England, so I got the vaccine and they flew it in by helicopter. Dr. Gift gave everyone the vaccine and Bingo! We both became heroes to the Ji-Hi tribe." Winston smiled as he remembered the tribe's adulation. "Ho Goo called us the saviors."

"Damn, that's quite a story," Cheyenne said. "And I believe every word."

"No reason to doubt me, old chap. That's exactly what happened."

Cheyenne grinned. "I'm impressed, and I sure would like to meet this Dr. Gift and his daughter."

Suddenly, Ebony shot up from her bed and said, "I don't care about you meeting up with Dr. Gift, but I sure don't like that daughter stuff." She had been listening to the whole story.

Cheyenne and Winston broke into laughter.

"That's quite a girl you've got there, old chap," said Winston. "She doesn't miss a trick."

"Right in one, *old chap.*"

The next morning they joined some of the tribespeople for breakfast. Winston chatted amiably with them, while the others concentrated on their food. Breakfast was exactly the same as last night's supper: cooked fish and berries, with wedges of coarse bread. Afterwards, they all walked back to the jeeps, and Cheyenne strapped on his pistols. Ho Goo joined them later, and seemed to be very interested in the guns. He exchanged a few whispered words with Winston.

"I say, old chap," said Winston, approaching Cheyenne. "Ho Goo would like a demonstration with your guns."

"Geigy, who is this guy, my agent?"

Geigy smiled. "We can do that, no problem," he said, recalling Cheyenne's last demonstration.

"Yes," agreed Cheyenne, looking at Geigy, "we can give the chief a demonstration."

The words had barely escaped his lips, when a tribesman came hurtling towards them, screaming at the top of his lungs. He stopped in front of Ho Goo and spoke rapidly, the words tumbling from his mouth. Cheyenne and the rest of the group looked on anxiously, waiting for Winston to tell them what had happened.

"What the hell's going on?" said Geigy.

"I dunno, but it sounds serious," said Willie.

"Let's wait and see what Winston has to say," said Cheyenne, patting his trusty pistols. "Look, here he comes now."

Winston strode towards them, his face set in a tight grimace. "Okay, chaps. Let me tell you what has happened. This man takes care of a big herd of cattle, which are very important to the Ji-Hi tribe." He pointed to the tribesman who had now calmed down, and was being comforted by Ho Goo. "Two healthy cattle were found dead not too far apart, and he doesn't know why."

"Hmm, that does seem strange," said Cheyenne. "Two healthy cattle turning up dead for no reason. We had a few cattle on our ranch in Wyoming, and they were very tough."

Ho Goo motioned for a few men to join them as they followed the cattleman, to take a look at the two dead cows. Although still quite early, the sun's ferocity blasted them as they trudged to the cattle site. Ebony spotted the first dead animal. "Look, its tongue is sticking out. Poor thing."

"Yes, it is, but that happens with most animals, when they die," Cheyenne explained. As he bent down to examine the cow, Goo came running towards them, waving his arms and shouting.

"What has happened to the cattle?" he asked his father. He had just heard the news.

"Calm down, my son," said Ho Goo. He too could speak perfect English when he chose to. The good doctor's daughter had taught him well. "We will find out, but I hope it's not some kind of virus. Cheyenne and the cattleman will check out the first animal."

Cheyenne examined the carcass carefully. "I don't see a thing wrong with this animal," he said. "Let's take a look at the next one."

"They both look the same," said Winston.

"Yes, they do, except for one thing - one is lying on its right side and this one's lying on its left side." Cheyenne placed his hand on the second animal and felt through the hair.

"It looks like you're petting the animal," said Ebony as Cheyenne ran his hand over the cow from head to hind quarters.

"What's that on your hand?" exclaimed Geigy, stepping back. "It looks like blood. Has it been shot or something?" Instinctively, they glanced over to the trees, where the cattle had come from.

"No, this animal has not been shot," said Cheyenne. "Let me check it one more time." Running his hand over the carcass again, he stopped at the animal's hindquarters. "There's a little blood and swelling here," he said as he gently parted the hair to get a better look.

"Do you see anything?" asked Ebony.

"Sonofabitch!" exclaimed Cheyenne, suddenly realizing what he was looking at. "It's some kind of snake bite Be careful where you step! Snakes are hard to see." Startled, the whole group took a step backwards and checked the ground around them.

"The Black Mamba! The Black Mamba!" cried Ho Goo, drawing Goo close and placing a protective arm around him.

"What the hell is a Black Mamba?" Geigy asked.

"It's one of the most aggressive, deadliest snakes in Africa," Winston shouted.

"Everyone stay close, I want to check out that first animal again," said Cheyenne. "Help me roll it over on its side. I just want to make sure that I'm not mistaken."

Winston, Geigy and Willie rushed forward and helped Cheyenne to roll the carcass over. Repeating the same process, he felt the animal from head to foot. "There it is," he said as he parted the hair to show the cattleman and Ho Goo the snake bite. "Judging by the height of these snake bites, I think the Black Mamba are hanging out in those trees." Once again, all eyes swiveled in the direction of the nearby trees.

"Let's get out of here," urged Ebony, "snakes remind me of the devil. I want to go back to my hut."

"You're right, Ebony," said Cheyenne, placing his arm around her. "Winston, could you ask Ho Goo to send a man back with Ebony."

"Certainly, old chap," replied Winston.

Ebony grabbed Cheyenne's hand and held on tight. "Please come with me, Cheyenne," she begged, squeezing his hand even tighter. "I don't want you messing with those Black Mambas, it's too dangerous. If you get bitten, you will die."

Cheyenne looked deep into her beautiful opal eyes, now filling with tears. "Look, Ebony," he began, "you may be right, but women and children and men and cattle walk these paths every day, and they have to be protected. Now is the time to do this." He kissed her gently. "I have to do this. Now go with Ho Goo's man, back to the hut, and watch your step."

Ebony saw the steely determination etched on his face and knew it was pointless arguing with him. He would not be deterred from his mission. Shrugging, she released herself from his embrace and set off down the path with her guide. "Stay safe. I'll be waiting for you."

Ho Goo turned to his son. "Goo, stay right beside me," he commanded in his deep voice.

"Yes, Father," Goo replied.

Ho Goo turned to address to the small group, in perfect English. "Be careful, everybody," he warned, "these snakes may look like branches, so watch out for any low hanging branches." The others nodded. "Now, let's follow the path of the cattle, there may be more than one."

As the small group slowly worked their way through the trees, they met a tribesman who told Ho Goo that one of the cattlemen had stumbled onto a nest of baby Black Mambas and killed them all with a club.

"So now we know we have a male and female Black Mamba that are really pissed off," Cheyenne said to Winston.

"Bloody right, old chap," agreed Winston.

The group spread out, searching the brush and vegetation, and looking in the trees.

"I imagine it took a while before the snake venom killed the cattle," Willie asked Cheyenne. "Maybe one hour?"

Cheyenne scratched his head. "I don't know for sure how long it takes to kill a good sized animal like that. We should be coming on that hour about now," he replied.

Suddenly, Geigy yelled out, "I think I saw something move in a tree in front of me.

Cheyenne was at his side in a flash. "Where, Geigy? Where?"

Geigy pointed to a tree overhanging the path where the cattle traveled.

"Stay still, everyone!" said Cheyenne.

They stood like statues in the vast African rain forest, only their eyes moved, searching for any sign of movement in the trees.

"Let's get a closer look," said Cheyenne, bending his knees to examine the lower branch more closely. Suddenly, the branch sprang alive and the Black Mamba struck!

Chapter Twenty-Eight

The Black Mamba had missed Cheyenne by inches! The deadly snake hissed as it opened its mouth, and Cheyenne was close enough to see why it was called the Black Mamba. The inside of its cavernous mouth was completely black. Cheyenne blanched and stumbled backwards.

"Damn, it almost got me," he said with a shudder. Steadying himself, he drew his weapon and fired one shot, blowing the head off the Black Mamba. Still visibly shaken, he fired off two more shots to make sure that the snake was well and truly dead.

"Are you okay, Cheyenne?" asked Geigy, patting him on the shoulder.

Cheyenne sighed in relief. "Yeah, I'm okay *now*. That damn snake scared the hell out of me."

"Take a few deep breaths, old chap," said Winston. "That was a close shave."

"Tell me about it," said Cheyenne, wiping the sweat from his brow.

They were all amazed at the size of the snake, not to mention the speed and precision of Cheyenne's marksmanship. "You are a dead shot," said Ho Goo, moving forward to shake his hand. "I learned those words from the good Dr. Gift."

"Thank you, chief," said Cheyenne. "I learned how to shoot at a young age, ever since I saw Black Bart at the circus."

"Well, thank God for this Black Bart," said Ho Goo with a smile. Then, turning to one of his men, he said, "Bury that snake, and let's find the other one."

In all the commotion, no one had noticed that Goo was missing. As they buried the snake and continued talking about the accuracy of Cheyenne's shots, Ho Goo suddenly turned around and realized that Goo was no longer by his side. "Goo, Goo," he called, "where are you? Goo!"

"I think I saw him playing with a stick," said Cheyenne. "Look, here are his tracks." And he flew down the trail like a bat out of hell. He knew that another pissed-off Black Mamba was out there! Racing down the cattle path, he noticed another path running parallel, separated by brush and trees. Then he saw it – the other Black Mamba slithering down the path with its head high in the air. *It's after something. A Mamba on a mission!* He increased his speed, panting heavily. *God, I could use a horse right now; I'm getting a little tired.*

Glancing over at the snake, he spotted Goo sauntering along ahead, stick in hand, hitting at a stone without a care in the world. Little did Goo know that he was the snake's next prey! But Cheyenne knew. And he had to act quickly, otherwise it would be too late. The thick brush and trees prevented him from firing off a shot, so his only option was to yell.

"Goo! Goo!" he shouted, "run for your life, there's a Black Mamba coming after you!"

The Black Mamba hesitated momentarily, when it heard Cheyenne's voice. Startled, Goo dropped his stick and shot off down the path as fast as his small legs could carry him.

"Keep running! Keep running!" yelled Cheyenne as the young boy looked over his shoulder to see the Black Mamba rapidly gaining on him.

Cheyenne prayed he would soon reach a clearing, allowing him to cross over to the other path. Bathed in sweat, his limbs aching, he pushed his exhausted body forward, stumbling with every tortured step. The Black Mamba was now ahead of Cheyenne, hot on the trail of Goo. He knew that one bite from the venomous snake would mean certain death for the young boy.

"Oh, my God," he panted, "I don't think I can take another step." Grimacing in pain and sheer exhaustion, he dragged himself along, urging his body to go on. He couldn't lose this battle; otherwise the young boy would die. *Just a few more steps. I must reach Goo before the Black Mamba does!*

Goo knew he was running for his life. As he raced down the stony path, he looked over his shoulder and tripped over a branch, falling flat on his face in the dust. *Oh, my God, this is the end,* he thought as he struggled to rise to his feet. He knew it was just a matter of seconds before the Black Mamba reached him, and he quietly accepted his fate. He would die face down in the dust and dirt. Closing his eyes, he waited for the deadly snake to strike.

Suddenly, he heard the thunderous crashing of heavy brush and trees tumbling to the ground. *What's that noise?* Opening his eyes, he stared in amazement at the sight of a huge elephant charging down the pathway, directly toward the Black Mamba. Cheyenne saw it too. *My God, would you look at that! It's Monsoon! Monsoon has come to save us!*

The Black Mamba raised its head higher as it confronted the large elephant and hissed fiercely. Monsoon stopped in a cloud of dust and threw his trunk in the air, bellowing loudly. The snake stood her ground, hissing as loud as she could and raising herself even higher. Instinctively, Monsoon knew that he could crush this small, hissing animal with one stamp of his giant foot. He also knew that he would pay a big price. So he turned and crashed back through the brush. *Oh no!* muttered Cheyenne as he watched the huge elephant disappear through the brush. *But he did the right thing, the Mamba's venom would have killed him. At least he has bought us some time. The snake has stopped, but she'll soon be back in pursuit of Goo. I have to find a clearing to get to that other path.* Panting and sweating heavily, he stumbled forward. Pure adrenaline drove him onward. *I see a clearing. Thank God! Thank God!*

As he hit the clearing to the other path, he was now ahead of Goo and the Black Mamba, thanks to the intervention of Monsoon. Goo had risen to his feet and was now limping along, leaving behind a trail of blood. "I'm coming, Goo! I'm coming!" yelled Cheyenne as the two limped and stumbled toward each other.

Goo's foot was bleeding profusely as a result of his fall. Now he fell into Cheyenne's outstretched arms, breathing heavily. "I've got you, Goo. You're safe now." *But were they safe?* They both looked down the path, hoping that the deadly snake would turn off the path after its close encounter with Monsoon. But it was not to be. The Black Mamba was out to avenge her babies, and she would not be deterred from her mission. Hissing loudly, she raised herself high and opened her mouth to reveal the blackness inside. She was not going to stop.

Cheyenne pushed Goo behind him and pulled out his gun, hoping to kill the snake with the first shot. But the shot veered wild. The deadliest shot in Africa had missed his target.

"Damn!" he cried, sucking in air like a person who had almost drowned. *This miss could cost us our lives.* His hands were shaking as he struggled to control his breathing. *Stay calm.*

"I can see its fangs and beady eyes," cried Goo, in sheer terror.

Steadying himself, Cheyenne took aim again. The snake was moving its body back and forth, and Cheyenne missed again. The Black Mamba struck! Cheyenne staggered backwards. The force of the strike and the snake's speed sent the Black Mamba flying past Goo and Cheyenne, onto the path behind them.

"Did he bite you?" cried Goo.

Cheyenne had no chance to answer. The Black Mamba had regained its balance and was readying itself for a second strike. Mouth wide open, it sprang forward. And showing its fangs and devil-like blackness, the deadly Black Mamba struck again!

Chapter Twenty-Nine

Cheyenne stood straight and fired another shot. *This time the shot met its mark!* The snake's head rolled by Goo's foot. The mouth was still open, poisonous venom dripping from its fangs. Cheyenne sagged and breathed a huge sigh of relief. "Thank God, we finally got her," he said, wiping the sweat from his brow.

Goo reached for the head.

"Don't pick that head up!" warned Cheyenne, kicking the head from his reach. "That snake may be dead, but those fangs are sharp and the venom dripping from them can still kill you."

Goo shrank back. "I didn't realize," he said.

Just then, Geigy, Willie and Ho Goo came running up.

"You killed the snake!" Ho Goo exclaimed. "Did it bite anyone?"

"Cheyenne saved my life," Goo said, "and the snake bit him!"

"Oh, my God!" cried Geigy. "The snake bit you?"

Cheyenne shrugged. "It got me some place, but I don't feel a thing," he said, pulling up his shirt.

Geigy and Willie checked his entire body, from head to toe, but they didn't find any bite marks.

"I don't see any marks," said Geigy.

"I saw the snake bite him in the stomach area," said Goo.

"I'm telling you, I don't feel like I've been bitten by a snake," said Cheyenne.

"Maybe you can't feel it at first, but we have to find out. This is no laughing matter," said Geigy. "If that snake has bitten you, its venom could kill you within minutes."

"Okay, okay, I'm all yours. Take another look," said Cheyenne.

Once again, Geigy and Willie checked every inch of his body and found no bite marks. Geigy threw his hands up in the air. "Nothing. There's nothing there," he said in exasperation.

"I know what I saw," Goo insisted. "The snake bit him." They examined his body again.

"Wait a minute," said Geigy, "I feel some wetness and it doesn't feel like sweat. It's on your gun belt, Cheyenne. Take it off," he urged.

Cheyenne slid off the gun belt and checked it carefully. "Well, I'll be damned!" he exclaimed, "there are two fang marks right here on the belt. But it was too thick for them to penetrate, thank God." He wiped his brow and sighed deeply. "I am one lucky man."

"You sure are," agreed Geigy.

"Ain't that the truth," said Willie.

Ho Goo walked over and enveloped Cheyenne in his giant arms. "You saved my son's life," he said, practically squeezing the breath from Cheyenne's body. "I will never forget this. You are now one of us." He smiled proudly. "You are now a Ji-Hi tribesman."

Cheyenne struggled to release himself from the big man's grasp. "I am honored, chief, to be a member of your tribe," he said finally, gasping for breath. "Deeply honored."

Ho Goo smiled. "And now we will return to the village." He pointed to the dead snake. "Pick up the Mamba and bring it back to the village," he ordered one of his tribesmen. "We will show it to our people."

As they entered the village, all the tribespeople gathered around them, shouting and cheering. They had been preparing for the big festival that night, and now they had even more reason to celebrate.

Ho Goo stood in front of his large white hut and beckoned for Cheyenne and his group to join him, along with his son. Placing his massive arm around Cheyenne, he addressed his people.

"I name this man here *Hands of Lightning,*" said Ho Goo in his booming voice. "He and his friends are now members of the J-Hi tribe."

The tribespeople cheered wildly, waving their hands in the air and stamping their feet. Ho Goo motioned for them to be quiet. "Minutes ago, this man saved my son's life by killing this Black Mamba," he said, gesturing to the tribesman, who raised the headless snake high in the air for all to see. An astonished moan swept through the tribe as they pressed forward to get a closer look at the large deadly snake.

Ho Goo continued on. "If any of these new tribe members ever need help, or if they become sick or too old to take care of themselves, we must all help them in any way we can." His words resulted in a collective nod of heads and a resounding cheer. "Now, continue working on the festival," he said. "This will be an extra special night. We have much to celebrate."

The tribe quickly scattered. Each of them had a specific task and there was still much to do in preparation of the evening's festivities. The friends watched from their hut as they built a huge pile of wood in the center of the village. A group of women were roasting a pig while others roasted a slab of beef. Others were painting their faces and bodies in a myriad of bright colors.

Later a tribesman approached the friends' hut and motioned for them to follow him.

"Please have a seat." He pointed to a row of wooden chairs to the right of a big thronelike chair.

"The big chair is for Ho Goo," Winston told them, "and the chairs on the left are for different leaders of the tribe."

"Look at all the people," said Ebony, pointing to the hundreds of tribespeople surging forward.

"I didn't realize there were so many people in this tribe," said Geigy, amazed.

They took their seats and watched as the center of the village filled with singing, chanting people, eager for the festivities to begin. "Ho, Ho, Ho," chanted the villagers as they danced around the pile of wood. Suddenly they stopped in mid-step, their chants fading to a whisper.

"Why did they stop?" asked Ebony, who had been enjoying the spectacle.

Cheyenne pointed to Ho Goo's hut. "That's why," he whispered as the door opened and Ho Goo emerged from his hut.

"Look! The people are forming a line to the big chair," said Willie.

Ho Goo greeted everyone by raising his hands in the air and nodding to his people.

"Ho, Ho, Ho," yelled the tribe as Ho Goo made his way through the milling throng.

On reaching his *throne* he greeted the five friends with a wave of his hand and a smile that stretched from ear to ear. "My friends," he said with a slight bow.

He sat down on his *throne* and the tribe fell silent. Five men emerged from the throng and sat to the left of Ho Goo. They were followed by six women who sat down in front of Ho Goo.

Ebony turned to Winston. "Who are all those women on the ground, in front of Ho Goo?"

"His wives."

"Six wives!" exclaimed Ebony in amazement as she looked over at Cheyenne.

Ho Goo rose to his feet. "Let the festivities begin!" he boomed.

Wild cheering swept through the tribe. They were ready to party! Darkness had fallen. The aroma of roasting meat and burning wood filled the air.

"That smells delicious," said Geigy, smelling the air. "The meat, I mean, not the wood fire."

"Look at all those jugs being passed around," said Willie. "What's in them, Winston?"

"Those jugs are full of fruits and herbs," he said, "and believe me, they pack some punch."

Six jugs were placed in front of Ho Goo. "Pass out the jugs to me and my guests," he ordered.

Ho Goo raised one of the jugs to his lips and took a long drink. "Let the drinking begin," he boomed again, holding the jug aloft.

The tribe cheered, and stamped their feet in appreciation. "Ho,Ho,Ho," they sang. "Ho, Ho, Ho."

Ho Goo beamed and passed the jug to the leaders on his left. Then he turned to Cheyenne.

"Here, this jug is for you," he said, handing him one of the jugs.

"Thanks," said Cheyenne. "Here's to you, chief."

He was about to raise the jug to his lips, when Geigy grabbed the jug. "Here, let me try that first," he said, "it might be poison."

They all laughed as Geigy took a long swig from the jug and started coughing. "My God, that is mighty potent," he said, between coughs.

Winston patted him on the back. "It takes a bit of getting used to. I warned you that it packed a punch," he said, tipping the jug to his lips. "Ha," he said as the fiery liquid passed down his throat. "Whoa, that really burns." He thumped his chest. "Damn good stuff, chaps!" He passed the jug to Cheyenne. "Here, old chap, take a swig, it's very tasty."

Cheyenne grabbed the jug and took a big gulp. "It may take a little getting used to, like you say, Winston, but it's not bad," he said, wiping his lips.

"Give me that jug," ordered Ebony, snatching it from Cheyenne's hand. She took a small sip and grimaced. "Ugh! It's terrible," she said, taking another small sip.

Everyone was laughing as the jugs were passed back and forth.

"Look at all the dancers, dancing around the fire," said Ebony. All eyes swiveled in the direction of the glowing fire.

"Those are the ones who were getting all painted up this afternoon," said Cheyenne. "Look at all the colors from their bodies, gleaming in the firelight."

"It's dazzling, isn't it, with all the colors?" Ebony whispered to him.

"Yes, it is," replied Cheyenne as he turned and kissed her gently on the lips.

A drum started beating and a hush fell over the gyrating tribe. "What's happening?" said Ebony.

"I dunno, let's wait and see," said Cheyenne.

They all watched as the drum continued to beat and the crowd parted to make a path for two tribesmen. "What are they carrying on their heads?" asked Geigy, turning to Winston.

"Just watch," he replied.

The drums continued their solemn beat as the two tribesmen drew closer.

"Why, it's the Black Mamba!" Cheyenne exclaimed. "They're carrying the Black Mamba on their heads." A chill ran down his spine as he remembered how close he had come to being killed by this snake.

The two tribesmen strode up to the fire and tossed the snake into the flames. Cheyenne shivered as he watched the Black Mamba disappear into the ashes.

Thank God, he said to himself, *it's finally gone.*

Chapter Thirty

The drums finally stopped and the festivities resumed.

"Here comes the food," said Ebony as the first plate was served to Ho Goo.

Ho Goo stood and handed the plate to Cheyenne. "If it wasn't for you, my friend, we would not be having this festival," he said with a smile. "We are in your debt and we will never forget it."

Once again the tribe cheered wildly, waving their arms in the air and jumping up and down. Ho Goo called for quiet. Turning to his wives, he said, "Serve Cheyenne's friends now, and then I will have my mine."

The festivities continued into the night. And the five friends were feeling no pain as the jugs were passed back and forth between them. Winston tapped Geigy on the shoulder.

"I say, old chap," he slurred, "why don't you get out your harmonica and play some tunes."

Geigy nodded. "Let me have a few more drinks first."

"These jugs seem to be endless," said Willie, taking a quick slug from one of the jugs and passing it to Geigy.

Ebony laughed. "Come on, Cheyenne," she said, tugging his arm, "let's dance."

"Yes, ma'am," he saluted as she led him onto the dirt floor. They danced around amidst the whirling mass that was now dancing with wild abandon.

Winston glided past with a pretty native woman. "I say, chaps," he said, pointing to Geigy. "He plays a mean tune." They looked over at Geigy who was now blasting out tunes on his trusty harmonica. Ho Goo and his wives clapped their hands in appreciation.

"Well, that's it for me," said Geigy, bowing to his audience. "I'm going to have me a dance." And placing the harmonica in his pocket, he strode toward the gyrating dancers and asked the nearest woman to dance.

A big roar erupted as Ho Goo and one of his wives swept into the middle of the happy throng and joined in the dancing. For a large man, Ho Goo was very light on his feet.

"Just look at him move," Cheyenne whispered to Ebony as they watched the chief swaying back and forth to the rhythm of the drums.

Ebony nodded. "He's quite a mover," she agreed.

"I wonder if he'll dance with all his wives," said Cheyenne, and they both burst into laughter.

After several hours of dancing and drinking, the crowd started to thin out. The blazing fire had dwindled to a few burning embers as if to say, *It's time to go home now!*

Ho Goo yelled something to the remaining people that Cheyenne and the others could not understand. The friends were sitting by the ebbing fire, feeling relaxed and happy. They had wined, dined and danced, and were now ready for bed.

"What did he say to the people?" Ebony asked Winston.

"He asked all the widows to come forward, if they would like to," Winston replied.

"What happened to their husbands?" she asked.

"Some were killed by lions and snakes, others died in hunting accidents, and others fell ill," Winston explained to her.

The friends watched as dozens of women inched forward and stood in front of Ho Goo. Some were still dancing to the pulsating drumbeat.

"I can't believe that there are so many widows," said Ebony.

Ho Goo called Winston over and whispered something in his ear.

"What's going on?" asked Geigy, slurring his words. He had been drinking heavily all evening, and was still clutching a jug.

Winston returned to the group and whispered in Geigy's ear. Geigy's face lit up. "That's wonderful," he said. "That's great." He looked over at the widows and smiled. "I'll take that one," he said, pointing to a young woman with jet black hair and sparkling black eyes. He walked over to the woman, placed his arm around her and disappeared into the night.

Willie followed suit, choosing a doe-eyed woman with a fetching smile. Winking at the others, he, too, disappeared into the night.

That does it, muttered Ebony as she strutted over to Cheyenne. "Don't you be looking at any of those widows," she said to him, her dark eyes flashing. The widows looked disappointed as Ebony grabbed Cheyenne by the hand and led him away to their hut.

"Will Winston end up spending the night with one of those widows?" she asked Cheyenne, looking over her shoulder and glaring at the assembled women.

Cheyenne shook his head. "I dunno, honey, you'd have to ask Winston."

She stared at him long and hard. "You weren't really thinking about going with one of those women, were you?"

"Of course not, honey," Cheyenne reassured her as he opened the door to their hut. Ebony did not see him turn and glance longingly at the attractive native women, all lined up in a row. He winked at them and disappeared into the hut.

The next morning a nubile young girl with long, dark hair brought food and water to Cheyenne and Ebony's hut. Cheyenne winked at her.

"Thank you, honey," he said. The young girl smiled and fluttered her eyelashes at him.

Ebony slapped his arm and waved the girl away. "Don't you be honeying her," she scolded.

"Oh, I was just teasing," he said, pulling her close. "You are my only honey."

After they had bathed, Winston came to their hut. "We can stay as long as we want," he said.

Then Geigy and Willie showed up, grinning from ear to ear. Ebony glared at them as if to say *Wipe those silly grins off your faces.*

"How long do we want to stay?" Cheyenne asked the group.

"Forever!" replied Geigy.

The men burst out laughing, but Ebony remained stony-faced. She was not amused.

"All right, we'll stay for a few days. Is that okay with you, honey?" he said, giving her a quick peck on the cheek.

"I guess so," she said reluctantly.

Chapter Thirty-One

A few days later, the five friends were awakened early by a loud commotion in the village.

"What's going on?" Ebony asked Cheyenne as they rushed from their hut. "What's all the excitement? I'm still half-asleep."

"Me too," replied Cheyenne, rubbing the sleep from his eyes. "I've no idea what's going on."

Geigy, Winston and Willie joined them a few moments later, staggering from their hut half-asleep. "What's with all the yelling?" said Geigy.

"We've only had a few hours' sleep," moaned Willie, struggling to keep his eyes open.

"And whose fault is that," demanded Ebony, glaring daggers at him. She knew that he and Geigy spent most of their nights with the young widows.

Willie hung his head. "Dunno," he said sheepishly.

Winston took charge. "Follow me, chaps," he said, marching forward. "Let's find out."

"Lead on, MacDuff," said Geigy with a quick bow.

Chattering excitedly, the natives jostled each other as they headed for the far end of the village.

"Look! Look! It's a baby elephant," cried Cheyenne.

Ho Goo emerged from his hut and joined the five friends as the bustling crowd surrounded the young animal. Turning to Winston, Ho Goo explained, in hushed tones, what was happening. Winston nodded his head as if to say *I see.*

"What's going on, Winston?" asked Cheyenne. "What did Ho Goo say?"

"Yes, tell us," said Geigy.

Winston scratched his head and sighed. "Well, it appears that two native hunters far out in the bush heard a shot in the distance. When they investigated, they found the mother elephant shot and her tusks missing."

"Oh, no!" gasped Cheyenne, shaking his head.

"Are you all right, old chap?" asked Winston, touching his arm.

"I'm fine," replied Cheyenne. "Go on."

Winston continued. "Well, the baby elephant was nudging the mother, trying to get her up. It took the two hunters some time to get the young elephant away from its mother. Eventually, they herded the baby to the village."

Cheyenne sighed. "Thank God the little guy survived."

"Yes, poor baby," said Ebony, nodding her head.

For a few moments, Cheyenne seemed lost in thought, then he looked up and addressed his friends. "Listen, I'm glad everyone is here. I think we should leave tomorrow."

"Tomorrow! That's a bit sudden, isn't it?" said Geigy.

"Yes, old chap, why the sudden rush?" asked Winston.

Cheyenne rubbed his head. "Well, maybe we could have saved this baby elephant's mother if we'd been out in the bush."

"And maybe not, old chap," said Winston. "It's impossible for us to save every elephant."

"He's right, honey," said Ebony.

"Well, at least we can try," said Cheyenne. "We're not going to save any if we stay in the village."

"You're right," said Geigy, "let's move out tomorrow. All in favor, raise their hands."

Five hands rose in unison. "It's a done deal," said Cheyenne. "We leave tomorrow."

Meanwhile, Python and the Russian and their small army of soldiers were ready to go on the hunt. A thick blanket of fog hugged the parched ground as Python and the Russian stepped out of their hut. Ego followed behind, a sickly yellow smile etched on his gnarled face. Python grabbed an iron ring and banged it with an iron pipe. "I want all you men standing in front of me in five minutes, no exceptions," he yelled.

Ego and the Russian smiled as they heard the men hustling to get dressed. Five minutes later they were all standing in front of Python.

"Good, good," he said, surveying the motley crew, an eclectic bunch of rogues and misfits. "That's what I like to see."

"Very good," said the Russian, nudging Python.

Python picked his teeth and turned to Ego. "Ego, I want you to take six men and two jeeps, and find that cowboy and his miserable group."

Ego nodded. "Okay, boss."

"Good. Now pick out six men to go with you. The two jeeps have already been set up for you. You have enough gas and food to last you for a week."

"Thanks, boss," said Ego. "I won't let you down." He turned and singled out six men. "You six, come with me," he ordered, pointing at each man in turn.

One of the chosen men raised his hand. "What the hell do you want? This better be good, because you are holding us up," shouted the Russian, pointing his pistol at the *soldier*.

"I have a pretty good idea where this cowboy and his group may be," replied the man. "In the Ji-Hi region, or by the mountain."

The Russian lowered his pistol and looked over at Python. Python stared intently at the man. "You seem to know what you're talking about, so you will be driving the lead jeep." He turned to Ego and wagged his finger. "Do not cause any problems with the Ji-Hi tribe," he warned. "They are brave but vicious warriors, so we don't want any trouble."

"You got it, boss. We'll be careful not to ruffle any feathers."

The Russian turned to Python. "We have to get rid of that cowboy so he doesn't spoil our plans. We will both be rich if nothing happens."

Python nodded and rubbed his palms together. "Yes, rich beyond our wildest dreams."

They both waved goodbye to Ego and his small band of soldiers. "Good luck!"

Ego yelled back. "We will bring them back alive so you can personally say hello to them."

The Russian licked his lips in anticipation. "I can't wait to cut out their tongues and pull out their fingernails and listen to their screams of agony," he drooled. "And watch the blood pour from their wretched bodies." His eyes glazed over as he pictured the bloody carnage. "Yes, yes, Ego, bring them back soon. We will be waiting for them, won't we, Python. And, oh, what a party we'll have!"

Python took out his knife and ran his finger across the sharp blade, drawing blood. "Oh yes, one helluva party," he said, licking the blood from his finger. "One helluva *bloody* party!"

Chapter Thirty-Two

Back in the Ji-Hi village, a thin veil of early morning mist shrouded the cluster of huts and surrounding trees.

"Are we all packed and ready to go?" Cheyenne asked Ebony.

"I think so," she said, looking around the hut. "I'm glad we packed most of the stuff last night."

"Yes, now we can make an early start. It's barely dawn; most of the village is still sleeping."

Taking one last look around the hut, they walked outside into the brisk morning air. Cheyenne looked up at the sky to see the faint silhouette of the sun. Soon this fiery ball of fire would devour the mist – it promised to be another brutally hot day.

Winston, Geigy and Willie greeted them outside with a cheery good morning. Cheyenne smiled. "Good morning, guys, are you ready to get back in the bush?" he said. "We should get moving soon before that sun eats us up."

"We're all packed and ready to go," said Geigy. He hesitated then blurted out, "I sure wish we could take our women with us, but I know there's no room."

Cheyenne looked at him, but said nothing. It was impossible for them to take the women. They were about to slip away silently when Ho Goo and most of the people suddenly appeared to say goodbye and wish them good luck. Ho Goo placed his massive arms around Cheyenne.

"Cheyenne, my good friend, you and your friends are always welcome here," he said.

Gasping for breath, Cheyenne struggled to free himself from Ho Goo's strong embrace.

"Thank you, chief, it has been an honor to meet you. You and your tribe have made us very welcome, and we thank you all for your kind hospitality," he said.

Ho Goo beamed. "Do not forget us, dear friend. We will not forget you, will we, my son," he said, pulling Goo towards him and lifting him into his arms.

"I will never forget," said Goo solemnly as he held out his hand to Cheyenne and touched his arm. "Thank you for saving my life, Cheyenne; I will never ever forget you."

Cheyenne's eyes misted over. "And I will never forget you, young Goo," he said, shaking the small boy's hand. "Take care of your father and the baby elephants."

"I will," said Goo. "I promise you, I will."

Cheyenne nodded to him and then turned to the others. "Okay, let's hit the road." He started the Rover and Winston fired up the jeep and the two vehicles moved slowly through the crowd.

"Lordy, I didn't realize that there were so many Ji-Hi natives," said Ebony as she waved goodbye to the milling crowd. "Look, how far they are lined up – right to the end of the village."

"I guess we made quite an impression on them," said Cheyenne. "This is one heck of a farewell."

Ebony smiled wistfully. "I'm going to miss them all," she said, wiping back the tears.

As they reached the edge of the village, they turned one last time to wave goodbye, then sped off into the bush. Leading the way, Cheyenne drove for several miles and then pulled off to the side of the dusty road. He walked back to the other vehicle.

"What's up, Cheyenne?" asked Geigy. "Why are we stopping?"

"Make sure you have your weapons loaded and ready to shoot. You never know what you might run into, out here in the bush," he replied.

Geigy patted his rifle. "We're all locked and loaded and ready for any problem."

"Yes, don't worry, old chap, we won't let you down," said Winston.

"Good, I just wanted to make sure," said Cheyenne as he turned and walked back to the Rover.

They traveled slowly through the bush for most of the day, absorbing the sights and smells of this vast outdoors in central Africa. As the sun sank lower, leaving in its wake an array of vivid colors, Cheyenne looked around for a place to camp for the night. Nudging Ebony, who had fallen asleep against his shoulder, he pointed to a cluster of nearby trees. "That looks like a nice sheltered spot to set up camp."

Ebony nodded sleepily as Cheyenne waved for the jeep behind to stop. Tired from their long day of traveling, they were asleep as soon as their heads hit the ground. And at the crack of dawn, they were back out on the road again, looking for elephants and poachers. It was nearing midday when Ebony suddenly sat up straight and pointed ahead. "I think I saw a cloud of dust in the distance," she said, squinting against the sun's penetrating glare.

"It's probably just the wind," said Cheyenne. "Or perhaps herd of animals." He had barely mouthed the words when they came face to face with a camouflage jeep carrying four men armed with guns. A similar jeep followed behind carrying three other men, also armed.

These men are definitely not friendly! thought Cheyenne. As he surveyed the seven hostile faces, his eyes were drawn to the small man driving the second jeep. There was no mistaking that sickly yellow smile. "My God, that's Ego," he exclaimed as he reached for his gun. "Take cover!" he yelled, waving to Geigy and the others.

Cheyenne shot two of the men before they could open fire. But it was impossible for him to take out all the assailants. The driver of the lead jeep had him in his sights. Ebony reacted instinctively. "Look out, Cheyenne!" she cried, pushing him to the side. The driver's shot veered wide and embedded itself harmlessly in a nearby tree.

Quick as a flash, Ebony raised her gun and shot the driver right between the eyes. He slumped forward against the wheel, blood and brains oozing from the gory wound. Cheyenne looked at Ebony in amazement. "Now I know why I love you. How did you get to be such a good shot?"

"I had a good teacher."

Meanwhile, Winston had taken out a fourth man as two others jumped out of their jeep, rifles blazing. Geigy's jeep had slid sideways leaving him wide open. Before he could take cover, a shot blasted his leg and sent him flying over the side of the jeep. Clutching his shattered leg, he managed to crawl to the safety of some nearby bushes. Willy rushed over to help him.

"Geigy, Geigy, are you okay?" he cried, bending over to examine his friend's bloody leg.

"I'll live," said Geigy weakly, "but I need something to stop the bleeding. Without missing a beat, Willy tore off his shirt and wrapped it tightly around the gaping wound, staunching the flow of blood.

"Great tourniquet," said Geigy. "I just knew your old shirt would come in handy someday," he quipped. Although faint and weak from loss of blood, he still hadn't lost his sense of humor.

"Same old Geigy," said Willie. "Always coming up with the funny lines."

"Yep, that's me, funny to the last drop…of blood!"

"Hey, Cheyenne, Geigy's been shot," cried Willie over the hail of gunfire. "The big guy with the scar did it," he said, pointing to a hefty man with a jagged scar running down his left cheek.

"I'll handle him," shouted Cheyenne. His steely blue eyes focused like lasers on the swarthy assassin, and taking careful aim, he blasted the man who had shot his friend. Right through the heart. "That's for Geigy," he said as he watched the man topple forward and collapse in a bloody heap on the dirt track.

"Five down, two to go," said Ebony.

"And one of them is that slime ball, Ego," said Cheyenne. "Look! he's making a run for it."

Ego had put the jeep in reverse and screeched off down the road, in a cloud of dust, leaving the last remaining man to fend for himself. This man, shielded by a large boulder, was perfectly placed to take out Willie and Geigy who were still huddled by the bushes. Unaware of the danger, Willie tended to Geigy's wound, leaving his back exposed. The gunman raised his rifle and fired off a shot, hitting Willie in his right shoulder and sending him reeling to the ground.

"Willie! Willie!" screamed Geigy, reaching out to his wounded friend. "Cheyenne! Winston! Willie's been shot! We're both exposed out here. The guy is shooting from behind that boulder." And he pointed in the direction of the massive boulder.

"I'll take care of him," said Cheyenne. "Winston, cover me while I try to sneak up behind him."

"You've got it, old chap."

"We've got to get Geigy and Willie back here before they bleed to death," said Ebony.

"No, Ebony," said Cheyenne, "it's too dangerous." But before either man could stop her, she had darted off in the direction of the bushes.

"Winston, lay down some heavy fire on that boulder. I've got to take this guy out now before he kills them all."

Winston nodded and fired off several rounds, while Cheyenne darted out from behind the jeep. Crouching low to the ground, he circled the boulder, edging closer to the lone gunman.

Ebony had reached Geigy and Willie, and was examining Willie's shoulder. Tearing off his shirt, she probed the bloody wound. "What's the damage?" asked Willie weakly. His face was sickly pale, and he had lost a lot of blood.

Ebony patted him gently. "Fortunately, it's just a flesh wound," she said soothingly, "but you've lost a lot of blood. Grabbing his torn shirt, she fashioned a tourniquet and wrapped it round his shoulder. “There, that should stem the flow until we get some medical help. How are you holding up, Geigy?”

“I’m okay, thanks to Willie. He acted fast and wrapped this tourniquet around my leg, otherwise I’d probably have been a goner, from loss of blood.”

“Good work, Willie,” said Ebony. “Let me just take a look.” She unwrapped the blood-soaked shirt and checked the wound. “You’re lucky too, Geigy. The bullet just grazed your leg and didn’t hit any bones. You’ll be limping for a while, but I think you’ll live.”

Winston was still exchanging fire with the gunman behind the boulder, making sure the man’s attention was fixed on him and not on his friends. Cheyenne, meanwhile, had circled the boulder. He crept up behind the gunman, silent as a mouse. *I’d like to take him prisoner if he would surrender,* he thought as he edged closer and closer. In his heart, he knew the shooter and his slain friends had probably been brainwashed by Python and the Russian. Cocking his two six shooters, he leveled them at the man’s back. “Put your hands in the air, you’re surrounded.”

The man swung round in surprise and aimed his gun at Cheyenne’s heart. Cheyenne had no choice but to kill him with one shot between the eyes. The force of the shot blasted the man against the boulder. He slithered down the rock and fell face forward in the dirt.

“Sorry, buddy, you should have surrendered,” Cheyenne whispered to the dead man. He crouched down beside him and then yelled to Winston. “Hold your fire! He’s dead. I shot him.”

Winston shouted to the others. “It’s all over.”

Ebony raced toward the boulder and threw her arms around Cheyenne. “Thank God, you’re all right,” she cried.

“He wouldn’t surrender,” he said as he stared at the motionless body. “When they work for Python they have no other choice.”

Ebony nodded. "Python owns them, body and soul," she said.

Cheyenne walked back to the jeeps to check out the damage, while Ebony grabbed the first-aid box from inside the glove compartment and ran back to Geigy and Willie.

"I have some clean dressing and bandages here," she said, holding the first-aid kit aloft.

Diligently, she carefully dressed and bandaged their wounds, with the skill of a trained nurse.

"How did you learn to do that?" asked Geigy.

"Ever since I was a little girl I wanted to be a nurse. Never happened. But I did take a few first-aid courses – practiced on my friends and stuff. And don't forget my mother was a nurse – she taught me a lot."

"Well, you'd make a wonderful nurse," said Geigy.

"Sure would," agreed Willie.

Winston walked over to them and took a plastic bag from his pocket. "I'm going to put their things and any identification they may have in this bag," he said, looking around at the six slain men. "When we see Jocko, I'll give it to him, so he can tell their families what happened."

"If they have families," said Ebony as she surveyed the bloody carnage.

Winston tried to call Jocko on his phone. "I can't reach Jocko; he must be in a dead zone."

Cheyenne wandered over after examining the vehicles. "I see they shot out one of the back windows in the Rover, and the tire on Geigy's jeep," he said. "We'll have to fix them as best we can, and I guess we'll have to bury these guys."

"May as well start now, old chap," said Winston.

"Let's start digging…"

Chapter Thirty-Three

It took them half a day to repair the jeeps and to bury the six *soldiers.* Not a pleasant task, but at least they had given their assailants a decent burial.

"We have to return to the mountain and get some of that dynamite," said Cheyenne.

"Why?" asked Geigy, frowning. His leg was hurting, and he was hoping to rest for a few days.

"Yes, why do you need the dynamite, old chap?" said Winston.

Cheyenne looked at each of them in turn. "Ego," he said simply.

"Ego?" said Ebony. "What's he got to do with the dynamite?"

"Remember, he got away and he's now on his way back to give Python and the Russian our whereabouts," he explained. "We have to protect ourselves."

"The sooner the better," said Geigy, rubbing his aching leg.

"Let's go," said Willie.

"Okay, grab the ammunition and gas from the soldiers' jeep and we'll hit the road," said Cheyenne.

"Don't forget the first-aid kit," said Ebony. "We'll need the extra bandages and dressings for Willie and Geigy."

Cheyenne gave her a quick hug. "Good thinking, Ebony," he said, pecking her on the cheek. "Now I know why I love you so much."

They drove through the night without stopping, anxious to reach the mountain.

"The fog is getting heavier and heavier," said Cheyenne, straining his eyes to see through the thickening mist. "We must be getting closer to the mountain."

Ebony dozed beside him, her eyes half-closed. "Thank God," she said. "I'm so sore after driving along these bumpy roads."

Geigy lay slumped behind them in the back seat trying to rest his wounded leg. "Tell me about it," he said. "My leg feels as if it's gonna drop off if we drive over one more bump." He turned and looked at Winston and Willie who were following behind in the second jeep. "I wonder how Willie's holding up. His shoulder must be mighty sore."

"We're almost there, Geigy. Try to hold on for a bit longer. I'll avoid as many bumps as I can."

"Thanks, Cheyenne," he replied. "Appreciate it."

The first slivers of dawn were poking through the shimmering rain forest as they approached the base of the mountain. The sun's early morning rays chased away the last fingers of mist and bounced off the treetops.

"Look!" cried Ebony, pointing to the mountain looming in the distance. "Isn't it beautiful with the circles of fog surrounding it like a halo."

Cheyenne and Geigy turned to look at the shrouded edifice. Its ghostlike appearance was eerie yet awesome. "It's truly magnificent," said Cheyenne.

"Sure is," said Geigy, staring at the mountain, in wonder.

"I can't wait to get there," said Ebony. "The first thing I'm going to do is clean the wounds of Geigy and Willie. Then I'm going to have something to eat and then…" She yawned and rubbed her eyes. "…I'm going to sleep for the whole day!"

Cheyenne laughed. "Sounds like you've got your day all planned out."

"Think I'm gonna sleep too," said Geigy. "And rest this sore leg."

On reaching the mountain, they hid the two vehicles under a clump of overhanging vines, and then brushed out their tracks to avoid detection.

"There, I think we've covered our tracks pretty well," said Cheyenne, surveying their handiwork. "Tomorrow morning, Winston and I will be leaving to get some of that dynamite from the cave." He looked over at Ebony. "Ebony, you stay here and take care of Geigy and Willie."

Both men protested, but Cheyenne was adamant. "I know you would like to come with us, but you've both been wounded. It's a hard slog up that mountain and you're in no shape to tackle such a climb."

Geigy tried again. "I can handle it."

"Me, too," said Willie, although he didn't sound too sure.

"I'm sorry, guys, but it's best if you stay here with Ebony. You've both lost a lot of blood and you're probably weaker than you think."

"Okay," said Geigy reluctantly. "I guess you're right."

"Good chap," said Winston, patting him on the shoulder. "We'll be back before you know it."

"Yes, we should be back in about 4 or 5 days," said Cheyenne. "We'll spend at least one night in the cave, and we can't move too fast with the dynamite."

"Don't worry about us, I'll take care of these two," said Ebony. "Now, where's that bottle of whiskey; I want to clean off those wounds."

Geigy looked at her in horror. "That's a waste of good whiskey." And they all broke into laughter.

Ego jammed his foot on the accelerator, pushing the jeep as fast as he could. He knew that the cowboy could pick him off at a far distance with his long range rifle. Spirals of dust billowed up behind him as he muttered incoherently, over and over again. "I had no choice but to leave those soldiers. Python and the Russian will understand." Still trying to convince himself, he continued mumbling. "After all, I couldn't get myself killed – I have to report back to Python.

Puffing himself up as tall as his small stature would allow, a greasy yellow smile crossed his face. "Now that I know their location, we can hunt them down. Python will be pleased."

He drove on for several more miles, whistling and singing to himself. *Python will be pleased! Python will be pleased! Eeiaddyo, Python will be pleased!*

Then, suddenly, he slammed on the brake, bringing the jeep to a screeching halt. "Goddammit, I can't hold it any longer," he said aloud, holding his crotch. "I gotta take a piss." Sliding out of the jeep, he unzipped his pants and sprayed the ground in front of him in a zigzag pattern. He sighed deeply. "Oh, that feels better. My bladder felt like it was gonna burst."

He looked around. Apart from a few birds and a couple of lizards, he was totally alone.

Thank God, I don't have to squat out here in the bush, he thought, shaking himself off and zipping up his pants. *Don't want no snake slithering up and snatching my privates.* He rubbed his crotch and smiled slyly. *I need my tackle for other things.*

He walked around some more, surveying his surroundings, and now, by God, he did have to squat! *What the hell brought that on?* He dropped his pants and squatted down over the dusty earth. As he was about to take care of business, he heard the terrifying bellows of an elephant.

"Aw shit," he cried aloud, looking down the road. *Shit being the operative word!* What he saw scared the shit out of him. *Monsoon!*

"It's that goddamn crazy elephant and he's coming for me."

Chapter Thirty-Four

Monsoon had been munching on leaves from a tree, when he heard the noisy jeep barreling down the road. Startled, he stopped mid-munch and cocked his huge head, letting out a thunderous bellow. Birds perched in the nearby branches flew off into the sky; wildlife scattered in all directions. Monsoon was angry – very angry that his leisurely lunch had been interrupted.

He raised his trunk and flapped his huge ears. Monsoon hated the noisy moving thing that sounded like a lion's roar, and belched out smelly black smoke. He remembered that it carried the people who had hurt him so badly that day, when he was shot. He would never forget the searing pain.

He remembered how he had charged after the two men in the moving thing. But, alas, he couldn't catch up with them. So, now when he saw the man pass by in the moving thing he just watched and waited. Then he let out a deafening trumpet. Monsoon was angry! Very angry indeed! Elephants never forget!

With his pants halfway down to his knees, Ego waddled to the jeep like a penguin.

"I have to grab my rifle, otherwise I'm a dead man."

Now his pants had dropped to his ankles. Tripping over, he fell face down in the mud.

"I'm gonna die! I'm gonna die!" he yelled to the wide blue yonder. "I'm gonna die and Python and the Russian will never find the cowboy and his gang."

Monsoon's loud trumpeting echoed closer and closer. Ego froze. "To hell with the rifle, I have to get my jeep going." Grabbing his pants, he scrambled to his feet and jumped into the jeep. His hands shook as he fumbled with the ignition, the elephant's bellows still echoing in his ears. The engine spluttered and died.

"Damn," said Ego, looking down the road. "That big ass Monsoon sure can move. He's getting closer and closer." Trying to steady his trembling hand, he turned the ignition again and pumped the gas. "Oh, God, I hope I don't flood the engine. Please God, let it start," he begged, looking up at the sky. Although not a praying man, he needed all the help he could get. This time the engine stuttered and then fired up.

"Thank you, God," sighed Ego, exhaling. He looked up to see the lumbering elephant almost upon him, its razor sharp tusks gleaming in the hot sun. Icy fingers of fear ran through his body. He shuddered. "Sonofabitch!" he exclaimed, "why did I park sideways?" He had no time to lose and now he had to back up. Precious moments lost.

Revving the engine, he reversed the jeep and reached for his rifle. "I'll fix your ass now," he said, raising the rifle. He took aim and found himself looking into Monsoon's glinting eyes, now red with fury. Ego shuddered again. Monsoon was so close that Ego could smell his breath. The giant tusks were only a few feet away.

Monsoon hit the back of the jeep, jolting it back and forth. The force of the blow knocked the rifle from Ego's hands. "Oh no!" he screamed as he watched the rifle fall to the side of the road. "I'm a goner." He jammed his foot on the accelerator as the wheels spun trying to get traction. Monsoon hit the jeep again. "I'm gonna die! I'm gonna die!" Ego yelled.

Fortunately, this second jolt pushed the jeep forward freeing the back wheels from the dirt. Ego hit the gas pedal and sped away in a cloud of dust. Heaving a sigh of relief, he looked through the rearview mirror. "Look at that damn elephant standing on his back legs," he cried aloud. "What the hell is he doing?"

Monsoon raised himself high, lifted his trunk in the air and let out another booming roar. Ego gripped the steering wheel tightly and almost drove off the road. *Get a hold of yourself, Ego, he can't catch you now.*

With each passing mile, Ego finally relaxed. An hour later, he reached the village, screeching to a dead stop in front of Python's hut. "Python! Python!" he yelled, blasting the horn.

Hearing the commotion, Python and the Russian rushed outside from their hut. "What the hell's going on?" said Python, shaking his fist at Ego. "Why are you blowing the horn and acting like a damn maniac?" He sniffed air. "And what the fuck is that smell?" he said, crinkling his nose.

The Russian started gagging. "Yeah, what the fuck is it?"

Ego ignored their questions. "I saw the cowboy and I almost got killed," he said.

"By the cowboy?" asked Python.

"No, by Monsoon," replied Ego. "He's one big motherfucker and he's got bad breath."

"The cowboy has bad breath?" said Python.

Ego shook his head furiously. "No, no, no, Monsoon has bad breath."

"Okay, quiet down, quiet down," said Python. "Where are all the men I sent with you?"

"They're all dead, the cowboy killed all of them," he said rapidly.

"Slow down, you're talking so fast that it's hard to understand you," said Python. He sniffed the air again. "And what the hell is that stink?"

Ego looked shamefaced. "I had to take a shit and my pants were half down, when Monsoon tried to kill me." He tried to change the subject. "The cowboy, I know where he's at."

"All right, calm down," said Python. "Did you shit outside the jeep or inside the jeep?"

"Both," Ego told them, averting his eyes.

"Go and get cleaned up," said Python. "We can't take that smell anymore."

Ego ran inside the hut as Python motioned to three of his men who were standing nearby, smoking. "Get that jeep cleaned up right now," he ordered.

An hour later, a somewhat cleaner Ego emerged from the hut.

"That's better," said Python. "Now, tell us what happened and talk slow."

"We couldn't understand a word you were saying before," said the Russian, picking his teeth.

"Start with the patrol and the men that were with you," said Python. "And remember, sloooow!"

Ego nodded. "We were traveling along this curved path when we came head to head with the cowboy and his group. I was in the second jeep with two of the men." He took a deep breath. "We all started shooting about the same time. All the men in the first jeep got killed pretty fast. That damn cowboy is fast and he don't miss." Python glowered but said nothing.

"What happened next?" asked the Russian.

"One of the guys in my jeep got shot and then there were only two of us. I stayed in the jeep and the other guy managed to get behind a big boulder."

"Did you return fire?" asked Python.

"Sure I did," lied Ego. He had cowered in the jeep without firing a single shot.

Python knew he was lying, but he let it pass. "Continue," he said.

"I saw two of cowboy's group go down. Then I put my jeep in reverse and got the hell out of there. Then I damn near got killed by that killer elephant Monsoon when I was taking a shit."

"You did good, Ego," said Python. "Do you think you could find them again?"

Ego nodded. "I think so."

"This time I want you to bring in the whole group alive, or just Ebony," said Python.

Ego looked puzzled. "Just Ebony?" he questioned, thinking he had misheard.

"Yes. I'm pretty sure the cowboy would not like us having his woman," he sneered, licking his lips suggestively. "Don't you agree, Russian?"

The Russian threw back his head and laughed his evil laugh. "Yes, comrade, the cowboy would be most upset. We could have a lot of fun with her," he leered.

Ego sniggered and rubbed his hands together. "I see what you mean," he said.

"Yes, we have a big surprise for the cowboy and his group," said Python as he handed Ego and the Russian two fat Cuban cigars. "Let's go and swig a bottle of whiskey, or maybe two, to celebrate. We will soon be rid of that pesky cowboy and his friends."

They sat up most of the night, drinking and conspiring. And in the morning a bleary-eyed and half drunk Ego awaited his next orders.

"Ego, I have a special guide who knows that area like the back of his hand," said Python. Take ten men this time, and an extra jeep. And these," he said, passing Ego a pair of binoculars. "And make sure you have plenty of gas and water and food supplies."

Ego nodded his throbbing head. He had a king-size hangover.

"I don't want you killing anyone unless you have no choice, understand?" demanded Python.

Ego nodded again. His headache was getting worse by the minute.

"Good, now get your men ready. You'll be leaving tomorrow morning."

Thank God for that, Ego said to himself. *Now I'll be able to sleep off this damned hangover.*

Chapter Thirty-Five

At dawn Ego and his men prepared to hit the road as Python and the Russian looked on.

"Don't forget, I want you to bring them back alive," said Python, wagging his finger. "Unless, of course, you have no choice."

"Don't worry, boss, you can count on me," said Ego, flashing his rotten yellow teeth.

The blistering hot sun bore down on the small convoy. They traveled all day in the relentless heat, and were soon bathed in sweat from head to toe. Ego kept his eyes peeled. No sign of the cowboy. By the end of the second day, Ego began to lose patience. They had covered miles of terrain without spotting a single track. And now they were approaching the mountain.

"I don't see hide nor hair of 'em," he snarled, scanning the horizon with his new binoculars. "Where the fuck are they? We're close to the mountain now, does anyone see anything?"

A tall, burly man with rippling muscles and tattooed arms rushed over to him. "Ego, Ego," he panted, "one of the men has spotted a flashing light at the bottom of the mountain."

"Let's find out where it's coming from," said Ego excitedly. "It might be them."

The man pointed. "See the light when the sun hits whatever it is," he said.

Ego followed the direction of his finger. "Yes, yes, I see it!" he exclaimed. "It might be from a mirror or a windshield." He turned to the men. "Now, listen, we have to be very careful and quiet. If it's the cowboy and his group, we don't want to alert them."

The men nodded, trying to hide their disdain. They knew more about tracking than Ego ever would. Python was their boss, and they resented taking orders from this little runt. Oblivious to their resentment, Ego continued. "Men, we have to walk this one. We have that flash of light pinpointed and it's by a large tree. I'm going to call Python and let him know." Taking out his phone, he dialed Python and told him about the light.

Python was pleased. "That sounds like it just might be that fucking cowboy and his miserable friends. Now listen carefully, Ego. I want you to send two of your best men in, to see what's going on. And I want you to bring them in alive. Do you hear me? Alive!"

"I hear you, Python. Don't worry, we'll get them. We'll move closer today and then tomorrow morning I'll send out the two best men."

"Don't let me down, Ego. I want them *alive*!"

Ebony was missing Cheyenne already as she watched him disappear into the bush. *He's going to be gone for four or five days. That's a long time.* She shook her head sadly and turned to Geigy and Willie. "How are your wounds doing?"

"Mine's healing quite well," said Geigy.

"Mine, too," said Willie.

Ebony smiled. "I'm going to change both your bandages before we have lunch, and dab them with whiskey."

Geigy grimaced. "I still think that's a waste of good whiskey," he said.

Willie and Ebony laughed. "You're right about that," said Willie.

That night they huddled together in the Rover for warmth. Although the days were blistering hot, at night the temperature dropped considerably. The next morning as they were emerging from the vehicle, Willie inadvertently knocked a tree limb off the windshield. Little did they know that this would have dire consequences.

After breakfast, Ebony dressed their wounds again. She was about to dab Geigy's leg with whiskey, when he grabbed the bottle from her hand. "Damn it, Ebony, give me that bottle. I need a drink," he said, taking a large swig.

"Geigy, Cheyenne's not going to like this," scolded Ebony.

"Oh, don't worry, by the time they get back, I'll be all sobered up." He took another slug of the fiery liquid, and then handed the bottle back to Ebony. "Come on, Ebony, lighten up and take a drink. We've got maybe a whole week of boredom, just sitting here waiting for them to return. May as well enjoy ourselves while we wait."

Ebony laughed. "You're right, Geigy, it is boring. Give me that bottle."

And they all started laughing, unaware that they were being watched by two sets of bulging eyes.

Chapter Thirty-Six

The drinking continued for many hours. Geigy laughed drunkenly as he tried to dance around on his one good leg.

"Be careful, Geigy. Watch your injured leg, or you'll open up the wound again," said Ebony.

"Don't worry, I'm okay, as long as I have my whiskey," he slurred. "Hey, I bet Cheyenne and Winston are counting those tusks right now."

"Yeah, and they're probably throwing dynamite sticks at each other," laughed Willie, trying to lift Ebony's spirits. She was missing Cheyenne.

"I just hope they have no trouble finding the cave," she said. "I do miss them."

"Come on, dance with me," said Geigy, holding out his hand. "You, too, Willie." And the three of them joined hands and danced around in a circle. *Still watched by the two sets of eyes.*

Ego and his men were resting in the shade, waiting for the two scouts to return.

"I wonder if they've found them yet?" he said, picking his yellow teeth.

"They're the best trackers," said one of the men, averting his face from Ego's foul breath. "If anyone can track them down, they can." He covered his mouth, almost gagging on the stench.

"They've been gone a long time," said Ego impatiently as he lifted the binoculars and pointed them in the direction of the mountain. Off in the distance, a dark figure was running toward him.

"It's one of the scouts!" he exclaimed, jumping to his feet. "I wonder what happened to the other one? Let's find out."

The exhausted man raced toward the group and collapsed in a heap on the ground. Sweat poured from his face; his chest heaved. The other men crowded round him.

"Give him some room, men," said Ego. "It looks like he's been running for some distance."

The men stepped back and looked down on their exhausted colleague. He was in bad shape.

"Please give me some water," he panted.

"Quick, get him some water," Ego ordered. "This man is on his last legs. Hurry! Hurry!"

One of the soldiers scuttled off and returned with a flask of water. "Here, drink this," he said, holding the flask to the scout's parched lips.

The man sipped the water and then lay back, catching his breath. "That's better. I feel almost human again."

"Let's get him into the shade," said Ego. "He's burning up."

They moved the man to the cool shade of a nearby bush, and Ego squatted down beside him. Although eager to interrogate the man, Ego knew he had to take things slowly. "What happened to the other scout," he asked finally.

"He's staying at the spot, hoping to pick up some more information," the man replied.

"What information? Did you see the cowboy?" asked Ego, his excitement rising.

"We didn't see the cowboy, but we saw the others," replied the scout. "They kept talking about thousands of tusks in a cave. And lots of dynamite, too."

Ego's eyes gleamed. "Tusks! Dynamite! What else did they say?"

The scout took another sip of water and wiped his sweaty brow. "They said that the cowboy and a man by the name of Winston would be gone for four or five days."

Ego rubbed his hands together. "Is that so," he said. "What else?"

"The three of 'em are drinking whiskey and getting' drunk as skunks."

"This gets better and better," said Ego, smacking his greasy lips together. "Go on," he urged.

"I could use a drop of whiskey myself," said the scout.

"Well, you're only getting water," said Ego. "Now continue with your story."

The scout sighed and took another sip of water. It was worth a try. "They are dancing around, even though the two men have been wounded. I guess they're too liquored up to feel the pain."

"Good job. I think you've earned a drop of whiskey. But first, can you lead us to this spot?"

"Sure can," said the man, smiling. "Give me a few more minutes' rest and I'll lead the way."

Ego grinned. "We'll drive as close as we can so they don't hear us." Turning to the other men, he said, "Okay, guys, let's gear up and take a look at our dancing and drinking enemy."

The men jumped to their feet; they were ready for some action, after lounging in the sun all day.

"And don't forget," said Ego, wagging his finger, "we have to take them alive."

"Alive!" shouted the men in unison.

Standing up in his jeep, like General Patton leading his troops into battle, Ego waved his hand and cried, "Follow me, men."

The scout climbed in the seat beside him, and the convoy of soldiers moved out. As they neared the mountain, the scout held up his hand. "That's as far as we can go," he cautioned. "We'll have to walk the rest of the way."

"How far is it?" asked Ego.

"About a mile and a half."

They walked on in silence for a mile, when the other scout suddenly emerged from out of the bush. "Ssh," he warned, holding his finger over his mouth. "You have to be very quiet; they are just over that little rise." The troops nodded and moved slowly forward.

"I see them," whispered one of soldiers in the lead. "The two men look like they are sleeping, and the woman is just wandering around."

Ego grabbed two of the soldiers by the arm. "I can't see," he whined. "Lift me up, you idiots."

The soldiers stifled the urge to tell the little runt to shut his trap, but they feared Python's wrath. He and the Russian would be merciless if anything happened to Ego. Grudgingly, two of them hoisted him up on their shoulders.

"Okay, okay, I see them; put me down, you idiots."

As they lowered him to the ground, the two soldiers winked at each other and then 'accidentally' dropped Ego in the mud.

"Oops, sorry, Ego," they said, "our hands are so sweaty, we lost our grip."

"Idiots," snarled Ego as he picked himself up and wiped off the dirt. "You did that on purpose."

"Nah, it was an accident, Ego," said the shorter of the two, trying hard not to laugh.

"Yeah, and I'm the Queen of England," replied Ego. He turned and addressed the whole group. "Men, I want you to be very quiet and surround the whole camp. Crawl on your bellies and wait for my call. Understand?" The soldiers bristled, but they would do as he ordered. "We must do this before the cowboy gets back," said Ego. "And remember, we have to take them alive."

The men edged forward on their stomachs, and circled the entire camp. They lay motionless waiting for Ego's command. After about fifteen minutes, he yelled at the top of his lungs, "Charge! Let's get them."

Still half-drunk, Geigy staggered to his feet. "What the hell's going on?" Then his eyes fastened on Ego and the soldiers. "You bastards," he cried as he took a wild swing at one of the men and fell to the ground. Down but not out, he struggled to his feet again, and was hit viciously in the head with a rifle butt.

"Get them! Get them!" yelled Ego. "Take them alive."

Willie, aroused from a drunken sleep, joined the fray and was promptly kicked to the ground. Still half-asleep he thought he was in the middle of a nightmare. Ebony tried to grab a rifle, but it was yanked from her grasp and thrown to the ground.

"Grab her," shouted Ego, "but don't hurt her. Remember, we have to take them alive!"

"You sonofabitch!" screamed Ebony, her eyes on fire, "you're not taking me without a fight." She fell back against one of the jeeps and crawled underneath. "That bastard Python and that creepy Russian ordered you to take us," she cried.

Ego just stood there smirking and said nothing.

"You foul smelling cretin," she yelled. "You're nothing more than Python's lap dog. If he told you to jump off a cliff you probably would."

"Shut up, bitch," Ego snarled, revealing those rotten yellow teeth again.

"Make me!" shouted a defiant Ebony.

Some of the soldiers sniggered as they listened to this exchange, secretly pleased that Ebony was challenging their so-called 'leader.' After ten minutes of kicking, cursing and screaming, they finally pulled her out from under the jeep.

"I told you to stop that yelling and screaming, bitch," said Ego as two soldiers held her firmly in their grasp. "You may be Python's woman, but I don't have to take any shit from you."

Quick as a flash Ebony raised her right leg and kicked him squarely in the balls. "Take that, you yellow-bellied dwarf," she cried.

Ego screamed in agony and crumbled to the ground, clutching his crotch. "Agh…"

"Why are you crying, you yellow-mouthed freak," Ebony taunted. "After all, you have no balls, so you shouldn't be in pain."

The soldiers looked at Ebony with newfound respect. *This woman definitely did have balls!* Many of them laughed openly as Ego writhed in the dirt, in pain, and if not for Python, they would have changed sides in an instant. Ego finally staggered to his feet, still clutching his crotch. "Hold her legs, you idiots," he ordered, swinging around to face his men. "And I'll shoot anybody who's laughing," he warned.

The soldiers clammed up. Python's far reaching shadow loomed large – cross his sidekick and they crossed him. Obediently, they did as he ordered.

"Make sure you have her this time, you fools," he said. "Put her on her knees."

The soldiers pushed Ebony to her knees, gently. Their respect for this fiery woman was overwhelming. Ego looked her straight in the eyes. "That wasn't too smart," he said.

She glared back at him and spat in his face. Ego flinched and wiped the phlegm from his eyes. "Why, you little bitch," he yelled, striking her in side of her face. "Take that!"

Blood trickled from her mouth. The soldiers on either side of her stiffened, itching to smack Ego, but the image of Python restrained them.

"Hold her fast," said Ego, "I'm not finished yet." And he punched her twice in the stomach. Ebony grimaced in pain, but she didn't cry out. *What a warrior,* thought the soldiers. *She has more guts than that cowardly dwarf ever will.* They wanted to help her but forced themselves to stand firm.

"Let her go," said Ego. The two soldiers released her arms and she fell limp to the ground. "Now tie her up and put her in the jeep with the other two." Geigy and Willie had been bound and thrown in the back of one of the jeeps.

Ego called Python on the phone. "I have good news for you, boss," he said excitedly.

"What?" said Python.

"I have Ebony, Geigy and Willie. They're tied up in the back of the jeep," he replied.

"Where the fuck are the cowboy and Winston?" demanded Python.

Ego flinched. "As far as we know, they won't be back for four or five days. It has something to do with thousands of tusks…and dynamite," said Ego.

"Tusks and dynamite?" said Python. "Where the hell are they getting all this stuff?"

"The men overheard them talking about some cave up in the mountains. That's all I know."

"All right, now this is what I want you to do," said Python. Ego nodded as if Python were standing right in front of him. "Leave a phone on the front seat of their Rover, I'm going to keep calling until the cowboy answers the phone. We have a big surprise for him, that may put him six feet under," said Python. "Now hurry back, the Russian is waiting for your arrival."

The Russian rubbed his hands together as he heard the news.

"I guess you can't wait until they get here," said Python.

The Russian's dark eyes flashed with evil. Even Python was a little afraid of him. "Yes, yes, I can't wait," he said eagerly. "I'm thinking of all the ways I'm going to torture them." He ran a finger up and down the sharp edge of his knife. "Especially the woman," he leered, his wicked eyes bulging. And he laughed an eerie laugh that sent shivers down Python's spine.

Python walked outside, the maniacal laughter, ringing in his ears.

I better not mess with the Russian. He's crazy!

Chapter Thirty-Seven

Cheyenne and Winston were exhausted as they pulled the dynamite on a wooden handmade sleigh.

"We sure were lucky to find this wood in the cave," said Cheyenne. "This may be how they got all those tusks and dynamite into the cave, in the first place."

Winston nodded. "I'm pretty sure you're right, old chap." He wiped the sweat from his brow. "Thank God, we'll be back at the camp tomorrow."

Cheyenne straightened and felt his aching back. "Yeah, me too. I don't like sleeping in trees that much. My back is killing me."

"Mine, too, old chap," said Winston. "I'm not as young as I used to be, and sleeping rough doesn't suit me."

"We should arrive back tomorrow afternoon, around two," said Cheyenne, checking his watch.

"I'm sure we'll have a warm welcome, especially from Ebony," said Winston, winking at his friend.

Cheyenne blushed. "I can't wait for her to cook us a nice hot meal and to see her smiling face."

"I bet that's not all you can't wait for, old chap," said Winston, nudging him in the ribs. "I wish I had a hot woman like that waiting for me."

"Don't get any ideas," said Cheyenne, laughing.

"Wouldn't dream of it, old chap," he replied, joining in the laughter.

Several hours later, they were within a few miles of the camp. The closer they got, the faster they moved, eager to be reunited with their friends. Finally they reached their destination. *The wanderers had returned.*

"What's going on here?" said Cheyenne as he looked around the camp. "Where is everybody?"

"Perhaps they took a walk," said Winston. "Or they may be collecting wood for a fire. Must have been pretty boring sitting around here for five days."

"Yeah, you're probably right," said Cheyenne, but he looked doubtful. "Ebony! Geigy! Willie!" he shouted. "Where are you?"

Winston joined in, but their shouts were met with silence. The only noise was the rustle of the wind through the trees and the chirping of nearby birds.

"Where the hell are they, Winston," said Cheyenne, scratching his head. He was starting to worry now. Bile rose in his throat and a sick feeling of dread invaded his stomach.

Winston patted him on the arm. "Don't worry, old chap, I'm sure they're around here somewhere," he said, always the optimist. "Let's check out the jeeps to make sure they're still there. Who knows, they could have driven off somewhere."

Cheyenne looked at him, puzzled. "Why would they do that?"

"Perhaps Geigy's leg got worse, or Willie's shoulder, and they had to get help. Find a hospital or something."

Cheyenne nodded. "Okay, let's take a look. Striding over to the jeeps' hideout, he pulled back the tree branches. "They're still here," he shouted to Winston. And then he noticed a black telephone lying on the front seat. *That's odd, I've never seen that phone before.* He was about to pick it up, when Winston's cries startled him.

"Cheyenne, come quick!" yelled Winston. "I've found something."

"What is it?" said Cheyenne, rushing over to his friend.

"Look at all these footprints," said Winston, pointing to the ground. "And see over there, it looks like blood." The two men examined the bloodstains.

"Could be from Willie's shoulder or Geigy's leg," said Cheyenne.

"But what about all the footprints, old chap?" said Winston. "There are dozens of footprints here and there are only three of them."

"You're right," said Cheyenne. The bile rose in his throat again. "I don't like the look of this, Winston. I don't like it at all."

"And look, there are a couple of empty whiskey bottles," said Winston. "I think I know what happened here, old chap."

Cheyenne examined the blood again. "If that bastard Python and his sicko Russian friend have taken them, I'll kill them," he said, through gritted teeth. "If they have hurt one hair on their heads, I'll kill them with my bare hands." His steely blue eyes glinted with anger as he flung his cowboy hat in the air. "I promise you, I'll kill them all."

Winston patted him on the arm. "All right, take it easy, old chap. There's not that much blood, and I doubt very much that Python would want them dead. He probably wants to use them as leverage to get to you."

"He's nothing but a lowdown sniveling coward – hiding behind two wounded men and a defenseless woman."

"Oh, I wouldn't call Ebony defenseless, old chap. I bet she put up a helluva fight, Geigy and Willie, too," said Winston.

"Yeah, she's a tigress," said Cheyenne. He bent down again and examined the ground. "That little bastard Ego was here, too," he shouted, pointing to a tiny footprint. "I'm gonna to kill him too."

Before Winston could reply, they heard the ringing of a phone. "What the hell?" said Cheyenne, and then it suddenly dawned on him that it was coming from the black phone. "That's the phone in the Rover. I noticed it lying on the front seat."

They both rushed over to answer it. "Hello," said Cheyenne warily, placing the phone to his ear.

"Is that the cowboy?" asked a raspy voice at the other end.

"Who wants to know?" demanded Cheyenne, already knowing the answer.

"This is Python."

Cheyenne felt the bile rise yet again. "What have you done with them?" he screamed.

"Done with who?" Python taunted.

"Stop playing games, Python."

"Oh, you mean *your friends.*" Python paused for effect and then continued. "Ego and my men are taking great care of them, so don't you worry."

Cheyenne slammed the phone. "Listen, you crazy bastard, if you hurt them in any way, I'll kill you. If it takes me until my dying day, I will track you down and kill you. And that's a promise."

Python laughed. "Oh, dear me, cowboy, I'm shaking in my boots. Do tell how you would go about killing me." He turned to the Russian and smirked. "The Russian is standing right next to me and he'd like to know, too."

"I'd break your scrawny neck with my bare hands," he said, waves of anger suffusing his face. "Snap it right in two." And he clicked his fingers SNAP!

Python shuddered and looked over to see if the Russian had noticed. Deep down, he was afraid of Cheyenne, and knew that the cowboy would make good on his threat if anything happened to his friends. Controlling his fear, he said, "Oh, I'm so scared."

Cheyenne shouted down the phone. "I saw blood on the ground. They better not be hurt or else you're a dead man."

Python shuddered again. "Well, to tell you the truth, I haven't seen them yet. They'll be arriving in a couple of days. As I said, my men are taking great care of them."

"You keep that sicko Russian away from them," snarled Cheyenne. "I've seen his brutality."

Python ignored him. "Now you listen to me, cowboy, I will call you again as soon as they arrive. Wait for the call, and if you don't answer I may have to kill them. Bye Bye, for now…" and he hung up the phone.

"Go to hell, Python," screamed Cheyenne but Python had gone.

Winston looked at him quizzically, and Cheyenne related what had happened. "Now all we can do is wait," said Cheyenne.

"It's going to be okay, old chap," said Winston. "We'll get them back safe and sound."

"I wish I shared your optimism," said Cheyenne sadly.

"Yes, that's me, the eternal optimist," said Winston.

Chapter Thirty-Eight

That night they lay by the phone, taking it in turns to sleep, in case they missed the call. By the second night, Python still hadn't rung.

"Oh, God, why doesn't he ring," said Cheyenne. "I'm afraid that something has happened to them. Perhaps we missed the call and he's killed them all."

"Relax, old chap. Nothing has happened to them. Remember, Python said it would be a couple of days before they arrived at the village. And we haven't missed the call – that phone hasn't been out of our sight or hearing for the past 48 hours."

"Yes, you're right, Winston, as always. I just can't help worrying."

Winston patted his shoulder. "Try to get some sleep. I'll listen for the phone."

"Thanks, Winston, you're a true friend. I could use a few hours' sleep."

But Cheyenne couldn't sleep. Myriad thoughts churned through his head as he gazed up at the stars. *Please God, don't let any harm come to my beautiful Ebony and my dear friends. I don't think I could live with myself if anything happened to them. We never should have left them alone. Two wounded men and a woman are no defense against a posse of soldiers, even though they probably put up a good fight. Why are there such evil people like Python and the Russian, and Ego, in the world? Why do they get kicks out of hurting others?* He remembered what his parents had taught him. *There will always be God and Satan, and they will never get along.*

Finally, he drifted off into a fitful sleep as Winston kept a silent vigil. The phone never rang.

"Did he call?" asked Cheyenne as soon as he awoke.

Winston shook his head. "Sorry, old chap. I was willing it to ring, but nothing. Just the sounds of the jungle."

They were about to have breakfast, when the phone suddenly sprang into life. Cheyenne grabbed it on the first ring. "Python," he said urgently. "Are they all right?"

"What, no hello?" said Python.

"Quit playing games, Python," he cried. "Are they all right? Let me talk to them."

"Calm down, cowboy. They're fine, except for a rifle butt to the head and a few kicks and punches. They didn't seem to like the idea of being captured," he smirked.

Cheyenne was furious. "I told you not to hurt them," he yelled.

"Nothing to do with me," said Python innocently. "I guess things got a little out of hand when they wouldn't come quietly."

"You bastard, Python. I'm gonna get you. As God is my witness, I'm gonna get you."

"Yeah, yeah," said Python, masking his fear. "As I said before, I'm quaking in my boots. Now listen to me, and listen good. Your little girlie's life is on the line, and your two friends. If you don't comply with what I say, they will all be hung at noon, on a day of my choosing." Python looked over at Ebony and Geigy and Willie who were still tied up in the back of the jeep. "Did you hear what I said, cowboy?"

"I heard you loud and clear," said Cheyenne, struggling to contain his anger. If he pissed off Python now, he'd only take it out on his friends.

"I'm looking at your precious friends now and I don't know what's so special about them," continued Python. "Has-been drunk, deadbeat nobody and a two-bit whore."

Cheyenne bristled. He wished he could reach down the phone and strangle the bastard, but he kept his cool and said calmly, "What do you want me to do, Python?"

Python grinned. "That's better. Now you can save your miserable friends if you just show up here on the day I tell you."

"Just tell me when and I'll be there," said Cheyenne.

"Now you're being a very good boy," said Python, grinning at Ego and the Russian who were standing next to him. "Write down these directions to my village."

Cheyenne did as he asked, trying hard to stay calm, for the sake of his friends. Winston stood by his side, nodding and offering encouragement.

"Why are you doing this, Python? What have I ever done to you?"

Python had been waiting for this question. His face brightened. "I want to prove to Ebony that you're not the man she thinks you are," he sneered.

"So that's what this is all about," said Cheyenne. "Ebony. You're angry because I stole your woman."

Python stiffened. "Shut up, you clapped-out cowboy," he bellowed, his face clouded with anger.

"Easy, old chap," said Winston. "Don't make him angry."

Cheyenne nodded. "Okay, Python, what do you want me to do?"

"I want you to camp out about two hours from my village, and I will call for you the day before the hangings," he replied. "That is, if you're man enough to save your friends. And come alone, otherwise they're dead!" Before Cheyenne could respond, he hung up. *Click!*

"What's the story, old chap?" asked Winston, tugging on his sleeve. "What does he want us to do?"

"Not *us*," said Cheyenne, *me."* And he told Winston what Python had said.

"It's a goddamn trap, old chap, and I hope you're not fool enough to fall for his bullshit."

"Winston, I truly believe that he will hang them all, if I don't do as he says."

"And end up dead yourself," said Winston. "What good will that do? You won't be saving them – you'll all be dead."

"I have to try to stop him. What else can I do?"

Winston shook him by the shoulders. "Listen to me, old chap. You might as well commit suicide, because they're going to kill you as soon as you step into that village."

"I have to go, Winston, otherwise they'll all die."

Winston tried again. "You can't save them. You are walking right into their trap, and you will all end up dead."

Cheyenne shook his head sadly. "You're right, Winston, as you always are. But I have to take that chance. I couldn't live with myself if I didn't try to save them."

"Then I'm going with you, old chap. Two heads are better than one, eh?"

"No, Winston," said Cheyenne sharply. "Python was adamant that I come alone, otherwise he'll kill them."

"So I'll hide in the bush," said Winston. "They'll never see me."

"I'm sorry, but I can't take that chance. I have to go alone."

Winston realized that it was no use arguing with him any longer. Cheyenne was determined to go alone, and there was nothing more he could do to stop him.

"You're a good friend, Winston," he said, patting his shoulder. "Thanks for understanding. I'll leave first thing in the morning."

Winston nodded. "I'm not a religious man, but I'll be praying for you. May God go with you."

Chapter Thirty-Nine

Early the next morning, they buried all the dynamite and wrapped up the firing caps to prevent it from getting damp. And after a hearty breakfast, Cheyenne was packed and ready to go.

Winston walked over and shook his hand. "Well, old chap, I know you won't listen to me. You have to do what you have to do. I understand."

"Thanks, Winston. There's no sense both of us getting our heads blown off, is there?" he said, trying to keep things light.

They made eye contact for second. "Take care of yourself, old chap. As I said last night, I'll be praying for you." And sighing deeply, he jumped into the jeep and took off down the trail, in a cloud of dust.

"Goodbye, old friend," said Cheyenne softly as he watched Winston tear down the road at breakneck speed. *I wonder if I'll ever see him again?* Banishing the thought, he walked over to the Rover and set off in the opposite direction. *Friends going their separate ways.*

He drove along the dusty trail, planning his next course of action. *I'm going to take my own sweet time. Whatever those guys have planned for me, they can't start without me. I'm the star attraction.* He stopped frequently along the way, and practiced his draw, over and over again. *Practice makes perfect. You can never have enough practice.* Stones and bushes were his targets. He would take aim and holler: *Take that, Python; Right between the eyes, Ego; You are toast, Russian,* imagining that the three thugs were standing there before him. He was about to shoot an imaginary Python through the heart, when the phone rang. He placed it to his ear.

"Hello there, cowboy." There was no mistaking the caller's raspy voice. "This is Python."

"What a surprise," said Cheyenne sarcastically.

Python ignored his comment. "So, are you man enough to come for your woman and your friends?" he said.

Cheyenne gripped the phone tightly. "Now you listen to me, Python. I know how your sicko Russian sidekick likes to torture people. Keep him away from my friends or else."

"Or else what?" sneered Python. "You're in no position to make demands. I'm holding all the cards, and you'll do as I say if you want to see your miserable friends again."

Cheyenne stood firm. "I'm warning you, Python. The deal's off if you don't do as I say. I won't come in. Do you hear me?"

Cheyenne was bluffing. He would come to the village, no matter what, to save his friends. But Python didn't understand such loyalty. He would abandon his friends in a second to save his own skin. And they would do the same to him. No honor among thieves and cutthroats.

"Yes, yes, I hear you," said Python. "I'll talk to my Russian friend, because I would hate to see you miss what I have in store for you." He ran his finger across his throat and winked at Ego and the Russian, who were standing nearby, listening to the whole conversation – at least Python's side of it. "Now, listen up, cowboy, here are the rest of the directions to my village."

Cheyenne jotted them down and Python hung up abruptly again.

Showtime! said Cheyenne to himself.

Back in the village, Python took the Russian aside. "The cowboy won't show if he sees a mark on any of his friends, so leave them alone," warned Python.

"But how will he know?" argued the Russian. "Does he have ESP?"

"What the fuck is ESP?" asked Python.

"Extra sensory perception," replied the Russian.

Python stared at him as if he were speaking a foreign language. "Extra fucking what?"

"Oh, forget it," said the Russian. "You wouldn't understand. He can't see them, so how would he know if they're marked or not?"

Python stared at him. The Russian was right, how would he know? Still, his instincts told him to keep his word.

"Just a couple of hours," the Russian pleaded. "I won't leave a single mark on them, promise."

Python's face was like thunder. "Don't you understand English, you Slavic prick. I said, don't lay a hand on them, and I'm not going to repeat myself. Lay off! Comprendre!"

"Okay, okay," said the Russian calmly, backing off. "It's no big deal. I just wanted to have a little fun." But underneath, he was seething. Python had promised that the three would be his, to do with as he wished. And now he would have to wait. Slamming his fist on the table, he grabbed a bottle of vodka and stormed outside.

Python and Ego decided to pay a visit to the prisoners. "Snap to it," he yelled at the guards as he caught them smoking and laughing together. "You're supposed to be keeping your damn eyes on the prisoners."

The guards stood to attention. "Yessir," they replied in unison. "Sorry, sir." Python pushed past them and approached the tiny cell.

"Let us out of here right now, you black devil," screamed Ebony, banging on the cell door.

Python looked at her through the iron bars. "What has come over you, Ebony? You used to call me sweetheart and honey, and tell me how much you loved me, and now you are cursing me to high heaven."

"Go to hell, Python," she yelled. "That was before I found out what you were really like."

"Is that so?" sneered Python. "Or was it because you met the cowboy?"

"He's worth ten of you. I know he's on his way, so you'd better look out. He'll kill all of you."

Python turned to Ego. "Listen to the bitch, lovesick for her crappy cowboy." Ego sniggered.

"Yes, Ebony, you stupid bitch," he snarled, "we know he's on his way. And we have a big surprise for him." He grinned wickedly.

"Bastard," she yelled.

"Oh, watch your language, sweetheart. The cowboy would be shocked if he heard what a foul mouth you have."

"Go to hell," she cried.

Ignoring her, Python said, "Oh, and talking of shock, he's going to be so shocked that he might have a heart attack."

Ebony grabbed the cell bars, straining to reach Python. "I swear I'll kill you, if you harm cowboy," she yelled. "And you, too, Ego, you little weasel. Payback time is coming soon."

Ego flinched. *Thank God, there are steel bars between us,* he thought as he and Python walked away. *She would kill me in an instant.*

After they had left, Ebony burst into tears. Geigy consoled her. "Don't worry, Ebony, Cheyenne is on his way. He'll get us out of this mess."

"But there are dozens of them and only one of him," she sobbed.

"Oh, he'll find a way," said Geigy, wiping away her tears. "He always does."

Chapter Forty

The Russian met them in the hut. He had swigged almost a full bottle of vodka, and was feeling no pain. "I was thinking about putting some knockout pills in a bottle of whiskey, and giving it to the guards," he said.

Python glared at him. "Oh, yeah, why would you do that?" he asked.

"Well, after they passed out, I was going to torture our three prisoners," he slurred. "Have a little fun with them, especially the little lady."

"I told you to lay off them," shouted Python, "and I won't tell you again." He shook his fist at the Russian, the blood vessels on his neck and face bulging with anger.

The Russian remained unfazed. Taking another chug from the vodka bottle, he wiped his lips and smirked at Python. "Don't worry," he said, waving the now empty bottle in front of Python's face. "I won't touch them. Since the cowboy is going to die anyway, I changed my mind."

Python unclenched his fists and relaxed his facial muscles. "That's good, that's good," he said, visibly relieved. "Let him walk into our trap." He patted his friend on the shoulder. "Now let's get another bottle of vodka and talk about our retirement plan."

Cheyenne was taking his time. Now close to a week since his last conversation with Python, he was waiting for that second phone call to arrange *his special day at noon.* Cheyenne knew he was walking into a trap, but he had no choice. What else could he do? He had to save his friends. *What could Python possibly have in store for me? Except to kill me.*

Cheyenne spent hours practicing his draw every day, making sure that everything was in place. He checked and rechecked his holster – one loose string could mean a missed shot. And that one missed shot could mean life or death.

In the distance, he could hear the insistent beating of drums. At first he welcomed the noise, which helped to break the monotony of his lonely days. He missed the companionship of his friends and somehow the drums made him feel closer to them. But after a while, the incessant beat began to get on his nerves.

The constant beat, beat, beat is driving me crazy. I wish I knew what they were saying. He gazed up at the starry sky. Out here in the bush, with a zillion stars looking down on him, he felt as if he were the only person in the world. *Just a lonely cowboy from Wyoming and a galaxy of faraway stars. How many times will I gaze upon their starry beauty?* One star in particular drew his attention. Brighter and larger than the others, he felt as if he could reach out and pluck it from the inky sky. *From now on, that will be my lucky star.*

At night, he counted the heavenly bodies, to help him fall asleep. He usually fell into a dreamless sleep, but one particular night he had a nightmare, so vivid and violent that he awoke in a cold sweat. "No, no," he shouted, punching the air around him. Finally he realized that it had only been a dream.

He was walking into the village, to meet Python, and as he walked, he noticed that there were high walls on either side of him. There was no escape. Python's voice rang out, urging him to keep walking. 'Come, come, your friends are dying to see you,' cackled the disembodied voice. Cheyenne looked around, but there was no sign of Python. He walked on, towards a large gate at the end of the village. Suddenly the gate sprang open and a herd of elephants charged towards him at full speed. Cheyenne froze. Python's voice rang out again, and he heard the Russian laughing. 'He came to save the elephants and now they are going to crush him like a sardine.' Cheyenne ran like the wind, but he was no match for the stampeding elephants. They were gaining on him with every step, and just as they were about to crush him, he woke up...

Wiping the sweat from his brow, he reached in his backpack for a bottle of water and took a large gulp. *Thank God, it was only a dream,* he muttered.

Just as he was beginning to relax, the shrill of the phone jolted his nerves, and he dropped the bottle, spilling water all over his trousers. "Damn," he shouted, jumping to his feet as the water ran down his legs. He grabbed the ringing phone. Python's hoarse voice bellowed in his ear.

"Make sure that you show up tomorrow at noon."

"I'll be there," said Cheyenne. "Just don't harm my friends."

"Your *friends* will not be harmed," he said, *"if you show up.* But if you are a no-show, they will be shot and hung, and we will also cut their throats to make sure they're dead."

Cheyenne shuddered inwardly. "How do I know you're telling me truth? For all I know, my friends might already be dead. Put them on the phone and let me talk to them," he demanded.

"Shut your mouth and listen," shouted Python angrily. "You're in no position to make demands on me. I'm in the driver's seat, Cowboy, and you will do as I say, otherwise you can kiss *your little friends goodbye, especially your little sweetheart."*

Cheyenne gripped the phone tightly and struggled to control himself. "If you hurt one hair on her head, I swear I'll tear you apart, limb from limb," he said, through clenched teeth. "And that's a promise."

"Oh my, I'm quaking in my boots," said Python as Ego and the Russian tittered in the background.

"Be warned, Python, if you hurt any of my friends, you're a dead man."

"Don't you be threatening me, Cowboy, just shut up and listen. I ain't telling you again."

Cheyenne took a deep breath and calmed himself. "Okay, I'm listening."

"That's a good boy," said Python. "Do as your daddy tells you and everything will be okay."

"Get on with it," said Cheyenne.

"Shut your damned mouth and listen," snarled Python.

Cheyenne bit back his words, struggling to stay silent.

"That's better," said Python. "Now, here's what I want you to do. When you arrive at the village, toot your horn as you're approaching so that we know you are coming. Got that?"

Cheyenne nodded into the phone. "Yeah," he replied.

"Good," said Python as he picked at his rotten teeth with a twig. "Then I want you to park your vehicle and walk into the village slowly." Cheyenne remained silent. "Do you hear me, Cowboy?" demanded Python, throwing the twig to the ground and crushing it under his boot.

"Yes, I hear you," said Cheyenne.

"Good boy," smirked Python as if he were talking to his dog.

"Now you listen to me, Python. You better keep your word, or God help me, I will kill you," he said calmly and deliberately. There was no mistaking the steely determination in his voice. And Python knew the threat was real. If he crossed the cowboy, he'd be a dead man!

"If you want your three friends alive, show up tomorrow or they will die," he warned, slamming down the phone.

"Nice talking to you, too," said Cheyenne.

Chapter Forty-One

Might as well try to get some more shuteye, thought Cheyenne as he lay back down and gazed up at the illuminated heavens. He knew that this could be his last night on earth. The threat from Python and his cohorts was real, and tomorrow he and his friends could be dead. *Stop it! Stop it!* he muttered, struggling in vain to banish the negative thoughts from his head. *I will beat those thugs and I will free my friends. I will, I will,* he yelled, slamming his fist against the ground.

Unable to sleep, he appealed to the heavens. *Dear God, with your help, I will succeed. Please help me to defeat these evil men.* Praying as he had never prayed before, he finally fell into a fitful sleep, lulled by the dull beat of the distant drums.

The next morning he was jarred awake by the noisy purr of a motorcycle. Two burly men sat astride the bike while many others walked alongside. Cheyenne rubbed his eyes and watched them from his hiding place, behind some large bushes. He had wiped out his tire tracks so as not to be seen from the road.

Many of the people wore hats, and their necks were adorned with sparkling gold and silver. *I wonder where they're going? If only I knew what the drums were saying?* As he continued to watch the procession, his thoughts strayed to his three friends. *Would he be holding Ebony in his arms tonight? Would he see Geigy and Willie, with their smiling faces, or would they all be dead? I must stay focused. And with God's help, I will be victorious.*

Cheyenne had already checked out the village with his binoculars. He figured that he was now about a mile away. All seemed quiet. He checked the time on his wristwatch. It was 10:30 am. *I have an hour and a half. Ninety minutes and it will all be over. How did I get myself in this predicament? I'm just a simple cowboy from Wyoming. And all I wanted to do was to save the elephants. Now, here I am, facing death as I try to save the lives of my three friends.* Once more he looked up to the heavens and prayed. *God help me to save them all.*

Around eleven, the long procession of people had finally passed by. Cheyenne scanned the area with his binoculars. No one was in sight. Removing the brush and branches from his jeep, he jumped in the driver's seat and started the engine. *Okay, this is it! Showtime!*

He drove slowly, checking his watch every few minutes to make sure he would not be late. And as per Python's strict instructions, he blew the horn as he approached the village. The rhythmic sound of clapping met his ears. *Clap! Clap! Clap!*

What's that all about? he thought as he drove slowly down a small slope and parked the jeep near a clump of trees. Espying the first few huts of the village, he blew the horn once more and waited. But all was deserted. The only noise was the steady clapping and the dull beat of the distant drums. Despite the blazing sun, an icy chill ran down his spine and he shuddered.

I don't like this. It's creepy…very creepy.

Cheyenne patted his trusty guns. His lightning fast hands were ready to draw at anything that moved. A dog emerged from between two huts and scampered down the path towards him. Surprised, Cheyenne's hands flew to his pistols, and then relaxed their hold when he realized that it was only a harmless dog. *Stay calm. Stay calm and breathe.*

Taking a deep cleansing breath, he inched forward, struggling to stay calm. With each step, he could feel himself getting tenser and tenser as the *clap, clap, clap* grew louder and louder. And the beating drums moved in rhythm with his beating heart. *Thud! Thud! Thud!* His eyes scanned the village, scrutinizing every hut, every door. Nothing. No one. Not even another stray dog. *Where is everybody?* he called out loud.

And then he saw them. His three dear friends tied to posts, buried deep in the ground. Bound and gagged, their eyes wide with fear. "Dear Lord," he cried out, "what have they done to you?" Thin and haggard, their faces caked in dirt, his friends were barely recognizable. But they recognized him. Instant joy replaced the fear in their eyes. Cheyenne had come to save them. He was here. He had come. Their prayers had been answered.

Cheyenne gulped back his shock and called out to them. "Ebony, Geigy, Willie, hang on, I'm here to get you."

As he rushed forward, a familiar raspy voice stopped him in his tracks. Python!

"Not so fast, Cowboy," he yelled. "You have to earn that." Python stepped out from the shadows into the bright sunshine and faced Cheyenne. For a few seconds the two men stared at each other. Python finally broke the silence. "All right, people, you can come out now."

Dozens of people joined Python and gathered on either side of the street, surrounding Cheyenne. "Look at all the people on both sides of you," said Python, a huge smirk creasing his ugly face. "I have them blocked off so you have a clear view of the road."

Cheyenne looked puzzled. *What was Python up to?* He glanced over at his friends who were burning up in the hot sun. *There's no time to lose. I must save them.* "What do you want, Python?" he said, turning to face his enemy.

Python smiled and rubbed his hands together. "All in good time, Cowboy," he said, beckoning to his two cronies. Ego and the Russian emerged from the shadows and stood on either side of him. Ego smirked at Cheyenne, revealing his rotten yellow teeth, while the Russian laughed out loud.

Cheyenne stared them down. "Okay, so now it's three to one. I can handle that." He patted his guns. "What do you want?"

Python spat on the ground. "We're having a little competition at noon, just like we had at the *African Queen.*" Cheyenne still looked puzzled. "Let me explain," said Python. "Some people are betting on you and some are betting against you."

"So I have to shoot those twelve whiskey glasses again," said Cheyenne.

A wicked grin lit up Python's face. "No, this time, it's going to be much more exciting. Now, stay where are you," he commanded, pointing his finger at Cheyenne.

Cheyenne stole another quick glance at his friends. Their eyes locked. *Don't worry, I'm here to save you,* his eyes seemed to say. *I won't let you down. With God's help we'll beat these guys. Good always triumphs over evil.* They nodded their response, hope shining in their eyes.

Cheyenne had come to save them.

The silent exchange did not go unnoticed. "Don't be looking to them for help," sneered Python. "They ain't gonna be much use to you."

The Russian laughed heartily. "I'll drink to that, comrade," he said, raising a half-empty vodka bottle to his lips and taking a hefty swig.

"Yeah, they ain't going nowhere," said Ego, looking over at the haggard trio and laughing.

"Ain't that the truth," said Python, joining in the laughter.

Cheyenne stiffened. Time was running out for his friends. A few more hours and they would be burned to a crisp under the brutal African sun. "Can you at least give them some shade and water," he pleaded.

"No time for that, Cowboy," said Python dismissively. "We have to get this show on the road. Everyone's waiting." He belched loudly and let out a smelly fart. Ego and the Russian wrinkled their noses and turned away. "Oops, sorry about that," chuckled Python. "Must have been those refried beans I had for breakfast."

Filthy swine, thought Cheyenne. *I'd like to blast him off the face of the earth. The world would be a better place without him.*

As if he could read his mind, Python said, "Hope I haven't offended your nice sensibilities, Cowboy. I must remember to mind my manners from now on." Cheyenne said nothing.

Python reached over and opened the door of the nearest hut. "I want you to meet someone."

What the devil is he up to now? wondered Cheyenne as he stepped forward towards the hut.

A man of medium height, dressed all in black, emerged from the shadows of the hut. He wore a black cowboy hat and two pearl-studded pistols hung around his waist, the leather straps tied tightly around both legs. Black cowboy boots with small heels and silver spurs covered his feet.

Cheyenne stared at the black figure as he strutted from the hut, the silver spurs making a clicking sound as he walked. *Who is this guy dressed all in black in this cowboy outfit? Probably one of Python's cronies.*

The man faced him now and Cheyenne looked straight into his dark eyes. Although the temperature hovered around 105 degrees in the shade, Cheyenne suddenly felt very cold. An icy chill wracked his body, sending shivers up and down his spine. He knew this man who stood before him. And his blood ran cold. He was looking into the eyes of Black Bart!

Chapter Forty-Two

"May God have mercy on my soul," Cheyenne whispered as he silently crossed himself.

Black Bart's fierce black eyes bore down on him. Cheyenne cringed under his evil stare.

"Black Bart!" he exclaimed, finally finding his voice. "What are you doing here in Africa?"

Behind him, Python and his thugs sniggered behind their hands. They enjoyed seeing the look of dread on Cheyenne's face.

"I came here to kill you, Cheyenne," replied Black Bart in a slow drawl. His words hung in the air. And for several moments no one spoke. Finally, Cheyenne found his voice.

"I have no problem with you, Black Bart," he said. "You have been my idol since I was a little boy. You still are." He stared intently into the dark man's eyes without blinking. "I have always looked up to you." Black Bart stood silently, returning Cheyenne's unflinching gaze.

Cheyenne tried again. "I came here to save the elephants, not to have a gun battle with you."

"He came here to save the elephants," mimicked Python. "What a good little soldier he is."

Ego and the Russian burst into laughter. "Such a good little soldier," they repeated.

"Shut up, Python," snapped Black Bart, whirling around to face him. Python clammed up immediately. "And control your moronic friends. Or I'll control them for you," he said, patting his guns.

Python punched them both hard, in the ribs. And the laughter stopped abruptly.

My God, thought Cheyenne, *I don't think I've ever heard anyone talk to Python like that.* The thought amused him. *He's afraid of Black Bart. Deathly afraid.*

Black Bart turned back to Cheyenne. "You have no choice, Cheyenne. One of us has to die, and that will be you."

"But I don't understand," said Cheyenne. "I have no quarrel with you. Why would I want to have a shoot-out with you?"

Black Bart's withering gaze seemed to bore a hole right through his head. "You're not listening to me, Cheyenne. As I told you before, you have no choice. A lot of money is riding on this gun fight." He turned and pointed to the gaggle of people lined up on both sides of the street. "Look at all these people. They are betting a lot of money on us, and I would say that most of the money is riding on me."

The crowd cheered loudly. "Black Bart! Black Bart! Black Bart!" they chanted as they danced up and down, waving their arms in the air. Black Bart smiled at them, basking in their adoration. "Now, we wouldn't want to disappoint them, would we?" he said, turning back to Cheyenne.

"So, this is all about money?" said Cheyenne.

"You got it, Cowboy," said Black Bart. "I have two hundred and fifty thousand dollars in my bank account, and…" he nodded toward Python…"I will double it if I kill you. Thanks to Python and his Russian friend."

Cheyenne shook his head in disgust. "Can't you see they're using you for their own evil ends?"

"Seems to me that everyone benefits, except, of course, you," said Black Bart.

Cheyenne looked over at his friends who were slowly wilting like flowers in the midday sun. Their eyes were begging him to do something; to save them before it was too late. Time was running out. He tried once more. "I don't want to draw on you, Black Bart," he pleaded. "As I said before, you're my idol, always have been. I have always looked up to you." He took a deep breath and continued. "You're the one that made me want to be the fastest draw in the West."

Black Bart stamped his foot angrily sending up a cloud of dust. "You're wrong there, Cowboy. I AM the fastest draw in the West, and I'm here to prove it."

Cheyenne was about to reply when the clapping suddenly reached a thunderous roar.

"What the fuck is all that clap, clap, clap, Black Bart?" asked Python, holding his ears to block out the deafening noise.

Black Bart turned around and scanned the horizon, shading his eyes from the sun's intense glare. "I have no idea, but the drums have finally stopped beating."

Cheyenne stared long and hard at Black Bart. A small skull hung around his neck, which he hadn't noticed before. "What does that skull represent?" he asked. "The one round your neck?"

Momentarily caught off guard, Black Bart spun back around and gently touched the skull with his fingers. "It was given to me by a witch doctor. He swore to me that if I wear this, I will always be protected. Which means, Cowboy, that I will live and you will die."

Cheyenne stood his ground. "Well, I'm sorry to inform you, but I don't believe in witch doctors and all that mumbo-jumbo," he said defiantly. Black Bart opened his mouth in amazement, but no words came out. Cheyenne continued on. "Now, why don't you get Python to release my three friends over there, before they die in this blistering heat, and we'll forget all about who is the fastest gun in the West."

"Sorry, Cowboy, no can do," replied Black Bart, touching his guns and looking over at Python. "Tell him, Python."

"See this bell above my head," broke in Python as he pointed to the small golden bell dangling from the hut door. "At the third ring, we will find out who really is the fastest draw in the West."

On hearing these words, the crowd began chanting, "Ring the bell. Ring the bell," as they worked themselves into a frenzy, jumping up and down, and flailing their arms and legs.

"See, Cheyenne, we can't let the people down," said Black Bart softly. "A lot of money is riding on us. They're here to see a show, and by God, we're gonna give 'em one."

"But..." began Cheyenne.

"No buts, Cowboy," interrupted Black Bart. "I can feel the adrenaline running through my body." His black eyes glazed over. "What a feeling! Now I can prove that I'm the fastest draw in the West."

"No, wait, you haven't thought this through," cried Cheyenne.

"The time for waiting is over, Cowboy. It's Showtime!" exclaimed Black Bart. His black eyes glittered. "You'd better draw on the third ring, Cowboy, because I'm gonna kill you."

It's Showtime! Black Bart's words hit Cheyenne like a ton of bricks. He knew the man was serious. This was no game. He had to draw at lightning speed, otherwise he'd be a dead man. Adrenaline surged through his body and he suddenly felt lightheaded. *I have no choice but to kill Black Bart. I know I wanted to be the fastest draw with a gun, but I never thought I would have to prove it here in Africa. And against Black Bart of all people. The man I have looked up to all my life – my inspiration and my idol!* He shook his head in an effort to clear his thoughts. *I must stay focused. If I turn my back on that third ring, I know that Black Bart will shoot me in the back. It's either him or me. I have no choice.*

Once more, Cheyenne looked over at his friends who were frying in the blazing sun. Time was swiftly running out for them. He had to act quickly and get this over with. All three had now passed out from the heat, their heads slumped against their frail bodies. Without water and shade, they would soon be dead. One look was all it took to galvanize him into action. *I have to act now, I have to save them.* He turned to Black Bart and the waiting crowd.

"Ring the bell! Ring the bell!" they chanted, louder and louder.

"Okay," he said, patting his guns. "I'm ready when you are, Black Bart. It's now or never. Ring the bell, and may the best man win."

Black Bart chuckled and patted his holster. "I am the best man, Cowboy, which you'll find out in a few seconds," he said, turning to Python. "Okay, Python, I'm ready."

Python nodded and then addressed the crowd. "Okay, people, shut it!" he shouted, trying to make himself heard above the noisy din. The crowd continued chanting. Python tried again. "I said shut the fuck up," he bellowed. The crowd finally fell silent.

"That's better," said Python. He turned to Cheyenne and Black Bart. "Now, I'm gonna ring the bell, and on the third ring, we'll find out who has the fastest draw. May the best man win!" But under his breath, he muttered, *You're a dead man, Cowboy. In a few minutes the vultures are gonna be feasting on your scrawny carcass. And me and my friends are gonna be celebrating. You'll be dead and we'll be rich!*

Cheyenne steadied himself. *This is it! Stay focused! Think of Ebony, Geigy and Willie! This is your last chance to save them.* He watched as Python reached for the bell. Simultaneously, he reached for his gun when, from behind, a thunderous roar met his ears, like the sound of a herd of stampeding elephants. "What the hell," he said as the spun around. "Oh, my God," he cried, shaking his head in disbelief. "I don't believe what I'm seeing."

Python's hand dropped to his side and his eyes widened in horror.

"Fuck me!!"..

Chapter Forty-Three

"Now that's a sight for sore eyes," said Cheyenne as he shook his head in amazement.

A dust covered jeep raced into the village at breakneck speed, and there in the driver's seat sat his old friend Winston. Beside him sat Ho Goo, a beaming smile creasing his massive face. And behind them followed hundreds of brightly painted natives wielding spears and machetes.

"My old friend Winston – I might have known that crazy Englishman would come through for us," said Cheyenne. "And here he is with Chief Ho Goo and the entire Ji-Hi tribe. This is truly amazing – the cavalry has arrived just in time."

Winston slowed the jeep to a stop, and Ho Goo raised his hand. The advancing tribe stopped in mid-step and waited for his next command. *Surely Python would stop the gun battle now,* Cheyenne thought as he looked first at Black Bart and then at his sworn enemy.

Python stood in shock, his mouth wide open as he surveyed the small army of tribesmen. For once in his life, he was speechless. He looked from the Russian to Ego to Black Bart and then back to the Russian, as if to say: *What the fuck are we gonna do now?*

The Russian shrugged. Ego giggled nervously. And Black Bart, cool as a cucumber, polished his silver pistols.

Winston jumped from the jeep and ran over to Cheyenne. "Are we in time, old chap?" he said, giving Cheyenne a big bear hug.

"Winston, old buddy, am I glad to see you," replied Cheyenne, smiling. "And I see you brought the cavalry with you."

"Of course, old chap, you don't think I would let you walk into Python's trap alone, do you? Wouldn't be much of a friend now, would I?" he said, looking around. "Who the hell is that," he whispered, pointing to Black Bart who was still polishing his pistols.

"It's a long story," said Cheyenne. "You'll find out soon enough."

"And where are Ebony, Geigy and Willie?"

Cheyenne pointed to their three friends who still lay unconscious.

"Oh, my God!" exclaimed Winston. "We have to free them – there's no time to lose. They are frying to death in this brutal heat."

"There's something I have to take care of first," said Cheyenne. And he briefly told Winston about the imminent shoot-out between himself and Black Bart. "Python won't free them unless I agree to go up against Black Bart. He has a lot of money riding on the outcome, and so do all these others," he said, pointing to the assembled crowd.

"But how are you going to free them if you're dead, old chap? This gunslinger could outdraw you."

"That's a chance I have to take – I have no choice."

"We'll just overpower them. We have Chief Ho Goo and the whole tribe behind us now."

"No, it's too risky. One of Python's men has a gun trained on them, with orders to shoot them if I make one false move."

"He'll probably kill them, even if you do play ball, old chap. I wouldn't trust that snake as far as I could throw him."

"I know, but I've got to try – it's our only chance."

"Okay, old chap. I'm right behind you.

Meanwhile, Chief Ho Goo had now stepped out of the jeep. He and his tribe of painted warriors stood and faced Python and his men. Mexican standoff. On one side of the street stood the Ji-Hi tribe and on the other, Python and his motley crew of deadbeats, thieves and misfits.

"So, the cowboy's friends have to come to rescue him," jeered Python, attempting to put on a brave face. Outwardly, he seemed totally in command, but inside he was quaking in his boots. *These warriors look mighty fierce,* he thought as he surveyed their painted faces and lethal looking weapons.

"Well, Cowboy," he shouted, "are you gonna keep your part of the bargain. Black Bart is waiting. And don't forget *your three little friends* - they are definitely counting on you."

Cheyenne nodded.

"You don't have to do this, old chap," said Winston, placing a restraining hand on his arm. "We can take them."

"Sorry, Winston, but I can't take that chance – Python would shoot Ebony, Geigy and Willie in a nanosecond."

Ring! Python rang the bell once. "Black Bart! Cowboy! Take your places, pistols at the ready."

Cheyenne and Black Bart stood and faced each other in the dusty street. Their eyes locked. Steely confidence met steely determination. One man confident of victory, and the other determined that victory would be his.

Ring! Python sounded the bell for the second time. The crowd fell silent. Watching and waiting. Winston held his breath. Beads of sweat ran down Cheyenne's face as he struggled to remain focused.

Will I be too slow on my draw?

Will this be my last day on earth?

Will I die at the hands of Black Bart?

And then he heard the sound of an elephant calling to his mate, off in the distance. That was all it took. A soothing calm descended over his body and he felt himself relax. The elephant's call had restored his confidence. The old Cheyenne was back. His whole body was now burning for the showdown.

Like hell I'm gonna to lose to this bunch of killers!

This is for Ebony, Geigy and Willie!

This is for the elephants!

Ring that bell, Python – this cowboy is ready!

Chapter Forty-Four

Python's hand hovered near the bell. All eyes were focused on the two gunmen as they stood facing each other, legs spread apart. *Who would live and who would die!* In a few seconds, they would have their answer. Python smiled as he touched the bell for the third and final time.

R*ing!* Two shots rang out, and before the crowd could react it was all over.

What happened? We didn't even see the guns being drawn! Quicker than lightning! Who won? Who was shot? Did our man win? Did we lose our money? Are we rich? Is it over? Are they both dead? These questions and more rippled back and forth through the crowd.

Python craned his neck above the mob to see what had happened. The scene that greeted his eyes brought a cruel smile to his face. His lips curled in a sneer. Cheyenne had fallen down on his left knee.

"Oh no!" cried Winston, rushing forward to help his friend.

"Oh yes!" cried Python, rubbing his hands together in glee. "The cowboy is down! Finish him off, Black Bart!" His words echoed throughout the crowd. *The cowboy is down! The cowboy is down! We won! We won! Black Bart is the winner!*

All eyes swiveled toward Black Bart. His hat had blown off, and he seemed to stand in suspension for several moments. Then he toppled forward and hit the ground with a resounding thud. Blood oozed from his forehead and trickled down his face to mix with the dust and dirt.

Black Bart is down! They've both been shot! Who's the winner? What about my money?

"Oh shit!" yelled Python as he watched Black Bart crash into the ground. He turned to Ego and the Russian. "Go check him out, Ego. See if he's dead."

Ego waddled over to the fallen gunslinger as fast as his small legs could carry him. Black Bart had been shot right between the eyes. Ego checked his pulse and listened for a heartbeat. Nothing! "He's dead, boss," he yelled to Python.

"Are you sure?"

"Yep. Clean shot right between the eyes. He's dead as a doornail."

Python stamped his feet in anger and looked over at Cheyenne. "Sonofabitch," he screamed. "He said he was the fastest draw in the West."

"Well, he ain't the fastest anymore," observed Ego, looking down at the dead gunslinger.

Meanwhile, Winston had raced over to Cheyenne, and was now tending to his fallen friend. "Cheyenne, old chap, are you all right? Are you wounded?" he asked.

Cheyenne grimaced and held his left leg. He had been shot in the calf, but fortunately, the bullet had missed the leg bone. Blood poured from the open wound and trickled down his leg.

"I got shot in the leg, but I think I'll live," he said, trying to force a weak smile.

"Thank God for that, old chap, for a moment there, I thought you were dead."

"Nah, it would take more than that to finish me off. What about Black Bart? Is he okay?"

Winston shook his head. "Sorry, old chap, but it looks like you were a mite faster than he was, thank goodness. You got him right between the eyes. He's dead."

Cheyenne closed his eyes tightly and let out a deep sigh. "Oh no! Black Bart was my idol – I had no quarrel with him."

Winston patted him on the shoulder. "You had no choice, my friend," he said gently. "You said so yourself. It was either him or you."

Cheyenne nodded. "I know, but I'm sorry I had to kill him. I just meant to wound him and instead I shot him right between the eyes. I just drew my gun as fast as I could and fired."

Winston tried to comfort him. "Black Bart knew the score. He was a seasoned gunslinger, and one day he knew he would meet his match. And on this day, he met more than his match."

"It doesn't make me feel any better," said Cheyenne. "I'm still sorry that he's dead."

"You did what you had to do," said Winston. "He would have killed you, old chap. Now let me take a look at that leg. I have a first-aid kit in the jeep."

"No, first you must check on Ebony and Geigy and Willie. You must release them now. They won't last much longer in this hot sun. Please, Winston. HURRY!"

Ho Goo and his tribe had taken control of the village. They had already released the three friends from their bonds and were now tending to them in one of the nearby huts. Winston rushed over just as they were regaining consciousness. Looking at their frail, dehydrated bodies, their faces badly burnt by the sun, he stifled a cry. *In God's name, what have those monsters done to you?*

"Are they going to be okay?" he asked Chief Ho Goo.

"They are very dehydrated, their bodies covered in burns, but they will be all right. Our tribe has remedies for their ailments. Do not worry, my friend, we will take good care of them."

"Thank you, chief," said Winston. "I feel comforted knowing that they are in such good hands."

Ho Goo smiled. This was his chance to pay back his friends for saving his son. "You are very welcome," he said simply.

Ebony was the first to speak. She smiled weakly as she saw Winston's face. "What happened? I remember Cheyenne coming to our rescue and then everything went blank. Where is he? Is he okay?" she said anxiously, struggling to sit up.

Winston stroked her head and pushed her back down gently on the bed. "He's fine, don't worry. Just a slight flesh wound."

Her eyes widened. "A flesh wound? What happened? Is he all right? I must see him."

"It's nothing to worry about. Fortunately, the bullet missed the leg bone and passed right through the flesh. Cheyenne was lucky. You should see the other guy," said Winston, in an attempt to lighten the mood. And then he told them all about the shoot-out, and how their lives had depended on the outcome; how he had arrived with Chief Ho Goo and his tribe, and how Cheyenne had been victorious. "He is now indisputably the fastest draw in the West!"

"My God," said Geigy, "you guys arrived just in time. If not for you and the Ji-Hi tribe, and Cheyenne's expert marksmanship, we'd all be dead meat now. Fried dead meat at that! I couldn't have lasted much longer in that heat."

"Yeah," said Willie. "I know what they say about getting a sun tan, but that was ridiculous. I'm already blacker than the ace of spades, but now I'm blacker than black."

The others couldn't help but laugh. Trust Willie to see the funny side.

"You're all severely sunburnt and dehydrated," said Winston. "Just take little sips of water, not gulps, otherwise you'll be sick. The Ji-Hi tribe will take of your burns. The chief said they have this special ointment made from the leaves of a special tree which works wonders for burns."

"Thanks, Winston," said Geigy, "you're not half bad for a crazy Englishman."

"I'll drink to that," said Willie.

"Me, too," said Ebony.

"Drink! Drink! Did someone say drink?" said Geigy. "Forget the water, does anyone have a slug of whiskey?"

And they all broke into laughter.

Chapter Forty-Five

Leaving the others in the capable hands of Ho Goo's wives, Winston grabbed the first-aid kit and dashed back to Cheyenne. "I'm back, Cheyenne," he said breathlessly, holding the first-aid kit aloft. "Let's get you fixed up." But Ho Goo had beaten him to it again, and already one of his wives had dressed and bound the wound. "Thanks, chief, you did it again," said Winston.

"Yes, chief," said Cheyenne. "Thanks for all your help. You and your people really came through for all of us. Thank God, we're all alive."

Ho Goo had told Cheyenne about his friends' release, and how they were being cared for by his other wives "You and your friends saved my son," said the chief, smiling. "And I told you that if you got into any trouble, or fell sick, we would come to your aid. When Winston told us about Python and how he had kidnapped your friends, we dropped everything and rushed to help you. Didn't you hear the drums beating? And all the clapping?"

"So that's what the drums and the clapping were all about," said Cheyenne. "You were summoning all your people. I wondered what they were saying."

"You Westerners have your phones and your internet, we have our drums."

"Amen to that," said Winston with a grin.

Just then, one of Ho Goo's men raced over to him and whispered in his ear. Ho Goo's face darkened and he shook his fist angrily. Winston and Cheyenne looked at him, concerned.

"What's the matter, chief?" asked Cheyenne. "Has something happened to our friends?"

"No, it's that damn Python and his cutthroat friends!" said Ho Goo.

"What happened?" asked Winston. "Have they escaped from the village?"

"No, my men have sealed off the village – there's no way out," he replied, still shaking his fist.

"Then tell us why you are so angry?" asked Cheyenne.

"~~One of~~ my men had to kill two of Python's men," Ho Goo said finally. "We don't like to kill, but this was necessary."

"Why?" asked Winston. "What did they do?"

"They were hiding up in the trees, with their rifles trained on Cheyenne," he said.

"Oh my God," gasped Cheyenne.

"I say, old chap, it looks like Python and the Russian were going to make sure that you lost one way or another," said Winston.

"They are the lowest of the low, with no respect for human life," said Ho Goo. "I intend to have a talk with Python and his cronies." And he stormed off down the village in search of his prey.

Python and the Russian had now joined Ego, and all three were looking down at the dead body of Black Bart. "What the hell went wrong?" asked Python. "Check his holster, Ego."

Ego knelt down and checked the body. The holster was empty. "Look! He got his gun out of the holster," exclaimed Ego, pointing to a silver pistol lying by Black Bart's side.

"Dammit! He didn't do the job like I thought he would," said Python. "I thought he was supposed to be the fastest draw in the West."

The Russian knelt down and examined the body more closely. "Look at that hole in his forehead! It's dead center, right above his nose," he said. "That cowboy is a dead sure shot."

Python looked on in amazement. "And we have one dead body. Only problem is the body is Black Bart's and not the cowboy's," he observed wryly.

"What are we gonna do now, boss?" asked Ego.

Before Python could answer, Ho Goo strode up and confronted him. "What have you to say for yourselves," he said angrily, wagging his finger in front of Python's face.

"What the fuck are you talking about?" said Python.

Ho Goo signaled to his men who were standing nearby. "Men," he called, "bring those two bodies over here."

Four scantily-clad natives, their faces smeared with war paint, carried the bodies of the two dead snipers and lay them down in front of Python. "What the fuck's going on?" ranted Python, his eyes darting from the Russian to Ego and then back to Ho Goo.

"You tell me," said Ho Goo. "Are these your men?"

Python bristled. "I never saw them before in my life," he said indignantly. But his eyes betrayed him. Ho Goo knew he was lying.

"Are you sure about that?" said Ho Goo. "How about your friends, do they know them?"

Python turned to his two loyal sidekicks. "Russian, do you know who these men are?" he asked.

The Russian shook his head. "Niet."

Now it was Ego's turn. "Ego, have you ever seen these men before?" he asked.

"Never, boss. On the grave of my dear departed mother, I swear I ain't ever seen 'em before."

"You heard them, chief," said Python, "and me. We ain't seen 'em before."

"Is that so," said Ho Goo.

"You have our word," said Python, adopting a solemn pious look which looked incongruous on his evil face.

"From what I hear," said Ho Goo, "your word isn't worth very much around here."

"Are you accusing me and my men here of lying, Chief Ho Goo?" said Python.

Ho Goo pointed to the two dead bodies lying at his feet. "These men were perched up in those branches," he said, pointing to a nearby tree, "and they weren't pointing their guns at the birds."

"Is that so?" said Python sarcastically. "Perhaps they were trying to bag themselves an elephant."

Ego and the Russian burst into gales of laughter. "Nice one, boss," said Ego.

Ho Goo did not find their humor funny. "I believe those men were under your orders to shoot Cheyenne if Black Bart failed to do so," said Ho Goo. "Fortunately, we spotted them just in time, and my men killed them before they could fire their guns."

Python continued to maintain his innocence. "Prove it," he said boldly. "As I said before, I have no idea who those men were." Inside, he was quaking with fear. He and his two cohorts knew that with just one word Ho Goo could massacre them and the entire village.

Ho Goo stared intently at the three men. "I want you to know one thing," he said, wagging his finger in front of Python's face. "Cheyenne and his friends are all sacred members of my tribe – the Ji-Hi tribe. Cheyenne saved my son's life, and Winston saved many of my people from certain death." Python nodded but said nothing. Ego and the Russian looked down at their feet.

Ho Goo continued on. "And as members of our sacred tribe, if they should ever be in trouble, or need our help, we will always come to their rescue. ALWAYS!" said Ho Goo, his voice rising.

"Of course, chief," said Python meekly.

"And any enemy of theirs is our enemy," said Ho Goo, locking eyes with Python. "Do you understand me?"

"I understand, chief," replied Python. "We all do, don't we, fellas," he said, looking over at Ego and the Russian.

"Yessir, absolutely," said Ego and the Russian nervously.

"Good," said Ho Goo. "I'm glad that we now understand each other." He knew that Python and his friends were lying, but for the time being he decided not to challenge them. "Okay, I'm going to take you at your word that you did not know that the two snipers were going to shoot my friend Cheyenne."

Python heaved a sigh of relief. Ego whistled through his teeth. And the Russian whispered to himself *Nostravia!*

"And you can thank my English friend, Winston, for my decision," said Ho Goo. "He told me that he wanted no violence, he just wanted his four friends safe. And they had better stay safe, otherwise you will have to answer to me. Do I make myself clear?" he boomed.

"Loud and clear, chief," said Python as Ego and the Russian nodded their heads up and down like clockwork soldiers. They could scarcely believe their luck. The chief was going to leave them in peace. They were home free.

"Remember, should any harm befall my friends, I will be back," warned Ho Goo, shaking his fist.

Holding their breath, the three thugs stood like statues, afraid to move should they anger the big native. Afraid to respond should the big man change his mind. Winston had witnessed the exchange from a distance. He walked over and whispered in Ho Goo's ear. "You do know that they're lying, chief?" he said.

"I know, my friend," he said. "But I am heeding your words - *No Violence*. We will meet these three again, out in the bush one day, and then we will settle the score."

Winston nodded. "You're a wise man, chief."

"We have what we came for," said Ho Goo. "Our friends are safe. Now we can leave in peace."

He raised his hand to summon the rest of the tribe. "Stay safe, my friend," he said, enveloping Winston in his massive arms. "Please tell the others that we have to take our leave. My wives have taken good care of their wounds. They should heal quickly."

Winston smiled. "We are in your debt, chief. How can we ever thank you?"

Ho Goo shook his massive head. "No, my friend, you do not have to thank me. You and your friends are part of our family, part of our sacred tribe. And we will always come to your aid. You owe us nothing," he said, shaking Winston's hand. "And now we must take our leave. Until we meet again, may the great God in the sky hold you all in the palm of his hand." And before Winston could respond, Ho Goo and his tribe had disappeared as quickly as they had arrived.

Winston glared at the three thugs. "You don't know how lucky you are," he said angrily.

"I don't know what you're talking about, Englishman," said Python. With the tribe's swift departure, his cockiness had quickly returned.

"You know exactly what I'm talking about," challenged Winston. "We may have let you off the hook this time, but as God is my witness, this is not over."

"I'm quaking in my boots," said Python, shrugging, his old defiance back on display.

Winston threw him a look of disgust and then turned on his heel and walked away. Shouting over his shoulder, he left the motley trio with these parting words: "Mark my words, Python, this is definitely not over. Someday, somewhere, sometime, we will settle the score."

Chapter Forty-Six

The people sighed in relief as they watched the retreat of Ho Goo and the Ji-Hi tribe. The dust finally settled, and soon they were chattering excitedly about who had won and who had lost.

"Black Bart has lost this gun battle," bellowed Python, the trademark smirk plastered across his ugly face. Now that Ho Goo and his tribe had departed, Python was back in charge with a vengeance. No longer feeling threatened, he had reverted to his bullying, arrogant self.

"All you winners, come up and get your money," he shouted. "And all of you miserable losers, grab some shovels and dig graves for Black Bart and the two snipers."

The winners surged forward to collect their winnings, while the losers looked on dejectedly. They had been convinced that Black Bart would win the gun battle. *A sure bet* most of them had thought.

"Hand me Black Bart's hat and take off his gun belt," ordered Python. One of Python's men quickly obeyed and passed the two items to his boss. Python snatched them greedily. "Damn if it don't fit me perfect," he said as he plunked Black Bart's hat on his head and straightened out the rim. "It's like it was made for me."

Ego and the Russian laughed. "Sure looks good, boss," said Ego.

"Very sharp," agreed the Russian.

Python smiled like a cat that had swallowed the cream and then fastened the gun belt around his waist. "Another perfect fit," he laughed. "Now let's have a bottle of vodka so I can drown my sorrows," he said, turning to Ego and the Russian. "My plan to get rid of that pesky cowboy didn't work. We will have to think of something else."

Meanwhile, at the far end of the village, Cheyenne and the others were discussing their next plan of action. For the time being they knew they were safe. Python and his cronies wouldn't try anything yet, with the threat from Ho Goo hanging over them. The big man had scared them.

"So how are you all feeling?" said Winston, looking around at his injured friends. "It seems that I'm the only one who came through this adventure unscathed."

"Oh, we'll survive," said Cheyenne. "Ho Goo's wives patched us up really well."

"Yeah," piped in Geigy. "I'm not sure what kind of ointment they put on our wounds, but it sure feels good. I can feel myself healing already."

"It must be some kind of miracle drug," said Ebony, "because my burns don't feel so sore anymore."

"Yeah, and that shot of whiskey helped too," said Willie.

"Ain't that the truth," said Geigy. "Pass me the bottle again, Willie, I need another quick slug."

The others laughed. Geigy was his old self again. They had all come through this ordeal with flying colors.

"Now, we have to decide on our next plan of action," said Cheyenne, rubbing his sore leg. "Python and his thugs won't dare to challenge us at the moment."

"Yes, the cowards are too afraid of Ho Goo and his tribe," said Ebony.

"I agree," said Winston, "we are safe for the time being, but we had better get going as quickly as possible. Are you up to traveling?" he asked, looking at each of them in turn.

They all nodded their heads vigorously. "I think that's a resounding yes," laughed Cheyenne.

"Jolly good! Now, Cheyenne, I saw your jeep when I entered the village with the tribe. Do you have any gas in the vehicle?" asked Winston.

"Yes, it should be just about full," replied Cheyenne.

"Excellent, old chap," said Winston. Now, Geigy, do you think you're strong enough to drive Cheyenne's jeep?"

"With another shot of whiskey, I could drive a tank," said Geigy, laughing. "But I sure could use a nice bath and something to eat first."

"Me too," said Ebony.

"And me," said Willie.

Ebony turned to Cheyenne. "Let me take a look at that wound and see how it's doing," she said, unraveling the bandage on his leg. "Thank God, it's just a flesh wound. It seems like I'm always taking care of something connected to your body. It's getting be a habit."

Cheyenne laughed. "A nice habit," he said, locking eyes with her. Ebony blushed.

Winston saved her from any further embarrassment. "Ho Goo thought you might be hungry," he said, "so he left about twenty men to hunt down some food. They are camped right next to a small lake, so you will have food and water and be able to bathe yourselves."

"That's wonderful, Winston," said Ebony. "Ho Goo thought of everything."

"He certainly did," agreed Winston. "Thank God, he is our friend."

"Here's to Ho Goo and the Ji-Hi tribe," said Cheyenne, raising his arm in a salute.

"Hear! Hear!" shouted the others, following his lead. "To Ho Goo and the Ji-Hi tribe!"

Chapter Forty-Seven

"Okay, let's see if this thing starts," said Geigy, climbing into the jeep and plunking down behind the wheel. The others gathered around the vehicle, fingers crossed. Geigy cranked the engine. Nothing. Ebony gasped.

"Don't worry," said Cheyenne, pulling her close. "It never starts on the first try."

"I hope you're right," said Ebony.

Geigy cranked the engine once again, and this time it sputtered into life.

"Told you," said Cheyenne, squeezing her hand.

"There she goes!" cried Geigy, pumping the gas. "Come on, Willie, let's go get that food and water."

"I'm with you, Geigy," said Willie, climbing in alongside him. "Let's go."

Winston smiled and turned to Cheyenne and Ebony. "Okay, you two, I guess you're with me," he said, pointing to his jeep. "Jump in, or should I say, climb in slowly. None of you are well enough to jump yet. Here let me give you a hand."

Once they were settled in his jeep, Winston called over to Geigy. "Follow me, and don't go too fast. Remember, the tribesmen are out there, walking and running, and they're also exhausted."

"Thank God for them," cried Geigy. "They saved our lives."

As they drove out into the bush, they all waved and thanked the brightly painted tribesmen who rewarded them with beaming smiles.

"Now I know what that clapping noise was," Cheyenne said to Winston, eyeing the natives' colored shields.

"What, old chap?"

"It was their weapons clapping on their shields."

"Ah, well spotted, old chap," said Winston, patting Cheyenne on the back.

Suddenly Winston spotted a large familiar figure silhouetted in the hazy distance. He recognized him immediately. No mistaking that huge frame. "Well, I'll go to the foot of our stairs, as they say in my beloved England," said Winston, blinking rapidly. "I don't believe my eyes."

Cheyenne and Ebony turned in their seats to look at him. "What is it, Winston?" said Ebony anxiously. "What's the matter?"

"What do you see, Winston?" asked Cheyenne.

"Do you see that massive figure up ahead, almost blotting out the sun," said Winston, grinning like a Cheshire cat.

Cheyenne and Ebony leaned forward, straining their eyes to see against the gleaming sun.

"Is that who I think it is?" said Cheyenne, slapping his thigh.

"The one and only, old chap."

"Who is it? Please tell me," pleaded Ebony, shielding her eyes from the sun's piercing glare. "I can't see anything in this damn sun; it's too bright."

"It's Ho Goo," said Winston finally. "He must have stayed behind with his contingent of men.

"Ho Goo! Ho Goo!" they shouted as they drew level with the big chief.

"What are you doing here, chief?" asked Winston. "We said our goodbyes a while ago and I thought you had left with the rest of the tribe."

Ho Goo grinned from ear to ear, his dark brown eyes sparkling in the sunlight. "Forgive me, my friends, but I don't trust the evil Python and his henchmen, so I decided to stay close by with a few of my men. Just in case…" he said, winking at them.

But, chief…" began Cheyenne.

Ho Goo raised his hand to stop him mid-sentence. "No buts, my friends, my men and I are here to offer assistance should you need it. Now move over and make room for me in your jeep. My feet are killing me!"

"You got it, chief," said Winston. "Hop in." And they all burst into laughter.

Ho Goo clambered in and plunked himself down next to Winston. "Ah, that's better, I'm not used to walking in the hot sun. Too much exercise for me," he grinned, patting his fat belly.

As they moved slowly through the bush, Ho Goo spotted the binoculars lying on the floorboard.

"Could you show me how to use those things," he said, pointing to the binoculars.

"Of course, chief," said Winston, slowing the jeep to a stop and showing Ho Goo how they worked.

Ho Goo held the binoculars to his eyes and scanned the horizon. "By all the spirits of my dead ancestors!" he exclaimed, "I can't believe how far I can see with these so-called binoculars. Look, there's a water buffalo! And there's a herd of gazelles!" he cried, his chunky body wobbling with excitement. "I feel as if I can reach out and touch them."

The others smiled. They enjoyed watching the chief with his new toy.

Suddenly, Ho Goo held up his hand and cried out, "Stop the jeep!"

"What's the matter, chief?" asked Winston, slamming his foot on the brake. "What do you see?"

Ho Goo passed him the binoculars. "Take a look way over there, by that bunch of trees," he said. "Do you see the two elephants?"

"Yes! Yes!" exclaimed Winston. "I see them. And I'll be damned, it's Monsoon getting ready to breed that female elephant. Take a look, Cheyenne," he said, handing over the binoculars. "Near that bunch of trees."

"You're right, it is Monsoon," said Cheyenne, "and he's heavy in musk."

"Give me those binoculars, I want to see also," said Ebony.

"Oh, my God," she gasped as she focused in on the two elephants. "Monsoon is trying to mount her now. Just look at the size of that thing, it's enormous," she said, shuddering. "Now I can't see it any more."

Cheyenne snatched the binoculars from her. "Give me those binoculars," he said, laughing. "We don't want a minute by minute report on Monsoon having sex with a female elephant. It's perfectly natural."

"Way to go, Monsoon old chap," yelled Winston. "Bloody good show!"

Chapter Forty-Eight

Ebony nestled back into Cheyenne's arms and promptly fell asleep as they moved slowly to their destination. "Wake up, Ebony, we're here," said Cheyenne, pointing to the glistening lake. Ebony rubbed her eyes and stared ahead. "Oh, just look at that heavenly water. "I'm starved to death, but I must take a bath first." And before anyone could respond, she gathered her things and scampered off to a remote spot on the lake. Everyone else headed for the food and water. Several of Ho Goo's men were huddled around a camp fire, roasting pieces of fish and meat.

"That smells delicious," said Winston. "I'm so hungry, I could eat a horse."

"Me, too," said Geigy.

"And me," agreed Willie.

"I am always hungry," said Ho Goo, patting his stomach. "This fat stomach of mine needs a lot of food to fill it up," he chuckled.

Cheyenne lagged behind the others. Although, he, too, was starving, he was worried about Ebony being all by herself.

"Come on, Cheyenne," called Winston over his shoulder. "Aren't you coming to eat, old chap? The food smells scrumptious," he said, wrinkling his nose.

"Yes, come on, Cheyenne," said Geigy, "let's go eat."

Cheyenne shook his head. "I'll catch up with you all in a few minutes. I think I'd better check on Ebony. I don't like the idea of her being all alone in such a remote place. You never know what could happen. I'll keep an eye on her, just in case." And he limped off in her direction. As he neared a small bend in the lake, he heard some splashing. And there was Ebony in all her naked splendor, her lithe bronzed body glistening in the sunshine.

God, how beautiful she is, he thought as he watched her frolicking in the sparkling water. He felt himself grow hard as he watched her bathe one full breast and then the other, trickling the water around her cherry nipples. How he would like to suck off the water right now. *Dear God, I want to take her right now,* he muttered, his erection growing even larger.

Unaware of his presence, Ebony continued bathing her body, singing softly to herself as the water splashed over her tawny frame. Cheyenne stood transfixed, unable to tear his eyes away. She held him in her spell. *If I should die right now, I would die a happy man.* Finally, feeling guilty for being a voyeur, he yelled out her name. "Ebony! Ebony! are you all right out there?"

Startled, Ebony froze like a deer caught in the headlights. "Oh, Cheyenne," she cried, relaxing when she recognized him, "you frightened me. How long have you been standing there? I bet you got quite an eyeful, didn't you, you naughty boy."

Cheyenne blushed and struggled to hide his erection. "Oh, not long," he replied. "I'm sorry for disturbing you, Ebony, but I just wanted to make sure you were safe. This is quite a remote place, and you never know who could be hiding in the bushes."

"Oh, just a few monkeys, I should think, wondering who this strange woman is," she said, smiling. "I'm perfectly all right and the water feels so wonderfully refreshing."

"Yes, you are definitely *all right,*" muttered Cheyenne.

"What did you say?" she called.

"Oh, nothing," he mumbled. "Just admiring the view."

"Yes, I can see that," she said, jutting out her large breasts. "By the way, I hope you came by yourself. I don't want to be the main attraction."

"Yes, I'm all alone. You look so beautiful, I just can't take my eyes off you. I feel as if I'm in a trance. You're like a magical water nymph and I've fallen under your spell."

Ebony laughed heartily and continued splashing around in the water. Then she noticed Cheyenne's erection. "I'm not sure about casting a spell on you, but I do notice that you're definitely glad to see me," she said saucily. Cheyenne blushed and quickly covered his groin.

"Oh don't be shy. I'm very flattered. Why don't you come and join me. We can bathe each other or *whatever*," she said, stressing the last word. *Whatever*.

Cheyenne did not need a second invitation. Dragging his wounded leg, he lumbered over to her and stood at the water's edge. Transfixed. Her beauty literally took his breath away.

"Okay, my randy cowboy," she said, breaking his trance. "Why don't you take your shirt off so that I can bathe you."

Cheyenne stripped off his shirt and stepped into the water. Ebony looked at his leg. "You must have limped all the way here. I know that wound was just a nick, but I don't want to get it wet – it may get infected," she said. "Here let me cool you off," and she dunked her blouse in the water and dabbed it over his face and chest.

"Ah, that feels good," murmured Cheyenne.

"I have something that will make you feel even better," said Ebony coyly. "Why don't you take off your trousers and I'll show you."

"I can't wait," said Cheyenne as he struggled to shed his trousers.

"It's hard getting my pants over this," he said, pointing to his erection.

"Here, let me help you," said Ebony, stroking his groin as she deftly pulled down his trousers. Cheyenne's cock sprang forward, stiff and ramrod straight. "My, oh my, what do we have here," she crooned. "This little fella has a mind of his own. Almost hit me in the face."

"Not so much of the little, if you please," said Cheyenne.

"I'm only teasing, lover," she said, taking his member in her mouth and gently caressing it with her lips. Cheyenne moaned softly. "Tastes good," she purred, licking her lips. "The taste of a strong, healthy lover – my lover."

"Jesus, Ebony," groaned Cheyenne. "I think I'm gonna explode."

"Easy, lover, let's take this nice and slow," she said, running her hot tongue up and down his throbbing cock.

Cheyenne reached down and slid his finger into her wet pussy. Ebony rocked back on her feet and almost lost her balance. "Oh, cowboy," she whispered huskily, "that feels soooo good."

"You feel good," said Cheyenne, his other hand now massaging her breasts.

"Take me, take me now, cowboy," she pleaded. "I can't wait any longer."

"Oh, honey," groaned Cheyenne, lying her down by the lakeside, "I thought you'd never ask."

Ebony spread her legs wide, urging him to enter her. Cheyenne lowered himself over her and with one swift thrust, plunged inside her quivering mound.

"Faster! Harder!" cried Ebony breathlessly. "I want to feel every inch of you."

Cheyenne rammed her harder and harder as she wrapped her legs tightly around his body.

"Oh, Ebony, I just want to keep fucking you forever," he said hoarsely.

"Promise me you will," she said, struggling to hold on.

Moaning in ecstasy, the couple rocked back and forth, both of them lost in the throes of frenzied lovemaking. "I can't hold on much longer. Come with me now!" urged Cheyenne.

"Oh, yes, yes," she cried. Now!" And shouting out each other's name, they soared to a peak, exploding in an exquisite burst of passion. The climax for both was indescribable.

"I feel as if I've died and gone to heaven," said Cheyenne as they sauntered back to the camp later, arm in arm.

"Me, too," said Ebony, looking at him adoringly.

With silly grins plastered across their faces, and the look of love in their eyes, it was obvious to anyone who encountered them that they were hopelessly in love. Obvious to anyone, that is, but their friends, who had not even noticed their absence.

"Just look," said Ebony, indignantly, "they haven't even missed us." She pointed to the others who were huddled around the campfire, gobbling down their food as if there were no tomorrow. "Look at them, Cheyenne, you would think it was their last meal."

Cheyenne laughed and drew her close. "I'd rather have you, any day, than a plate of food," he said, winking. Ebony blushed. "Even if I was dying of starvation, I would rather have you."

"Hush," she said, pushing him away, "they might hear you."

Cheyenne drew her into his embrace again and kissed her softly on the lips.

"I don't care if the whole world hears," said Cheyenne. He was still on cloud nine after their joyful union. "I want to shout it from the hilltops; you are my woman and I love you."

"Oh, Cheyenne, I love you, too," she said, smiling. Her heart literally overflowed with love for this man. Her man. "You are my cowboy, my wonderful, crazy cowboy."

Chapter Forty-Nine

Everyone slept well that night, except for Cheyenne. Plagued by nightmares, he tossed and turned, occasionally calling out in his sleep. Exhausted after their long journey and the bout of passionate lovemaking, Ebony slept soundlessly beside him, unaware of his anguished calls.

Cheyenne dreamt about Wyatt Earp, Billy the Kid and Jesse James. He felt that they now shared a common bond. The gunfight. *But did they share the same thoughts and fears,* he wondered, *when they went up against their next opponent, mano a mano? Did they feel as I felt when I faced Black Bart? Did they say to themselves, 'Will I see my friends again?' 'Will this be my last day on Earth?' 'Is he faster than me?' Then if they were victorious, as he proved to be against Black Bart, did they worry about the man's family and friends left behind? Would Black Bart's friends and family come after him? Would they hunt him down? Would he always be looking over his shoulder? In the street? In a restaurant? A saloon bar?In the bush? In the jungle? By the mountain? Would he never be safe? Would they harm Ebony? His precious love?*

"No! No! No!" he cried out. "No! No! No!"

Ebony shot up. "Cheyenne! Cheyenne!" she called, shaking him gently. "Wake up, you're having a nightmare."

Cheyenne bolted upright, his body drenched in sweat. "What happened?" he said, rubbing a hand through his wet, tangled hair. "Are you okay?"

"Of course, I'm okay, silly. Why wouldn't I be?" she said, touching his face. "You just had a nightmare."

"Oh, it seemed so real."

"What was it about?"

"Oh, nothing really. I can't remember much about it now," he lied.

"Well, whatever it was, it certainly scared the life out of you. Thank God, it was only a dream."

"Yes, only a dream," he said. And then under his breath, "I hope…"

After a hearty breakfast, they broke camp and decided to head back to Ho Goo's village with Ho Goo and his tribesmen.

"Your wounds need time to heal," said Ho Goo. "Why not come back to the village with me and my men. My village is your village. My people are your people. We will take good care of you. You are part of our family now."

"Sounds good to me," said Geigy, thinking of the woman he had left behind.

"Me, too," said Willie, thinking the same thought.

Winston nudged Cheyenne, who was still thinking about his dream. "What do you think, old chap?" he said. "Should we take the chief up on his offer?"

Before he could respond, Ebony piped in. "Oh yes, that sounds wonderful, doesn't it, Cheyenne? Rest and relaxation and plenty of quality time together," she said, tickling him in the ribs.

"What? Yeah, whatever the rest of you decide is fine by me," he replied, sounding distracted. He couldn't stop thinking about the ancient gunfighters and his duel with Black Bart. He had just shot a man, and even though it was fair fight, he somehow felt responsible. *It was him or me. I had no choice,* he thought, still trying to convince himself.

"Are you okay, old chap?" asked Winston, noticing the distant look on Cheyenne's face. "You look as if you're far away."

"What? Oh yes, I'm fine, thanks," replied Cheyenne. "My leg's just bothering me, that's all."

"No need to be sorry, old chap. You took a bullet for all of us," said Winston, patting him on the back.

"I was lucky it was just a flesh wound," said Cheyenne. *It could have been my heart.*

Two days later, the weary travelers finally reached the Ji-Hi village.

"Now that's a sight for sore eyes," remarked Geigy, pointing to all the villagers who had come out to greet them with open arms.

"I think they're glad to see us," said Ebony, returning their waves.

"Of course, they are," said Hoo Goo proudly. "You are all part of our tribe now."

"Thank you, chief," said Cheyenne humbly. He was truly moved by the rapturous welcome. "If not for you and your people we probably wouldn't be here now."

"We are even now," said Ho Goo. "And should you ever need our help again, we will be there for you. Now, let us celebrate your return with a huge feast."

The villagers cheered wildly. "A feast! A feast!" they shouted.

"But first we must wash off the dust," said Ho Goo, turning to his fellow travelers. "After two days in the bush, we smell to high heaven!"

"I'll drink to that," said Geigy, turning to Willie and laughing. "First a wash, and then we find our women!"

Chapter Fifty

For the next two weeks, the five friends took full advantage of Ho Goo's hospitality. Rested and relaxed, their burns and wounds tended to by the local women, they slowly began to heal, body and soul. Python had subjected them to a vicious kind of cruelty and it would take a while for them to forget their ordeal.

Cheyenne continued to fight his demons. He had killed a man, but he was slowly coming to terms with his actions. He had had no choice. And when he looked over at his cherished friends, he knew he had made the right decision. He had done what he had to do to save them.

He and Ebony spent their days taking long walks in the jungle, frolicking in the lake, and making passionate love at night. It was apparent to everyone that they were hopelessly, helplessly, in love, and becoming more so with each passing day.

As for Winston, Geigy and Willie, they had reunited with their women and passed their days in a state of blissful contentment. This is just what they all needed right now. A chance to recuperate, refresh and regroup before they hit the road again.

"Ah, this is the life," Winston would say daily.

"I'll drink to that, old chap," Geigy would reply, mimicking his friend.

And Willie would offer his familiar rejoinder, "Me too!"

Cheyenne had not used his guns since his encounter with Black Bart. His trusty pistols were a constant reminder of that fateful day – a day he was not eager to relive. But the tribespeople had other ideas. They were eager to see the cowboy in action, to witness his superior marksmanship and rapid fire speed. And so, he finally caved in to their gentle urgings. After all, he and his friends were living in their village, being waited on hand and foot. How could he disappoint them? If they wanted a show, he would give them one. And what a show it was! They could not believe his speed, his accuracy. He hit every single target, never missing once.

"I never even saw him draw his gun," said one villager in disbelief.

"He's faster than the speed of light," said another.

"How fast is the speed of light?" asked another.

"I dunno," came the reply. "I just heard Dr. Gift say it one day."

"The cowboy is amazing."

"What a show!"

On that they could all agree. The cowboy was the fastest draw they had ever seen. And here he was in their little village, deep in the heart of Africa!

The five friends would often visit Goo and his big friend Kia.

"I can't believe how attached I've gotten to that big friendly elephant," Cheyenne told his friends. "I watch them every day."

"Goo looks so small riding on Kia's massive back," said Ebony, laughing.

"You can see how much Kia loves Goo," piped in Winston. "Goo could do practically anything and Kia would love it. They have such a strong bond. I bet that elephant would give his life to save Goo should the need arise."

"I read in a book that elephants are extremely intelligent and they can hear certain noises from miles away," Geigy told them.

"Yes," agreed Cheyenne, nodding his head vigorously. He considered himself an authority on his beloved elephants, and became animated when talking about them. "They are highly intelligent, due to their large brain. And they can communicate over long distances by sending and receiving low frequency sounds." His eyes shone as he continued on. "The sound is felt by the sensitive skin of an elephant's trunk and feet, which pick up vibrations through the ground." The others looked at him in amazement. Cheyenne didn't miss a beat. "They keep in contact with each other using these calls which are too low for us humans to hear," he continued. "The calls are even able to travel through thick vegetation."

"How do you know all that?" asked Ebony, her mouth wide open in astonishment.

"I know practically everything about the elephants," said Cheyenne proudly. "I have read dozens of books about them, and my father taught me many things. As you all know, they are my favorite animals."

"I'm impressed, old chap," said Winston.

"Me too," added Geigy. "I've read a few things, but not to that extent."

"Carry on, Cheyenne," urged Willie. "I never had much schooling, never cared for much teaching, but this is interesting."

Cheyenne continued. He was on a roll now. "Remember when we saw Monsoon mating with that female elephant?"

They nodded.

"I won't forget that in a hurry," laughed Ebony, blushing.

"Well, when the female is ready to mate, which can happen anytime during the year," said Cheyenne. "She starts sending out infrasounds – sort of growling sounds - that attract the males, sometimes from many miles away."

"Monsoon must have heard that female growling," said Willie.

"Yes," said Cheyenne, "and other adult males probably heard her too. Monsoon probably fought off her other *suitors,* probably injured a few and broke a few tusks. It's a case of *the best man* winning, so to speak."

The others laughed.

"To the victor go the spoils," said Winston.

"Exactly," said Cheyenne. "The animal world isn't that different from the human world. Boy meets girl, boy fights over girl, boy gets girl."

"Winner takes it all," said Geigy.

Cheyenne nodded his head. "Yes, and the female accepts the victor by rubbing her body against his."

"Just like us women," laughed Ebony as she pretended to rub her body against Cheyenne's.

"Later, Ebony," said Cheyenne with a wink.

"Then what happens, Cheyenne?" asked Willie, hanging on to Cheyenne's every word. "What happens after they rub bodies?"

"What do you think?" said Geigy

"Well, they mate, and then both go their own way," said Cheyenne.

"Just like us humans," said Geigy.

"Exactly so," said Winston.

"Huh, Huh," said Ebony indignantly. "Sometimes the male sticks around, isn't that so, Cowboy?" she said, playfully digging him in the ribs.

Cheyenne smiled at her. "Yes, honey."

"Does the female always get pregnant?" asked Winston.

"Usually," replied Cheyenne. "And after 22 months, the female gives birth to a calf."

"Twenty-two months!" exclaimed Ebony. "That's almost two years. I'd hate to be pregnant for two years. Nine months is bad enough."

"Yes, the elephant's pregnancy is the longest among mammals," said Cheyenne. "The baby calf feeds on the mother's milk until the age of five, but also eats solid food when it's about 6 months old. And just a few days after the birth, the calf can follow the herd by foot."

The others stood there in astonishment, amazed at Cheyenne's vast wealth of knowledge on the elephant.

"And to think we thought you were just a greenhorn cowboy from Wyoming," said Geigy.

"You certainly know your stuff, old boy," said Winston, patting him on the back.

"You never cease to amaze me, Cowboy," said Ebony, loving him even more. "I don't know what to say."

"Me neither," said Willie. "I've lived here all my life, surrounded by elephants, and I never knew that about them. I have definitely learnt something today."

"We all have," said Winston.

"I'll drink to that," said Geigy.

"Me, too!" said Willie. And they all burst into laughter.

As the laughter subsided, Cheyenne looked over at Kia and his eyes filled with sadness.

"I will do everything in my power to save them from extinction," he said softly. "Kia was just a little calf when he lost his mother to poachers. Fortunately, he didn't have any tusks, otherwise he would have been killed too."

His friends nodded in agreement, but said nothing.

"How could anyone harm such gentle creatures?" he said, letting the question hang in the air. Then heaving a huge sigh, he continued. "Because of their huge size, they have no natural enemies other than man. But the calves, especially the newborn, are vulnerable to lion and crocodile attacks." He sighed again and clenched his fists in a tight ball. "Yes, man is their major enemy. And if no protective measures are taken, my beloved elephants will soon be extinct," he said, shaking his head sadly.

"We must keep fighting to save them," said the others in unison.

Cheyenne looked at each of them in turn, his eyes filling with tears. "Yes, my dear friends, we must." He looked over at Kia and Goo who were romping happily around the big grassy savannah. Boy and animal joined as one, without a care in the world. It was a sight to behold.

"Kia would give his life for Goo," he said simply. "And I would give my life for Kia. Until my dying day, I will fight to save my beloved elephants."

Chapter Fifty-One

For several minutes, the friends stood in silence watching the boy and his best friend frolicking in the dusty African bush. From time to time, Kia would raise his trunk and gently caress the small boy. Goo would squeal in delight. "Oh, that tickles," he cried, patting Kia's tough hide.

"Look!" said Cheyenne, pointing toward the carefree pair, "Goo is teaching Kia how to stand on his back legs."

The big elephant stood tall, and looked around proudly as if to say: 'Look how smart I am.'

"Look how tall Kia is, standing on his back legs," said Ebony. "He almost blocks out the sun."

"Not quite, Ebony," said Cheyenne, laughing. "He's big, but not as big as that."

As they were about to walk over to greet Goo and Kia, loud shouting and cries off in the distance stopped them in their tracks.

"What the hell is all that commotion?" asked Willie. "Sounds as if it's coming from the village."

"Well, old chap, there's only one way to find out," said Winston, taking charge. "Let's go!"

The five friends turned and headed back to the village, with Goo and Kia bringing up the rear.

"I wonder what's going on," said Ebony, clutching Cheyenne's arm.

"We'll soon find out," said Cheyenne as they approached the village. The villagers were standing in a circle, looking at something on the ground.

"Excuse us. Pardon us," said the five friends as they pushed their way through the crowd.

"Look!" Willie cried as they reached the opening. "It's a pygmy and he looks like he's dead."

The others crowded around, straining their necks to see above the milling throng. Ho Goo stood over the pygmy and held up his hand. "Stand clear," he boomed, "give him some air."

"What happened here, chief?" asked Winston, staring down at the fallen man.

"He came staggering into the village and then he fell to the ground," replied Ho Goo.

Winston bent down and felt the little man's pulse. "He's still alive! Quickly, fetch some water."

Two jagged scars ran down either side of the man's face from forehead to chin and an ivory bone pierced his squat nose. He was naked, except for a simple loincloth, his feet bare. Dust and grime covered his leathery body, and his dark curly hair hung in matted tangles around his face.

"Initiation scars," said Ho Goo, pointing to the deep grooves. "Probably etched into his face when he reached manhood. The ivory bone too," he remarked.

"Ouch! That must have hurt," said Geigy.

"A lot of the pygmy tribes do that," said Willie. "That is when a boy becomes a man. The bones and the scars are a sign of his reaching manhood."

"I think I'd prefer to stay as a boy," said Geigy. "Don't think I could handle someone sticking a bone through my nose, and cutting grooves into my face."

"Me neither," said Willie.

"How come Ego doesn't have any scars or bone a sticking through his nose?" asked Geigy.

"He never became a man," said Willie simply.

Ebony and Cheyenne bent down to help Winston. "Is he going to be okay?" asked Ebony.

"I don't know," said Winston, turning to one of the native women. "Let me have that water."

The woman smiled timidly and handed him a large jug of water. "I'm going to give him a few sips of water until he comes around," said Winston, tilting the man's head forward.

"He seemed to be very frightened about something," said Ho Goo. "Scared to death almost."

Ebony gently dabbed the pygmy's forehead and chest with the cold water. "He's so tiny," she observed. "No more than four and a half feet at the most."

Winston continued giving him small sips of water and eventually the little man's eyelids fluttered open. He coughed a few times, spitting out the water.

"Look! He's coming around," said Winston.

The pygmy looked around with terror-filled eyes, thrashing his head back and forth.

"It's okay, little fellow," soothed Winston. Don't be afraid. You're among friends."

The pygmy began to scream and yell in a strange language.

"I don't think he understands you, Winston," said Cheyenne. "And we certainly don't understand him." He turned to Ho Goo. "Have you any idea what he's saying, chief?"

"No," said Ho Goo, shaking his big head. "There are many pygmy tribes in the rainforest and each of them has their own individual language.

"Well, something has really shaken him up," said Cheyenne. "Just look at his wild bloodshot eyes. The poor little guy is absolutely petrified."

"Let me give him some more water," said Ebony. "It might settle him down." Whispering to him in gentle, soothing tones, she continued dabbing water on his face and body. The little man finally relaxed.

"You're a regular Florence Nightingale," said Winston.

"Who's Florence Nightingale," asked Geigy, puzzled.

"Oh, a very famous nurse who lived in England in the 1800s. Her patients used to call her the Lady with the Lamp," said Winston. "Ebony here seems to have the same magical touch."

"Oh, don't exaggerate, Winston, I'm no Florence Nightingale," she said. "I'm just trying to make him feel more comfortable."

"Well, whatever you're doing, it's working," said Cheyenne.

Just then, the crowd parted and Goo and Kia came into view. The pygmy turned his head to see what was happening. His eyes bulged. Terror-stricken, he waved his arms furiously and pointed at the small boy and his elephant. "Agh! Agh!" he cried, practically gagging on his words.

"I think he's afraid of Kia," said Winston.

"Why?" asked Cheyenne. "That gentle creature wouldn't hurt a fly."

"His village may have been set up right in the middle of the path where the elephants have been traveling for hundreds of years on their quest for water."

"Yes, I read about that," said Cheyenne. "So you do know a bit about the habits of elephants."

"Just a little, old chap," said Winston.

"Or the elephants may have been targeted by poachers and in their rush to get away, they may have trampled the village," said Cheyenne.

"Yes, that's a possibility, too," said Winston. "I wish we could understand what the little man is trying to say."

Ho Goo turned to his son. "Goo, take Kia away, so the pygmy cannot see him," he ordered.

"Yes, Father," said Goo meekly. "We will return to the savannah. Come on, Kia, let's go."

On Goo's command, the big elephant backed up and turned around. Raising his trunk, he trumpeted loudly, flapped his large ears and then lumbered off toward the grasslands.

"Look! The pygmy's coming around again," said Ebony as she offered him another sip of water.

"He probably hasn't had water for several days," remarked Winston. "He looks as if he's dehydrated."

"I think he's getting stronger with every sip," said Ebony.

"And he doesn't have those wild-looking eyes anymore," said Cheyenne.

The little man struggled to get to his feet.

"Stay down. Stay down," Ebony told him. "You're too weak to stand yet."

"I don't think he understands you, Ebony," said Cheyenne.

"Yes, he does," she replied. "Look, he's lying back down. And now he's smiling. He must realize that we're trying to help him."

The pygmy was indeed smiling broadly, revealing a crooked gap-toothed grin. His two front teeth were missing. Once again, he tried to stand up.

"Let's help him to stand up, Winston," said Cheyenne. "He's still weak, but I think he'll be okay."

Between them, they lifted the pygmy to his feet and held on to him as he tried to walk. After a few tottery steps, he managed to keep his balance and was soon able to walk without assistance. Pleased with this accomplishment, he flashed his crooked smile, then knelt down and started drawing pictures in the dirt with his finger.

"What's he doing?" asked Geigy.

"Well, he doesn't speak our language, and we don't understand him," said Willie, "so he's talking to us through his pictures."

The group studied the pygmy's drawings carefully. At first, they couldn't make any sense of them and then suddenly Cheyenne's face lit up. He had recognized the rough sketch.

Look!" he exclaimed, pointing to the pygmy's rough sketch. "That's the big mountain where the cave is. Don't you recognize it?"

"Yes, yes, I see it now, old chap," said Winston. "But the pygmy is pointing way over on the other side of the mountain."

Cheyenne was about to respond when he heard a loud ringing.

"What's that noise?" asked Ebony.

"It's the phone ringing in the jeep," he replied. "It must be Jocko. Let me see what he wants."

Pushing his way through the crowd, he strode over to the jeep and grabbed the phone. Sure enough, it was Jocko. "Hi, Jocko, what's going on? We haven't heard from you for a while."

"I'm glad you're still alive, Cowboy," replied Jocko. "I heard about your shoot out with that so-called Black Bart."

Cheyenne shivered. He was still struggling to shake off the demons. "Yes, I was just a mite faster than he was, but he did hit me in the leg."

"I hope it wasn't too serious."

"Nah, just a flesh wound. It's all healed up now."

"How's the rest of your group?" asked Jocko.

"Everyone is fine. Thanks for asking."

"Listen, Cheyenne, the reason I'm calling is to ask you to check on a village that got hit by a herd of stampeding elephants. They need your help."

"You got it," replied Cheyenne.

"One of my men will meet you halfway with some medical supplies that were ordered by a Dr. Gift. The doctor's out at the village now."

"We'll be glad to help," said Cheyenne.

"Thanks, Cheyenne. I knew I could count on you and your friends. I just hope you can find this place. The tribe moved from their regular village, because they were being threatened by another tribe who wanted to make them their slaves.

"That's terrible," said Cheyenne, shocked at the thought of slavery in this day and age.

"Yes," agreed Jocko. "The tribe has been living in fear for many years. They are a friendly tribe of pygmies who just want to be left in peace. I hope you can help them. Make sure that no one takes advantage of them. They have enough problems."

"You got it, Jocko. We'll leave first thing in the morning," said Cheyenne. "As it happens, a pygmy came stumbling into Ho Goo's village today, and I think he may be from that village. Hopefully, he can help us find his home."

"That's great, Cheyenne. I hope he can help," said Jocko. "One more thing, my man is going to meet you with the medical supplies at your campsite by the mountain. He'll be there tomorrow, about sunset."

"Okay, Jocko, we'll be there."

"Good luck!"

"Thanks, Jocko. Goodbye."

Cheyenne walked back to the group, who were still studying the pygmy's sketches.

"Who was on the phone?" asked Ebony. "Was it Jocko?"

"Yes, he wants us to check on a pygmy village," and he proceeded to tell them what had happened.

"So, this little guy here must be from that village," said Geigy.

"I think so," said Cheyenne. "I just hope he will be well enough to travel."

"He seems much stronger now," said Winston.

The pygmy looked up from his drawings and grinned at them.

"He doesn't really understand us, but he knows that we're talking about him," said Cheyenne. "I hope he'll be able to lead us to his village. Dr. Gift is waiting for those medical supplies."

"When are you leaving?" asked Ho Goo.

"First thing in the morning," replied Cheyenne. "We have to meet Jocko's man at sunset."

"I will make sure that you have enough food and water for your journey. And my wives will look after the pygmy until it's time for you to leave."

Cheyenne shook his hand warmly. "Thank you, Ho Goo. I don't know what we'd do without you."

"You are all part of our family now," said Ho Goo. "And we will do everything we can to help you."

"Thanks, Ho Goo, we're going to miss you," he replied.

"Oh, I think our paths are going to cross again very soon," said Ho Goo, smiling.

Cheyenne returned his smile. "I hope so. Well, I guess we'd better start packing now. We have a long journey ahead of us."

Chapter Fifty-Two

They awoke the next morning to a curtain of fog, which shrouded the entire village.

"Okay, guys," said Cheyenne, nudging his sleeping companions, "let's hit the road."

Although the weather was gray and dismal, their spirits were high, and after a hearty breakfast they gathered at the edge of the village to say goodbye. Practically every villager had come to bid them farewell. They called out greetings and waved enthusiastically.

"Goodbye – hurry back soon."

"Take care of yourselves."

"Our village is your village."

"Safe journey."

"Watch out for the bad people."

"Don't step on any snakes."

Ho Goo and his son embraced the five friends as the pygmy looked on. "May the Great Spirit in the sky guide you and watch over you, my friends," said Ho Goo solemnly. "And don't forget, if you should ever need our help, we are right here."

"Thank you, Ho Goo," said Cheyenne, returning his embrace. "You are a true friend. You have already come to our aid once; I hope we don't have to call on you again."

Ho Goo raised his right arm. "Go in peace and return to us in one piece," he said, winking.

The friends chuckled, while the pygmy looked at them all in amazement. He had no idea what they were talking about, or why they had all suddenly burst into laughter. But the laughter was contagious, and soon he was laughing along with them.

"Bravo, little man," said Winston. "It's good to see you smile after all you've been through."

The pygmy nodded as if he understood. Still laughing, they piled into the two vehicles and pulled away from the village. Cheyenne, driving the Rover, led the way, with Ebony seated beside him, and Winston and the pygmy in the backseat. Geigy and Willie followed in the jeep.

"Goodbye," they shouted to Hoo Goo and the assembled villagers. "Thanks for everything."

They trundled down the potholed trail and were soon swallowed by the twirls of swirling mist.

They rode in silence for several miles, cautiously maneuvering their way through the tentacles of dense fog. Cheyenne glanced up at the sky and spotted a faint glimmer of sunlight.

"Look! The sun is coming up. It will burn up this goddamn fog. I can hardly see a darn thing."

"I know what you mean, old chap, it's a bloody pea-souper, as they say in dear old Blighty."

"What's a pea-souper?" asked Ebony, "and what the heck is Blighty?"

"Blighty refers to dear old England," replied Winston with a smile, "and a pea-souper is thick fog. You knew that, didn't you, little man?" he said, nudging the pygmy.

The little man grinned crookedly and nodded his head up and down. He had no idea what Winston was talking about, but he liked to smile.

"Well, pea-souper or no pea-souper," said Cheyenne, "I don't want to keep Jocko's man waiting. We have to get those medical supplies to the village as soon as possible."

The sun's piercing rays gradually cut a swath through the blanket of mist and soon the friends were racing toward their destination. They made up the lost time, but Jocko's man had beaten them to it. Cheyenne screeched to a halt and jumped out of the Rover to greet him.

"I'm Cheyenne," he said, holding out his hand. "Nice to meet you."

"Likewise," said the man, returning a hearty shake. "I'm Jimmy." His shaven head gleamed in the midday sun as his dark eyes darted back and forth from Cheyenne to the other four strangers. Cheyenne made the introductions.

"Nice to meet y'all," said Jimmy, bowing his head slightly.

"How long have you been here, Jimmy?" asked Cheyenne. "I hope we haven't kept you waiting too long. That darn fog was a killer."

Jimmy smiled, flashing his pearly white teeth. "No problem. I've only been here about ten minutes or so. Just got out to stretch and limber up my legs some." He pointed to several boxes perched on the dusty ground. "Here are the supplies that Jocko promised."

"Thanks, Jimmy, we'll take good care of them," said Cheyenne.

"Dr. Gift needs them ASAP," said Jimmy.

"We'll be taking off first thing in the morning," said Cheyenne. "Hopefully, the pygmy here will be able to lead us to his village."

Jimmy nodded. "I sure hope so."

"Winston, you've forged a bond with the little man. See if you can figure out what he is saying, so we can find his village," said Cheyenne.

"I'll do my best, old chap," said Winston, turning to his little friend. "Come on, little chap, let's sit down and have something to eat and drink."

The little man smiled and followed Winston to the nearby brush. The Englishman had gained his trust, even though he couldn't understand a word Winston was saying.

"Just look at the two of them," smiled Cheyenne. "Bosom buddies."

"Yes," laughed Ebony. "Little and large."

"Or the odd couple," sniggered Geigy.

"Well, odd or not, they're communicating," said Cheyenne, "and that's the main thing." He turned to Geigy and Willie. "Could you guys put the medical supplies in your jeep."

"Sure thing, Cheyenne," said Geigy. "Come on, Willie, let's do it."

The two men hefted the boxes into the back of the jeep, and then Geigy wandered over to Cheyenne and tapped him on the shoulder. "Could I have a word with you?"

"Sure thing, Geigy. What's up?"

Geigy rubbed his chin. "Well, I was thinking about the dynamite we have hidden. It just might come in handy."

Cheyenne threw him a puzzled look and then the penny dropped. "Good thinking, Geigy. You're absolutely right." Geigy beamed. "It may be a while before we come back here," Cheyenne continued. "And you never know, we just might need it with Python and his men roaming around."

"Yeah, that Python gives snakes a bad name," said Geigy.

"That's funny, Geigy," laughed Cheyenne.

Geigy nodded. "I'm known for a joke or two," he quipped. "We have room in the jeep. Let's load it up, Cheyenne."

The next morning at the crack of dawn, they were packed and ready to roll. Winston had now spent many hours with the pygmy, and between them they had established a rudimentary form of communication: hand signals, nods and blinks. Hopefully, it would be enough to get them to their destination.

"Jimmy, it's been a pleasure meeting you," said Cheyenne, extending his hand. "Say hello to Jocko for me."

"Will do," said Jimmy. "Goodbye and good luck."

"Thanks, Jimmy, something tells me we're gonna need it," Cheyenne replied as he jumped into the Range Rover. The others were seated and ready to go. "Okay, gang, let's hit the road," he said, pumping the gas. "Bye, Jimmy, take care of yourself." Waving goodbye, Cheyenne and his friends took off in one direction, Jimmy in another.

"Well, our little man is looking much better," observed Cheyenne, looking at the pygmy through his rearview mirror.

"That he is, old chap," said Winston, patting the little man on the back. "I think I'm going to give him a name. Any ideas?"

"How about Noddy," said Cheyenne, "as he keeps nodding his head up and down when you talk to him."

"Perfect, old chap," said Winston. "Noddy it is. What do you think, little chap…er, Noddy?"

The pygmy smiled and nodded his head vigorously. "Noddy, Noddy," he said in broken English.

"He seems to understand," said Ebony, smiling.

"Yes," agreed Winston, "and I think he likes his new name. Thanks for suggesting it, old chap."

"You're welcome," said Cheyenne.

Noddy grinned widely, pleased with his new name. Feeling comfortable with his newfound friends, he relaxed back in his seat knowing he was in safe hands.

"Does he understand that we are looking for his village?" asked Ebony.

"Yes, I think so," said Winston. "We've become quite close over the last few days, and I think I've been getting through to him."

"Well, time will tell," said Cheyenne. "Try and ask him if we're going in the right direction."

"Okay, I'll give it a go," said Winston, and through a series of nods and hand gestures, he somehow managed to get the message across.

The *newly-christened* Noddy nodded his head again and pointed to his left. "Ayou! Ayou!," he said excitedly.

"What's he saying? He seems to be getting very excited?" said Ebony.

"I've no idea," said Winston, "but he's pointing over there to his left. Look! the ground is all padded down."

"It's an elephant trail," said Cheyenne. "This must lead to his village."

Noddy bobbed his head up and down and flashed his gap-toothed smile.

"Yes, that's right, he understands us," said Winston. "All we have to do is follow the trail."

Winston patted the little man on his back. "Thank you, Noddy."

"Ayou! Ayou! said Noddy, beaming brightly.

They followed the worn down trail for several hours, but there was still no sign of the village.

"How much longer?" complained Ebony. "We've been following this trail for about three hours. Do you think Noddy is leading us on a wild goose chase?"

Noddy sat up in his seat and frowned as if he knew what she was saying. Then he turned once again and pointed to his left.

"Look! the trail is curving off to the left," said Cheyenne. "And I can see trees and brush ahead."

"I think we are on the right trail," said Winston, smiling at Noddy. "Good chap, Noddy."

Ebony turned in her seat and faced Noddy. "Sorry I doubted you, Noddy." Noddy grinned and gently touched her hand. "I think he understands," she said.

"Yes, in his own way, he does," said Winston.

"I'm going to take it a little easy," said Cheyenne as he drove the Range Rover deeper into the thick brush. Geigy and Willie slowly followed in the jeep. As they approached the rise of a small hill, Noddy jumped up and down in his seat, waving his hands furiously.

"I think we're close," said Winston.

"You think so," said Ebony facetiously.

Sure enough, cresting the hill, they looked down to see the devastated village spread out before them in the valley below. Ebony gasped in horror. "Look at the damage that herd of elephants did to the village," she said, pointing. "They trampled right through the center of it."

"Yes," agreed Cheyenne, shaking his head, "it looks like a cyclone hit it smack in the belly."

"Most of the huts have been destroyed," said Winston sadly. He turned to Noddy who was scrambling to get out of the Rover. "Hold on, little fellow, where are you going?" He tried to grab hold of the pygmy's arm, but Noddy had already jumped out of the vehicle and was racing toward his village. "Stop! Watch you don't run him over, old chap," cried Winston as Cheyenne quickly slammed his foot on the brake.

"He must be anxious to get back to his family and friends," said Ebony.

"Poor little guy. Come on, let's go and assess the damage and get these supplies to Dr. Gift," said Cheyenne.

"I just hope we're in time," said Winston.

Chapter Fifty-Three

As they approached the village, they were spotted by several children who raced toward them, shouting excitedly and waving their hands in greeting. Noddy had already alerted his tribe to the strangers' arrival, and was now surrounded by his family and friends. Cheyenne and Geigy drew to a halt and the five friends jumped out of the vehicles.

"Now, that's what I call a hearty welcome," said Geigy, surveying the cheering children.

"Yes, they are definitely pleased to see us," said Cheyenne, smiling at the sea of dark faces.

A tall lean man with a silver beard and flowing white hair emerged from a large hut in the center of the village and walked toward the waiting group. Noddy followed behind.

"My name is Dr. Gift," said the bearded man, extending his hand in greeting. "Thank God, you are here. Picu here has told me all about you." The doctor smiled down at the little man.

So that's his real name, thought Cheyenne *Picu. Noddy suits him much better.* He stepped forward and introduced himself and his friends. "It's a pleasure to meet you, Doctor," he said, shaking the doctor's hand. "My friends and I are here to help in any way we can. We have the medical supplies from Jocko here in the jeep."

"Thank God," said Dr. Gift. "Now we must hurry – time is of the essence." He waved to some of the pygmies who had gathered around the group and ordered them to unload the medical supplies. Geigy and Willie rushed forward and helped them with the heavy boxes.

"Excellent," muttered the doctor as he rummaged through the boxes. "Penicillin, chloroform, antiseptic, bandages, etc. Yes, yes, everything is here. Quickly, bring everything into the hut."

Once again, Geigy and Willie rushed forward to help, along with Cheyenne and Winston.

"I'm sorry for being so rude," said the doctor, "but I have a patient who has to have one of his legs amputated, otherwise he will die."

"Oh, my God," gasped Ebony.

"Do any of you have any medical experience?" asked Dr. Gift, looking at each of them in turn.

"I do," said Geigy, raising his hand. "I'm an ex-Marine and I've helped out in such situations."

"Excellent! Please come with me," said the good doctor.

As they walked toward the large hut, a woman's voice rang out from inside. "Father! Father! Please hurry! I don't want the gangrene to spread any further."

As Dr. Gift and Geigy hurried into the hut, Picu walked over to Cheyenne and grabbed him gently by the hand. "What is it, Noddy, I mean, Picu?" he asked, looking down at the little man.

"I think he wants us to follow him," said Winston. "We'll have to get used to calling him Picu now. I still prefer Noddy – suits him better." The others nodded in agreement.

As Picu led them through the shattered village, the other pygmies stood in silence, shyly watching them. Compared to them, the four strangers looked like giants. Ebony waved at the silent villagers who returned her greeting with nods and shy smiles.

"Well, at least they seem friendly," whispered Ebony. "They're just shy. Not used to strangers, especially big strangers like us. Just look, not one of them is over four feet."

"Yep, they're all the size of Ego, and Picu here," said Cheyenne.

Standing as tall as his small size would allow, Picu led them to a hastily dug burial site at the far end of the village.

"Oh, no, he's taking us to the graves of the pygmies who must have gotten trampled by that herd of wild elephants," said Cheyenne.

Winston surveyed the burial site. "I count ten graves. Let's say a prayer for these poor departed souls and for the pygmy who is having his leg amputated." They bowed their heads.

"Okay, let's head back," said Cheyenne.

Retracing their steps through the village, they spotted Geigy and Dr. Gift standing outside the big hut. "The operation must be over," said Ebony. "I hope that everything went well."

"We'll soon find out," said Cheyenne as they approached the hut. "How are his chances, Dr. Gift? Will he live?"

The doctor rubbed the sweat from his forehead with a white cloth. "Well, thanks to those medical supplies, he has a fifty-fifty chance of pulling through," replied the doctor with a wan smile. "I'm pretty sure that we got all the gangrene."

"That's good," said Ebony.

"I gave him some penicillin," continued the doctor, "and something to stop the bleeding. He's in good hands with my daughter Tara, whom you will all be meeting soon." Still wiping his brow, he turned to Geigy. "I have some other patients to look after. Would you care to join me, Geigy? You provided invaluable assistance with my last patient. In fact, I don't think we could have managed without you."

Geigy beamed. "By all means, Doc," he replied. "Lead the way."

As the two men walked away from the group, they heard Geigy's whispered aside to the doctor. "Now, Doc, are you telling me that you have a couple cases of whiskey for your patients?"

"Yes, that's right. You heard me correctly, Geigy."

"Leave it to Geigy to ferret out the whiskey," said Cheyenne, laughing.

"I'll drink to that," said Winston. "Nothing wrong with a good healthy shot of whiskey."

Cheyenne surveyed the damaged village. "Look! they are starting to rebuild their huts. Let's give them a hand."

They walked over to the villagers who were busy gathering tree branches, brush and leaves.

"Let's check out one of the huts and see how they do this," said Cheyenne.

"I used to live in a similar kind of hut not too long ago," Willie told them. "They're made of tree limbs and branches and tied together to make them strong. Then on top, they put these big frondlike palms." Willie thought for a second. "I can't think of the name right now, but they stop the rain from coming in," he explained.

"They seem to have a very effective system," said Winston, admiring the tribe's speed and efficiency in re-erecting their damaged homes. "So in a few days, I expect the village will be back to normal."

"Yes, these huts have been built like this for generations," said Willie proudly, "all the way back to our ancient ancestors, hundreds of years ago."

"Wow, that's amazing," said Ebony.

"The huts are called 'mongulu' and they are usually built by the women," said Willie.

"But the men are helping to build them now," observed Ebony.

"Yes, because this is an emergency," said Willie. "The village was practically ruined. On a normal day, the men would usually be out hunting for food."

"What do they hunt for?" asked Geigy.

"Monkey, antelope, crocodile, and pangolin, among other things."

"What on earth is a pangolin?" asked Ebony.

"It's like a lizard covered with horny scales," said Willie.

"Agh!" said Ebony, wrinkling her nose.

"Actually, it's very tasty," said Willie, smiling.

"What weapons do they use to hunt these animals," asked Cheyenne. "They don't have guns, do they?"

Willie shook his head. "No, I guess most of them have never even seen a gun. They hunt with bows and poisoned arrows, crossbows and spears. They also use traps."

"I guess if they don't hunt, they don't eat," said Winston.

"That's right," said Willie. "The women and children also help by gathering fruit and berries and catching fish."

"Hunters, gatherers and builders – I like that," said Cheyenne.

"Talking of builders, let's go and ~~go and~~ give them a hand," said Winston.

The group of friends tried to help as much as they could, but they seemed to be more of a hindrance than a help.

"Thank you so much for trying to help, but just like myself, you are getting in the way more than helping," a soft voice told them.

They turned around to face a striking young woman of medium height, with flowing red hair and piercing blue eyes. The sunlight danced and glinted in her fiery hair, throwing off a halo of burnished gold.

"Hello, I'm Tara, the daughter of Dr. Gift."

Chapter Fifty-Four

For a few moments, they stood like statues, hypnotized by the sudden appearance of this golden specter. Winston was the first to break the spell. "It's a pleasure to meet you, Tara," he said with a small bow. "My name is Winston."

Cheyenne was the next to step forward. He held out his hand. "Nice to meet you, Tara. I'm Cheyenne."

She shook his hand and then stepped back to look at him. "So, you're the one they call *The Cowboy*," she said, batting her eyelids flirtatiously. "*The Hands of Lightning.*"

Before Cheyenne could respond, Ebony had planted herself firmly between Tara and *her man.* "I'm Ebony," she said defiantly, throwing Tara a stony glare, "and this here is Willie. It's a pleasure to make your acquaintance."

The look that passed between the two women was unmistakable. *Hands off! He's mine!* Tara had received Ebony's message loud and clear. Cheyenne was off-limits. Tara shrugged it off and threw her a dazzling smile. "The pleasure is all mine," she said, although her eyes said otherwise.

Winston now thrust himself forward in an attempt to diffuse a potentially volatile situation. It was obvious to the three men that the two women had taken an instant dislike to each other. Taking Tara's hand in his, he said politely, "We are all happy to meet you, my dear lady."

"Likewise, my dear sir," replied Tara. "I am happy to meet *all* of you," she said, stressing the word *all* and staring directly at Ebony. "Now, please come with me, I have some tea heating on the fire, if you would care to join me."

They followed her back to the big hut and sat down by the fire.

"Excuse me for just a second," said Tara, disappearing into the hut, "I have to check on my patient. Please help yourself to the tea." She was back within minutes.

"How is he?" asked Cheyenne.

"Poor man, I understand that his leg was amputated just below the knee," said Ebony, squeezing Cheyenne's hand.

"He'll be fine in a few days," Tara told them. "My father will fashion a leg for him out of a tree branch, and he'll soon be up and walking again as best he can. The pygmies here are very resilient. Over the years, they have survived many hardships, but they always come through smiling. Just look at them now, their village was practically destroyed, many were killed and injured, but here they are picking up the pieces and starting again." She waved her hand in the direction of the pygmies who were busily rebuilding their homes. "They don't ask for much," she continued. "Food, water and a safe, warm home for themselves and their children. Material things matter little to them. They live very simply."

"In some ways, I envy them," said Cheyenne. "There are some in this world who would do well to take a leaf out of their book."

"Well said, old chap," said Winston. "I couldn't agree more."

"I think I was happiest when I lived simply in my hut," said Willie. "Now I seem to be caught up in the material world." Shaking his head sadly, he stared into the fire.

Ebony patted his hand. "It happens to most of us, Willie," she said softly. "The material world entices us and suddenly we're trapped on the treadmill. There's no going back to the simple life."

"Wisely spoken, Ebony," said Winston.

"You never cease to amaze me, Ebony," said Cheyenne, drawing her close.

Even Tara was impressed.

As the profundity of Ebony's words sunk in, they all sat in silence for several minutes, staring into the fire. Tara was the first to speak. "Forgive me, I haven't thanked you yet for bringing those medical supplies. Without them, my patient in there" – she pointed toward the hut – "would be with the rest of them at the burial site."

"It's lucky that we were in this area, or others may have died," said Cheyenne.

"God must have answered our prayers. We are thankful to all of you," she said as she poured hot tea into round wooden bowls and passed them around. "And I don't know what my father and I would have done without Geigy's help. His assistance was invaluable."

The others nodded. "Here's to Geigy," they said, raising their cups in a toast.

"Talk of the devil, here he comes now," said Cheyenne.

"Who's taking my name in vain?" asked Geigy as he and Dr. Gift approached the group.

"We were just toasting your health, old chap," said Winston.

"Yes, it was a toast to your expert medical skills, Geigy," said Tara. "My father and I couldn't have performed the operation without you. Isn't that so, Father?"

"Absolutely," said the doctor, patting Geigy on the back. "We've just been treating the injured, and Geigy here has been my right-hand man."

"So here's to you, Geigy," said Cheyenne, once again raising his cup.

The others followed suit. "To Geigy," they said.

Honored by the toast, but slightly embarrassed by all the attention, Geigy looked at their wooden bowls. "Well, if you're gonna toast me, I wish you'd do it with something stronger than tea! A good shot of whiskey would have been more appropriate, don't you think?" he said. And they all burst out laughing.

"I see you have met my daughter Tara," said Dr. Gift as the laughter subsided.

"Yes, we have, and she's a wonderful hostess," said Winston, holding up his bowl of tea.

"Yes, she is," agreed Cheyenne as Ebony nudged him in the ribs.

Tara smiled. "Father, Geigy, please join us," she said, making room for them around the fire. "Here, have a bowl of tea."

"Thank you, my dear. Tea is just what the doctor ordered," he said with a wink.

"Thanks," said Geigy, taking the proffered bowl. "But I could still use a shot of whiskey."

Dr. Gift sipped his tea and sighed. "Ah, that tastes good."

"Wish I could say the same," muttered Geigy.

"What's that, Geigy?" asked the doctor. "My hearing is not what it used to be."

"Aw, nothing, Doc, just thinking out loud," replied Geigy.

"Well, let me tell you all, the natives are preparing a special supper to say thanks for bringing the medical supplies."

"They don't have to do that," said Cheyenne. "We were happy to help."

"They are a very proud people," said Dr. Gift, "and it is their way of expressing their gratitude. They are very friendly and accommodating, but don't take that for granted," warned the doctor. "They value trust and loyalty above all else, and will die fighting for their families and fellow tribesmen."

"Worthy attributes," said Winston. "We have been observing them for the last few hours and have seen the close bond of brotherhood…and sisterhood," he added, looking at Ebony and Tara. "It's truly admirable."

"Yes, it is," said the doctor as the others nodded in agreement. He looked down at his watch. "And now, it's getting late. Tara, would you show our guests to their hut."

"Of course, Father," she replied as she stood up. "Please follow me. I will ask the natives to bring you some water so you can wash up before supper."

Tara led the way to another large hut nearby. "This should be big enough to accommodate all of you," she said. "My father and I will join you after you have bathed and eaten your supper."

"Thank you, Tara," said Cheyenne.

"You're very kind," said Winston.

"Tell your father not to forget that bottle of whiskey he promised me," Geigy blurted out.

Tara smiled at him. "My father is a man of his word. He keeps all of his promises, so I'm sure he will not forget. Enjoy your supper." And turning on her heel, she left.

"Tara and her father sure are wonderful people," said Cheyenne. "Tending to all the villagers and trying to keep them healthy."

The others agreed. And even Ebony had to grudgingly admit that this was true. "Just so long as you don't think she's too wonderful!" she whispered in Cheyenne's ear.

Chapter Fifty-Five

After they had bathed and eaten supper, they grabbed a couple of blankets from the jeep and settled down to wait for Dr. Gift and Tara.

"Perfect timing," said Winston as a knock sounded on the door. Jumping to his feet, he opened the door and welcomed in the two guests. "Come in! Come in!" he said, ushering them inside. "Doctor, Tara, we are delighted to have you as our guests. Please make yourselves at home."

"Thank you, my friends," said Dr. Gift settling down on the thick woolen blanket. "It's nice and cozy in here."

Tara was carrying a tray of wooden cups, which she set down before them. "See, I told you that my father always keeps a promise," she said, looking directly at Geigy. And with a flourish, Dr. Gift produced a large bottle of whiskey from inside his jacket pocket and held it aloft.

"The finest Johnnie Walker Black," he said with a grin.

Geigy's face lit up like a Christmas tree. He looked like a little kid in a candy store. "Superb! Superb!" he exclaimed, grinning from ear to ear.

"You look like the cat that just swallowed the cream," said Winston, laughing.

"I don't know about swallowing cream," said Geigy as he started handing out the wooden cups, "but I'll be swallowing some of this Johnnie Walker finest soon!"

"Good old Geigy," said Willie, punching him lightly.

"Now, does everyone have a cup?" said Geigy. "Let's get to it."

"Allow me to do the honors," said Dr. Gift as he filled each cup with three fingers of whiskey.

"Now raise your glasses, or in this case, your cups," he told them. "Here's to Africa and its people and to all the magnificent wildlife and wonders that it possesses."

"To Africa," they cried in unison.

"May I have just one more for Africa?" asked Geigy, smacking his lips. "That tasted mighty good."

"Of course, you may, my good friend," replied Dr. Gift, reaching over and filling Geigy's cup.

Geigy grinned in delight. "It looks like it's gonna be a fun night," he said, downing the drink in one.

As the evening wore on, Cheyenne decided to broach the subject of his father. Taking the doctor aside, he said, "Dr. Gift, I didn't want to bother you with this until you had taken care of your patients, but now I'd like to ask you: do you remember my father?"

"Your father?" said the doctor, looking puzzled.

"Yes. His name was Robert Cole. He told me to look you up if I ever came to Africa."

"Robert Cole!" exclaimed Dr. Gift. "Yes, yes, of course I remember him. He would read about elephants and Africa all the time."

Cheyenne nodded. "He loved the elephants," he said sadly.

"So Robert Cole is your father. The last I heard he was in the sales business and then I heard no more."

"Was," said Cheyenne. "He died last year."

"I'm sorry to hear that, son," said Dr. Gift, gently patting Cheyenne's shoulder. "He was a good man."

"He was the best," said Cheyenne. "Simply the best."

"Yes, he was," agreed the doctor. "I lost touch with him and then I joined the Peace Corps. That's when I met my beautiful Tamara, Tara's mother." The doctor stared off in the distance, temporarily lost in the past. A look of intense sadness creased his face.

"May I ask what happened to her?" said Cheyenne, jolting the doctor back to the present.

"She was killed by a swarm of African bees," he replied. "Hundreds of them attacked her with their stings. She didn't stand a chance." Tears filled his eyes and he reached for Tara's hand. "Tara was just a little girl."

"I remember her well, Father," she said tenderly. "And I have her flaming red hair and blue eyes."

"Yes, you do, my dear," replied the doctor. "As long as there's a Tara, there'll always be a Tamara. She lives on in you, my dear girl."

"And in you, Father," she whispered.

Wiping away his tears, the doctor turned once more to Cheyenne. "What happened to your father?" he asked.

"He had a sudden heart attack."

"I'm sorry to hear that. He was a fine man," said the doctor. "And your mother? Is she still alive?"

Cheyenne shook his head. "No, she died from a stroke six months later. Guess she couldn't live without my dad."

"Well, at least they are together now," said Tara, offering what she hoped were words of comfort.

"Yes, I guess they are," said Cheyenne. "I never thought of it that way before."

"Okay, okay, that's enough of the doom and gloom," said Geigy, who had been half-listening to their conversation. "This is supposed to be a party. Let's have another shot of whiskey."

"You're absolutely right, Geigy, my friend. Let's forget about the past and talk about things that are happening right now," said Dr. Gift as he poured another drink.

"I'll drink to that, Doc," said Geigy, holding out his cup.

Relaxed and happy, they passed the bottle back and forth, exchanging stories and enjoying one another's company.

"Dr. Gift, I've been meaning to ask you," said Ebony, "the food that the natives prepared for us was delicious. I have no idea what we were eating. Could you tell us what it was?" She was remembering what Willie had told them earlier.

Dr. Gift smiled. "Of course, my dear, although I'm not sure you will like what I'm about to tell you."

"How so?" she asked, looking puzzled.

"Well, my dear, the meat you were eating was monkey and crocodile. Fresh from the jungle today."

Ebony gagged. "Did you say monkey?" she asked in alarm. "And crocodile?"

"Yes, one hundred percent monkey, and crocodile. But didn't you say you enjoyed it?"

"Yes, but…," began Ebony.

"Well, then, my dear, that's the main thing, you enjoyed it," he said, patting her on the arm.

"I did tell you, Ebony," said Willie.

"Yes, I know, but I didn't realize that we would be eating it."

"Best meat I've tasted in ages," slurred Geigy, feeling no pain. He was several slugs ahead of the rest of them.

"The berries and fruit were picked fresh from the forest," added the doctor. "Surely you enjoyed the bananas and the honey?"

"Hmm, yes," said Ebony, but she was still thinking about the monkey and crocodile meat.

Cheyenne decided to change the subject. "Did anyone get a good look at the elephant that was leading the rampage," he asked Dr. Gift.

The doctor rubbed his chin. "Yes, many of the pygmies said he was extremely large – one of the biggest elephants they had ever seen – with a jagged scar running along the side of his head."

"Monsoon!" they all cried in unison.

"Who is Monsoon?" asked Tara.

"It's a long story," piped in Winston. "We crossed paths with Monsoon some time ago, and I'm responsible for the scar alongside his head. It was all my fault." And for the next hour he proceeded to tell Tara and her father all about their first encounter with Monsoon. "I still feel guilty about that scar," he finished. "An elephant never forgets."

"Enough of that," cried Geigy. "We're sliding back into the past again. Pass the bottle, it's time for another drink."

"Rightio, old chap," said Winston. "Sorry to be sounding so melancholy."

"Oh darn it," complained Geigy, "I think we just squeezed out the last drop. You don't happen to have another bottle, do you, Doc?"

Dr. Gift grinned. "As a matter of fact, I do," said the doctor, producing yet another bottle from his jacket like a magician.

"Doc, you are a scholar and gentleman," said Winston.

"I'll drink to that," said Geigy, chuckling. "Pass the bottle, Winnie, old chap."

"You're going to have one heck of a hangover in the morning, Geigy," said Cheyenne.

"Not to worry," said Geigy, taking a healthy slug. "The doc here will fix me up."

This time it was Tara's turn to change the subject. "At the last village my father and I visited, the natives were talking about a shoot-out between two Americans, because most Africans love the Old West and its gunslingers. Do you happen to know anything about that?" she asked.

Cheyenne frowned and rubbed his head. He wasn't sure how to answer her question. "Well, I guess you could say I was one of the gunslingers, but it wasn't how you think," he said. "I had to kill a man whom I idolized to save the lives of my friends here. He gave me no choice."

Tara stared at him transfixed. "Oh, my goodness," she said finally. "How terrible!"

Ebony reached over and gave Cheyenne a gentle kiss on the cheek. "Geigy, Willie and I would all be dead now if Cheyenne, Winston and Ho Goo hadn't come to our rescue," she said softly.

"Well, it sounds as if you've had quite an adventure," said Tara.

"It certainly does," agreed her father. "Thank God, you are all safe now."

Tara turned to Cheyenne. "I hope you don't think I'm being presumptuous, but my father and I would love to witness your shooting skills," she said. "And I'm sure the natives would, too. Could you possibly give us a demonstration tomorrow?"

"Well...," began Cheyenne, "I...

"Sure he can," interrupted Geigy, waving the whiskey bottle back and forth. "He'll put on a show for the whole village."

Cheyenne laughed and pointed at Geigy. "By the way, I'd like you all to meet my promoter."

"That's me," said Geigy, and promptly passed out.

Chapter Fifty-Six

The next day, as promised, Cheyenne strapped on his silver pistols and showed off his shooting skills. Many of the natives had never seen a gun before, let alone a real live cowboy. They pressed forward, chattering excitedly, and eager for the show to begin. For a few precious moments, they could forget about the despair and the destruction of their village.

A very hung-over Geigy presided over the spectacle, designating himself master of ceremonies as he called out for silence. "And now, my friends, you are about to witness the marksmanship of a man who has no equal; a man who is faster on draw than any other. I give you, ladies and gentlemen and children, Cheyenne Cole, otherwise known as the *Hands of Lightning*, the *Cowboy*, the fastest draw in the West."

The natives clapped and cheered, even though they had no idea what Geigy was talking about. What they did know was that something special was about to take place - something they would be talking about, around their campfires, for years to come.

Cheyenne stepped forward. Tipping his hat to the crowd, he bowed slightly to Dr. Gift and Tara, who were standing in the front row, and smiled at his waiting audience. "Okay, Willie," he called, "I'm ready."

Far off in the distance, Willie stood by a line of targets, planted firmly in the sand, and on several tree branches. "Okay, Cowboy," shouted Willie, "they're all yours. Just let me get out of the way first." Willie scrambled to the side, making sure he was well out of the line of fire.

Geigy took command once more. Although his head was beating like a drum, he managed to rise to the occasion. Banging two large stones together, which caused his head to throb even more, he called out, "On the count of three, let the games begin. One…two…three…"

Before the words were out of Geigy's mouth, Cheyenne had drawn his guns, faster than the speed of light, and destroyed every single target in the blink of an eye. The natives couldn't believe their own eyes. Dr. Gift and Tara stood wide-eyed, their mouths open in amazement. Cheyenne, the *Cowboy*, truly was the *Hands of Lightning*. They had all witnessed his marksmanship firsthand and would surely be talking about this day forevermore.

Dr. Gift stepped forward and shook Cheyenne's hand. "My God, Cheyenne, if I hadn't witnessed it with my own eyes, I would have never believed it. You are faster than the speed of light, and aptly named the *Hands of Lightning*."

"Thank you, Doctor," he said humbly. "I guess I'm just good at shooting, the way you are good at medicine."

"Well, that's one way of looking at it, son," replied Dr. Gift, patting him on the shoulder.

Now it was Tara's turn. She was practically speechless after witnessing such a show. "I don't know what to say," she began. "I thought the natives must have been exaggerating when they talked about this cowboy whom they called the *Hands of Lightning*, but now I know it to be true. That was truly amazing, Cheyenne, and I feel honored to have witnessed it."

Cheyenne shrugged. "All in a day's work," he said modestly. "I can shoot well, but you and your father perform miracles – you save lives, you look after the poor and the weak and the injured and that is far more important than shooting at sitting targets."

"Well, today, you gave these poor villagers the thrill of their lives. You took their minds off their sad plight, at least for a little while, and they'll be talking about this day for a long, long time," said Dr. Gift. "Now let's take a sip of whiskey to celebrate," he said.

"I'll drink to that," said Geigy, coming up behind them.

Several days later, the village was still abuzz about the *Hands of Lightning*. The natives huddled together practicing make-believe draws. The story of the cowboy from the American West would be passed from generation to generation.

The group of friends busied themselves, helping the natives to rebuild and repair their village, and soon they were experts at fashioning the wooden huts. During a well-earned break, Cheyenne's phone rang as they relaxed in the shade. It was Jocko.

"Hi, Jocko, what's up?" asked Cheyenne into the phone.

"There are reports that other villages have been attacked by this crazy bunch of elephants," he said "And they have to be stopped. The last I heard they were headed for Kilimanjaro."

"Kilimanjaro! But that's over two thousand miles way miles away in Tanzania."

"Yeah, I know, but Kilimanjaro has a high elephant population and they may be wanting to join up with more elephants. I want you to try and intercept them before they leave the Congo."

"We'll do our best," replied Cheyenne.

"You always do," said Jocko. "Did you find out if Monsoon was leading the rampage?"

"Yes, it was definitely Monsoon," replied Cheyenne. "Several witnesses described him to a T, including the trademark scar running alongside his massive head."

Jocko sighed into the phone. "Cheyenne, Monsoon has to be stopped. You must intercept the elephants before they leave the Congo, and you must destroy Monsoon."

"We're on our way, Jocko," replied Cheyenne without hesitation.

"Thanks, Cowboy, I knew I could count on you. Take care of yourselves, and be on the lookout for poachers – they've been killing dozens of elephants in that area," said Jocko.

"Will do, Jocko. Bye," he said, clicking off the phone.

The others looked at him expectantly. "Well, Cowboy, what's our next mission?" said Geigy. "We heard you talking about Kilimanjaro and Monsoon."

"Yeah, Jocko thinks Monsoon and the elephants may be heading for Kilimanjaro, to join with other elephants. He wants us to intercept them before they leave the country."

"And what about Monsoon?" asked Winston.

"We have to destroy him."

"But we can't kill him, Cheyenne," said Ebony, grabbing him by the arm. "Ho Goo told us that Monsoon had to be protected for saving his son. We can't destroy him. We just can't."

Cheyenne patted her hand. "I know, Ebony, but Monsoon is killing too many people and demolishing too many villages. Look around you," he said, pointing to the ruined huts, "he and his herd practically destroyed this village and ten natives were killed in the stampede. He has to be stopped."

Ebony nodded her head sadly and then she said in a soft whisper, "I think it will bring us bad luck if we kill him."

Chapter Fifty-Seven

The next morning they arose at dawn, and were soon packed and ready to go. Dr. Gift and Tara, accompanied by Picu and several other natives, stood by patiently waiting to bid them farewell. "It was our pleasure having you here. We will surely miss you. Thank you so much for all you have done for the village. Without those medical supplies, many more lives would have been lost," said the doctor. "I wish you Godspeed and pray that you will come back and visit us."

Tara stepped forward, the early morning mist silhouetting her flaming red hair. "As my father just said, words can't express how much we appreciate your help. It was a pleasure meeting all of you. It's not often that we get a chance to talk to people who speak English. My father and I enjoyed conversing with you all over a couple of bottles of whiskey," she said, winking at Geigy. "Take care of yourselves – you have a dangerous mission ahead. May God watch over you."

And with that, she and the doctor hugged everyone in turn and wished them luck.

Now it was Picu's turn. Although to them, he would always be Noddy. Tears glistened in his dark eyes as he looked up at them and smiled.

"Goodbye, little chap," said Winston, hugging him close. They were an unlikely couple, the tall pale Englishman and the short dark pygmy, but over time, they had forged a strong bond and now it was time to say goodbye.

Picu responded with a series of hand gestures that only Winston could understand.

"He wishes us good luck and Godspeed," said Winston. "Says he will miss us. Says that we saved his life and he will never forget us."

In turn, the friends stepped forward and said their goodbyes to Picu. Winston had not realized how hard it would be for him to say goodbye. Crouching down, he faced the little man and looked into his eyes. The tears now streamed down Picu's face as Winston struggled to keep his stiff upper lip. "Take care of yourself, little man. I will always hold a place for you in my heart," he said, touching his heart.

"Heart, heart," mouthed Picu in broken English, also touching his heart.

"Time to go," said Winston, wiping away the tears. Turning, he jumped into the nearby Rover, and with a final farewell wave, they disappeared down the trail in a cloud of dust.

"We have to take it a little easy until the mist clears," said Cheyenne as they rounded a sharp bend. "I almost missed that turn in the road."

"The sun will soon burn it off," said Winston who was sitting in the back seat. He was still thinking about Picu. "I miss Noddy…I mean, Picu – I got used to him sitting beside me."

"I'm glad we were able to deliver him safely back to his family," said Ebony.

"Wonder if I'll ever see him again," mused Winston.

"Hey, you never know," said Cheyenne.

The two vehicles wriggled their way down the trail, the occupants watching for any sign of elephants.

"How can we tell if we're on the right trail?" asked Ebony.

"Well, this trail leads toward the Congo, so if the elephants are heading for Kilimanjaro, they have to cross the Congo. Hopefully, we'll be able to intercept them before they reach the border," said Cheyenne. "Keep your eyes peeled for elephant tracks."

"You got it, old chap," said Winston.

On they traveled, stopping only to eat and refresh themselves at one of the many watering holes along the way. At nightfall, they set up camp by a small stream and by dawn the next day, they were back out on the road again. So far, they had seen neither hide nor hair of a single elephant.

"I do hope we're following the right trail, old chap?" said Winston. "Strange, don't you think that we haven't seen a single elephant?"

"Well, they do have a head start on us," said Cheyenne. "Remember, we stayed several days at the village. "My gut tells me that we're going in the right direction."

"And my gut tells me that I'm hungry," said Winston.

"Let's pull over here and have some lunch," laughed Ebony as she pointed to a cluster of nearby trees. "Those trees should provide some welcome shade."

"Good idea," said Cheyenne as he slowed the vehicle to a stop and signaled to Geigy.

As they relaxed in the shade, enjoying a light lunch of bread, cheese and berries, Ebony leaned over and touched Geigy on the arm. "Is that dynamite safe riding with you and Willie?"

Geigy seemed taken aback by her question. "Well, you would have to light the fuse with a match to make it explode, and we're not about to strike any matches. Don't worry, Ebony, the dynamite is perfectly safe."

"Okay, Geigy, if you say so," she said, although she still looked doubtful.

"Why are you suddenly so worried about the dynamite, honey?" asked Cheyenne.

"Well, I just thought that because the roads are so bumpy, it might cause a spark to jump from the exhaust and ignite the dynamite."

Cheyenne roared with laughter. "Not gonna happen, honey. So quit worrying. Okay?"

"Okay," she said, but she still wasn't convinced.

Back out on the trail, they continued to clock up the miles. Still no sign of the elephants. And then Ebony spotted something in the distance. "Hey, look, over there!" she cried, pointing off to her right. "See where all the brush is trampled down. You know that expression, *it looks like a herd of wild elephants has trampled through here.* Well, that's exactly what's happened here."

Cheyenne slowed the Rover to a stop, and held up his hand. Geigy stopped the jeep behind him.

"Let's take a look," said Winston, leaping out of the Rover to inspect the tracks.

"What do you see, Winston?" asked Cheyenne, bending down beside him.

"They look fresh, say about two hours ago," said Winston, prodding the dusty indentations.

"So they are not too far ahead," piped in Ebony.

Cheyenne hustled back to the Rover. "Let's keep on going while the light is still good," he said, turning around and signaling to Geigy and Willie. "Are you ready to hit the road again, guys?"

"Ready when you are, Cowboy," shouted Geigy. "Let's hit it."

Cheyenne fired up the engine again. "Okay, let's move out."

They followed the tracks until the sun slowly sank below the horizon, leaving a blaze of color across the inky sky.

"Let's get up as high as we can so that we can watch the valley below," said Cheyenne. "Maybe we'll spot Monsoon and finish our dirty deed before night falls."

Ebony shuddered. "I still don't like going against Ho Goo's word."

"What do you mean?" asked Cheyenne.

"That Monsoon is just like one of us," she replied.

Cheyenne stared off into the distance and said nothing.

Fate had brought him to this wild untamed country and fate would bring him face to face with Monsoon once again. Of that he was certain.

Chapter Fifty-Eight

They spent the night on a high ridge overlooking the valley below but saw nothing of Monsoon and his herd. Cheyenne lay awake whilst the others slept, gazing at the starry heavens. A myriad thoughts ran through his head denying him much needed sleep: his beloved father's dying wish, the circus of his boyhood, the sad fate of dear Nellie the elephant, his deadly shoot-out with Black Bart, the fights with the nefarious Python and his evil cronies, his first meeting with Ho Goo and the Ji-Hi tribe, and last but not least, his first encounter with Monsoon. By the time his eyelids fluttered to a close, the first fingers of dawn were drawing back night's black curtain to reveal a cloudless blue sky.

Cheyenne yawned and struggled to his feet. *I feel as if I could sleep for a week.* "Come on sleepyheads, it's time to hit the road again," he shouted to his sleeping friends.

One by one, they emerged from their sleeping bags rubbing the sleep from their eyes and squinting against the sun's glare. Ebony stared at Cheyenne and grimaced. "You look terrible, honey," she said softly. "Couldn't you sleep?"

Cheyenne shook his head. "Nah, too many thoughts racing through my head. I guess I won't rest properly until our mission is accomplished. But don't worry, I feel fine. Nothing a good strong cup of coffee won't cure." He smiled down at her. "You, on the other hand, my sweet," he said, ruffling her hair, "slept like a log. I could hear you snoring gently beside me."

Ebony slapped his hand away. "I do not snore," she said indignantly. But her twinkling eyes said otherwise. "Well, maybe just a little when I'm very tired."

Cheyenne kissed her lightly on the cheek. "I'm only teasing. Come on, let's get a fire started and make some breakfast. I sure could use that cup of coffee now," he said, laughing.

Several cups of coffee later they were all ready to hit the trail again. Cheyenne turned to Winston and Willie. "Could you take the two pairs of binoculars and check out the valley below," he asked them. "If we're lucky, maybe you'll spot Monsoon."

Willie and Winston nodded and hurried off to find the binoculars. A few minutes later, they were both perched against the edge of the ridge, scanning the distant horizon.

"I see a herd of elephants," cried Willie. "About twenty of them with several baby elephants."

"What about Monsoon?" asked Cheyenne. "Do you see him?"

Willie shook his head. "No sign of Monsoon."

"Keep watching and let me know what you see."

"We are taking turns watching so that our eyes don't start seeing things," said Winston. He raised the binoculars to his face and swiveled from side to side. "I can see a huge cloud of dust in the distance. It must be another herd of elephants," he said, lowering the binoculars.

"Just let me know if you see Monsoon," said Cheyenne.

Ebony came up behind and slipped her arm around his waist. "Cheyenne, I don't think you could shoot Monsoon, even if you did see him," she whispered.

Caught off guard, Cheyenne turned and stared at her. "What, are you a mind-reader now?"

Ebony smiled. "No, but I do know that you love elephants too much to shoot one of them, even that crazy Monsoon."

"Well, you might be right, but there again, you might be wrong. I'm just hoping that we never see Monsoon and I will not have to make the choice."

"I know it's bothering you," said Ebony, kissing him softly on the cheek.

"Yes, it is," he muttered almost inaudibly as he stared off into the distance, lost in thought.

Winston's excited cries snapped him back to reality. "Cheyenne! Come here quickly, old chap."

"What is it?" asked Cheyenne, running over to him.

Winston lowered the binoculars again. "I don't think I'm looking at a herd of elephants. It looks like some kind of convoy."

"Willie, let me have your binoculars so I can see what Winston's talking about," said Cheyenne.

Willie passed over the binoculars and Cheyenne raised them to his eyes.

"Take a look at that little dust cloud over to the left, down in the valley below," said Winston. "Is that a convoy or what?"

"Yes, yes, I see it now. You're right, Winston, it's a convoy of jeeps and two big trucks."

Geigy grabbed the binoculars from Cheyenne and scanned the valley in a sweeping arc.

"What do you make of it, Geigy?" asked Cheyenne.

"Well, there are two jeeps in front and two big diesel trucks pulling a heavy load," he said, still studying the valley below. "In fact, the diesel trucks are in heavy stress pulling these two heavy objects." He paused and then scanned the area again. "Behind the two diesel trucks there are two military trucks loaded with soldiers, and they don't look too friendly."

On hearing this, Cheyenne immediately took charge. "Okay, everybody, get behind the camouflaged vehicles," he ordered. "We don't want them to see us. For all we know they may have already spotted us."

As they huddled behind the vehicles, Ebony said, "Cheyenne, I think I recognized somebody in that first jeep. Hand me that rifle."

"Easy, easy, Ebony," soothed Cheyenne. "What's wrong with you? Are you trying to get us all killed," he said, wresting the rifle from her grasp.

"Give that to me," she yelled, struggling to grab the rifle again. "It's that goddamn filthy Russian and some of his comrades. I want to blow his head off for all he put us through."

"Easy, baby. Let me take a look." Cheyenne zeroed in on the convoy and let out a huge sigh.

"I'll be damned," he gasped. "It is the Russian and two of his military comrades."

"How do you know they are his military comrades, old chap?" asked Winston.

"Well, they're wearing Russian uniforms and insignia."

"Didn't know you were an authority on Russian military uniforms," said Geigy with a laugh. "I'm impressed."

"Yeah, I've always been a bit of a history buff," said Cheyenne. "Especially military history. And those guys are wearing the old Soviet Union uniforms."

"So much for end of the Cold War," observed Winston wryly.

"Well, Cold War or no Cold War, I want to blow his goddamn head off," cried Ebony, still struggling to grab the rifle. "He's up to no good."

"Relax, baby," said Cheyenne, folding her in his arms. "We will take care of this. Just let us live through the day."

Ebony relaxed in his embrace. "Well, since you put it that way, I'll let the Russian live one more day. But only one," she warned, wagging her finger.

Cheyenne laughed. "Okay, okay, I hear ya."

Geigy was still scanning the convoy. "The big trucks are coming into view now, but I can't make out what they are hauling."

Cheyenne patted him on the shoulder. "Geigy, I know, being a Marine, that you have seen many military convoys, so tell me what they have on those flatbeds?"

Geigy nodded, his binoculars still focused on the moving convoy. "Let them move up a little further and maybe I can tell you." The shape of the object finally came into Geigy's sight and he let out a huge gasp. "Oh, no! Dear God, no, it can't be! This must be a dream," he cried as he dropped the binoculars and fell to his knees trembling.

Winston rushed over to him. "Steady on, Geigy old chap," he soothed.

"It must be a dream. It must be a dream," muttered Geigy, still trembling.

"It's no dream, Geigy," barked Cheyenne. "What the hell is it?"

"Relax, Cheyenne," said Winston. "You can see the chap's in shock. Let me handle this."

"Sorry," said Cheyenne. "I don't know what came over me."

Winston turned to Geigy and patted his trembling shoulder. "What is it, old chap? What's got you in such a state? You're trembling from head to toe. Whatever it is, it can't be that bad."

"Oh yes, it is," said Geigy, pulling himself together.

"What?" said the others in unison. "What is it?"

Geigy stared at them long and hard. *"Missiles. They're carrying two long range nuclear missiles!"*

Chapter Fifty-Nine

Geigy's words were met with a stunned silence. Finally, Cheyenne found his voice.

"Missiles?" he said, almost choking on the word. "Did you say *missiles*?"

"Yes," croaked Geigy. "You heard me loud and clear. Long range nuclear missiles – two of 'em." He paused to wipe the spittle from his mouth. "And that's not the worst of it?"

"What do you mean, old chap?" said Winston.

Fear glinted in Geigy's eyes; his entire body shook. "I mean…" he began, struggling to control his trembling body, "that I know what their target will be." He broke off unable to finish, his voice quaking.

Cheyenne grabbed his shaking shoulder. "What do you mean, Geigy?" he asked in alarm. "What the hell are you talking about? What's their target?"

Four pairs of eyes locked on Geigy. Time seemed to stand still as they waited for his response.

"New York City!" he whispered. "That's where they're headed."

His words hung in the air. The fear was now palpable, shrouding them all like a veil of mist.

Surprisingly, Ebony was the first to speak. "You mean that these long range missiles will be able to reach New York City?"

Geigy nodded.

"But how do you know that New York is their target?" said Cheyenne.

"Yes, old boy, their target could be anywhere in the world," chimed in Winston.

Geigy stared at them, the fear still flashing in his grey eyes. "I just know," he said simply. "I just know that New York is their target. I can feel it in my gut. They want to wipe New York off the face of the earth."

His words resonated. Although they had no proof that New York was the target, they knew that Geigy was speaking the truth. If they didn't act soon, the entire world could be destroyed.

Cheyenne sprang into action. "Okay, we have to come up with a plan to stop them," he said, turning to survey the progress of the convoy in the valley below.

"Look how slow they are moving," said Willie, "making sure that heavy load don't turn over."

"We have to make sure that they don't see us, because we are way, way outnumbered," said Cheyenne. "The Russian would kill us all just like swatting flies; he would show no mercy."

"He's a cold-blooded killer," said Ebony, shuddering as she remembered their recent incarceration, and how close the Russian had come to torturing them. Ironically, it was Python who had intervened to save them from his deadly clutches.

They stood in silence, watching as the convoy moved slowly away from them. Although they were quite a distance from the convoy, their voices could still carry on the wind.

"Okay, we should be able to talk now – the sound of the diesels will cover our voices, but we should stay down for a while longer," warned Cheyenne.

Paralyzed by fear just a few moments earlier, Geigy was now back in Marine-mode – fighting fit and ready for action. "So, what the hell are we gonna do about these missiles?" he demanded, jumping to his feet. "What's our plan of action?"

The others stared at him in astonishment, amazed by his rapid recovery, from trembling wreck to man of action.

"Well, the first thing we are going to do is follow them at a safe distance," replied Cheyenne.

"Good idea, Cowboy," said Geigy.

"Then we should be able to find out what that goddamn Russian is really up to," said Ebony.

"Maybe we are getting all excited over nothing," said Cheyenne.

Geigy brought himself to his full height, standing tall. "I don't think so. Those missiles are definitely headed for New York City," he said adamantly. "I can feel it in my gut…and my water," he added. "We have to stop them, Cowboy."

"Okay, okay, relax, Geigy, I believe you – we all do," he said, patting his friend's shoulder. "Tonight, you and I will be going on a mission to find out what's really going on."

Geigy beamed. "You got it, Cowboy. I'm ready when you are."

"What can we do, old chap?" asked Winston.

"Yeah, we want to help, too," said Willie.

"Yeah, I want to tear that Russian's head off," said Ebony.

"Okay, guys, relax, we're all gonna do our bit. First, we're gonna move very quietly and carefully until it gets dark," said Cheyenne. "I'm pretty sure that they'll have a fire burning so they can have a hot meal." The others nodded. "Talking about a hot meal, let's have something to eat ourselves. I don't know about you lot, but I'm starving."

"It will have to be something cold, old chap," said Winston. "We can't risk making a fire, otherwise we'll give our position away."

"Good point, Winston. Cold beans, it is," he replied, laughing.

"And a coupla shots of whiskey to wash 'em down," added Geigy. "God knows, we could all use a stiff drink."

"Time to hit the road," Cheyenne announced after they had finished eating. "We'll follow the tracks of the two diesel trucks. The tracks are pretty deep, so they won't be too hard to follow."

"Won't they see our headlights, old chap?" asked Winston.

"Nah, we'll make sure that we stay well back," said Cheyenne. "And when the two diesels stop running, Geigy and I will crawl up beside them and listen to what the Russian has to say."

Without another word, they jumped into the vehicles and followed the deep groves of the moving convoy. Several miles later, Cheyenne held up his hand. "Whoa, stop the vehicles, I just heard one of the diesel trucks turn off its engine."

The others listened intently. "There goes the other one," said Ebony.

"Thank God, there's a breeze tonight to carry the sound," said Geigy.

They sat for a few moments listening to the silence.

"Oh, Cheyenne, it's so quiet and spooky," said Ebony, grabbing his arm. "I'm getting the chills just knowing that the Russian is so close."

Cheyenne drew her close. "Don't worry, Ebony, everything's gonna be fine. Trust me, we're gonna take care of that crazy Russian once and for all," he said, touching her cheek. He looked over at Geigy. "Are you ready to roll, partner?"

"Ready when you are, Cowboy."

"Okay, everybody, just be as quiet as possible. Geigy and I will be back as soon as we can."

Ebony grabbed his arm again, reluctant to let him leave. "Please be careful, Cheyenne. I'm so scared. That crazy Russian is pure evil."

"Don't worry, honey. We'll be back before you know it." And giving her a quick peck on the cheek, he and Geigy moved out into the inky darkness.

Geigy's Marine training instantly took over. "Okay, Cowboy, from now on we won't be able to talk," he whispered. "Just as we heard the purring of their trucks from several miles away, this breeze will also carry the sound of our voices. Everything has to be by touch, otherwise we both could be killed."

Cheyenne nodded. "It's a good thing that both of us have been in the military."

"Let me show you a little trick that I learned in the Marines," said Geigy as he started to dig a small hole with his hand, until the soil got a little moist.

Cheyenne watched, wondering what he was doing. Geigy passed him a handful of soil.

"Now, take this soil and rub it all over your face. Just a little camouflage which may come in handy before the night is over," he said.

"Damn smart trick," said Cheyenne as he rubbed the moist dirt on his face.

"Perfect," replied Geigy, following suit.

As they trundled along the deep tracks, Geigy suddenly grabbed Cheyenne's arm and pointed. In the velvet darkness, they could make out the faint glimmer of a fire. Falling to their knees, they crawled up a small incline overlooking the convoy and lay on their stomachs underneath a gorse bush. It was a perfect vantage point. Hidden by the sprawling bush, they could easily hear the Russians talking. Geigy held his index to his lips as if to say hush. Cheyenne nodded. The two friends surveyed the scene below, and listened.

The three Russians were in their element, tossing down shots of vodka as they waited for their meal. Chattering excitedly in Russian, they toasted each other's health, and roared with laughter. As their words floated upwards, Cheyenne and Geigy exchanged glances and grimaced. *What the fuck?* their eyes said. *If the Russians continued speaking in their native language, they would be well and truly fucked!*

Chapter Sixty

As if reading their thoughts, the Russian abruptly raised his glass and addressed his comrades in English. Cheyenne and Geigy smiled at each other, unable to believe their luck.

"Python and Ego are going to be so happy after this is over," he said, taking another slug of vodka. "The three of us will be sipping on champagne and vodka all day long on some island."

His two comrades looked at him and grinned.

"With many beautiful women waiting on us. They will be give us massages day and night, and whatever comes after that," he leered. Breaking into his crazy laugh, he patted his comrades on the back. "Yes, yes, I'm going to invite both of you for a month of pleasure," he said, licking his lips lasciviously

"Nostravia," replied the two men, raising their glasses.

"Nostravia!" cried the Russian. "I will be so happy when I hear that New York City has been destroyed by a nuclear missile. *Our nuclear missile!"* Laughing his crazy laugh again, he danced around the fire, waving the vodka bottle back and forth. "And then the next report will be that Israel has been wiped off the face of the earth," he slurred. "And good riddance, too."

"Ya, Ya," agreed his comrades, in Russian.

"What a great day it will be for us, comrades, when the United States finds out that the missiles came from the poor country of Somalia." He laughed loudly and chugged down another shot of vodka. "What can they do? If they attack Somalia, the United Nations and many other countries will accuse them of being big bullies picking on poor Somalia."

Cheyenne and Geigy exchanged glances again, scarcely able to believe their ears. *Somalia.* The word hung in the air between them.

The Russian continued holding court. He was enjoying this display of power as his captive audience hung on to his every word. "Here's to the KGB," he said, raising the vodka bottle to his greasy lips and downing another slug. "What a brilliant plan they came up with. The United States and Israel have always wondered what happened to all the nuclear bombs we had in our possession." He laughed loudly. "Now they will find out."

Cheyenne tugged on Geigy's shirt letting him know that it was time to leave. They had heard enough. As they started to crawl back down the incline, three soldiers strode around one of the diesels. The two friends froze.

"I have to take a piss so bad, I can almost taste it," said one of the soldiers, unzipping his fly.

"Hey, do you guys want to have a pissing contest?" said the second soldier.

"What's a pissing contest?" asked the third soldier.

"To see who can piss the farthest," replied the second soldier.

"All right, you're on, man," said the first soldier, "but hurry, I can't hold it much longer."

"Okay, do you see that bush up there, see if you can hit it."

"Hell, that's no problem," said the other two as all three of them pissed as hard as they could, sending a spray of urine over the bush.

"Damn, all three of us hit the bush, so it's a tie," said the second soldier.

The Russian and his two comrades rounded the diesel. "What's going on here?" he demanded, looking at the three soldiers with their cocks hanging out.

The soldiers stood to attention. "We're having a pissing contest to see if we can get over that bush up there," explained the second soldier, pointing.

The Russian smacked his hands together. "I had a pissing contest back at *The African Queen*, and I out pissed everyone," he bragged, grabbing his crotch. "Come on, comrades, let's show these guys what Russian piss can do," he said.

"Ya, Ya," nodded his comrades.

The three Russians unzipped their flies and leaned back, pointing their cocks at the bush.

"Russian vodka makes for strong pissing," laughed the Russian as the three men watered down the bush.

Meanwhile, Cheyenne and Geigy still crouched behind the bush were drenched with urine. Unable to move or cry out, for fear of discovery, they lay there motionless as wave after wave of piss soaked their bodies. Finally, the Russians zipped up their flies and walked away.

"I think we won that contest," said the Russian.

Swiftly and silently, Cheyenne and Geigy crept back down the incline and trudged back to the waiting vehicles. "Sonofabitch, that was close," said Cheyenne, clutching his dripping shirt.

"Goddamn, I thought I was gonna gag," said Geigy, wiping the sticky urine from his face. "Agh, I am now," he retched.

"Just the thought of that Russian's piss soaking us is enough to make anyone vomit," said Cheyenne and he too threw up alongside Geigy.

"Let's get outta here," said Cheyenne, wiping his mouth. "Are you okay, Geigy?"

"I've been better," said Geigy. "I just want to get out of these smelly clothes and wash off this piss. The stench is overwhelming." And he promptly threw up again.

"I wanted to get up and run, but I knew they would track us down," said Cheyenne.

"Yeah," agreed Geigy, coming up for air. "Thank God, we held our ground, otherwise we'd be dead by now."

They trudged on. "I think we're getting close to camp," said Cheyenne. "Ebony, Winston, can you hear me?" he called softly. "Willie?"

"I think they're gonna smell us before they hear us," Geigy deadpanned.

Cheyenne called out again. No answer. "Let's keep going, maybe we're too far away. It's hard to tell in the dark."

They continued on for about half a mile and this time Geigy tried his luck. "Winston, Willie, are you there?" he cried, a little louder. "Ebony!"

Cheyenne grabbed his arm. "Listen, I hear a voice and it sounds like Ebony."

"Cheyenne, Geigy, is that you?" she called.

"Yes, it's us," said Cheyenne. "We're both here."

"Oh, thank God, you're back safe and sound," she cried. "Where are you? I can't see you."

"We're right here, honey," said Cheyenne. "But please stay away from us."

"Why, what's wrong?" she cried, her voice filled with anguish. "Are you hurt or something?"

"No, nothing like that," said Cheyenne.

"Then why should we stay away from you? We want to see you both."

"I can explain…" began Cheyenne, but before he could finish Ebony interrupted him.

"My God, what's that smell," she cried, holding her nose. "It smells like piss."

"That's what I'm trying to tell you," said Cheyenne. "That's why you can't get close to us."

Ebony laughed. "So you pissed your pants. What's the big deal?"

"No, we did not piss our pants," said Cheyenne, "but the African soldiers and the Russians all pissed on us."

"Oh, my God, they saw you and both of you are still alive," said Winston. "I can't believe it."

"Me neither," chimed in Willie.

"Will you stop interrupting and let us explain," said Geigy. "The sooner we get out of these piss-soaked clothes the better."

"No, they did not see us," continued Cheyenne. "We were hiding behind this bush, and they decided to have a pissing contest. Unfortunately for us, they chose our bush as the target, and now we're dripping in piss and vodka."

On hearing these words, Ebony, Winston and Willie struggled to stifle their laughter.

"Now you know the story, could you bring me a shovel from the Rover," said Cheyenne. "And some soap and water and fresh clothes for both of us."

"Yeah, and hurry up, this piss is making me sick," said Geigy. "I think I'm gonna throw up again."

Winston stepped toward them. "Oh, you poor chaps. It's a wonder they didn't see you."

"We had to stay perfectly still, otherwise they would have seen us," said Cheyenne.

"Yeah, if we'd moved a single muscle we'd have been dead meat," added Geigy.

"Phew! You certainly do stink to high heaven," said Winston, holding his nose. "But you're alive and that's the main thing."

Ebony and Willie rushed forward and handed them the shovel and soap, along with two sets of clean clothes and a bucket of water.

"Thanks," said Cheyenne.

Struggling to suppress her laughter, Ebony stared at the two bedraggled figures, the urine still dripping down their faces. "Cheyenne, Geigy, I know you're both going to hate me, but I can't hold this in any longer," she said, doubling over in laughter.

"It's not funny, Ebony," snarled Cheyenne.

"I know. I know. Please forgive me. You poor things, even the Russian pissed on you," and she doubled over again. "It is quite funny if you think about it," she said as Winston and Willie joined in the laughter.

Cheyenne and Geigy glared at them. "I wonder if you lot could have kept still while a spray of foul Russian piss was raining down on you," said Cheyenne.

"Wouldn't have lasted a second," said Geigy.

Cheyenne took his arm. "Come on, Geigy, let's go and get cleaned up. Then we'll come back and join the three Stooges."

Chapter Sixty-One

Cheyenne and Geigy scoured their bodies with soap and water, and then buried their filthy clothes. Now groomed, and dressed in clean clothes, they strolled back to the camp.

"I feel like a new man," said Geigy, running a hand through his freshly-washed hair. "A good shot of whiskey and I'm all set."

Cheyenne laughed. "Me, too, Geigy," he said as they strode toward the others, arm in arm.

Their friends looked at them, shame-faced. "Sorry about all the laughter earlier, old chaps," said Winston, holding out his hand. "We just couldn't help ourselves."

"Yeah, sorry," said Willie, offering his hand.

"Sorry," said Ebony, but her blue eyes were still twinkling in amusement.

"Don't worry about it," said Geigy. "Just pass me a shot of whiskey and I'll be a new man. All is forgiven and forgotten."

"Yeah, forgiven and forgotten," said Cheyenne, throwing a look at Ebony and noticing the laughter still dancing in her eyes.

A few shots of whiskey later, they were feeling no pain.

"So tell us what you found out," asked Ebony, huddling close to Cheyenne.

"Well, it's not just New York that they're going to drop a nuclear bomb on," he began. "Israel is also a target." And he went on to explain how Somalia would take the blame.

"Oh my God," gasped Ebony.

"Very crafty," said Winston. "Never could trust those Russians."

Geigy banged the whiskey bottle against his hand. "They have to be stopped, and I know what has to be done," he told them.

The others looked at him, waiting to hear his plan of action.

"Well, how can we stop them?" asked Cheyenne. "We are way outnumbered, and they have a fifty caliber machine gun on one of those jeeps."

"They would mow us down like grass," said Winston.

"Yeah, like grass," agreed Willie, nodding his head.

Geigy took a long slug of whiskey and then turned to them and smiled. "I'm going to blow them to kingdom come with that dynamite in the back of our truck," he said with a flourish.

"Wow!" said Willie, his eyes like saucers.

"Ebony, you won't have to worry about that dynamite no more, after this is over," said Geigy.

Ebony cuddled closer to Cheyenne, her eyes locked on Geigy. "Cheyenne, baby, Geigy's getting that wild look in his eyes again," she whispered as her hand started to tremble.

Oblivious to her fear, Geigy rambled on, his face lit up like a Christmas tree. "Cheyenne, we have to go back one more time and take the binoculars with us," he said.

"Okay, I'm with you, Geigy," replied Cheyenne.

"Let's make it tomorrow night." Cheyenne nodded.

"I want to go with you this time," Ebony demanded.

Willie jumped to his feet."Let's all go."

"No," said Cheyenne firmly. "The more people, the more chance of being seen. And if they do see us, we'll all be killed."

Disappointment flooded their faces, but Ebony and Willie realized that Cheyenne's course of action was the only sensible way to handle the situation.

"If we don't stop them, can you imagine how many people will be killed in New York City alone," said Cheyenne. "The entire city will be wiped out – roughly 9 million souls destroyed in one fell swoop. It would be a catastrophe beyond anyone's imagination, so we have to tread carefully, and not make any mistakes."

"You're absolutely correct, old chap," agreed Winston. "We have to think smart and act smart. Our very civilization depends upon it. One false move on our part and the whole world could go up in smoke."

For several moments, they all sat in silence as Winston's words sank in.

One false move and the whole world could go up in smoke.

Cheyenne broke the silence. "Okay, so it's Geigy and me, tomorrow night," he said. "Now let's hit the sack – it's been long day."

They awoke at dawn and followed the big diesels chugging along with their heavy load.

"As soon as we hear the diesels shut down, and it gets dark, we have to move out," Geigy told Cheyenne.

"Why so early?" Ebony asked.

"We have to see what they do as soon as they stop," said Geigy.

"I guess, like last night, we won't be carrying any guns," said Cheyenne.

"That's right," replied Geigy. "Guns are too hard to crawl with, and we can't afford to make any noise. *Remember, one false move on our part, and the whole world could go up in smoke.*"

"You're right, Geigy, we have to act smart. Our only weapon will be a pocket knife."

Willie held up his hand. "Listen! The diesels just shut down."

Geigy snapped to attention. "Okay, Cowboy, it's Showtime! Let's get our camouflage on and hit the road again."

Ebony watched as they smeared their faces and heads with the moist dirt. "Damn, with your tan pants and shirts, and all that dirt smudged on your faces, they might just walk on you tonight," she said, giggling.

"If that happens, we'll be up and running as fast as we can," said Cheyenne.

"Come over here, the two of you," she beckoned, opening her arms wide, "and let me give you both a big hug." The two men blushed as she folded them in her embrace and planted a wet kiss on their cheeks. "Be careful out there," she whispered.

Cheyenne returned her kiss. "We'll be back before you know it," he said.

"Have the whiskey ready," grinned Geigy as he slung the binoculars around his neck.

"May God go with you," murmured Ebony as the two men disappeared into the night.

Neither man spoke as they edged their way along the deep grooves of the diesels. Steely determination etched their faces as they moved forward. This was their mission and they could not afford to fail. Winston's words rang in their ears. *Their very civilization depended on it.*

As the neared the convoy, Geigy nudged Cheyenne and pointed to the burning fire to the right of the parked diesels. Keeping one of the trucks between them and the Russians, the two friends crept silently by on the left.

Another truck pulled up to the big diesels. Cheyenne tugged on Geigy's shirt as three soldiers jumped out of the truck and pulled out fuel cans to fill up the powerful diesels. Geigy nodded his head as they crept closer and watched the soldiers. Crawling closer and closer, they heard the Russian's loud mouth. *He was talking to Python!*

"We are moving well, and are now in the back country of Kilimanjaro," he said. "In the distance, we are spotting many groups of elephants." The Russian cleared his throat and chuckled. "This would be a good place to have a few poachers – nice big shiny tusks some of these elephants have."

On hearing these words, Cheyenne bristled and doubled his hand into a fist. It took all of Geigy's strength to prevent his friend from charging forward and attacking the Russian. He knew the hatred that Cheyenne harbored for the poachers. Grabbing Cheyenne's face, he turned it toward his own. *One false move* said his eyes.

Cheyenne sagged against him and unfolded his fist. He knew he had come close to sabotaging their mission. If not for Geigy's intervention, he would have ruined everything and *the whole world could have gone up in smoke*!

Chapter Sixty-Two

"We will be rich soon, my friend," said the Russian as he licked his thin, greasy lips. "As soon as the nuclear missiles go *boom*!"

Cheyenne clenched his fist again, but made no move to spring forward. Geigy held on to his shirt, just in case. He wasn't taking any chances.

The Russian laughed loudly and continued his phone conversation. "We are getting ready to have a few vodkas. And after the two big *boom boom,* our mission will be completed."

Turning, he pirouetted on his heels and shouted out to the black, inky sky. *"Boom! Boom!"*

Cheyenne and Geigy stiffened. Their first instinct was to rush forward and throttle him with their bare hands. But common sense prevailed, Winston's words of doom ringing in their ears.

"We will get our money from the KGB," spouted the Russian, "and soon we will be sipping champagne on the beach, surrounded by beautiful women." He clapped his hands gleefully and danced a little jig. "I will see you soon, my good friends, Python and Ego."

Cheyenne and Geigy watched as the Russian drank a bottle of vodka with his two comrades, their anger mounting with every second. They wanted to crush him like an ant, squeeze the life out of his worthless body, but they had to bide their time. Wait to strike.

After their meal, the three Russians retired to a small tent that the soldiers had erected for them. Cheyenne and Geigy watched and waited as Geigy formulated his plan. They noticed that some of the soldiers slept on the ground by the fire, and others slept in the trucks. Only one soldier stood guard at a time, as they took it in turns to take three-hour shifts. Soon the soldiers were fast asleep, including the soldier who was supposed to be standing guard. Geigy and Cheyenne listened to their loud snoring, and then slowly crept away, back to the camp. Now it was time to grab some sleep themselves. They had seen all they needed to see.

The next morning, Ebony told Winston and Willie to let them sleep for a while. "They came back early this morning," she said. "It was after 4 when they finally hit the sack."

"But we want to hear what happened last night," complained Willie.

"We have all day to find out," said Ebony. "For now, let them sleep; they must be exhausted."

As she finished speaking, Cheyenne's head suddenly popped up from the nearby sleeping bag.

"No, no," he said groggily as he rubbed eyes, "we have to get up right now. Every moment is precious – we can't afford to lose a single second."

"But you've only slept for a couple of hours," said Ebony. "Surely you can sleep a little longer."

Cheyenne shielded his eyes from the sun's piercing glare. "No, we have plenty of things to talk about, and we have to be very, very precise, otherwise we could all end up dead," he said, leaning over and nudging Geigy who was snoring in the sleeping bag beside him.

"What's happening?" said Geigy, bolting upright. "Have they fired the missiles?"

"Relax, Geigy, old chap," said Winston, "the world is still here. It was only a dream."

"Thank God for that," said Geigy, rubbing the sleep from his eyes. "Where's breakfast – I could eat a horse. And a shot of whiskey wouldn't go amiss, just to get the juices flowing."

"Good old Geigy," said Cheyenne, nudging his friend again. "The end of the world may be nigh, but you're gonna make sure you're fed and watered."

A huge grin spread across Geigy's weathered face. "I'll drink to that!" he chuckled.

After a hearty breakfast, and a couple of shots, Cheyenne told them what they had witnessed last night. Now it was time to take their next step. "I will let Geigy take over now; he's the expert on dynamite and explosives."

"Where is Geigy?" asked Ebony, looking around.

"I'm over here by the truck," Geigy shouted, "getting some fuse to see how it works."

"What do you mean, how it works?" asked Ebony. "I thought you knew about explosives."

"That's right, I do, but this fuse is old and it has to be tested," replied Geigy as he examined the fuse and then pulled a match out of a jar with a lid on it.

"I'm not going to stand here and see if it's too old to work," cried Ebony as she ran off and hid behind a large tree. The others laughed, but she paid them no heed. "You won't be laughing if that thing blows."

Geigy continued his examination and then took about one yard of fuse and lit the end.

"Is it going to blow?" yelled Ebony from behind the tree.

Cheyenne called to her. "Ebony, come here, honey, this is just the fuse," he explained. "You have to put the fuse inside the dynamite before it goes boom."

Geigy looked at the burning fuse. "It burns pretty fast, so that could be good or bad," he said.

Willie threw him a puzzled look. "I don't know a damn thing about explosives, Geigy. What do you mean, that this could be good or bad?"

"Well, if it burns too slow, they might have a chance to put it out," replied Geigy. "And if it burns too fast, it could blow you up. Boom!"

"Whoa, I see what you mean," said Willie.

"So what do you think, Geigy?" asked Cheyenne.

Geigy scratched his head and thought for a moment before he responded. "Well, I can tell that this fuse is unpredictable, so I really don't know."

"So how do you plan to do this, old chap?" Winston asked.

"I don't care about blowing up the Russians' jeep. We have to get the two diesels carrying the missiles." He paused... "And if we plan on living, we have to blow up the truck with the soldiers and the truck with the fuel. They all have to go."

"I don't like the idea of blowing up the soldiers," said Cheyenne. "Those men are probably trying hard to feed their families. They just happen to be working for the wrong people."

"And they have to pay the price," Geigy said vehemently, his voice rising. "A few will die but millions will live. It has to be done at all costs."

The others nodded. "We're with you, Geigy," they said in unison.

"Good. I'm gonna need everybody's help to pull this off...if we can pull it off."

"We can do it, Geigy," said Cheyenne. "Just tell us your plan."

"Okay, listen up. I'm gonna bind four sticks of dynamite together with duct tape; the center stick of dynamite will have the fuse, and they will blow up together," he explained. "Now I'm very short on fusing and this might be a problem."

"How do we solve it, old chap?" asked Winston.

"Listen carefully, guys," said Geigy, "this is my plan." The friends drew closer hanging on Geigy's every word. "The vehicles will not be parked too far from each other. When the soldiers are sleeping, I'm gonna crawl under the trucks and place the dynamite close to the engine." He turned to Willie. "Willie, you will have the fuel truck."

"Me?" said Willie, in surprise. "But I told you before, I don't know nothing about no dynamite."

"You don't have to, Willie. You just have to crawl under the truck, find the fuse and light it."

"Okay…"said Willie nervously.

Geigy continued. "We have to be as quiet as mice. We cannot talk or make any sound. Give me about twenty minutes and then crawl up until you feel the fusing. Are you following me so far?"

Willie nodded, although he did not look too sure. "You unravel the fusing carefully so as not to pull it from the dynamite, and then try to find some covering if you can. Have your matches ready for my signal, and take a few extras ones, just in case." Geigy took a deep breath and then turned to Winston. "Winston, the same applies to you. You will have the soldiers' vehicle."

Winston nodded. "Absolutely, old chap, you can count on me – I won't let you down."

Now it was Cheyenne's turn. "Cheyenne, you'll get the first missile, and I'll get the second one."

"Sure thing, Geigy."

"How will we know when to light the fuse?" asked Willie, his voice shaking.

"After I have all the dynamite in place, I will crawl as far as I can from the second missile," said Geigy. "Then, in the dark, you will see me light up the fuse. That will be your signal to light your fuse."

"And then what?" said Willie.

Geigy grinned mischievously as he turned to face Willie. "And then you run like hell!"

Chapter Sixty-Three

Willie's dark face practically turned pale, if that were possible. "That's it? I just run like hell," he said, wiping the sweat from his forehead.

"That's what I said," replied Geigy. "You run like hell back to our vehicles and weapons."

Ebony tapped him on the shoulder. "What about me, Geigy? What am I supposed to do?"

Geigy looked at her and smiled. "Ebony, your role is the most important. You are going to cover us, if we get spotted by somebody."

Ebony returned his smile. "I can do that, Geigy," she said brightly. "I'll cut down anyone who tries to stop you, especially that crazy Russian. It will be a pleasure to shoot him."

Geigy continued on with his plan. "After the dynamite goes off, all hell's gonna break loose. The most important thing the rest of you have to do, *is find that fuse in the dark*," he said, emphasizing his words. "Do you understand?" The three men nodded their heads vigorously.

"Try and set the fuse with your first match. And please be patient, don't do anything until you see me light the fuse," Geigy warned. "I may have a situation where I cannot move for hours."

"Don't worry, Geigy," Cheyenne reassured him, "we'll be very patient. One wrong move could cost us our lives."

"Yes, old chap, we won't let you down," said Winston.

Willie didn't look too sure. He was still thinking about the *run like hell* part.

"Geigy, can we help you with anything else, old chap?" asked Winston.

Geigy shook his head. "No, this is very tedious and dangerous work, but I know what I'm doing. I just have to concentrate very hard." He patted Winston on the back. "But thanks for the offer."

All day long Geigy worked on his four dynamite bombs, totally absorbed in the task at hand. He neither ate nor drank, not even a sip of his beloved whiskey. The others watched him from afar.

"He hasn't had a thing since breakfast," said Ebony. "He's so absorbed with the dynamite that he doesn't even know we're around."

"I don't think we should bother him," said Winston. "He'll join us when he's good and ready."

Several hours later, as dusk was falling, Geigy approached the group. "Okay, guys, I think everything is set," he said, wiping his brow with the back of his hand. "Are you ready to roll?"

Cheyenne jumped to his feet. "Ready when you are, Geigy."

"Since I have the dynamite, I will be by myself in the jeep. The rest of you will ride together in the Rover," he told them. "It's just too dangerous for anyone to ride with me."

"Okay, old chap, whatever you say," said Winston.

"You're leading this mission, Geigy. We'll follow any orders you give us," agreed Cheyenne.

"Okay, just drive nice and slow until we hear the diesels shut down," said Geigy.

Ebony clutched Cheyenne's arm. "I'm really nervous about tonight, and worried about all of us."

"Don't worry, honey, everything's gonna be okay," he said, trying to reassure her, although deep down he was unsure of the night's outcome. "If Geigy can get the dynamite placed properly, we have a good chance of killing everyone in the convoy. That fuel truck alone will blow sky high."

"I hope you're right, Cheyenne," she said, staring off into the distance and wondering if they would all make it back safely tonight.

"Look, the sun is starting to go down!" exclaimed Willie, pointing at the red burnished sky. "They'll be shutting down the diesels soon."

"Damn, you're good, Willie," said Geigy as they listened to the silence after the diesels shut down a few moments later.

Willie stood tall and proud. "Thanks, Geigy." His nerves had vanished and he was ready to roll.

The two vehicles trundled along the grooved tracks. Cheyenne and the others led the way in the Rover; Geigy followed behind in the jeep, his only companions, four bundles of dynamite.

"I think it's best if we pull over here, behind this heavy brush," said Cheyenne as he brought the Rover to a stop and switched off the lights and engine. Geigy pulled in behind them.

"The dynamite is packed safely in the jeep, but when I leave, I'll be carrying it on my back," said Geigy as he walked up to them. "Right now, I'd like to check out what they are doing." He turned to Cheyenne. "Let's go, Cowboy."

"Please be careful out there," pleaded Ebony, grabbing their arms. "Come back safely."

Cheyenne and Geigy slipped off into the night. An hour later they were back.

"Okay, everyone, this is it," said Geigy. "Time to get started on our mission. You all know what you have to do, so let's do it."

Retrieving the bundles of dynamite from the jeep, Geigy carefully strapped them on his back and addressed the group once more. "Let's do this as quickly as possible," he said as the others lined up behind him. "We found a spot not too far from the soldiers, but you must be very careful," he warned. "If you're gonna talk, get real close to the person and whisper in his ear." He marched forward. "Okay, follow me and be as quiet as possible."

They crept along in single file, for several hundred yards, until Geigy signaled for them to halt.

"Here's the spot we found," he said, pointing to a grassy knoll. "Now I want you to check with each other that you have found your fuse. Willie, you are the first one, so you have to let Winston know that you have found the fuse, by patting him on the back, and so on and so on. *Remember, you have to be patient.*"

They nodded, their eyes telling Geigy that they wouldn't let him down.

"I will try to get this done as fast as I can," he said. "Now, all of you come over here and put your hands on top of mine. I ain't too religious, but it wouldn't hurt to say a short prayer. We need all the help we can get."

They stood in silence for a minute or so, each of them alone with their thoughts and prayers. Finally, Geigy said, "This is in memory of the eighteen Marines who died trying to feed and free people in Somalia. These nuclear warheads will not make it to Somalia. Let's do it!" And, like a shadow in the night, Geigy disappeared into the darkness.

Now it was Cheyenne's turn to address his friends. "Look, I know everyone is scared and nervous like me, but Geigy is right, these missiles cannot reach Somalia. The future of the world is in our hands."

"And remember," cautioned Winston, raising his hand, "*one false move on our part and the whole world could go up in smoke.*"

Chapter Sixty-Four

They waited for an hour and a half, giving Geigy enough time to plant the four bombs. Huddled close to each other, they whispered their innermost thoughts and fears.

"Ebony, is your rifle loaded and ready?" asked Cheyenne.

"You bet," replied Ebony, patting her trusty rifle, "and nobody is getting close to any of you. I'll blow their socks off."

"Listen," whispered Winston, "I can hear the Russians and the soldiers talking together."

"And they just put some more wood on the fire," said Willie, watching the flames rise higher, off in the distance.

"I wish we could hear what they're saying," said Ebony, shivering, her nails digging into Cheyenne's arm.

Cheyenne immediately took charge. "You're right, we have to get closer. Ebony and Willie, you stay put. Winston, come with me."

As Cheyenne and Winston edged closer, they could hear the Russian laughing, and offering his men more vodka. "Ah, Russia vodka, it is the best vodka in the world, is it not?" He waved the bottle in front of their faces. "Now, let us drink to our comrades-in-arms. They should be here soon with the fuel supplies. And once they hear the big boom boom, we will be very rich. Very, very rich."

He raised the bottle high above his head. "To Al-Qaida!" he bellowed, throwing back his head and roaring with maniacal laughter.

The others raised their glasses: "To Al-Qaida!"

Winston moved close to Cheyenne and whispered in his ear. "Did you hear that?" he said. "Al-Qaida."

"Al-Qaida!" gasped Cheyenne, taking a step backwards. "Python and the Russian are working with Al-Qaida! Are you sure?"

Winston nodded his head vigorously. "Sounds like it, old chap. You heard them."

Cheyenne looked stunned. "So that's who they are hoping to get their retirement money from," he said, still in disbelief. "Python and the Russian are one thing, but Al-Qaida is an entirely different matter. This changes everything, Winston. I still can't believe it. *Al-Qaida!"*

"Right again, old chap," replied Winston. "I guess they don't realize that Al-Qaida is just using them to get their hands on these nuclear warheads. As soon as they've achieved their goal, they'll squash them like flies, just like that," he finished, grinding his hands together. "Those bastards will stop at nothing – they are pure evil. To them, human life is worthless, especially the lives of the cursed infidels." He pointed to himself and Cheyenne, and smiled wryly. "And that includes you and me, old chap," he said, jabbing Cheyenne in the chest, "and Ebony, Geigy and Willie. We are the cursed infidels. To Al-Qaida, we are not fit for life on earth, and not fit for their so-called hereafter. Their blessed paradise."

"What are you saying, Winston?" asked Cheyenne, staring at his friend intently.

"Al-Qaida is filled with hatred – they hate anyone who is not a true believer," replied Winston, pausing for effect. "And I mean *anyone,*" he stressed.

Cheyenne stared at him, hanging on to his every word. "Go on, Winston," he said quietly.

"They believe that only they and their followers can exist in this world. The rest of us are expendable. We are the non-believers – the scum of the earth, in their eyes. Only the true believers, the true followers of Islam, will ascend to Paradise."

Cheyenne touched his arm. "Winston, are you sure about that?" he whispered. "Sounds crazy to me. What makes them so special?"

"Well, I've studied the Koran, old chap, and like the Bible, it is very confusing and conflicting in places, and hard to understand, but if you take it literally, I'm pretty sure that's what it says."

"I tried reading the Bible," said Cheyenne, "but gave up after Genesis." He sighed deeply. "But I consider myself a good Christian. I respect my fellow man and I try to lead a true, honest life."

"You're a good man, Cheyenne," said Winston, patting him on the back. "Unfortunately, Al-Qaida consider themselves to be good faithful Muslims, but they are misguided. They are fundamentalists who take the Koran literally, and believe that only the true Muslims who follow the Koran have the right to exist in the world."

"But most Muslims are peace-loving, aren't they?" said Cheyenne, looking puzzled.

"That's true, old chap, most Muslims just want to live in peace and harmony with their neighbors, but Al-Qaida are extremists who follow the Koran, word for word. To them, if you're a non-believer you are nothing."

"That's ridiculous," said Cheyenne. "As my dear old daddy used to say, 'Live and let live.' What right do they have to judge the rest of the world?"

"I hear you, old chap. But, ridiculous or not, that's what they believe," shrugged Winston.

"Like people who take the Bible literally. An eye for an eye and a tooth for a tooth, and all that."

"Right again, old chap. That's the trouble with religion - each has its own God or prophet – the Christian God, the Jewish God, Jesus, Mohammed, Allah, Buddha, Krishna, Shiva, etc., etc.,"

Winston shook his head sadly. "And each religion thinks that their God is the only true God, hence all the death and destruction in world in the name of religion. In my opinion, it would be better if there were no religion at all. The world would be a much safer, more peaceful place. Since time immemorial, death and destruction have reigned, all in the name of religion."

"I never thought about it like that before," said Cheyenne as Winston's words sunk in. "But I can't agree with you. I have met many religious people and most of them are kind and will help anyone. I think the leaders of the world love power, and in many instances that leads to war. You know that old saying by your fellow countryman: Power corrupts, and absolute power corrupts absolutely." He shrugged. "Religion or no religion, people do have the right to protect themselves and their families. But I understand what you're saying and respect your opinion - all the wars that have been fought, and are still being fought today. And now the terrorists have taken it to a new level."

"Exactly, old chap," agreed Winston. "And Al-Qaida is the worst. They will stop at nothing to achieve their ends. Life on earth means nothing to them. As I said before, to them, human life is worthless, especially the lives of the non-believers."

"The cursed infidels," said Cheyenne, looking into his friend's eyes. "Us."

"Exactly, old chap," replied Winston. "*Us.* And they will stop at nothing to get rid of *us*."

Cheyenne shuddered and crossed himself. "Dear Lord," he muttered under his breath.

"They believe that their true reward awaits them after death, in Paradise," continued Winston. "That's why there are so many suicide bombers – religious fanatics, martyrs - who believe that if they destroy the non-believers in the name of Allah, twelve virgins, or is it twenty four, will be waiting for them in paradise. Life on earth is meaningless to them – Paradise is their true goal."

Cheyenne stood in silence, absorbing Winston's words. But Winston wasn't finished.

"Al-Qaida grabs these young men and women at an early age and literally brainwashes them," he said. "Everything is done in the name of Allah, so in their eyes, it is okay to destroy and destruct. Slaughter, stoning, beheadings, hijacking planes and flying them into the World Trade Center, biological warfare, nuclear destruction – all are acceptable, as long as they're doing it in the name of Allah."

He paused for breath. "And look how they treat their women. To them, women are the lowest of the low. Having to wear those veils from head-to-toe, and walking several steps behind the men as if they are second-class citizens. And God forbid they should look at another man or commit adultery: for that they will pay the ultimate price: death by stoning. It's as if they still live in the dark ages," finished Winston. "They are well and truly indoctrinated."

For several moments, neither man said a word. Finally, Cheyenne spoke up. "So you're saying that after the Russians bomb New York City and Israel, Al-Qaida will turn on Ego, Python and the Russian."

"Absolutely, old friend, in a New York minute, as you would say. Now you see what we're up against. They place no value on human life. Not even their own lives. Their reward lies in heaven or Paradise, or whatever you want to call it. Life here on Earth is just a stepping stone – a means to an end. And they are willing to pay the ultimate sacrifice." Winston paused for breath. "Once they have got what they want from the Russian and his cronies and they don't need them anymore, they will destroy them." Winston rubbed his thumb and forefinger together. "Squash them like flies."

A look of steely determination lit up Cheyenne's face. "Well, I hope we can do our damndest to stop them and put a little damper on their hateful ways," he said, clenching his fists.

“I’m ready if you are, old chap,” said Winston, resolutely. “These men are evil – they use religion to justify their destructive actions, and we have to stop them.”

Cheyenne’s eyes burned with a fierce intensity. “Yes, at all costs, we have to stop them! Right now, Winston, I’m saying a prayer for all of us to come home safely.”

Winston patted his shoulder. “Well, I’m with you there, old chap. If there is a God watching over us, I hope he shows up tonight.”

Chapter Sixty-Five

"Let's do it!" exclaimed Cheyenne. "The soldiers will be going to sleep soon, so let's get back to Ebony and Willie." And with a backward glance at the huddled group, they crept silently back to their friends.

Ebony rose to greet them. "Cheyenne," she said, throwing her arms around him. "What the hell have you guys been doing? We were going half crazy thinking something had happened to you."

"Sorry," he whispered, squeezing her gently, "we didn't realize how long we'd been gone."

"You're forgiven," she said, pecking him on the cheek.

"Listen up," he said, "we've discovered that Al-Qaida is behind this brazen scheme."

"Al-Qaida!" gasped Willie.

"Oh, my God!" exclaimed Ebony, her mouth wide open.

"Yes," said Winston. "And it's up to us to thwart their plans. The world's very existence hangs in the balance."

"Well, if you put it like that," replied Willie, trying to lighten the somber mood. "But let me tell you, I ain't too happy about tangling with that Al-Qaida bunch."

Cheyenne took charge. "None of us are, Willie, but we don't have much choice. Now, they will be going to sleep soon, so you have to go and find your fuse. Take extra matches with you just in case the wind blows them out."

Willie chuckled nervously. "How about me being a little nervous and my hands starting to shake. Look, they're shaking now. Just the thought of Al-Qaida makes my whole body shake."

Cheyenne patted him on the back reassuringly. "Yes, that, too. But, don't worry, we will not be that far apart – they have the vehicles parked pretty close together."

Willie nodded, but already his nerves were starting to show. "Okay," he said quietly, struggling to control his shaking hands.

Cheyenne took his arm. "You'll be okay," he said as he turned toward the others. "Now, let's all move up cautiously so we can see the bonfire."

"We're right behind you, old chap," said Winston.

The four friends crept forward in single file, Cheyenne leading the way.

"Look, there's the bonfire," whispered Willie, pointing toward the smoldering flames.

Cheyenne motioned for them to stop and pointed toward a sturdy tree. "Ebony, you see that tree," he said, "that's where you should keep us covered."

Ebony nodded. "You can count on me."

"That's my girl," said Cheyenne, staring into her liquid ebony eyes. "Now, like Geigy said, be patient, this may take some time. And we can't afford to make any mistakes." He turned to Willie. "Willie, get ready to move out, and don't get frustrated if you can't find the fuse. Just keep feeling around."

"Okay, Cowboy," muttered Willie. "I'll do my best."

"That's the spirit," said Cheyenne. "When you find it, wait until you see Geigy light his fuse."

"Will do," said Willie, still struggling to control his nerves. Just the mention of Al-Qaida had put the fear of God in him, or in this case, the fear of Allah.

Cheyenne patted him on the back "You'll be okay, Willie. Good luck!" he said as the three of them watched Willie disappear into the darkness.

"I hope he'll be okay," said Ebony, "his hands were shaking pretty badly."

"He'll be fine," said Cheyenne. "Knowing that Al-Qaida is involved has shattered his nerves, but I have faith in Willie. I know he'll rise to the occasion."

"He's scared," said Winston, "but we're all scared.I, for one, am petrified. It's not every day we go up against Al-Qaida. It's enough to make the bravest of the brave quake in their boots."

"Ain't that the truth," said Cheyenne.

"Stop it, you two," she said, punching Cheyenne's arm. "You're really scaring me now, and I wasn't scared before."

"Sorry, Ebony, we didn't mean to scare you," said Cheyenne, kissing her softly on the lips.

"Now I'm ready for anything," she said flirtatiously, batting her lashes at him.

Cheyenne pointed to the tree again. "Now, Willie's out there and somebody might stumble over him, or hear him, so you have to go to that tree and cover him."

Ebony drew herself to her full height. "I know, and I will shoot anybody who tries to harm any of you. You can count on me," she said, patting her rifle.

"That's my girl," said Cheyenne, kissing her again. "I will see you when this is over, and remember, I love you."

"I love you, too," she said, returning his kiss. "And don't you forget it!"

Cheyenne laughed. "As if I could."

"Okay, you two lovebirds, time to say goodbye," said Winston. "It's my turn to find my fuse."

The lovers shared a last parting kiss, and Ebony disappeared into the night.

"Okay, Winston," Cheyenne whispered. "I'll see you at breakfast. Good luck."

"Breakfast, it is, old chap," replied Winston as he, too, was swallowed up by the night. Cheyenne stood alone in the darkness. *And then there was one.* A sudden shiver ran up and down his spine, as if someone had just walked on his grave. Standing there in the eerie stillness, he thought of his beloved Wyoming and wondered how Cheyenne Cole, a simple cowboy from the good old Wild West, had ended up in darkest Africa fighting Al-Qaida.

My dear old daddy would never have believed this. For him, I came here to save the elephants, and now my friends and I are trying to save the world! The question is, will we succeed? He shook off any doubt and turned toward the bonfire. *I wonder how Geigy is doing?*

Chapter Sixty-Six

Geigy was doing very well. Very well indeed! He was surprised at how well everything was going. Just like clockwork. *I can't believe how easy it was planting that first bomb underneath that fuel truck,* he thought, allowing a small chuckle to escape his lips. *It was quite lucky that they were hanging out by the fire. I just hope that Willie can find his fuse.*

He placed a second bomb underneath the soldiers' truck. *Easy as apple pie. My Marine training is coming in very handy,* he mused as he lay on the ground between the wheels. *I hope Winston can find his fuse. Are we really going to pull this off?* He placed a third bomb underneath the nuclear warhead, and looked over at the Russians. *Dear God, I'm so close to the Russians and the soldiers. Thank God, for these big dual tires – they'll never see me.*

Geigy lay there motionless as he heard the roar of a truck coming straight toward him, its blazing headlights glowing underneath the giant diesels. He froze. *What the fuck! My goddamn luck has finally run out. I might have known it was too good to be true.* The truck moved closer as he tried to make himself as small as possible. *They're gonna see me! I'm a dead man!*

The headlights flickered off his silhouette as the truck's wheels turned toward the bonfire. Geigy had the strongest urge to crawl from underneath the truck and run like hell, but he knew this would put their mission in jeopardy. It took every ounce of his willpower to stay motionless.

I have to stay put. If I run, they'll probably see me and then we're all done for. The whole world is done for.

He decided to put his faith in the power of prayer. *What was that old saying? Ain't no atheists on the battlefield. And I'm smack in the biggest battle of my life. The battle of all battles. Might as well give it a shot.* He closed his eyes and prayed softly. *Dear God, I'm not much of a religious man. Never have been. Never went to church or prayed much. I would rather have a shot of whiskey than say a prayer. But deep down, I have always believed in you. Always. Please, dear God, I'm begging you. Millions of innocent men, women and children will die if these evil terrorists see me. Please have their eyes looking in the other direction.*

Geigy's breathing became very light, and his heart started beating like a drum, as if it were about to burst through his chest. *Surely, they could hear the incessant thump, thump.* He lay there motionless, as if in a trance, practically willing his heart to stop. *Dear God, I'm leaving it up to you. The fate of the world is in your hands.* He closed his eyes tightly and held his breath as he heard the two men jump out of the truck and approach the Russians. *Showtime!*

"We have your gas and diesel fuel," said one of the Al-Qaida men, walking toward the Russians. "Where would you like it?"

Geigy opened his eyes and let out a deep sigh. The men had not seen him. *Thank you, God.* He gazed up at the inky heavens. *Thank you.* God had answered his prayers.

From her position behind the tree, Ebony was looking through the scope of her high-powered rifle. She could see the bonfire, and the silhouettes of the three Russians. Nagging thoughts filled her head as she struggled to keep them at bay. *Why don't I just pull the trigger and end their miserable lives? Those evil beasts are the scum of the earth – they don't deserve to live. Let me send them to their paradise now.*

She squeezed the trigger gently and took aim. *Just like that, and they'll be gone.* But then a little voice in her head said: *If you pull the trigger, you will give everyone away. They will win and the world will be lost. The soldiers will find your friends, and then they will find you.*

Ebony shook her head, trying to banish the thoughts from her mind. *Oh, my God, I almost pulled the trigger and ruined everything. What on earth was I thinking? This waiting is driving me crazy.* And then she remembered Geigy's parting words. *Be patient.*

Ebony looked over at the bonfire again and spotted the headlights. "What are those two headlights blazing through the darkness," she said aloud. "I had better get behind the tree and stay low." Ducking behind the tree, she continued surveying the floodlit scene. The lights were now shining under the big diesels, and she could see Geigy lying on the ground behind the two dual tires. Ebony gasped. "Don't move a muscle, Geigy. I pray to God they don't see you."

Over at his position, Cheyenne had dug himself a small hole in the loose dirt, and was now burrowed inside, with only his head and shoulders showing. *I don't want to crawl down there and not find the fuse. I'm going to give Geigy more time.* He looked over at the campsite. *There are too many soldiers still milling around, and the Russians have just finished their meal.*

He patted his dugout and ducked down inside. *This little dugout is the perfect hiding place. I can crawl up and nobody can see me, but I can see them.*

He watched as the men moved back and forth by the fire. Then, just as Ebony had done moments before, he spotted the headlights. "What the heck!" he exclaimed, watching as the lights came nearer and nearer. "What are those lights coming down the trail?" He burrowed down deeper in his hiding place. "I'd better keep my head down, those lights are lighting up everything."

Sneaking a quick peek, he noticed that the lights had now turned away from him. "Now I can look, the lights have gone off me." Straining his eyes against the darkness, he suddenly espied the prone figure of Geigy, lying behind the big dual wheels. "Oh my God, that's Geigy," he cried in alarm, "lit up like a goddamn Christmas tree. Oh, Jesus, they're bound to see him. The only thing separating him and the Russians are those big wheels." *Think, Cheyenne! What the hell can you do to save him? All will be lost if I don't do something soon!*

Then as quickly as they came, the lights veered away from Geigy, and Cheyenne watched as the truck drew to a halt. Two men jumped out and looked around. Cheyenne held his breath. *Will they see Geigy?* Every second seemed like an eternity. *Hang in there, Geigy, old friend, and whatever you do, don't move!*

Cheyenne sighed in relief. The men had killed the lights, and were now striding forward to greet the Russians. "Thank you, God," said Cheyenne, his heart pounding. "You did show up tonight. And thank you, Geigy, I bet you could use a strong belt of whiskey right now!"

Chapter Sixty-Seven

Cheyenne continued to observe the Russians and their two visitors. "Here's to you, Geigy," he said, paying silent homage to his old friend. "You held it together. I don't think I would have been so brave." He raised his hand in a mock toast. "I don't have any whiskey right now, old friend, but when all this is over, I swear that you will have all the whiskey you desire."

He scanned the area, looking for Geigy's figure, but apart from the bonfire's glow, all was in darkness. *Well, at least I know now that Geigy has planted the three bombs. And now I pray to God, that he stays safe, and they don't see or hear him.*

Cheyenne could hear the Russian's loud voice carrying on the gentle breeze. He was talking on the phone to his brother-in-crime. "Python, thank you, my old friend," he boomed, "they have just pulled in with the fuel. Now we can continue with our journey and join up with the Al-Shabab people." He paused and looked over at the two Al-Qaida men whose lips were drawn in a tight smile. "Are you ready for the two big Boom-Boom, Python?"

Roaring with laughter, he threw his arms around the two Al-Qaida men. They visibly squirmed. It was obvious that they detested him. Quickly, they drew away and brushed off their clothes trying to rid themselves of his touch. The Russian appeared not to notice, or if he did, he was too drunk to care. This was a time for celebration. Soon, he would be rich. *Very, very rich.*

His maniacal laughter echoed through the valley, simultaneously brushing the ears of the five friends. They shuddered. That eerie laugh none of them would ever forget.

After they had unloaded the fuel, the two Al-Qaida men returned to the bonfire where the Russians were still swigging their vodka and laughing loudly. Secretly, they despised these drunken louts with their foul-smelling bodies, sour vodka breath and sweaty palms. It would be an honor rid the earth of their presence. *Uncouth, uneducated pigs who deserved to die. Cursed infidels!* But right now, they needed their help. So they would smile brightly, and pretend to be their brothers-in-arms, united in a common cause – the downfall of America. *Ah, but afterwards it would be a pleasure to slit their throats and watch the blood drain from their unwashed bodies. Allah is good! Allah is great! Death to the non-believers! We spit on your vile carcasses! Allah is good! Allah is great! Death to the cursed Infidels!*

Attah, the taller of the two, stepped forward and addressed the Russian. A black beard covered most of his face, and his jet black eyes glinted in the firelight. Surprisingly his voice was soft and gentle, which belied the wickedness in his heart. Educated at Oxford, he spoke perfect English, but often pretended otherwise. *All the better to keep our enemies off guard. Let them think we are simple uneducated Arabs.* He suppressed a smile. *Little did they know, but soon they would find out. They would know the wrath of Allah. Allah is good. Allah is great.*

"We have unloaded all of the fuel, so we will be on our way back," he said.

The Russian nodded and offered him the vodka bottle. "Here, my good friend, take a slug. Celebrate with me and my comrades."

Attah dismissed the gesture with a wave of his hand. "No, no, as I told you before, I do not drink. We will see you in a couple of days, and then we will start setting up for the big boom."

The Russian threw back his head and took a large gulp of vodka, the fiery liquid dripping down his chin. "I'll drink to that," he slurped, wiping his mouth with the back of his hand. "Are you sure you and your friend won't join me, Attah," he said, once again waving the bottle in front of the man's face. "This is a time for celebration. We should drink to our great victory."

Attah struggled to hide his disgust. It took all his strength not to strike the filthy Russian. He coughed and hid his hatred behind a bright smile. "No, thank you, my friend, we must be on our way now." He turned to his colleague, who was glaring at the Russian, pure venom dancing in his dark eyes. "Come, Ali, let us be on our way – we have a long journey ahead."

But Ali did not move. He stood transfixed, his dark hooded eyes locked on the slovenly Russian. A jagged scar ran from his forehead to his chin and his thin narrow lips quivered with hatred. Unlike Attah, he made no attempt to hide his disgust.

The Russian wiped his mouth again, and rose to his feet. "Farewell for now, my dear friends," he slurred. "We will reach the missile site in a few days. Say hello to the Al-Shabab men."

Attah nodded curtly, while Ali continued to glare openly, the hatred evident on his swarthy face. Attah pulled him to one side, hoping that the Russian was too drunk to notice. Fortunately, none of the Russians had paid attention to Ali – they were too busy partaking of their beloved vodka.

"Come, Ali, we must go," urged Attah.

Still, Ali refused to move. *Cursed infidels,* he muttered under his breath as he watched the Russians pour the vodka down their throats. *I spit on your filthy Russian bodies.*

Attah grabbed his arm and pulled him backward. "Hush, Ali," he whispered, "they'll hear you."

"Cursed Cossacks, they will pay for their vile ways," continued Ali, oblivious to Attah's warning. Fingering the dagger hidden beneath his jalabi, he stroked the shiny blade.

"It will be a pleasure to slit their throats. To carve out their entrails and throw them to the dogs."

Attah tried again. "Hush, my friend, all in good time. We must go now."

"Nostravia!" shouted the Russians. They had already forgotten about the two Arabs.

Ali gritted his teeth. "Now they are rejoicing, but soon they will be squealing like pigs."

"Be quiet, Ali," warned Attah. "We need these men. Afterwards, you can do with them as you will, and as a present, I will give you the big Russian."

Ali smiled for the first time. "The big Russian will be the first to die," he purred. "Very, very slowly." He caressed the shiny blade as a lover would caress his sweetheart. "I will cut off his genitals and place them in his mouth and then I will drown him in his beloved vodka."

"Enough, Ali, it is time for us to go now," said Attah, hustling his friend to the nearby truck.

Ali continued to glare, still muttering obscenities as he climbed into the truck.

"Nostravia!" toasted the Russians as they watched the truck's rear lights disappear into the night.

The Russian took another swig and then rubbed his hands together. "I can't wait until the Americans and the Israelis hear that two nuclear missiles have blown up in their countries."

"Nostravia!" yelled his comrades.

"Yes, yes, it will be a great day," said the Russian, licking his bloated lips. "A great day, indeed." He patted himself on the chest. "And, we, my comrades, have made this possible. Thanks to us, the world, as we know it, will be no more."

Death to the Americans!

Death to the Israelis!

Long Live Russia!

Nostravia!

Chapter Sixty-Eight

From his vantage spot behind the two dual tires, Geigy watched the Russians carousing, and congratulating themselves. *Thank God, the Arabs have left. Those Al-Qaida guys give me the creeps. Now, I can't wait until the Russians go to sleep so that I can place the last bomb.*

His entire body was aching from head to toe. Who would have thought that lying motionless for the last hour would cause such excruciating pain. But he had to hang on for a little while longer, until the Russians finally called it a night. If he moved now, there was a chance they would see him. *Stay still!* he willed himself. *It won't be much longer. They're running out of vodka. And the fire has almost died. Hang in there, Geigy, you can do it!* He grimaced in pain, struggling to stay still. Then he heard the words that were sweet music to his ears.

"We are going to sleep now," yelled the Russian to one of the soldiers.

"Thank God," sighed Geigy, in relief. "I don't think I could have held on for much longer."

The Russian continued issuing orders. "You sit there and guard us through the night," he commanded, pointing to a nearby tree stump.

The soldier saluted. "Yessir," he shouted as he took up his position by the tree.

Oh, no! thought Geigy, *he's gonna be there all night long. And he has an AK-47, one of the best weapons that has ever been made. I'm trapped!*

"Goodnight, and don't you dare fall asleep," yelled the Russian as he stumbled into his tent.

Judging by the amount of vodka he's swigged, thought Geigy, *he'll be asleep before his head hits the pillow.* He rubbed his numb legs. *Thank you, Marines! Not moving a muscle for over an hour took all my strength and willpower. Best training I ever had – probably saved my life.*

He looked over at the guard who was sitting on the tree stump, and picking his teeth with a small twig. *Now how am I gonna get out of here? The sun will be coming up shortly, and then I will have to make run for it, otherwise they'll see me. I will have to light the fuse under the truck. The rest of them won't be able to see the fuse burning.*

A loud grunt followed by a groan interrupted Geigy's train of thought. He looked over at the campsite to see the Russian staggering from his tent. "I have to make a big one," he shouted to the guard. "Bring a torch and guard me. I don't want to be grabbed by a wild animal."

Yessir," cried the guard, running to fetch a torch.

Geigy's eyes lit up. *This is my chance*, he thought as he watched the guard follow the Russian to a clump of trees and then disappear into the brush. *My one and only chance*. He rolled over on his back. "Agh," he cried out in pain, "I can't feel my legs. Goddammit, I've got to get some life back into these suckers, otherwise I'm a dead man." He rubbed his legs vigorously for several minutes, flexing his ankles and toes. Then he repeated the motion on his arms and torso. Soon, he could feel the blood coursing back into the body. "Phew! that feels better. For a while there, I thought my muscles had died."

Geigy looked over at the clump of trees again, making sure there was no sign of the Russian and the guard. *Here goes, it's now or never*. Rolling over on his back again, he carefully placed the last sticks of dynamite underneath the missile. *That's the last one. Now I have to move in slow motion so that no one will hear me*. He looked over at the trees again. Still no sign of the Russian, or the guard. *That must be one helluva big dump he's taking. Either that or he's been snatched by a wild animal. I hope it's the latter! Poor animal would probably choke on his rotten vodka-soaked body.* Geigy gritted his teeth. *Now all I have to do is unwrap this fuse and get far enough away to light the end of it.* He fingered the end of the fuse, rolling it between his thumb and forefinger. Looking up at the sky, he glimpsed the first streaks of light breaking through the clouds. Dawn was approaching. *It's starting to get light out, so I better move a little faster. Here goes!*

Safe and secure in his little dugout, Cheyenne had been watching Geigy's every move. He had seen the Russian and the guard disappear into the bushes. *Poor old Geigy. he hasn't been able to move a muscle for ages. Must be as sore as hell. Don't think I could have kept still for so long. He's certainly earned his whiskey – goddammit, he's earned a whole crate of whiskey!* Cheyenne looked over the bushes. *Geigy is so close to the Russian and that guard. Thank God, that jerk had to take a dump. It will give Geigy enough time to set the last bomb. And it's almost dawn, so he should do it now.* Cheyenne strained his eyes against the dawn's early light. Something was moving. *What the hell is that? Some kind of animal? I could swear that I see a dark shadow moving slowly from underneath the truck.*

Opening his eyes wide, he stared long and hard at the dark shadow, trying to make out the shape. *Goddammit, it must be Geigy! Let me get my matches ready. I hope to hell that the rest of the group is ready,* he thought, fumbling with the matches. *If that's Geigy, this thing will be lighting up the whole valley. It will be like all our fourth of Julys rolled into one! Yep, that's Geigy all right,* he thought, now recognizing his old friend. *Now I know why he wanted the longer fuse, because he's the closest one to the Russians.*

Cheyenne watched as sparks suddenly crackled near the missile. *Damn, there goes Geigy's fuse. Now I have to light my fuse.* His hands shook as he broke the match. "Dammit," he cried aloud, "I broke the match." He looked around, hoping that the Russians hadn't heard him. *That was stupid. I could have given the whole game away.*

Steadying his hands, he grabbed another match and lit the fuse. "There it goes," he whispered as the fuse started to fizz. He looked over in the distance. "And there goes Winston's fuse, and Willie's. Thank God, they didn't fall asleep." Cheyenne smiled. "What a great group of friends. They're the best. The very best!" Then he noticed that Geigy's fuse was not burning anymore. "Oh, my God, Geigy's going back to light it!" gasped Cheyenne as he watched the dark figure of Geigy crawling back toward the truck.

Chapter Sixty-Nine

Cheyenne held his breath. A tiny light flickered in the darkness reminding him of the fireflies back home in his beloved Wyoming. *Hurry, Geigy! That sucker's gonna blow heavens high any second.* Straining his eyes, he spotted Geigy scurrying back for cover. "My God, he's done it! Goddammit, Geigy, my old buddy, you're a pistol!"

Before the words had tumbled from his mouth, Boom! the world exploded. Or so it seemed. To Cheyenne, it was like a million fourth of Julys rolled into one spectacular firework display. Night became day. And the sky was ablaze with a myriad colored lights.

"Jesus, the sky's on fire!" exclaimed Cheyenne, shielding his eyes from the brilliant glare. Pillars of black smoke and sooty debris wafted upwards. Boom! Another explosion ripped through the stratosphere, a hundred times more deafening than the last.

Cheyenne covered his ears. "Goddammit, I'm gonna be deaf and blind after this is over," he cried, still mesmerized by the magnificent firework display. A piece of falling debris narrowly missed his head and thumped harmlessly to the ground. Cheyenne prodded it with his foot. "It's the truck's steering wheel," he gasped. "That was a near miss." He looked up at the blazing heavens. Falling debris continued to rain down all around him. "Well, I guess I'm next."

Boom! Another giant explosion shattered the air as the dynamite under the first missile ignited, jettisoning the deadly weapon sky-high. Cheyenne continued to watch in awe, his eyes as wide as saucers. A sharp jab in the ribs brought him back to reality. "Ouch," he cried.

Geigy stood beside him grinning from ear to ear. "We did it, Cowboy!" His craggy, weather-beaten face beamed with joy. "I never would have believed it, but we did it."

Cheyenne smiled. "Yes, old friend, thanks to you, we did it," he said softly. "You orchestrated the entire show. And what a show! Just look at that fiery sky. You turned night into day."

Geigy beamed. "Everything went like clockwork. It was like the perfect storm."

Winston and Willie bounded over, their faces wreathed in smiles.

"What's that about a perfect storm, old chap?" asked Winston. "Looks more like Bonfire Night,

The others looked at him, puzzled. "Sort of like your Fourth of July," explained Winston, "except we burn a guy at the stake every Fifth of November." They continued to stare at him, shocked by his words. "Not a real guy," laughed Winston, "just a stuffed replica of Guy Fawkes who plotted to blow up the Houses of Parliament back in 1605."

They stood in a circle congratulating one another. High Fives all around.

"I still can't believe we actually pulled it off," said Geigy, shaking his head.

"It was pure magic, Geigy," said Cheyenne.

"Ain't that the truth," said Willie. "I was scared shitless, but we pulled it off. Magical!"

Just before the blast, the Russian was pulling up his pants. "Do you smell something burning?" he asked the guard as he sniffed the night air. The guard pointed to the burning torch. "Ah, yes, that must be it," smiled the Russian, fastening his trousers.

A fraction of a second later, the deafening blast shattered his eardrums, knocking him to the ground with a sickening thud. The guard landed in a twisted heap beside him.

"I can't see! I can't see," screamed the guard, temporarily blinded by the dazzling light.

"What the fuck," moaned the Russian, writhing in pain. Dazed and disoriented, he lay there frozen as a second explosion, then a third, and a fourth, rocked the night sky. "What the fuck," he repeated, shielding his eyes from the searing glare. "What the fuck is happening?"

Realization dawned. "The missiles!" he exclaimed. "That sonofabitch Cowboy and his crazy cronies have blown up the missiles!" Grabbing the AK-47 from the semi-dazed guard, he ordered him to attack with his burning torch.

"No, no," cried the guard, cowering in fear. "It is the Hands of Lightning. He is very angry. I leave now." And dropping the torch, he turned and ran like the wind in the opposite direction.

Disgusted, the Russian raised the AK-47 and took aim. "You rotten, lily-livered coward," he shouted at the departing figure. "I'm gonna blow you away." Squeezing the trigger, he shot the guard in the back, killing him instantly. "That's what you get for running away," he sneered. "Well, you ain't gonna be running no more. Cowards are the scum of the earth."

Fury enveloped the Russian like a warm blanket. The blast had affected his senses. Cradling the AK-47, he shouted at the top of his lungs. "I'm gonna kill every last person who did this."

But first, he had to call Python. Grabbing his phone, he keyed in the number and waited...and waited. "Goddammit, Python, pick up the phone, this is an emergency."

It seemed like an eternity before he heard a click at the other end. Hung-over and half-asleep, Python finally answered. "What the hell's going on?" he growled. "This better be good, Russian, you just interrupted my dream. I was dreaming about whiskey, women and MONEY."

"Well, you can forget about the money," shouted the Russian. "That effing Cowboy and his pals have blown up our nuclear missiles. Blown 'em sky high."

Python froze. "The Cowboy!," he exclaimed, his dream of riches rapidly disappearing.

"Who else could it have been? They must have taken the dynamite from that damn mountain cave, with all those tusks, and placed it under the trucks. It had to be them."

"Kill them all! Kill them all," thundered Python, banging his fist on the ground and drawing blood. "I want them all DEAD, DEAD, DEAD!"

"It will be my pleasure," replied the Russian. Dropping the phone, he ran through the debris of burning oil and gas, his eyes glazed with madness as he waved the AK-47 back and forth.

"You hear me, Cowboy. I'm gonna kill every last one of you. I know you're out there, you motherfuckers," he screamed, firing wildly through the black smoke.

The friends watched the crazy Russian from their hiding place as a bullet ricocheted from the AK-47, kicking up a cloud of dust in front of them. Another bullet slammed into the tree where Ebony was keeping watch. She quickly ducked behind it.

"That monster is not going to kill my friends," she said. Squinting through the dust and smoke, she zeroed in on the Russian. "Damn, it's hard to see him through all the black smoke."

Finally, the Russian stopped in his tracks and waved the AK-47 over his head. "Come out, you yellow-bellied cowards," he yelled. "Show yourselves, or are you too scared?" And brandishing the deadly weapon, he fired off another volley of bullets into the smoky darkness.

The light from the blast illuminated his burly figure, and Ebony took full advantage. Taking careful aim, she placed the crosshairs on the Russian's chest and squeezed the trigger, firing off two quick shots. The bullets hit their mark, and the Russian fell to the ground with a thud. He died instantly. "Gotcha!" cried Ebony.

Chapter Seventy

"Cheyenne! Geigy! Willie! Winston! Are you all alive?" yelled Ebony. "The Russian is dead! I got him dead center." Silence! Ebony's heart sank. "Oh, my God, was I too late," she sobbed. Dawn was breaking, the first fingers of sunlight glimmering through the smoky sky. Four hazy shadows emerged from the darkness. Her heart soared. They were safe. They were safe. Cheyenne reached her first, gathering her in his arms in a strong embrace. "Thank God, you're safe," he whispered, kissing her full on the lips. "You saved our lives, my darling girl. That crazy Russian was coming straight at us and he wasn't taking any prisoners."

Ebony nodded meekly as they all gathered around her. "I was worried that there might be more soldiers, but they were all killed in that first explosion," she said.

"Yes, that was a tremendous explosion," agreed Winston. "They never knew what hit them."

"I can't believe that we pulled this off and nobody got hurt," said Geigy. "It's a miracle."

Willie sighed. "My hands were shaking so much, it's a miracle I was able to light the fuse,"

"But you did it, my friend," said Geigy softly.

They stood in silence, thinking of what might have happened if they hadn't lit those fuses.

"It's been one blast of a night," said Winston, breaking the silent.

"You can say that again," agreed Geigy. One blast of a night, indeed!

Python and Ego sat facing each other. Two glasses and a half-empty bottle of whiskey sat on the table before them. Since the frantic call from the Russian, they had been drinking steadily since daybreak, and were now on their second bottle.

"Another shot," demanded Python, slamming his glass on the table.

Ego cowered in fear. "Sure, boss," he said meekly.

Python downed the shot in one quick gulp. "Ego, I want you to gather up all the soldiers. And I want you to hunt down the cowboy and his cronies." His dark eyes blazed with anger as flecks of spittle foamed on his lips. "Bring back their heads," he spat, "so that I know they're dead. Bring back their heads on stakes."

Ego smiled crookedly, revealing his rotten yellow teeth. "You got it, boss," he leered.

Python cackled and gulped down another shot. "I've been calling the Russian all morning, but he doesn't answer. I have a bad feeling that something has happened to our dear friend."

"Perhaps he's sleeping, boss."

Python wiped the spittle from his mouth. "Nah, my gut tells me that something is wrong." He slammed the table again, sending the whiskey bottle crashing to the floor. Ego lowered his head and waited. "Ego, even if you have to pay some of the natives, I want a large convoy of soldiers with trucks and machine guns."

Ego nodded again. "Your wish is my command, boss. Don't worry, I'll take care of it."

"See if you can find a couple of bazookas and some hand grenades. And make sure you take a couple of phones. I want you to call me every four hours so I know what's going on."

"You got it, boss," said Python, picking at his teeth. "You can count on me."

But Python wasn't finished. He continued issuing orders, the demands falling from his lips fast and furiously. "Make sure you have plenty of gas and water and extra rounds of ammunition."

He threw his glass at the wall for emphasis, shattering shards of glass everywhere. I WANT THEM DEAD, DEAD, DEAD!" he screamed, so I don't have to think about them anymore."

Ego cringed. "Okay, boss," he said in a small voice. He rose to his feet, anxious to leave, in case Python decided to take his anger out on him. "I'll be going now, boss."

Python continued to rant and rave, his voice reaching fever pitch. "Take that native who found them before," he bellowed, slamming the chipped table yet again.

Ego looked puzzled. "Which native are you talking about, boss?" he ventured timidly.

Another glass flew across the room and slammed into the wall. Ego closed his eyes, fearing Python's wrath. Any moment, he expected Python's fist to slam into his head.

"The one who drew us the map, you moron! The map where he thinks all the tusks are hidden," cried Python in exasperation.

Ego breathed a sigh of relief. "Ah, yes, now I know who you're talking about. We may have to pay him more than the other soldiers, though."

"So pay him whatever he wants," bellowed Python. "We need him."

"All right, boss," said Ego as he headed toward the door. "I'm going to find him right now." Under his breath, he muttered, "I've got to get the hell out of here before Python explodes just like the missiles."

"DEAD! DEAD! DEAD!" called out Python after him, the words ringing in Ego's ears.

"I WANT THEM ALL DEAD!"

Chapter Seventy-One

Monsoon was headed down that same valley with a small herd of elephants when he heard the first explosion rip through the air. Frightened by the deafening noise, the herd turned and stampeded toward the safety of the mountains. Three more explosions shattered their ears, and the cloying smell of oil and gas filled their nostrils. In the mad panic, Monsoon found himself separated from the rest of the herd. Trundling along alone, he sniffed the sulphorous air. The smell reminded him of the day he got shot. The excruciating pain. An elephant never forgets. After that dreadful day, he wanted to kill and crush anything or anyone that smelled of gas and oil. Raising his trunk, he trumpeted loudly. PAIN! An elephant never forgets.

As Monsoon's bellow pierced the air, the five friends slept soundly in their vehicles. It was now mid-afternoon and the searing African sun blazed down on the dry earth, scorching everything in its wake. Parked under a clump of trees and protected by the shade, the friends slept on. The last twenty-four hours had left them physically and emotionally drained.

Ebony was sleeping in Cheyenne's arms, her head nestled on his shoulder, when she felt a gentle tapping on her arm. "Cheyenne, honey, stop tapping me," Ebony whispered, "I'm trying to get some sleep, and you should, too."

Cheyenne grunted, but never opened his eyes. The tapping continued. *Tap! Tap! Tap!*

"Cowboy, you're starting to annoy me," scolded Ebony as she opened her eyes to see an M-16 pointing straight at her. "Agggh!" Ebony sat bolt upright and let out a piercing scream.

"What the hell," said Cheyenne, sitting up and rubbing his eyes. "What in God's name is..." His voice trailed off as he stared at a row of rifles pointed straight at him. He was wide awake now. Beside him, Ebony clutched his arm. Nothing like a row of rifles to grab one's attention.

A tall distinguished-looking man with a clipped moustache and short salt and pepper hair faced them. His erect bearing and ramrod straight stance gave him the look of a military commander, which is exactly what he was. Alongside him stood a shorter man with dark hair and eyes, his stance almost identical to that of his companion. They were like two peas in a pod.

"Do not be alarmed, dear lady," said the tall man, lowering his rifle. "Allow me to introduce myself. My name is Colonel Macken – they call me Colonel Max for short – and I'm with the United States Special Forces."

Ebony and Cheyenne said nothing – they were still in a state of shock.

Colonel Macken turned to his colleague. "This is Lieutenant Feldman from the Israeli Special Forces, or as it is more widely known, the Mossad."

Lieutenant Feldman clicked his heels together and bowed slightly. "At your service," he said.

Cheyenne and Ebony continued staring at the two military men, temporarily lost for words.

Colonel Max cast a glance at the other vehicle, which was surrounded by his men. "Don't worry about your friends," he said with a grin. "We have already made our introductions and I assure you, they are all wide awake now!"

Cheyenne looked over at the jeep, to see his friends staring at the surrounding soldiers in alarm.

"It's okay," he shouted, waving to catch their attention.

Cheyenne surveyed the sea of soldiers, all dressed in camouflage from head to toe, their faces smeared with black and brown marks. Their hats reminded him of the soldiers in the French Foreign Legion. Clearing his throat, he addressed the colonel. "What are you doing here, Colonel Max?"

"We could ask you the same question," replied the colonel. "In fact, since I have the upper hand here, I'm going to ask you a few questions." He paused and patted his rifle. "And I want the truth. Believe me, I'll know if you're lying."

Cheyenne nodded. "I understand, Colonel, fire away." And then realizing his poor choice of words, he added, "Not literally…"

Colonel Max laughed. "I see you have a good sense of humor – I like that. Now, let's begin. Are you an American?"

"Yes," replied Cheyenne without hesitation.

"How about the rest of the group?" asked the colonel, pointing to the others.

"Well, Geigy over there is an apple knocker from upstate New York," began Cheyenne, "and Ebony here is African, born and raised in Gabon."

The colonel nodded. "And the other two?"

"Winston hails from England, and Willie is African, from a small village in the rainforest."

Colonel Max scrutinized the group, looking from one to the other. "Quite a cross-section, wouldn't you say, Lieutenant Feldman?" he remarked, turning to his brother-in-arms.

Lieutenant Feldman nodded. "Exactly so, Colonel." He was a man of few words.

Colonel Max turned back to Cheyenne. "Now, what is your name and what in heaven's name are you and your friends doing here?"

Cheyenne rose to his feet. "My name is Cheyenne Cole – I come from a small town in Wyoming, and I'm here to save the elephants," he said proudly.

The colonel stared at him in disbelief. This was not the answer he was expecting to hear.

Cheyenne continued, unfazed. "My father's dream was to save all the elephants, but he passed away," said Cheyenne, shaking his head sadly. "I promised him that I would help make that dream come true. And so here I am…" He looked over at his friends. "Here we all are."

Colonel Max stood in silence for several seconds, absorbing Cheyenne's words. He knew the man was telling the truth. "Well," he said finally, "I don't think we need to hold these folks at gun point any longer. The soldiers took their cue from their commanding officer, and slowly lowered their rifles. "Now, please come out of your vehicles," ordered the colonel. "We just wanted to make sure that you were on our side."

The five friends breathed a collective sigh of relief and slowly emerged from the jeeps. For once, they had found the good guys, or correction, the good guys had found them.

"I see you have a sniper rifle in your jeep," remarked the colonel, his keen soldier's eyes not missing a trick.

"Yessir," replied Cheyenne.

"I take it you were in the military at one time?"

"Right again, Colonel," replied Cheyenne.

The colonel's eyes bore into him, as if taking his measure. "I have one sniper in my platoon, and Lieutenant Feldman has one in his." He turned and faced the soldiers. "One shot, one kill," he said simply. "Brad, Abram, step up here and meet a fellow sniper."

The two soldiers stepped forward and shook Cheyenne's outstretched hand.

"Nice to meet another sniper," said Brad.

"Likewise," replied Cheyenne.

"Shalom," greeted Abram.

"Likewise," replied Cheyenne.

"I will introduce you to the rest of the men later," said Colonel Max. "Now, we see lots of debris, smoke and fire," he continued, surveying the scorched earth and the charred trees. "It looks as if there's been a huge explosion. Can you explain what happened here? We are very curious."

Cheyenne coughed. Well, Colonel, it's a long story. I'm not sure where to begin?"

Colonel Max smiled. "I've always found that the beginning is the best place."

His men laughed.

Cheyenne looked from the colonel to his friends. "From the beginning then. Here goes..."

Chapter Seventy-Two

Colonel Max leaned forward as Cheyenne related his story so as to catch every word.

"As you can see, my friends and I are park rangers," Cheyenne began, pointing to their badges. "We set out on a mission to kill this crazy elephant Monsoon. He's been wreaking havoc everywhere and killing many people in the area we just came from."

"And where was that?" asked Colonel Max.

"Gabon."

"Go on," said the colonel.

"We thought Monsoon might come through this valley, and we were waiting for him. Then we spotted this convoy of soldiers, hauling two nuclear warheads."

Shock and surprise registered on the colonel's face, but he said nothing. Cheyenne continued. "We followed the convoy for several days, making sure they didn't see us. And then we overheard them saying that those missiles were headed for New York City and Israel."

Cheyenne paused for breath. Colonel Max and his men were following his story intently.

"One night a gas truck pulled up, driven by two Al-Qaida men. They were all laughing and joking about waiting for the big BOOM! BOOM!"

"Boom? Boom?" questioned the colonel.

"Explosion, sir," explained Cheyenne. "Detonation of the missiles.

Colonel Max nodded. "I see. Continue, Cheyenne."

"We recognized one of the men – a Russian arms dealer whom we had encountered earlier. But that's another story. Anyway, he was in cahoots with Python, another bad guy. So, we all agreed to blow up the missiles before they could reach their destination. That's it in a nutshell, Colonel," finished Cheyenne.

Colonel Max and Lieutenant Feldman and the other soldiers stood shock still for several moments, transfixed by Cheyenne's story. Then the colonel turned and addressed his men. "Soldiers, I think we should salute these brave men and woman for doing our job."

The entire contingent raised their arms in unison and saluted the five friends. The close knit group shuffled their feet and exchanged sly glances. Embarrassed but extremely proud.

What do you mean, your job?" asked Cheyenne.

"Well, through our intelligence services here in Africa, we found out that a couple of Russians hanging out near Kilimanjaro were acting suspiciously, and receiving dozens of coded phone calls," explained Colonel Max. "After intercepting their calls and pulling up their photos on Interpol, Intelligence found out their true identity." The colonel paused for effect. "Nuclear scientists! So they sent us here to find out what was going on. Looks as if you beat us to it."

"I guess so," grinned Cheyenne. "A far cry from our original mission."

Unfazed, Colonel Max continued. "Anyway, we found out that two large containers had been removed from a Russian tanker and loaded onto two diesel trucks. We had a hunch they would be headed for the United States and Israel. So, my friends," said the colonel, looking at each of them in turn, "thank you again for doing our job."

"Thank you, Colonel," replied Cheyenne. "And thank God, we were in the right place at the right time!"

That night they held a small celebration to celebrate their victory. Good versus evil, and this time good had prevailed. After a hearty meal, courtesy of the colonel's men who had killed and roasted three wildebeest, Winston and Geigy suddenly produced a few bottles of whiskey.

"Where on earth did they get those?" said the colonel.

"Who knows?" replied Cheyenne, shrugging his shoulders. "Geigy can sniff out whiskey a mile away. He's like a magician, but instead of pulling white rabbits from a hat, he pulls out bottles of whiskey."

Colonel Max laughed. "A man after my own taste," he said, slapping his thigh. "I'm always partial to a drop of whiskey, especially when we have something worthwhile to celebrate."

"Yes, it's good to celebrate," said Cheyenne flatly, his brow creased in a frown.

This did not escape the colonel's notice. "Is something troubling you, dear fellow?" Cheyenne hesitated. "Come on, out with it, man," barked the colonel. "A trouble shared is a trouble halved and all that."

"May I speak to you and Lieutenant Feldman in private?" he asked.

"Of course, my good man," said the colonel, beckoning for Lieutenant Feldman to join them.

The two officers searched Cheyenne's troubled face. "Now, what seems to be the problem?" asked the colonel.

"Well," began Cheyenne, "I told you earlier that the Russian had a partner."

"Python!" piped in Lieutenant Feldman.

"Yes, that's correct, Lieutenant," said Cheyenne, looking at him in surprise. "Python. He's one mean s.o.b., and when he finds out what has happened, he's gonna come looking for us."

The two officers nodded.

"Python and the Russian were in this together, and I know for sure that he's going to seek revenge. He'll be sending many armed soldiers to kill me and my friends." Cheyenne paused and looked directly at the two officers. "Could you help us?"

Colonel Max and the lieutenant exchanged glances. Cheyenne and his brave friends had risked their lives to save the free world from death and destruction. They had literally pulled it back from the brink of catastrophe. The least they could do was to help them in their hour of need.

"How long will it be before they get here?" asked Colonel Max.

Cheyenne scratched his head. "I would guess about three or four days," he replied, looking over at his friends who were dancing and drinking the night away, unaware of the lurking danger. Only he was looking forward, trying to stay one step ahead of his old nemesis Python. Holding his breath, he waited for the colonel's response.

"You have helped the United States and Israel, so it is only just and right that we help you," said the colonel.

"Yes," agreed Lieutenant Feldman, smiling for the first time. "You and your friends have been a friend to Israel and the free world, and now we will be a friend to you."

Cheyenne relaxed and breathed a sigh of relief. "Thank you, my friends," he said, grasping their hands.

"Now, down to business," said the colonel. "Do you have any idea how many soldiers will be coming, and what weapons they will have?"

Cheyenne thought for a moment. "I would guess about fifty to sixty soldiers, armed with rifles and 50-caliber machine guns. Perhaps a few grenades."

"Hmm," said the colonel, stroking his chin. "I assume they will be coming straight here to check out the missiles and hunt you down?"

Cheyenne nodded. "Yes," he said simply. "Without your help the five of us would be no match for such a large contingent."

Colonel Max patted his shoulder. "Don't worry, my friend. Lieutenant Feldman and I will take care of everything. Tomorrow, we will make the necessary preparations. Is that all right with you?"

"Yes, yes, that's terrific," said Cheyenne. "I feel better already."

"Good man," replied the colonel. "I told you that a trouble shared is a trouble halved. Now let's join the party before that little gal of yours causes a ruckus amongst my soldiers. Looks like they're all clamoring to dance with her."

Cheyenne looked over at Ebony who was flirting with a group of soldiers, all of them vying for her attention. She was like a pretty butterfly surrounded by moths. *Time to rein her in, before there's trouble.* Aloud, he said, "I'm with you, Colonel. Let's join the party!"

He approached Ebony, whirling her around to face him. "May I have the honor of this dance?"

"It's about time," she scolded. "Where have you been?"

"Just taking care of business, my love," he replied. "Just taking care of business."

Chapter Seventy-Three

Monsoon had joined a herd of rogue bull elephants after searching in vain for his original herd. Spooked by the explosions, they had scattered far and wide, most of them seeking refuge in the mountains. The other elephants had recognized Monsoon by the deep scar on his forehead, but once again, he had had to prove his dominance, fighting off several male bulls to become the undisputed leader of the herd. With Monsoon at the head, on and on, they trundled, slowly making their way across the vast valley.

A black and white jeep, its windows encrusted with dirt and grime, drew up alongside the migrating herd and stopped to take photos. Gus, a mean-spirited American with a shock of dark curly hair, sat in the back seat, puffing on his cigar. Beside him, sat his wife Marie, a slight frail woman with soft blue eyes and pale skin, a sharp contrast to her dark brooding husband.

Gus surveyed the herd, a dark scowl etched across his pockmarked face. "God, I hate all these animals," he sneered. "If I had my way, we would be aiming long range rifles at these smelly beasts, not poxy cameras. I'd rather kill them than take their goddamn photo."

"Elephants are gentle creatures," piped in Marie, "and that's why they have laws to protect these poor animals from people like you."

Gus turned to her, his hand raised. "Why, you bitch," he shouted, his face suffused with anger. "Who the hell do you think you're talking to, woman? I should smack you in the kisser right now," he snarled, balling his hand into a tight fist.

Marie cowered in fear. Her husband was a bully, and she had been putting up with his violence for years. Before she could protest, the jeep jerked to a halt and the driver turned around.

"Hey, Hey, Gus, cool it," said his cousin Mike. "Don't you be hitting anybody in this vehicle while I'm driving. What the hell's the matter with you, threatening little Marie like that?"

Gus scowled but said nothing. Mike shook his head. "I don't know what's gotten into you. You were all for coming on this safari. And now all you do is moan."

Gus muttered under his breath and glared at the nearby elephants.

"Thank you, darling," whispered Mike's pretty young wife, Kristen, "for defending Marie." Sitting beside him in the front seat, she gave his hand a gentle squeeze. Then, swiveling around, she turned to Marie who was still cowering in the backseat, trying to put as much space as possible between herself and Gus. "By the way, Marie, I'm curious, how did you get that black eye and those nasty looking bruises on your arms?" she asked, looking straight at Gus.

"I…I…," began Marie.

Gus jumped in before she could respond, cutting her off mid-sentence. "She fell and hit her eye on the edge of a chair, didn't you, honey?" he said, nudging her in the ribs. "She must have hit her arm, too," he added as he pinched her thigh with his powerful hand.

Fear clouded Marie's delicate features as she flinched from his painful grip. "Yes, yes, that's exactly what happened," she said timidly.

"Hell, she's falling all over the place," said Gus with a smirk. "Just like a drunken sailor. I keep telling her to lay off the liquor."

Kristen and Mike exchanged worried glances. They weren't buying his story, but for now, they decided to let it be. "Well, Marie, Mike and I will make sure you don't fall here," said Kristen, still glaring at Gus. "Won't we, honey?"

"Absolutely, we'll take care of you, Marie. Now, let's drive on, there's so much more to see."

They drove on in silence for several miles, three of them admiring the wildlife and scenery, and one of them gazing sulkily out of the window.

"Jesus, is it hot, or is it hot?" grumbled Gus, wiping his sweaty brow. "I never would have come on this trip, except for my stupid doctor. He told me it would be good for me and Marie. Well, I ask you, do you call this good?" He pointed to the herd of elephants now resting by the side of a nearby watering hole. "Just look at those filthy beasts, all covered in mud and dust," he growled. "Where's a gun or a cop when you need them?"

"Relax, Gus," said Mike. "Those elephants are magnificent. Just look at their gleaming tusks and massive bodies. Why don't you just sit back and enjoy the scenery and wildlife – perhaps you'll learn something. That's what a safari is all about."

"Scenery, my ass," sneered Gus. "I've had my fill of so-called *scenery and wildlife*. I'm hot, sweaty and tired, and I'm getting a goddamn cramp in my leg." Massaging his aching thigh, he thumped the car door. "Stop the jeep, Mike, I need to walk, and I have to take a piss like Niagara Falls."

Mike jolted the jeep to a stop and Gus clambered out. One hand held his sore thigh, the other his trusty brown cane.

"Gus, do you think it's safe here with those elephants so close?" asked his wife.

Gus glared at her. "Don't be so stupid, woman," he snarled. "I can beat off those big sissy bastards with my cane." Leering at the two women, he unzipped his fly. "Now don't you girls be looking when I pull out the fire hose," he said as he sprayed the dusty ground with urine. The elephants watched him with mild curiosity and then returned to spraying each other with water. Monsoon, however, never took his eyes off him.

Gus called out to them. "Get the hell back, you filthy beasts," he yelled, raising his brown cane. Still frolicking in the water, the elephants ignored him. Monsoon continued to watch and wait.

Gus persisted. "Why can't this cane have a rifle inside of it like in the movies, then I would shoot me a few elephants," he said, raising the cane and aiming it straight at Monsoon.

With their keen sense of hearing, the elephants paused in their water play and looked over at the noisy American. Fearful of men, some of the younger ones trundled off into the bush.

"See, what did I tell you," bragged Gus, waving his cane. "They're scared of me. Sissies."

Monsoon raised his giant head, his eyes still fixed on Gus. He had caught a whiff of gas and oil, and the smell that drove him crazy – the scent of man. Charging through the brush, Monsoon hurtled toward Gus, raising his trunk and trumpeting loudly. A man had hurt him badly, and here was a man. This man must pay for the hurt. *An elephant never forgets.*

Unaware of the approaching danger, Gus was still brandishing his cane and cursing the elephants. But the others had seen the thundering animal with the crazed eyes stampeding toward Gus like a runaway freight train.

"Gus, look out behind you!" cried Mike. "A massive elephant is heading toward you and he don't look too friendly."

Gus turned and waved his cane. "Don't worry, I'll take care of him and he'll run away just like all the others."

Monsoon hesitated as the thing on two legs faced him. Gus repeated his mantra. "Get the hell away from me," he shouted, shaking his cane angrily in front of Monsoon. One shake of the cane was all it took. Monsoon charged. Gus screamed in fear. "Get the hell away."

Monsoon stopped in front of Gus and rose up on his hind legs, blocking out the sunlight. Gus cowered in fear – he wasn't laughing now. Bellowing loudly, Monsoon came down on his front legs and caught Gus in the head, squashing it like a water melon. He died instantly.

Marie screamed and struggled to climb out of the jeep to help Gus. Too late! Monsoon swiveled his head in her direction. Another target.

"Marie, stay in the jeep," cried Mike, pulling her back. "We are all in great danger. That elephant is crazed – just look at his eyes."

They watched in horror as Monsoon crushed Gus's body with his huge knees.

"Oh, my God," whimpered Marie. Although Gus had been a brutal husband, she had always loved him, despite the years of the violent beatings. He didn't deserve to die this way.

Impaling Gus's broken body on his razor-sharp tusk, Monsoon let out another terrifying bellow and raised Gus high above his head. The brown cane still dangled from his hand.

An elephant never forgets.

Terror-stricken, Mike, Kristen and Marie beheld the grisly scene. Monsoon turned to them, his bloodshot eyes glazed over with madness. They were unable to comprehend the hatred; elephants were usually so friendly and docile. "Get the jeep started, Mike," screamed Kristen, clutching his arm, "or we're going to be his next victims."

"I hear you," said Mike, "that elephant is crazy. Something or someone has really pissed him off, big-time." He struggled to fire up the engine, his hands trembling with fear.

"Hurry! Hurry! Mike," cried Marie.

"I'm trying," said Mike, still fumbling with the ignition. "The engine must be overheated from the sun."

Monsoon edged closer and closer, readying himself to charge the smelly machine.

"For God's sake, Mike," yelled Kristen, "he's almost upon us. Do something!"

Miraculously, the engine sputtered and then sprang into life. "There it goes," sighed Mike as the jeep's tires spun in the loose dirt.

"Thank you, God," gasped the two women.

Monsoon knew that he could not keep up with this smelly thing. *An elephant never forgets.* Shaking his powerful head back and forth, he flung Gus's lifeless body high in the air. *Thump!* It landed with a sickening thud right on top of the jeep's roll-over bars.

"Get it away from me," screamed Marie as she passed out in the backseat. Gus's blood-soaked body lay sprawled across her lap.

Kristen grabbed Mike's arm as the jeep lurched forward. "Mike, you have to do something, Marie has passed out in the back."

"To hell with Marie, we have to get out of here before that crazy animal impales one of us." He pushed down hard on the accelerator and the jeep raced forward, scattering dust and debris in its wake. On and on they sped putting as many miles as possible between them and the crazed elephant. "Just tell me when it's safe to pull over," said Mike.

Kristen turned and looked behind them. "I think we're safe now. There's no sign of him. I don't think he tried to follow us. It was as if he knew that he couldn't keep up."

Mike sighed with relief. "He was one mad sonofabitch. I wonder what happened to set him off? I'm sorry, honey, but that damn beast scared the crap out of me."

"Me, too," replied Kristen, hugging her husband. "Something terrible must have happened for him to crush poor Gus like that. Elephants are usually so warm and friendly – they have no enemies, apart from the poachers who hunt them down for their tusks."

"Perhaps Gus reminded him of a poacher who tried to hack off his tusks."

"Yes, I bet that's it," agreed Kristen. "Talking of Gus, honey, what are we going to do with his body? Marie is still out cold."

"He has to go with us. We can't leave him here in the wild – the animals will tear him apart. Even though he was a miserable bastard, we have to give him a decent burial."

Kristen nodded. "You're right, honey, it's the least we can do."

Mike clambered in the back and gently pulled Marie from under Gus's battered body. As he lay her on the ground, her eyelids flickered open and she regained consciousness. "Where am I?" she cried in alarm. "I had such an awful nightmare. I dreamt that Gus had been attacked by a crazy elephant." Kristen and Mike exchanged glances but said nothing.

Marie sat up and rubbed her eyes. "Where is Gus, by the way?" And then she spotted his broken body sprawled across the backseat of the jeep, and it all came flooding back.

"Oh no!" she sobbed, "it wasn't a dream, was it? I remember it all now. Poor Gus, he was a brute at times, but he didn't deserve to die such a hideous death."

Kristen put her arms around her. "It's going to be okay, Marie."

Mike covered the limp body with a tarpaulin canvas – he didn't want Marie to pass out again.

"Okay, let's hit the road again," he said, "We've got a lot of miles to cover before night fall."

They took off in a cloud of dust, with Gus's body rolling around on the backseat, a constant reminder of their deadly encounter with Monsoon.

An elephant never forgets.

Chapter Seventy-Four

Back at Python's camp, Python had new orders for Ego. "Ego, you've done an excellent job rounding up all those soldiers and supplies.

Ego beamed. "Thanks, boss," he said, picking at his yellow teeth.

"I still haven't heard from the Russian, so I can only assume that he's dead."

Ego nodded solemnly, feigning sadness. "I'm sorry to hear that, boss." But secretly, he was overjoyed. He had always hated the Russian, jealous of his tight bond with Python. Now, he would be second-in-command – Python's right-hand man.

"So, are you ready to move out? You have all your supplies, arms and water, etc.?"

"Yes, boss, we're all set."

"Good. Now, when you get to the explosion site, I want you to be an observer. Just report back to me exactly what you see."

"You got it, boss."

"And don't forget, Ego, bring back their heads! Except for Ebony. Bring her back alive!"

Ego nodded. "Yes, boss, I'll try." Under his breath, he muttered, "Try, my ass, that bitch will be coming back dead with all the others." He didn't want that woman coming between him and Python. He was second-in-command now.

"What's that, Ego?" asked Python.

"Oh, nothing, boss, just going through everything in my mind before we leave. I want to make sure we don't forget anything."

Python patted him on the back. "Okay, good luck. Don't forget, bring back those four heads. Ebony can keep hers, at least for the time being. Now give the order to move out."

"Let's load up," Ego yelled as the soldiers piled into their vehicles. He held up his hand. "Okay, let's move out," he commanded, standing on tiptoe to increase his small stature. He felt proud and important, issuing commands, like a little Napoleon.

Dawn was breaking as Python watched the last vehicle disappear into the early morning mist. *Don't forget, Ego. Bring back those heads.*

Back at the site of the explosion, Cheyenne and the two officers had formulated the perfect plan. At least, Cheyenne thought it was the perfect plan – now he was having doubts. Smiling nervously, he turned to the two men. So, what do you think? Will our plan work?"

Colonel Max nodded. "Yes, it will work. It has to work, otherwise all is lost," he said firmly. "Lieutenant Feldman here has his soldiers well dug in and well camouflaged. And, more importantly, his snipers will play a pivotal role. Isn't that correct, Lieutenant?"

"Exactly so, Colonel," replied Lieutenant Feldman. "My best sniper will be at the very end, to my left. In addition, he will also have grenade launchers. As such, the enemy will have a hard time getting out of our ambush."

"Excellent," said Colonel Max.

"My other sniper will cover the other side to keep them from using their machine guns," continued the lieutenant. "Their job is a priority, making sure that our enemies do not fire those fifty caliber guns. Cheyenne you will be the sniper in the middle."

Cheyenne felt reassured. "Sounds as if we have all bases covered. Now we wait. It's been three days – they should be coming soon, if they're coming."

"I've sent out a spotter," replied Colonel Max, "to alert us if and when they come."

"Good thinking, Colonel," said Cheyenne.

Colonel Max cocked his ear. "That's strange, I can hear drums beating. Do you hear them?"

Cheyenne and the lieutenant nodded.

"I wonder what they're saying?" said the colonel.

"If we only knew," murmured Cheyenne. "Somehow, I don't think it's tidings of peace and joy."

Chapter Seventy-Five

On the fourth day, around noon, the spotter raced into the camp, disheveled and breathless.

"Catch your breath, man," said Colonel Max. "What is it? Have you spotted the enemy?"

"Yes, sir," sputtered the soldier, still struggling to breathe evenly. "I spotted a small dot moving slowly down the valley floor. It has to be the enemy."

Colonel Max patted him on the shoulder. "Good man. Well done, soldier, now go and rest for a while. You've earned it."

"Thank you, sir," replied the soldier, saluting.

The entire camp sprang into action, readying themselves for the onslaught. They had no idea of the size and nature of the enemy, but they were ready for them, and would fight to the last man.

"Lieutenant Feldman, are your men in position?" asked the colonel.

"Yes, Colonel, we are ready and waiting your command."

"Good, let's teach these scoundrels a lesson," He turned to Cheyenne. "I suggest that your lady friend takes cover," he said, pointing at Ebony who was nervously biting her nails.

"Yes, sir."

Cheyenne walked over to Ebony and gently led her to the safety of some nearby trucks.

"I'm scared, Cheyenne," she said, gripping his arm tightly. Her beautiful ebony eyes were as wide as saucers and her body trembled from head to toe. "If Python gets us again, God knows what he will do to us. It doesn't bear thinking about." She shuddered, and Cheyenne pulled her close to him, gently stroking her hair.

"Don't worry, honey, it's gonna be okay. As God is my witness, I won't let anything happen to you. We have come up with the perfect plan. There's no way that Python is gonna harm a single hair on your pretty head. You have my word." He kissed her softly on the lips.

Ebony melted in his arms, her fear gone. Cheyenne would protect her. He was her man.

Ego and his small convoy slowly snaked their way along the valley floor, eventually coming face to face with the missile site. Ego surveyed the site and then turned to the soldier sitting beside him in the truck. "Zuzu, you are in charge of all the soldiers," he said. "I want you to let me know everything that's going on."

Zuzu nodded, his dark eyes flashing. "Yes, Ego."

Ego was enjoying his role as commander-in-chief. Issuing orders made him feel ten feet tall, not to mention the wonders it did for his Ego!

"Remember, Zuzu, there are only five of them. You are an expert tracker, so get out there and find me some tracks so that we can follow them and hunt them down."

"Yes, boss," said Zuzu, jumping from the truck.

Boss. That has a nice ring to it, thought Ego. He was used to calling Python boss, but out here in the wild, he was the boss.

"I was hoping that the missiles might still be here," he said. "Are they in bad shape?"

"They are blown to hell along with everything else," replied Zuzu, surveying the shattered scene.

"I see what you mean," said Ego dejectedly, already feeling Python's wrath.

"Ego, I would like to have our fifty caliber machine guns firing on some of the trees and bushes, on both sides of the valley."

Ego scanned the area, his beady eyes moving from left to right. "Go ahead, you might flush them out if they are hiding in the bushes."

Zuzu signaled to the three machine gunners. "Fire up at those trees and bushes," he ordered, pointing to the targeted area.

Ego looked over at the gunners, and then braced himself for his call to Python. Taking a deep breath, he picked up the phone and spoke into the receiver. "The missiles are nothing but a useless pile of junk," he said quickly. No point in beating about the bush.

"Sonofabitch!" shouted Python, his loud cry practically shattering Ego's right eardrum.

Ego told him about the machine gunners who were already firing into the bushes.

"Just remember, Ego, I want to see four heads," he said. "As for Ebony, bring her back alive."

Colonel Max lowered his binoculars. "Everybody down! Pass the word, they are going to fire the fifty calibers. I have just seen the machine gunners take up their positions. Brace yourselves for the onslaught." No sooner had the words left his mouth than the staccato stuttering of three machine guns burst through and shattered the stillness. The colonel dropped to his knees. "Get down! Get down! Everybody down!" he repeated.

Cheyenne shielded Ebony with his body. "Stay down, Ebony," he said as dirt from the machine guns' blast sprayed over them.

"We can't let this happen again," whispered Colonel Max. "We have to get them before they get us. Snipers, you know which machine gun is yours – take them out. We cannot take another burst of machine gun fire."

"Yessir," they shouted in unison.

Cheyenne patted Ebony's hand. "Stay here, honey, and keep your head down. I'm going to take up my position."

"Be careful, Cowboy, I couldn't bear it if anything happened to you," she said softly.

"Don't worry, we're gonna take out those bastards once and for all. With Brad and Abram on either side of me, we should get the job done."

"Stay safe," she whispered.

"And you."

Cheyenne edged forward on his stomach and zeroed in on his target. Abram and Brad followed suit. "After three," whispered Cheyenne. "1…2…3…"

The three snipers pulled their triggers. Three shots rang out. Three men lay dead. Bingo!

They had taken out all three. Clean shots right through the middle of their foreheads.

Colonel Max jumped to his feet. "Quickly, men, we can't let three more gunners get behind those machine guns. Open fire!" he ordered. "Grenade launchers, I want you to take out that fuel truck, and the rest of the trucks. Okay, everybody, open fire!"

All hell was breaking loose. Ebony cowered behind the trucks, covering her ears to block out the deafening noise. Clouds of smoke filled the air. Tears streamed down her face as the acrid smell of gunpowder assaulted her nostrils. *Heaven knows what's happening. I've no idea if we're winning or losing. God help us! I pray that Cheyenne is safe. I will die if anything happens to him.* She curled into a small ball and prayed that all would be well.

Fortunately, the good side was winning. Colonel Max and his soldiers were so well camouflaged that Ego and his small army could not see their target. Some of his men tried to get behind the big fifty calibers, but they were cut down by the snipers. It was all over within an hour. Colonel Max and his brave troops were victorious.

As the shooting stopped, Ebony raised her head and waited for the smoke to clear. "Look! they're waving a white flag," she cried. "Some of them want to surrender."

Colonel Max swiveled round to face the band of soldiers who were frantically waving the flag back and forth. "Put down your weapons and place your hands on top of your head," he commanded. Without hesitation, the soldiers obeyed. "Now start walking up here in single file so that we can check you for weapons."

Hands on head, the soldiers inched their way forward and stood before Colonel Max. "Pat them down," he ordered his men. "Make sure they have no knives or weapons on them."

"Nothing, Colonel," said his sergeant. "We've checked them all and they're clean. All they have on them is their clothing. They are all frightened to death, but happy to be alive."

Colonel Max surveyed the ragtag group. They looked more like a bunch of hillbillies than a squad of trained soldiers. "Looks as if our enemies just rounded up what they could get and marched them off to battle. With the exception of the three machine gunners I don't think these men had any idea what they were doing."

Cheyenne nodded. "You're right, Colonel. Knowing Python, he probably forced them to fight for him – I don't think they had much choice. Coward that he is, he is probably at his safe house, issuing orders from the other end of a phone."

Cheyenne was exactly right. Throughout the heat of the battle, Ego had been talking to Python, on the phone! Giving him a blow-by-blow report of the firefight.

Our men have just fired off three big bursts from the fifty calibers, and you can see dust kicking up from the bullets. What the hell!

Goddammit, Ego, what's happening? Talk to me.

Now they have stopped firing, but it looks as if ZuZu is giving another command to fire. Oh, no!

Sonofabitch! What's happening, Ego?

They've just killed our three machine gunners – shot them clean through the forehead. Dead shots. And now they're firing hand grenades at the fuel and ammunition trucks. Oh, Jesus, there's gonna be one helluva explosion...

What the hell was that big bang, Ego?

That was the fuel truck, and there goes the ammunition truck. Clouds of smoke are shooting out of both trucks. I guess that's what they mean by up in smoke.

This is no time to joke, Ego. Are all our soldiers pinned down?

They are getting shot at from both sides of the valley.

This can't be true. How can five people put up so much fire power?

I don't know, boss, but our men are getting wiped out and they have hardly any cover.

How can that be, Ego? Stand your ground. Show them what a leader you are.

It's a goddamn massacre, boss. We don't stand a chance.

What are you talking about – there are only five of them!

They're hitting us from all sides, boss.

Stand your ground. Don't give up.

The men have already given up.

What do you mean?

Some of them are waving a white flag.

What the hell do you mean?

They've waving the white flag of surrender.

Surrender?

That's right, boss, surrender. They are walking towards the enemy camp as we speak.

Goddamn cowards!

Listen who's talking.

What was that, Ego?

Nothing, boss.

What's happening now, Ego?

Goddammit, I think I've just spotted that damn Cowboy.

Sonofabitch!

Sonofabitch is right, I'm getting the hell out of here before he puts his sights on me.

Stay put, Ego! That's an order

Order, my ass, I'm getting the hell away. That cowboy can shoot me from quite a distance.

Stay there, Ego, stand your ground. Don't you dare disobey me.

Sorry, boss, I'm outta here

Ego! Ego! Ego…………!

But Ego was long gone. All you could see was a swirling cloud of dust as he made a very hurried escape.

Egooooooooooooooooooooooo…..!

Chapter Seventy-Six

Colonel Max scratched his weather-beaten brow. "So, Cheyenne, what are we going to do with this shabby looking group of misfits?" He walked up and down the line of captured soldiers, his face like thunder.

Before Cheyenne had a chance to respond, Ebony sprang forward and raised her rifle. "I know what we should do with Python's cut-throat rabble," she shouted, her piercing ebony eyes blazing with anger. "Kill them right where they stand." And she aimed her rifle at the nearest man, lining him up in her sights.

"No! No!" cried the man, falling to his knees. "Please don't kill us, we were only following orders."

"Only following orders," sneered Ebony, "the orders of a monster." She gently pressed the trigger. "We have to kill them, or they will shoot us in the back at the first opportunity. Their allegiance is to Python – they are more afraid of him than they are of us."

The man turned to Cheyenne, his eyes pleading for mercy. "Oh, please, please, Great Hands of Lightning," he begged, "don't let them kill us. We had no choice - Python would have killed us if we didn't follow his orders."

Cheyenne stepped between Ebony and the fallen man, and gently pushed the rifle to one side. "Put the rifle down, Ebony," he said.

Ebony shook her head. "No way," she said defiantly. "Don't you understand, Cheyenne, Python won't stop until we're all dead, and these men are his hired assassins. It's them or us." And once again, she raised her rifle and took aim.

Once again, Cheyenne pushed the rifle aside. "I understand what you're saying, Ebony, but let's talk about it a little more." Turning, he addressed Python's hired hands. "Yes, what she is saying is true. What's going to stop you from shooting us in the back?"

The soldiers stared back at him but said nothing.

"Cat got ya tongue?" continued Cheyenne. "Why do you all work for Python – he's a money-grabbing murderer who would sell his own mother for the right price."

Still no response. The soldiers stared down at their feet, unable to look him in the eye.

Cheyenne continued on. "He kills poor elephants for money, and he was willing to drop two nuclear missiles on innocent men, women and children in countries that are at peace. Countries that are not even at war with Africa or Russia. Yet, you all work for him. Why?"

Shamed-faced, the soldiers continued staring at their feet. They knew that Cheyenne was speaking the truth.

"Nothing to say in your defense, eh?" said Cheyenne. "Perhaps Ebony is right – maybe we should kill all of you right now."

"No, no, Africa Hands of Lightning," begged the man who had fallen to his knees. "Please spare us. We are frightened of Python. He said he would kill us and our families if we didn't join his army. But we will never work for him again, or kill any more elephants." The shaking man crossed himself. "My name is Bolo, and as God is my witness, I swear it."

"Do you all swear to this?"

One by one they all swore to break away from Python and cease their relentless slaughter of elephants. "If you don't believe us, kill us all now," said Bolo.

Cheyenne looked at each of them in turn. "I may be making a big mistake, but I believe what you're telling me. You will not be killed."

Ebony was not convinced. "Well, I for one think you're making a giant mistake," she said, lowering her rifle. "How about you, Colonel Max – what do you think?"

The colonel scratched his head. "It's Cheyenne's call," he said. "I'm willing to give them the benefit of doubt."

"Thank you, Colonel. I don't believe these men will let me down," he said, turning to the captured soldiers. "But be warned, if I catch any of you working for Python again or killing a single elephant, I will blow your brains out. And that's not a threat, it's a promise."

All the soldiers fell to their knees. "Thank you! Thank you!" they cried in unison.

"Yes, yes," said Bolo, grabbing his hand and kissing it. "The great Hands of Lightning has given us back our lives. From now on, our allegiance is to him and only him."

"To our savior, the Great Hands of Lightning," shouted the others.

Cheyenne looked at them in shock. He had not expected such an overwhelming response, nor had he ever been called 'savior' before.

"Damn, I haven't seen anything like that since Patton," said Colonel Max, shaking his head.

"Me neither," said Cheyenne, and they burst out laughing.

But Ebony wasn't laughing. She was still seething with anger. "Give me a break," she muttered under her breath. "It's like the second coming! And it's no laughing matter. I still think we should shoot them all."

"Aw, come on, honey," said Cheyenne, trying to placate her. "I don't think they're gonna double-cross us."

He pulled her close, but she shrugged him off. "Once Python's men, always Python's men. I will be watching my back and I advise the rest of you to do the same."

"You really feel strongly about this, don't you?" said Cheyenne.

"Yes, I do. I think you're making a big mistake, but who am I? Just a poor lowly African woman. Who cares what I think?"

"I do," said Cheyenne. "But this time my gut tells me that these men won't turn on us. Python scared them into working for him."

Ebony rolled her eyes. "Well, don't say I didn't warn you," she said, turning towards the captured men. "And as for this bunch of cut-throats, they are not leaving here until they bury all their fallen comrades."

"You got it, honey," said Cheyenne. "Men, you heard what the lady said, start digging!"

"Yes, yes," said Bolo enthusiastically, "we will be happy to dig a big hole to bury our friends."

Grabbing the proffered shovels, they fell in line and began digging furiously. But moments later, one of the diggers dropped his shovel and pointed to one of the blown-up jeeps.

"Willie, why don't you go down there and find out what's going on," said Cheyenne.

"Sure thing, Cowboy, I'll be right back." But instead of coming back, Willie motioned for Cheyenne and Colonel Max to join him.

"What is it, Willie?" asked Colonel Max as they drew close.

"One of the diggers thought he heard moaning sounds coming from one of the jeeps."

"Let's check it out," said Cheyenne as they headed towards the jeeps.

Colonel Max held him back. "Now, let's be careful here, Cheyenne," he warned. "Somebody could be sitting there with an AK-47 aimed right at us." Turning to his men, he barked out a string of orders. "Surround that jeep, men. And proceed with caution! It could be the enemy."

With guns pointed at the jeep, the soldiers slowly inched their way forward.

"It's all clear, Colonel," shouted his sergeant. "We've found a badly wounded soldier who's hanging on for dear life. I'm not sure he's gonna make it."

"Call for the medic, Sergeant, let's see if we can save him."

"Medic! Medic!" yelled the sergeant. "Over here on the double, we need your help."

Bag in hand, the medic rushed over and knelt down to examine the wounded soldier who was now groaning loudly. "Well, medic, what's the prognosis?" asked the colonel.

The medic shook his head. "I don't think he's going to make it, sir. Half of his stomach has been blown away. He's still alive because he had the presence of mind to tear off a piece of his shirt and place it over the wound to staunch the bleeding."

The other soldiers gathered around, looking down at the wounded man.

"I know him," said Geigy. "He's one of the soldiers who kidnapped us, and took us to Python."

"I wonder what his name is?" said Cheyenne.

"Zuzu," piped in Bolo. "He was second-in-command to Ego on this mission.

Cheyenne knelt down beside the dying man. "ZuZu," he whispered, "do you have a family?"

ZuZu groaned softly and tried in vain to raise his head. "Easy, man, easy," said Cheyenne.

"I have a beautiful wife and two children," he said, struggling to speak. "A son and a daughter."

"I'll make sure your family knows that you fought a brave battle," said Cheyenne, "and that you were a special soldier."

ZuZu raised his arm and placed his hand on Cheyenne's shoulder. "I know I am dying, Cowboy," he said weakly. "I always seem to be fighting on the wrong side – the side that likes to see things die. I should have been on the side that likes to see things live." He squeezed Cheyenne's shoulder with some force. "Now, as I lay dying, I want to do something for the living. I want to do something for you, Cowboy."

"What is it, ZuZu?" asked Cheyenne.

ZuZu looked straight at him and their eyes locked. "Python knows…," he whispered as his hand fell from Cheyenne's shoulder.

"Python knows what, ZuZu? What does Python know?"

Too late – ZuZu had taken his message to the grave.

"He's gone, Cheyenne," said Colonel Max.

Cheyenne looked up at the colonel and shook his head. "Well, I guess I'll find out soon enough what Python knows." Rising to his feet, he turned and addressed ZuZu's soldiers. "Dig a single grave for your brave leader. He deserves a special place of rest." The soldiers nodded.

"And make sure that his family knows that he died a hero."

Bolo stepped forward. "It will be done. I promise you, Hands of Lightning."

After the graves had been dug and white crosses placed on both, Colonel Max beckoned for Python's men to come forward. "Gather around, soldiers, Cheyenne has something important to say to you."

The men dropped their shovels and exchanged anxious glances. *Perhaps the Great Hands of Lightning had changed his mind about setting them free.* Falling into line, they stood to attention, and waited patiently for Cheyenne to begin.

"Soldiers, it's time for you to go home to your families."

The soldiers broke into a loud cheer. "Thank you, thank you, Great Hands of Lightning," they cried. "Thank you again for setting us free."

Still unable to believe their luck, the men grabbed their water canteens and turned as one to wave goodbye. Bolo was the last man to leave. Approaching Cheyenne, he held out his hand.

"Goodbye, Great Hands of Lightning, I will never forget you."

"Nor I you, Bolo," replied Cheyenne. "Go in peace."

"From now on, we will live in peace, not war. We owe our lives to you. You have given us a second chance, and we will not let you down. Peace be with you Great Hands of Lightning."

Chapter Seventy-Seven

Cheyenne and the others watched silently as Bolo and his group became distant specks, finally disappearing into the great African horizon.

"We'll be leaving in a couple of days," said Colonel Max, his booming voice cutting through the eerie silence. "We have to get the serial numbers off all those blown-up jeeps, as well as all the guns, rifles, and those two nuclear missiles." He scratched his balding head. "Not an easy task."

Cheyenne nodded. "You got that right."

"If they can trace the numbers, it will lead to the big weapons supplier. Would I like to get my hands that monster," said the colonel, shaking his fist angrily.

"It could be a huge cartel, or perhaps a foreign country," offered Cheyenne.

"Or even some big shot in the United States. It's all greed you know...greed, greed, greed."

"Yes, I know," said Cheyenne. "The world is a corrupt place and I believe it's getting worse."

"I like to believe that there are more good people than bad," said Ebony naively.

"Don't count on it," said Colonel Max. "There are more bad 'uns out there. Just ask my men."

"Well, thank God for you and your men," said Cheyenne. "Here's to the good old US of A!"

A couple of days later, a black African helicopter swooped down along the valley floor like a ravenous vulture scavenging for food. Its steel blades whirred noisily, cutting through the stillness.

"Break out the smoke flares so that they know where we are," ordered Colonel Max.

"Yessir," came the reply.

A funnel of red smoke whirled up in the sky, and a few moments later the big black bird circled and landed with a dull thud on the valley below.

"Well, that's our ride," said Colonel Max, turning to address the entire group. "It's been a pleasure meeting you and your friends, Cheyenne. I hope our paths cross again one day soon."

"Likewise, Colonel Max," replied Cheyenne, shaking the colonel's hand. "Godspeed."

The colonel and his men boarded the huge CH-47 Chinook, and with a final wave, the five friends watched as big bird disappeared into the clouds.

Cheyenne turned to his friends. "Well, I don't think Monsoon will be in this area with all the shooting and smells."

"I agree, old chap," said Winston. "He'll be long gone."

"Let's head back to the mountains in the morning," said Cheyenne. "Nothing to keep us here."

"And we can pick up some more dynamite, in case we need it," said Geigy.

"Good idea, Geigy. Something tells me we will be needing it."

Ebony sighed. "It will be nice to get back to the mountains," she said, twirling her hair. "Maybe we can relax for a few days and take a nice shower in one of the mountain streams. My hair is filthy, not to mention the rest of me."

Cheyenne laughed. "Too much information, honey," he said as the others joined in the laughter.

She punched him playfully. "Well, a girl's got to do what a girl's got to do, and I need a bath," she said, batting her eyelids.

"As long as I can wash your back," replied Cheyenne with a grin.

"Too much information, old boy," said Winston, laughing.

"After that, maybe we can pay Ho Goo a visit," said Geigy, winking at Winston and Willie.

"Yes, yes, good idea," said Willie.

"A brilliant idea, old chap," said Winston. "Absolutely spiffing."

They were all thinking of the women back at the village.

Ebony stared at them in surprise, and then burst out laughing. "Men!!"

Meanwhile, Ego was speeding through the bush as fast as the terrain would allow, spewing up clouds of dust in his wake. "I wish this damn jeep would go faster," he said, jamming his foot down hard on the accelerator. "Damn sand and dirt slows me down."

Although he feared Python's wrath and knew he would be blamed for the failed mission, he couldn't wait to get back. "How was I to know they'd have a goddamn platoon of soldiers with them," he shouted out loud. "Not to mention three or four snipers. Python ain't gonna be pleased, but heh, there weren't nothin' we could do."

He drove on for several more hours, muttering to himself, and cursing the hot stifling air.

I better call Python. Might as well get it over with. Here goes... Bracing himself for the onslaught, he braked to a screeching halt and grabbed the phone from the glove compartment.

Python had been waiting for the call. *I can just picture him. Face like thunder. God help me!*

He gulped. "Hey, boss, how's it goin'?" *Easy, easy, stay relaxed. What's he gonna do? Kill me?*

"How's it going? Is that all you have to say for yourself," Python boomed. "It ain't going nowhere, that's how it's going."

Ego cowered in his seat. Although Python was many miles away, his reach was overwhelming. "But, boss, it weren't my fault. I told you what happened – they had reinforcements."

"Reinforcements, my ass, you should have taken 'em out."

"We tried, boss, we tried, but those goddamn snipers took out our best men. And they captured the rest of them. Probably killed them all now. I don't think they would let any of them live."

"Yeah, yeah, who cares," sneered Python. "They didn't do the job, so I don't care if they live or die." His voice was calm now. "How far are you from the village?"

"About a day's travelling, I guess."

"Good, I'll have a bottle of vodka waiting for you."

He's forgiven me. "Thanks, boss, looking forward to it. See you tomorrow."

Breathing a sigh of relief, he placed the phone back in the glove box and turned the ignition. The engine sputtered into life and Ego hummed to himself as he resumed his journey. *The boss ain't angry with me no more. I can't wait to taste that vodka. One more day...one more day.* Several miles on, Ego passed a herd of elephants. *What the hell! Would you look at those goddamn elephants. Must be about twenty of them. I wonder where they're headed?* He grabbed the phone again. Dead. *What the fuck? Now I have no way of reaching Python.* Suddenly, the jeep jerked abruptly and sputtered to a stop. *What the hell's going on now. Damn jeep is playing up now.* He turned the ignition. Nothing. *Dead as a door nail. Just my luck.* Ego checked the gas gauge. *Son of a bitch! Empty. I'll have to walk the rest of the way.* He jumped out and checked the gas containers in the back. Empty. *Damn! Damn! Damn!*

Unbeknownst to Ego, Monsoon was among the herd of elephants that he had just passed. Stopping to munch on a tree limb, Monsoon had paid no attention to the speeding jeep. Now, his stomach full, he raised his giant head and looked around. A dark spot in the distance caught his eye. A dead animal? A fallen tree? Monsoon decided to investigate.

Separating from the rest of the herd, he set off in the direction of the mysterious *dark spot.* As he drew closer, he recognized the jeep. This strange, moving noisy thing was his enemy. It had hurt him before. *An elephant never forgets.*

Monsoon hit full stride and charged toward his deadly foe. Clouds of dust and debris scattered in his wake as he thundered onward. His eyes blazed with anger. *An elephant never forgets.*

Now level with *the thing,* he raised his trunk and sniffed all around the jeep. When the tip of his trunk touched the driver's seat, he let out a blood curdling bellow that echoed across the vast African plain. Still bellowing, he rose up on his hind legs, and plunged down with all his weight, breaking off the steering wheel and crushing the driver's seat. His eyes blazing with anger, he continued to smash the jeep, flinging bits and pieces everywhere. As the tires popped, he paused momentarily, the sound reminding him of the day he was wounded by Winston.

An elephant never forgets.

Lowering his massive trunk, he sniffed the tracks leading from the jeep and looked around. He had spotted a small moving object ahead of him. Letting out another blood chilling bellow, he charged forward. *An elephant never forgets.*

The relentless African sun beat down on Ego as he trudged through the parched brush as fast as his small legs could carry him. Cursing himself, he pounded his chest and cried out to the vast stillness. *What is wrong with your head, you idiot?* He pounded his chest even harder. *Why the hell didn't you fill up the jeep with gas?* He stopped mid-rant and took a slug of water.

At least I remembered to fill my canteen with water. But I'll have to make it last. God knows how many miles I have to go in this damned heat. Patting the canteen, he placed it in his pocket and continued swearing at himself. *If that damn phone hadn't died on me, I could have called Python and he could have picked me up. I may have to spend the night out here.*

He looked around and shuddered. Just the thought of spending the night alone in the African wild sent shivers down his spine. *I'd make a tasty meal for some of those wild critters.* He shuddered again and then stopped in his tracks. His ears had picked up Monsoon's loud bellow. *What the hell was that noise?* Spinning around, he looked behind him, his beady eyes scanning far and wide. Nothing. *Must be imagining things,* he muttered, scratching his head. *This damned heat is sending me stir crazy.*

Ego picked up his stride and even tried to run, but the sun was too hot. *I'll die of exhaustion if I go any faster. I must stay calm. Try not to panic, otherwise I'm a dead man.* Another blood curdling bellow assaulted his ears. Ego stiffened. *There it is again. What the hell is that noise?* He turned around again and looked behind him, squinting his eyes against the sun. This time he spotted a large black outline rapidly approaching. *What the hell is that?* His hopes were running high. *Could it be a jeep or a truck? Please let it be Python coming to rescue me.*

Another loud bellow ripped through the stillness. *What the hell is that sound?* And then realization dawned, and his entire body shook with fear. He had heard that sound before. *That's no goddamn truck or jeep, it's that goddamn elephant Monsoon!* Swallowing hard, he struggled to control his shaking body. *Oh, my God, I'm out here in the open, with that crazy elephant. I have to outrun him otherwise it's curtains for Ego. Don't panic! Stay calm!*

Ego was so frightened that he tripped and fell to the ground with a resounding thud. Sneaking a quick look behind, he gasped in fear. The big elephant was charging forward scattering billows of dust and debris in his wake. Monsoon was on a mission and nothing or no one was going to stop him. *God help me!* cried Ego, spitting dirt from his mouth. *He's gaining on me. I have to find some sort of protection from this mad beast, and fast!* Scrambling to his feet, he scanned the horizon and spotted a large boulder in the distance. *Thank God! Thank God!* He raced toward to the boulder and fell behind it in a breathless heap.

Sweat poured down his face. The merciless African sun took no prisoners. But Ego was immune to the heat – his mind was concentrating on the huge elephant now standing on his back legs and bellowing crazily. Chills ran up and down Ego's spine like a freight train speeding down the tracks. Crouching behind the boulder, he closed his eyes and hoped for the best. A pungent smell assailed his nostrils.

What the hell is that smell? Opening his eyes, he looked around. And froze in fear. Ego was now face to face with Monsoon. The elephant's red and yellow eyes blazed with anger as he pushed the boulder forward with his powerful front legs.

"Why, you bastard!" screamed Ego, coming to his senses. "You're trying to crush me with this boulder." Jumping to his feet, he swung his arms wildly, trying to scare Monsoon away. "Get away, you crazy bastard!" he yelled at the top of his lungs.

But Monsoon wasn't listening. Raising his trunk, he knocked Ego to the ground with a single swipe. Dazed but not seriously hurt, Ego staggered to his feet not knowing what had hit him. Monsoon rose up on his hind legs again, knowing that he had his enemy cornered. Still dazed and disoriented, Ego ran right underneath Monsoon, whirling his arms and screaming. As he emerged from between Monsoon's back legs, he unknowingly hit the elephant's testicles. Monsoon bellowed in agony, shaking his massive head backwards and forwards and stamping his feet. As the pain subsided, he continued his attack on Ego.

Having shaken off the first trunk blow, Ego was now running for his life, heedless of the hot sun bearing down on him. On and on he ran, like a footballer racing to the touchline, weaving left and right to stay out of Monsoon's reach. Elephants can move rapidly and Monsoon was soon gaining on Ego, the gap becoming smaller and smaller with every stride.

Panting for breath, Ego looked behind him to see the big elephant closing in on him. "Go away! Go away!" he yelled, flapping his arms in terror.

Too late. Monsoon swung his trunk and knocked Ego to the ground again. From somewhere within Ego's cowardly body a thread of fighting spirit sprang forward and he faced the elephant without fear. "You big, ugly bastard," he yelled. "Leave me alone."

Defiant to the end, Ego looked right into the elephant's wild bloodshot eyes as Monsoon plunged a razor-sharp tusk deep into his stomach. Ego let out a death defying scream as Monsoon raised his impaled body high in the air and flung it against ground. Eyes wide open, yellow teeth exposed, Ego lay dead in the dirt.

Stomping over to Ego's lifeless body, Monsoon smelled it with his trunk and with another loud bellow raised his front legs and crushed the body flat to the ground. He sniffed Ego one more time, then turned and sauntered slowly into the African sunset.

An elephant never forgets.

Chapter Seventy-Eight

Back at the village, Python was pacing back and forth as he waited for Ego's return. "What the hell could have happened to him?" he muttered aloud, as he took a long slug of whiskey. "I've been calling his phone every fifteen minutes, but I get no answer."

Taking another slug, he slammed the bottle on the table. Python had been drinking heavily all day and now his speech was becoming slurred. "I can't get one decent night's sleep because of those goddamned villagers. Those damn women are out to kill me."

Swaying drunkenly on his feet, he grabbed the bottle again and raised it to his lips. Empty. "Goddamn!" he screamed, flinging the bottle across the room. "Now I've run out of whiskey." The bottle shattered against the wall sending shards of glass flying. Python shook his head. "I've tried telling those women that the cowboy and his group were the ones that killed their husbands and sons, but they blame all of this on me." He hung his head, feeling sorry for himself. "I can't even walk outside without my AK-47 ready to shoot."

The villagers were afraid of Python. He would often single out a villager and kill them for no reason. Afterwards, he would blow on the end of his AK-47 and simply say *I shot them because I felt like it.* No one dared to challenge him or they would be next.

Python had lost the Russian and his army. All he had left was his little buddy Ego. "Thank God, for Ego," he slurred, still feeling sorry for himself. "He's my only friend left in the world. But where the hell is he?"

Python passed another sleepless night, tossing and turning, and dreaming of Ego. The next morning there was still no sign of his little buddy. Python made up his mind. "That's it. If Ego doesn't turn up today, I'm going to jump in my jeep early tomorrow morning and go looking for my little buddy. I just hope and pray that nothing has happened to him."

The day passed. Still no sign of Ego. That evening, Python sprang into action, placing food, whiskey and supplies in several pack bags. The villagers had already let him fill his jeep with gas, along with half a dozen gas containers.

"That should last me for a few weeks," he told himself, patting his supplies.

After another sleepless night, he left at the crack of dawn. The villagers slept on, unaware of his departure, except for one early riser who had seen his jeep speed off in a cloud of dust. The man ran through the village, shouting excitedly. "Python has gone! Python has gone!"

Python screeched through the brush, weaving the jeep in and out of stray bushes and boulders. Bleary eyed and still half-drunk from the night before, he drove erratically, jamming his foot on the brake and then pumping the accelerator. The jeep lurched forward like a drunken sailor.

"I should have left that village sooner," he muttered. "What a relief. They wanted to kill me."

Turning the steering wheel sharply, he veered to the left, just missing a tree. "Now, let me see," he said, wiping the sweat from his brow. "I have a pretty good idea where Ego is, from his last phone call. If I keep travelling south, I should meet up with him soon. But first I need to bed down and get some sleep."

The next morning Python awoke from a deep sleep, refreshed and rested. Rubbing the sleep from his eyes, he felt like a new man. "Now that's what I call a good night's sleep. No dreams, no nightmares – I slept like a baby for the first time in days. Must be all this fresh air."

Shading his eyes from the glaring sun, he stared off into the hazy distance. "I should be getting close to Ego by now. Let me push this jeep a little faster," he said, slamming his foot on the accelerator. "I'm anxious to see my little buddy."

As Python drove along, his thoughts drifted to the Russian. *He told us that the money from Al-Qaida would go into a private account that could be accessed by us at any time.* The Russian's exact words sprang to mind. *This way when you need money, you just take it out when you need it. But the Russian was a master poisoner. He could have poisoned our drinks at any time and taken off with all the money. This has always bothered me. No honor among thieves.*

All thoughts of the Russian and his poisons quickly vanished from his mind as he came upon the wreckage of Ego's jeep. "What the hell is that?" he cried, squinting against the sun. "My God, it's Ego's smashed-up jeep, but where the hell is Ego?" Turning, he surveyed the surroundings – no sign of his little buddy anywhere. "He's got to be here somewhere – he can't have vanished into thin air."

Python jumped out of the jeep and bent down to examine the wreckage more closely. "Wow, look at the size of those elephant tracks!" he exclaimed, measuring the tracks with his hand. "That's one helluva big elephant!" Realization dawned. "Monsoon!"

And then he spotted Ego's tiny imprints alongside the giant tracks. "Those are Ego's footsteps leading away from the jeep. That goddamn crazy elephant is following my little buddy. And he must have crushed the jeep. I just hope that Ego escaped in time."

Python jumped back in the jeep and stepped on the gas. "No time to lose, I must find Ego…" a cold chill enveloped his body and he shivered in the 100 degree heat…"before it's too late!"

As he followed the tracks, myriad thoughts ran through his mind. Although not a religious man, nor a man who cared for anyone but himself, he suddenly realized that he did care for his little friend, and he prayed that Ego would be safe. "Don't worry, little buddy, I'm coming. Just hold on, I'll be there soon. And then we'll find the cave with all the tusks, and we'll be rich." His eyes gleamed and for a moment he forgot about his friend. "Rich beyond our wildest dreams!"

The sight of dozens of buzzards circling the skyline brought him back to reality with a thud. "Oh, no!" he gasped, fearing the worst. Slamming on the brake, he quickly grabbed his AK-47 and approached the preying birds, firing at random and killing several of them.

"Get away!" he shouted, still firing wildly. And then he saw it – the mangled remains of his only friend. "Oh, my God," he screamed, "what have they done to you, little buddy."

Tears filled his eyes and for the only time in his life, he showed genuine compassion, genuine love for a fellow human being – for his only friend in the world – Ego.

Python sobbed openly. "My little buddy, my little buddy!" he repeated. What have they done?" The buzzards had feasted well. Ego was barely recognizable, except for his yellow teeth exposed in a grimace of death. They had eaten his eyes and his face was half-gone; the rest of his body ravaged and bloody, a mass of mangled muscle and tissue. The sight would haunt Python for the rest of his days.

Python hung his head as the buzzards circled overhead, watching and waiting. "You bastards didn't leave much," he shouted, shaking his fist at the scavengers. Carefully cradling what was left of his dead friend, he carried Ego to the boulder that he had hidden behind. "The least I can do is give you a decent burial, little buddy," he whispered softly. "I owe you that."

Python slowly dug a grave and lowered Ego into the ground. "Goodbye, little buddy, you were a loyal friend and I will never forget you. Rest in peace." Tears rolled down his cheeks as he stood in silence for several seconds, honoring his fallen friend. This was a side of Python that the world had never seen, and would probably never see again.

Chapter Seventy-Nine

Python's momentary lapse did not last long. Sweeping aside sentiment, he was all business again, bound and determined to find the cave. Heading straight toward the mountain, he drove for days before he finally caught a glimpse of the big rock. His eyes widened in amazement. "Just look at that maze around the mountain. I have to find those elephant tusks before somebody else gets their hands on that precious ivory."

He rubbed his hands together as he anticipated the riches that lay before him. "I just hope this is not a bunch of bullshit. I have never seen these tusks – the only thing I have to go on, is when we captured Ebony when they were all drunk." He laughed as he remembered the scene.

"Ego and the soldiers heard them talking about all these beautiful ivory tusks. Thousands and thousands of ivory tusks." He smacked his lips together, imagining the sight. "I hope it wasn't drunken talk. Only one way to find out, but first I have to find a good place to hide my jeep."

Spotting a clump of heavy brush, he carefully guided the jeep through the tangled undergrowth. "Okay, this is a good place. Now, let me get my machete." He reached under the front seat to grab the deadly weapon. "Yep, no one will be able to see it," he said as he covered the jeep with more brush. "It's the perfect hiding place."

Satisfied with his work, he spent the next hour searching all around the mountain, until he came upon an area of flattened down undergrowth. "Aha, this must be the campsite of the cowboy and his group. The trail has to be close by," he said, looking around. "It's got to be here somewhere." And then he spotted a narrow path leading off to the left of the campsite. His dark eyes gleamed. "That path has to be the trail to the cave. I would bet my last dollar on it."

Python followed the narrow trail for several hours as it wound deeper and deeper into the shade of the looming mountain. Sharp twigs and overhanging branches scratched at his face, his feet swelled and sweat poured in rivulets down his face and aching body, but Python felt nothing. He was a man on a mission. Walking the road to riches.

And then he was there, standing at the entrance to the cave. He sighed and patted his left pocket. "Thank God, I remembered to bring these matches – it's darker than hell in there. Stepping gingerly inside, he lit one of the torches hanging on the wall of the cave and looked around. "Agh, it smells musty in here, and it's so cold and damp," he said, shivering, "especially after that brutal heat outside." He swung his arms in an attempt to keep warm. "Okay, time to find those tusks. This place is enormous – I wonder what room they're in?"

Carefully making his way through the innards of the cave, he discovered a medium-sized opening that led into a brightly lit chamber. "What the hell? Where is that light coming from?" As he hoisted the torch higher, he gasped in astonishment. There before him, lay thousands and thousands of gleaming ivory tusks. The light from the torch danced off the shimmering treasure, casting a rainbow of lights across the cave walls and ceiling. He had found the precious tusks!

Python stood transfixed. Shocked and speechless, his eyes feasted greedily on the glistening ivory. "I can't believe it," he said, finding his voice again. "They were right. Look at all this beautiful ivory. I'm rich, rich, rich," he yelled, his voice echoing throughout the cavernous chamber. "Rich beyond my wildest imagination."

He gently caressed one of the ivory tusks as a lover would caress his sweetheart. "Just making sure they're real. I still can't believe this," he whispered, shaking his head in wonder. "I have to take one back with me to the jeep."

For the next twenty minutes, he stood there surveying the treasured tusks. "My God, there's a fortune in this cave – an absolute fortune – and it's all mine. Mine! Mine! Mine!"

Tugging at one of the heavy tusks, he dragged it carefully back to the entrance of the cave.

"Looks like I'll have to spend the night here," he said, as he watched the fiery African sun sink slowly below the horizon. Giving the tusk another tender pat, he raised his arms to the sky and cried out. "I'm rich! Rich! Rich! Rich!"

That night, Python slept fitfully. Vivid nightmares of stampeding elephants and Ego's bloody, broken body pervaded his sleep and he awoke in a pool of sweat. As the sun rose, he swept the nightmares aside and concentrated on getting the tusk down the mountain to the jeep.

"This is going to be some task," he said, scratching his head. "Why can't the tusk be straight like an arrow, then if I stand it up the right way, it will slide right down the mountain. Instead, it keeps tipping over."

Python spent all day struggling with the heavy tusk. And finally, at sunset, he had the tusk nestled safely in the back of the jeep. "Phew, that was some workout," he said wearily, wiping his sweaty brow. "And that was only one tusk!"

Python dreamed of hearing voices. Awaking at dawn, he stretched his arms over his head and yawned. "That dream seemed so real. Could have sworn those voices were close by." He stretched and yawned again. "Now, what am I going to have for breakfast?"

Rummaging in his backpack, he pulled out a plastic bag containing three wedges of salted beef. "Guess this will have to do," he said, chomping down on the salted beef. He stopped mid-bite. "What the hell? I do hear voices," and he reached for his AK-47.

Unaware of Python's presence, Cheyenne and his friends had pulled into the campsite the night before. "Wow, that was some trip," said Ebony. "It's good to get back to our little retreat by the mountain."

"Sure is," agreed Cheyenne. "Let's grab something to eat and then get a good night's sleep."

The next morning they all awoke bright and early.

"I feel like a new man," said Winston, stretching his legs. "That sleep was most refreshing."

"I'll get the fire going, so we can have breakfast," said Willie, gathering some wood together.

After a hearty breakfast, they discussed their plans for the day. "Maybe we should go to the cave and grab some more dynamite," said Geigy.

Ebony glared at him. She was about to respond when a volley of shots shattered the morning stillness.

"Get down! Get down!" yelled Cheyenne as another burst of gunfire rang through the campsite. "That was an AK-47. Stay down and get your weapons if you can."

Ebony darted to the jeep and grabbed two rifles from the backseat.

"Stay down, Ebony," cried Cheyenne, as another burst of gunfire kicked up dirt around the camp.

"I'm hit! I'm hit!" yelled Geigy as a bullet ricocheted off a tree and hit Geigy in the upper leg.

Winston tried to get to his rifle, but tripped on a branch and twisted his ankle. He fell to the ground, whimpering in pain.

"Ebony, I told you to stay down," said Cheyenne.

"I know, I know, but I'm worried about Willie. He went to take a whiz and never came back."

"So am I, Ebony," replied Cheyenne as he took his rifle from her, "but if you don't stay down, you'll get yourself killed. The shots are coming from over there." He pointed to a clump of trees and thick bush. "Now what we're going to do is put as many shots in that area as we can."

Ebony nodded.

"Geigy, Winston," he shouted, "are you all right?"

"I got hit in the thigh," said Geigy, "but I have a tourniquet to stop the bleeding."

"Good man. How about you, Winston?"

"I'm just a clumsy Englishman," joked Winston. "I fell and twisted my ankle, so get whoever is out there. I can take care of myself."

Cheyenne turned to Ebony. "Looks like it's down to you and me, sweetheart. Are you ready?"

"Ready when you are."

"Okay, ready on three. One, two, three…"

They let fly with a relentless barrage of gunfire, and then stopped.

"Look!" shouted Ebony, "someone's running over there."

"It's Python," said Cheyenne. Before they could get a bead on him, he had disappeared into the heavy brush. "Ebony, you go and check on Willie. I'm going after Python."

"Be careful, Cowboy," she said, placing a hand on his arm.

"Don't worry, I'll be okay." He fired a few shots into the undergrowth. "I'm coming after you, Python. I've had enough of your bullshit."

No answer. *I bet he's heading for the cave.*

Approaching the narrow trail, Cheyenne spotted Python's fleeing figure on his way to the cave. *There he is.* Cheyenne lined him up in his sights. *Can I hit him from here?* As he zeroed in on Python, he disappeared into the bush. Cheyenne lowered his rifle. *I'll take care of him later. Right now I have to get back to the camp. I'm really worried about Willie – he never came back.*

As he hurried back to the camp, he saw Ebony kneeling down on the ground. Her face was wet with tears. "Ebony! Ebony! What's wrong!" he cried.

She raised her tear-stained face and looked at him with sad, swollen eyes. "Willie's dead!"

She started crying uncontrollably, the tears flowing down her face.

"Oh, no!" gasped Cheyenne, pulling Ebony close to him and holding her tightly. "It can't be."

His tears joined with hers as they stood clutching each other.

"Python killed him, Cheyenne," she repeated. "Python killed him."

Cheyenne looked down at Willie's lifeless body. "Please God, no, not Willie," he said, choking back sobs. But it was too late. Willie was dead.

Chapter Eighty

"What's going on out there?"

"Everything okay?"

The cries of Geigy and Winston snapped them from their sorrow. "We have to tell them about Willie," said Cheyenne, wiping his eyes.

Ebony gripped his hand. "Yes, we'll do it together," she said softly.

They walked back into the camp, arms entwined. Winston took one look at their faces. He knew. "Willie's dead, isn't he?"

Cheyenne and Ebony nodded. "Yes," was their simple response.

"No! No!" pleaded Geigy, his eyes begging them to say it wasn't true. "Not Willie."

"Yes, it's true, Geigy," said Ebony, taking his hand in hers. "Python shot him twice."

She fell to her knees, pulling Geigy with her. Winston and Cheyenne knelt down beside them and the four friends huddled together in a circle, mourning their dead friend. Cheyenne was the first to break the spell. "I know that we are all very upset, but Willie would want us to be stronger than ever." He turned to Geigy and Winston. "The first thing we have to do is check you two out. Ebony, you have to take care of Geigy's wound so it doesn't get infected."

Ebony nodded. "Yes, don't worry, I'll take care of it."

"The bullet went straight through," said Geigy. "It was a clean shot, if there is such a thing."

"That's good, Geigy," said Cheyenne, "and you've managed to stop the bleeding with the tourniquet. Now, Winston, I think your boot has to come off that twisted ankle."

"Yes, old chap. I'm ready when you are. At least, I think I am."

Cheyenne took hold of Winston's boot. "This is going to hurt," he said as he pulled off the boot.

Winston yelped in pain. "Sorry…"

Winston smiled. "Not at all, old chap. It feels much better getting that pressure off my ankle."

"Now I'm going to make you a crutch so that you can get around," said Cheyenne. He turned to Ebony who was tending to Geigy. "How does that wound look on Geigy's leg?"

"It's not that deep, but he won't be doing any running for a while."

About fifteen minutes later, Cheyenne walked back into the camp, carrying a wooden stave.

"Here's your crutch, Winston. We can make it shorter if you like."

"Thanks, old chap," said Winston, taking the crutch. "You cut this from a tree?"

"Yes, now let's see how it fits," said Cheyenne, helping Winston to his feet.

"I would say this crutch is bloody remarkable. Thanks again, old chap."

Cheyenne looked at each of them in turn. "This afternoon, I'm going to dig Willie's grave. Ebony, I want you to pick out the best spot for him," he said, turning his head so that they couldn't see the tears brimming in his eyes.

"Let's do it now," said Ebony, walking over to comfort him.

They walked slowly out of the camp, arms clasped around each other, as Geigy and Winston looked on, the tears flowing freely down their faces.

"I think he should be buried right here, where his spirit left his body" said Ebony. "And there's a nice tree here to protect him." She broke down again, the sobs wracking her slim frame.

Cheyenne knelt down and examined Willie's body. "I don't believe it!" he exclaimed.

"What is it, Cheyenne?" asked Ebony between sobs.

"Python shot Willie in the back. He was a perfect target, standing still." He shook his fist angrily. "You bastard, Python," he shouted. "I'm going to get you for this."

Late that afternoon, they buried their dear friend where he had fallen. They took turns praying, and each of them said a few words in honor of their friend. In the evening, they built a big fire and reminisced about their beloved Willie.

"I wonder if Willie was really Ego's half-brother?" said Geigy.

"I guess we'll never know," Cheyenne replied.

"It's been a terrible day," said Ebony - one we will never forget."

Later that night, as she and Cheyenne lay cuddled together in the jeep, she asked him, "Why are you so restless? And where did you go before?"

"To check out Willie's grave."

"Oh, you really cared for him. I miss him too," she said, curling closer.

The next morning as Ebony was preparing breakfast, Geigy pulled her aside. "What's with Cheyenne? He keeps walking to Willie's grave. We have to move on, we all miss Willie."

"Yes," replied Ebony quietly. Then in a loud voice, "Breakfast is ready."

During breakfast Cheyenne addressed the group. "Python didn't walk here. We have to find his vehicle. Geigy, will you and Winston be all right for a few hours? Ebony and I have to find his jeep, and then we'll be back."

"We'll be fine, won't we, Winston?" said Geigy.

"Of course, old chap. I just wish we were fit enough to help you search."

Within the hour, they had located the hidden jeep.

"He didn't do such a good job of hiding it," remarked Ebony.

"No. And look what that greedy sonofabitch has in the backseat – a tusk. He thinks that all those tusks in the cave are his. Greedy, murdering bastard!"

Ebony touched his arm. "Let's get back to the camp. Geigy and Winston are waiting for us."

Cheyenne was boiling over with anger. Rivulets of sweat poured down his face, and his eyes blazed. "I'm going after Python. I won't rest until I've killed the bastard."

"Please, Cheyenne," begged Ebony. "Please don't go after him alone."

But Cheyenne remained resolute. "This is between me and Python," he said firmly. "I have to avenge Willie's death. I can't have a man out there, ready to shoot us in the back."

Ebony continued to plead with him, but his mind was made up. "Who's next, Ebony? You? Me? Geigy? Winston? We will never be safe, with Python sneaking around out there."

"I know you're right, Cheyenne, but I still don't want you to go alone. Let me come with you."

"No, this is something I have to do by myself. Besides, Geigy and Winston need your help."

Back at the campsite, Cheyenne told Geigy and Winston what he planned to do. "I'm going after Python, and I won't rest until he's dead. I have to do it for Willie…for all of us."

Geigy and Winston put up no resistance. They understood.

"I'm not a religious man, old chap," said Winston. "But may God hold you in the palm of his hand and bring you safely back to us."

"I'll second that," said Geigy.

"Me, too," said Ebony, drawing him into her embrace.

Cheyenne kissed her softly on the lips. "Thank you, my friends. I'll be back."

He grabbed his long range rifle and strapped on his six shooters. Then he packed a backpack with food and water and slung it over his shoulder.

"If I don't come back…and it's a big *if*…one of you will have to kill Python. You will be avenging Willie," he said, pausing,…and me." And before they could respond, he was gone.

Chapter Eighty-One

Cheyenne plunged into the thick bush, and was soon consumed by the heavy undergrowth. He stopped briefly at Willie's grave and saluted his fallen friend. "I will not let you down, Willie. I promise I will avenge your death. Python's days on this earth are numbered."

He moved quickly, knowing he would have to spend at least one night in the bush. He made camp that evening at sundown, and was up at sunrise, ready to face the day. Two days earlier, Python had been a man on a mission. Now it was Cheyenne's turn. And Python was the mission.

The morning mist cast a shroud around the dark mountain. Tall and forbidding, it reminded Cheyenne of a sentinel guarding the gateway to heaven.

I want to get to the cave by noontime. He wiped the dampness clinging to his hair and clothes. *At least, this damp air will be much cooler for traveling, so I should make good time.* He patted his trusty weapons. *I know that Python has an AK-47, but I have my long range sniper rifle which is just as deadly,* he mused as he carefully wiped the rifle. *My six shooters will be no good unless I get close enough. But I have a plan.*

As anticipated, he made excellent time, and reached the cave about noon. Standing at the entrance, he peered into the darkness and then yelled at the top of his voice. "Python, I'm here to arrest you for the murder of Willie."

No response.

"You are also on the most wanted list for dozens of heinous crimes, so come out with your hands on your head." Cheyenne's voice echoed throughout the vast chambers of the cave and bounced back to him like a boomerang. "I know you're in there, Python. Show yourself, you murdering coward."

Python's voice rang out in eerie silence. "I've been waiting for you, Cowboy," he shouted, letting fly with a volley of shots that whizzed by close to Cheyenne's head. "Come on in and get me, if you dare."

Cheyenne ducked and took shelter by the side of the mountain. Standing at the entrance of the cave, he was a sitting target. Python let off another burst of gunfire.

"I'm not going to jail, no how," he hollered. "I know all about your shooting capabilities, Cowboy, but first you have to get in the cave, and I'm gonna be ready for you."

Another burst of gunfire blasted from the cave's entrance, kicking up dust and dirt everywhere, and scattering the birds from the trees below.

"If he keeps this up," thought Cheyenne, "he'll run out of ammunition."

Slowly, Cheyenne edged his way back to the cave, stopping to pick up stones and several pieces of wood. Python had told him just what he wanted to hear. *I know all about your shooting capabilities.* This meant that Python definitely did not want him in the cave. So Cheyenne would trick him. Selecting one of the stones, he threw it in the cave and stepped back. As expected, a volley of shots rang out from Python's AK-47.

Cheyenne smiled. "Just what I was hoping for." He kept throwing rocks and wood into the cave, and Python kept answering with a burst of gunfire. *Not only is he a murdering, thieving coward, he's also very, very stupid,* thought Cheyenne. *He's playing right into my hands.*

As Cheyenne threw the next piece of wood, Python responded with a single shot.

"Gotcha!" said Cheyenne. "He might be trying to trick me, but something tells me he's out of ammunition." Just to make sure, Cheyenne threw some more stones and wood. No response. Nothing. It could be a trick, but he decided to risk it. "Time to go in."

Running to the other side of the cave, Cheyenne looked in. The entrance was dark, but in the distance he could see that the cave was illuminated with burning torches. "Okay, this is it – Showtime!"

Taking a deep breath, he sprinted into the cave, fired off two shots as he hit the dirt, and then rolled three times. He came up with his gun pointed at the entrance to the tusks. Python's raspy voice pierced the stillness. "All right, Cowboy, so you outsmarted me. Give yourself a gold star. I thought I had more ammunition, but I guess I was wrong. I'm all out." He paused, waiting for Cheyenne to respond. But Cheyenne remained silent. Watching…Waiting…

Python decided to try a different approach. "Listen here, Cowboy, you and me could become very, very rich, if we join together and sell all these tusks. What do you say?"

"Before we start talking, Python, where's your little friend, Ego? You two are usually joined at the hip."

Python gulped, thinking of his little buddy. "Ego's dead," he replied, his voice faltering. "Killed by that crazy elephant Monsoon."

"That's funny, I saw Ego when we blew up the missiles."

"Yes, he was there. By the way, thanks for blowing up the missiles," said Python sarcastically. "Me and Ego and the Russian were going to retire and spend the rest of our lives on some beautiful island, chugging down vodka and being waited on by gorgeous women." He sighed, thinking of what might have been.

"I guess you didn't care about all the innocent lives that would have been lost," said Cheyenne angrily. "Millions of men, women and children. Especially the children."

"Nobody is innocent in America," retorted Python, "or Israel – those rich pigs."

"Yes, but isn't it ironic that those people you call pigs help out countries like yours. And you just try to destroy them."

"What do you mean, help out? If you mean with money, I've never seen any money."

"No, because corrupt thugs just like you are in charge, and they steal all the money." Cheyenne shook his head in disgust. "Anyway, enough of this, I have to take you in, Python."

"No, wait, Cheyenne, we can still make a deal."

Cheyenne shook his head. "No deals, Python. You shot my good friend Willie in the back. I don't make deals with cold-blooded killers.

"Willie was nothing but a half-bred pygmy," snorted Python. "Half brother of Ego."

"How do you know that?" asked Cheyenne in surprise.

"Because I was the one who raped and killed their mother." Python smiled at the recollection.

"I rest my case," said Cheyenne. "A killer and rapist of the worst kind."

"I had to kill her because she recognized me – I had no choice, she had to die."

"You're a monster, Python. You'd probably kill your own mother for a slug of vodka."

Python shrugged. "What's the big deal? Willie and his like are only good for slaves. They do anything you tell them."

Cheyenne's face suffused with anger. "Why, you sonofabitch, I should kill you right now," he shouted, his grip tightening on his six-shooter.

"Hold on, Cowboy, I have no weapon," cried Python. "You wouldn't shoot an unarmed man, would you?"

"You're no man. More like a snake, hence the name Python. I guess your momma knew what she was getting."

"Leave my momma out of this," snarled Python.

"Not such a tough guy now, are you?" taunted Cheyenne.

"How tough are you without those guns strapped to your side," said Python as he strode out with his hands in the air. "See, Cowboy, no weapons."

Cheyenne watched him carefully, his guns trained on Python's forehead.

"Come on, Cowboy, don't be a wuss. Put your guns down and let's go at this man to man."

Eyes flashing with anger, Cheyenne tightened his grip on the gun's trigger. *I should blow him away now. Rid the world of this poisonous vermin.* He squeezed the trigger tighter.

"Come on, Cowboy, cat got ya tongue?" taunted Python, licking his lips. "What do you have under those pants, little girlie tights?"

Cheyenne stiffened. Graphic images of Willie's blood soaked body flashed through his mind. He could see the gaping holes where the two bullets had shattered his spine. His dear friend lying motionless in the dirt, the flies and mosquitoes already feasting on his wounds. The time for talking was over. He was ready.

"You've got it, you murdering bastard," cried Cheyenne as he tossed his guns to the ground. "I'm ready when you are. It will be a pleasure to beat you to a pulp."

Their eyes locked.

"I'm going to give you one more chance, Cowboy," said Python, fear radiating from his eyes. Cheyenne had stepped up to meet his challenge and he knew he was outmatched. "Just think about it, we could both be rich if we become partners. Rich, Cowboy." Python's dark eyes glittered with greed as he thought of the riches awaiting them.

"No dice, Python. I wouldn't be your partner for all the riches in the world. These tusks are going to flood the market, so killing elephants for their tusks will be a forgotten business. It's a question of supply and demand."

Python looked puzzled. To him, economics was a foreign language. "Supply and demand? I ain't gotta clue what you're talking about, Cowboy. But listen up, if you don't come on board with me, I'm gonna have to kill you."

Cheyenne continued on as if Python had never spoken. "And all the money from the sale of the tusks will go to the "Saving the Elephants" foundation."

Python exploded. "Saving the elephants! What the hell are you talking about. I ain't saving no elephants. That goddamn Monsoon killed my little buddy Ego – crushed him and stamped on him, and practically tore him apart." His eyes welled with tears as he pictured Ego's bloody, battered body. "I ain't interested in saving no elephants – I wanna avenge my little buddy and kill the whole damn lot of them."

"You'll have to kill me first," said Cheyenne.

"That's what I intend to do," growled Python as he started circling Cheyenne.

They looked like two professional wrestlers getting ready for battle. Cheyenne knew he was in the fight of his life. He hadn't forgotten how Python had come by his name; he had killed a man by crushing him to death. And he would try to do the same to him.

Let's hope and pray that my military training will come in handy. If not, I'm a dead man.

Chapter Eighty-Two

The two men continued circling each other, neither one ready to make a move.

"I'm taking you in for the slaughter of all those natives," said Cheyenne, "and for the murder of my friend Willie."

"You sonofabitch," yelled Python as he charged forward. "You ain't taking me anywhere. I'm taking you straight to hell." Grabbing Cheyenne's shoulders, Python tried to clinch him in his famous bear hug, but Cheyenne was ready for him. Placing his leg behind Python's leg, he pushed him to the ground.

"Not bad, Cowboy, not bad," said Python as he scrambled to his feet. "You took me by surprise, that's all. I'll get you next time. You're a dead man."

"Promises, promises," said Cheyenne as the two men circled each other again.

Although Cheyenne could not match Python in bone-crushing strength, his powerful legs, and his speed gave him an edge. He was much quicker on this feet than the heavier Python.

Python suddenly lunged forward and delivered a crushing blow to Cheyenne's head, knocking him into some of the tusks. Python lunged again, but the scattered tusks prevented him from getting closer. It was as if they had formed a protective barrier around Cheyenne.

"Goddamn tusks," yelled Python as the sharpened end of a stray tusk pierced his leg. Howling in pain, he grabbed the offending tusk and flung it to the far corner of the cave.

Cheyenne grinned. "It appears that the tusks hate you just as much as I do."

"Why, you sonofabitch," snarled Python, his face like thunder. "I'm gonna squeeze the life out of you and then impale you on one of your goddamn precious tusks."

He charged forward again, but Cheyenne was ready and waiting. His fist connected with Python's jaw and sent him sprawling to the ground again. Python rubbed his bruised chin. "You are dead now. Dead! Dead! Dead!" he screamed.

As he struggled to his feet, Cheyenne pounced and hit him hard in the gut. Python gasped and doubled over in pain. Cheyenne had knocked the wind out of him, and he could barely speak.

"Why…why, you…" he panted, trying to catch his breath.

"Not such a hot shot now, are you, Python? How does it feel to be on the receiving end for a change?"

"I'm gonna squeeze you like a lemon and then tear you limb from limb," gasped Python. "No one hits Python and then lives to see another day. I'm sending you to hell right…"

But before he could finish, Cheyenne delivered another stinging blow to Python's stomach, knocking him backwards. Python hit the dirt again, clutching his middle in agony. His screams echoed off the cave walls and reverberated through the darkened chambers.

"Got you again, Python," teased Cheyenne, dancing around him like a trained boxer.

"You just got lucky," said Python, gasping for air.

Cheyenne could have gone in for the kill, but instead he hung back, content to taunt his enemy. He was enjoying watching Python squirm. But Python wasn't finished yet. Sensing a lull in Cheyenne's concentration, he sprang forward and enveloped Cheyenne in a viselike bear hug.

"Gotcha!" yelled Python triumphantly.

Caught off guard, Cheyenne could feel Python's powerful arms crushing his chest and ribs, and cutting off his air supply. He felt lightheaded from lack of oxygen. *Is this how it's going to end? Crushed to death just as Python predicted.* Snap! One of his ribs cracked, and then another.

"I'm gonna crack every single rib in your body," cried Python as he squeezed tighter.

I've got to do something before I black out. I can't move, he's too strong for me. Think, Cheyenne, think, otherwise you're a dead man.

Struggling and squirming in Python's grasp, Cheyenne felt himself slipping away into oblivion. *This is the end. I can't hold on much longer. Forgive me, Ebony... Forgive me, Willie, I'm going, going... Forgive me, my old friends Geigy and Winston... I'm slipping away...Forgive me, elephants...Please forgive me...*

Stars danced before his eyes, Python's face became a blur, and he could hear his father's voice calling from beyond. *Don't give up, son. Remember your promise to me. Don't forget the elephants. Don't give up... Save the elephants... Save the elephants...* And as if by magic, he suddenly remembered an old trick from his Marine days. *It's now or never.*

Drawing on his last ounce of strength, he slipped his hand under Python's chin and then pressed down hard on Python's windpipe, cutting off his air supply. The tighter Python squeezed, the more pressure Cheyenne exerted on his windpipe, essentially choking him. Python released his grasp and stumbled backwards, gasping for air.

"Why, you...!" choked Python, holding his throat.

Dazed and disoriented from lack of oxygen, Cheyenne struggled to stay on his feet. He had three cracked ribs and his entire body ached. But he was free from Python's deadly embrace. He backed away from Python's reach, and once again the two enemies faced each other, eyes locked.

"I'm gonna grab you again, Cowboy, and after I've crushed every bone in your body, I'm gonna start on your little sweetheart Ebony."

Cheyenne bristled. "You leave Ebony alone," he shouted, shaking his fist angrily.

Python laughed. "Yeah, I thought that would get your attention. Do you know what I'm going to do to her," he said, pulling a knife from his boot and running his finger along the razor sharp edge. "Now look here what I have?"

Cheyenne stared at the knife and shook his head in disgust. "I should have known not to trust you. I might have known you'd have a weapon hidden somewhere."

Python continued to stroke the knife lovingly. And then, without warning, he suddenly charged at Cheyenne. "You're gonna die, Cowboy," he shouted, brandishing the knife above his head. "And you're going straight to hell."

"The only person going to hell is you, Python, and the devil's going to welcome you with open arms. You're gonna be burning in hell for ever more." And raising his arms to protect himself, he stepped to the side.

Die!" screamed Python as he lunged forward and slashed a deep cut in Cheyenne's arm.

"Agh!" cried Cheyenne as he grabbed his arm, and tried to fend off Python's deadly onslaught.

Python threw his head back and let out a roar. "Just look at all that blood. What a beautiful sight. And there's gonna be a whole lot more when I'm finished with you," he chortled. "I'm gonna finish you off right now. Hell is waiting for ya." And with another deafening roar, he charged at his prey.

This time Cheyenne was ready for him. Sidestepping to the right, he landed a swift blow to Python's head, knocking him to the ground. "Sonofabitch!" screamed Python, spitting out blood and debris. Before he could scramble to his feet, Cheyenne kicked the knife from his hand and tossed it into the sea of tusks. "Goddamn you, Cowboy."

"Now we're even again, Python, you shameless bastard. Let's finish it here and now."

"Damn right," cried Python staggering to his feet. "Make no mistake, this time I'm gonna crush you like an eggshell."

Thundering toward Cheyenne like a 300-lb linebacker, he let out a bloodcurdling scream, his dark eyes glittering with hatred. As he drew level with his arch enemy, Cheyenne suddenly dropped to the ground, thrust his powerful legs up into Python's chest, and flung him high in the air and into the sea of tusks. Python let out another bloodcurdling scream, but this time it was a scream of agony.

"What the hell?" cried Cheyenne, turning to look over his shoulder.

The elephants had got their revenge. Python lay impaled on a single tusk. The tusks which were meant to bring him wealth and riches had brought him death. The sharp edged tusk now stained red with blood protruded from Python's chest. Cheyenne stared at the grisly scene in disbelief. Python struggled to speak, and with his last dying breath, he uttered one word: *Monsoon.*

"No, Python," whispered Cheyenne. "The elephants have spoken. You tried to take their tusks, and now they have taken your life. The word is: *Karma.*"

Chapter Eighty-Three

"You are one lucky guy," muttered Cheyenne as he tore his shirt and fashioned a tourniquet for his wounded arm, strapping it tightly to stanch the bleeding. The cut was deep and he had lost a lot of blood, but he was alive. "Unlike you, Python," he said, looking over at the impaled body sprawled across the tusks. "The elephants got their sweet revenge and you're burning in hell right now." He turned and looked around the cave. "I should just leave you here to rot – it's a fitting resting place – Python and the tusks, together for eternity. But I guess I have to bury you somewhere. But where?"

Grabbing Python by the feet, he dragged his heavy body to side of the cave and prized off the bloody tusk. "You got what you deserved, Python. It was a fitting end," he said, chuckling at his joke. "A fitting end, excuse the pun. There's no escaping karma."

After burying the body in a sheltered spot by the cave, he placed Python's AK-47 on top of the grave. "I don't know why I'm giving you a decent burial, Python. God knows, you don't deserve it. And you certainly don't need this gun. I should have just let you rot, but it's not my way. No cross for you, though, it would be an insult to God. You're the devil's child."

That night, Cheyenne dreamt of elephants – dozens and dozens of elephants. Dancing elephants, baby elephants, big bull elephants, pink elephants, and prancing elephants. Elephants, elephants everywhere.

"I guess they were celebrating the demise of Python," he said as he woke up. "Dancing elephants - now that's what I call a nice dream." Rubbing the sleep from his eyes, he reached for his backpack and strapped on his guns. "And now it's time for me to hit the road."

Ebony paced up and down as she guarded the path leading to the cave. Cheyenne had been gone a long time, and her nerves were at breaking point. The more time that passed, the more she feared the worst. A sudden chill ran through her body and she shivered in the hot African sun. "Oh, my God, I hope that's not an omen – I feel as if somebody just stepped on my grave. Or God forbid, Cheyenne's grave." She shuddered again. "Who will come down that path? Will it be my beloved cowboy, or will it be that monster, Python?" She put her hands together and prayed a silent prayer. *Please God, let it be my cowboy.*

Two more hours and still no sign of anyone. And then she heard it, the sound of breaking twigs, and muffled footsteps thudding down the pathway. Raising her gun, she took careful aim. "Who's that? Show yourself!" she cried, struggling to control her shaking hands. "I hope I don't have to kill anybody." She squinted her eyes against the sun's glare and glimpsed a shadowy figure hurrying along the path. "Cheyenne, is that you?"

No response. Her finger tightened on the trigger and she took careful aim. *If that's you Python, you bastard, I'm ready for you. And I'm gonna blast you to kingdom come.* She called out again. "Cheyenne, is that you?"

And then she saw that old familiar cowboy hat. Her beloved Cheyenne had come back to her - battered, bruised, and bloody, but *Alive!* "Cowboy! Cowboy!" she shrieked. "You're alive!"

Dropping the rifle, she ran to him and grabbed him around the waist, pulling him close and planting wet kisses on his face.

"Okay, okay," he said, laughing. "You're gonna smother me with your kisses."

"I thought you were dead," she said, squeezing him tighter. "Thank God, you came back to me."

Cheyenne flinched. "Ouch, watch my ribs. Python snapped a few of them when he tried to crush the life out of me?"

"Oh, I'm sorry," she said, tenderly massaging his chest. "What happened? Where's Python?"

"He's dead."

"Dead?"

"Yes, the elephants killed him."

Ebony looked puzzled. "What do you mean, the elephants killed him? What elephants?"

Cheyenne sat her down and related the entire story. "It's like the elephants got their revenge," he said. "Karma."

"Yes," said Ebony, nodding her head. "Karma. What goes around comes around."

"Yep, Python took their tusks, so the tusks took his life. He met his end impaled on a single ivory tusk. Sweet revenge."

"Sweet indeed," agreed Ebony. "Now let's get back to the camp, I want to take a look at that cut on your arm. It looks nasty."

"That's my girl," said Cheyenne. "I'm all yours."

"Promises, promises," said Ebony, winking. "Come on, let's get going."

They walked back to camp arm-in-arm.

"Cheyenne, you're alive," cried Geigy, limping over to welcome him.

"What happened, old chap?" said Winston, looking at Cheyenne's battered body.

That night, Cheyenne told them the whole story. The friends sat transfixed, hanging on to his every word. "I'm very lucky to be alive," said Cheyenne, poking the dying embers of their campfire. "I believe the elephants were watching over me."

"Yes, the elephants and the tusks," said Geigy, laughing.

"Here's to the elephants and the tusks," said Winston, raising his water flask.

"I'll drink to that," said Geigy, grabbing his whiskey bottle.

"To the elephants and the tusks," they all said in unison.

Early the next morning the phone rang jarring them all awake. Yes," said Ebony drowsily, putting the phone to her ear. "Who is this?" She was still half-asleep.

Jocko's voice boomed at the other end. "It's Jocko, Ebony. Is Cheyenne there?"

Ebony nudged Cheyenne. "It's Jocko," she said, passing him the phone.

"Hello, Jocko, what's up," said Cheyenne, rubbing the sleep from his eyes.

"Monsoon is still attacking villages, but he seems to be moving back this way," replied Jocko. "I would like you to go back to the Ji-Hi village and stay in that area."

"You got it," said Cheyenne. "Maybe we'll get lucky and find Monsoon."

"He attacked a bar in Uganda – killed several people, and destroyed the place. He's on a rampage."

"He's one angry elephant," said Cheyenne.

"I'd like you to get back to that area right away," said Jocko. "Could you move out now?"

"Will do. But I have some other news for you – Python is dead."

Jocko could hardly believe his ears. "Python is dead? You mean we can take him off Africa's Most Wanted list?"

"Yep, he's dead as a doornail." Cheyenne briefly told him what had happened.

"Good work, Cheyenne. Perhaps I'll run into you soon. Over and out."

"We have to head back to the Ji-Hi village," said Cheyenne, turning to the others. "Jocko thinks that Monsoon might be in that area."

After a quick breakfast of fruit and dried meat, they loaded up the two vehicles, and hit the road. The sun's relentless heat beat down on their weathered faces and after a few minutes, they were bathed in sweat. It was going to be a long, exhausting journey.

Around midday, Ebony pulled over the Rover to the side of the road. Cheyenne followed suit behind her. "What's going on?" he shouted.

"I see a jeep in front of us, parked at the side of the road," she said. "I just want to check it out."

"Okay," said Cheyenne, "stay put. I'll take a look through the binoculars." He turned to Geigy. "Hand me the binoculars. Let's see what they're doing." He raised the binoculars to his eyes and scanned the jeep.

"What do you see?" asked Ebony.

"Well, I'll be damned, it's Dr. Gift and his daughter Tara, and it looks as if they're fixing a flat tire. Let's go and lend a hand."

Dr. Gift and Tara looked up in surprise as the four friends pulled up alongside them.

"Need a hand there, doctor?" called Cheyenne, jumping out of the jeep.

"My, my, my, this is a surprise," said Dr. Gift, wiping the sweat from his brow. "We never expected to bump into you."

"Likewise," said Cheyenne.

"We just had a flat tire, but it's all fixed now, thank you," said the doctor.

"We're headed to the Ji-Hi village," said Tara with a shy smile.

"Well, what a coincidence," replied Cheyenne, "that exactly where we are headed."

Geigy limped over and patted Dr. Gift on the shoulder. "Hey, Doc, great to see you," he said. "You don't happen to have an extra bottle of whiskey with you by any chance."

Dr. Gift smiled. "Why, Geigy, I thought you'd never ask," he said as he reached into the back of the jeep and pulled out a full bottle of Johnny Walker.

Geigy beamed. "Why, Doc, you're a scholar and a gentleman. I think this calls for a drink, don't you? Let's see how it tastes."

Dr. Gift passed him the bottle. "Still the same old Geigy," he said with a grin. "Let's all have a drink – I can assure you it was a very good year when this was bottled."

"I'll drink to that," said Geigy.

Catching up on all the news, the friends passed the bottle back and forth, until Dr. Gift finally called a halt to their reminiscing. "Well, it's time to get back on the road," he said. "We need to reach the Ji-Hi village before nightfall."

"We're right behind you, Doc," said Cheyenne, jumping into the jeep.

Dusk was falling as they entered the village. Brightly dressed native women were huddled around blazing fires, busy preparing the communal evening meal.

Geigy nudged Cheyenne and winked. "I hope my woman hasn't gotten married," he said as he took a long slug from the whiskey bottle.

"Don't worry, Geigy, there are plenty of women in the village. By my reckoning, the women seem to outnumber the men," he said, looking around.

A steady drumbeat heralded their arrival as the smiling villagers gathered around to greet them. Ho Goo waddled towards them, a huge grin plastered on his florid round face. Arms outstretched, he greeted them warmly. "Welcome, welcome, my dear friends," he said, hugging each of them in turn. "You all must be tired from your long journey. Come, come, follow me, and I will show you where you are staying, and then we will eat, yes?"

"Thank you, Chief," said Cheyenne, shaking Ho Goo's hand. "It's good to be back here."

"You are always welcome here, my friend. We consider you all chosen members of our tribe," he said as the crowd of villagers opened up to let them through. "But tell me, where is my good friend Willie? I don't see him."

Cheyenne shook his head sadly as tears pricked at his eyes. "I'm sorry to say that Willie was killed by Python. He shot him in the back."

Ho Goo sighed deeply and thumped his head with his fist. "Oh, no! I had a feeling he was lying about those two snipers. I should have killed him that day, but I took him on his honor." He sighed again and hung his head in shame. "I am deeply sorry, my good friend, if I had followed my instincts, Willie would still be alive today."

"Don't beat yourself up, Chief," said Cheyenne, "that wily Python had us all fooled. Anyway, he and his cronies are all dead now, so I hope Africa will get a little more peace." He raised his eyes heavenward. "And Willie's death has been avenged – may he rest in peace."

"Yes," said Ho Goo softly. "May Willie rest in peace, and may their evil spirits burn in hell."

Cheyenne smiled. "Oh, they're burning all right – that's one helluva bonfire!"

Chapter Eighty-Four

Later that night, snuggled up in their cozy hut, Ebony was feeling amorous. "Make love to me," she whispered huskily as she stroked his thick cock. "I want to feel you inside me."

Cheyenne didn't need to be asked twice. His cock hardened. He was ready. But just as he was about mount her, there was a gentle tap on the door. The lovers sprang apart.

"Who is it?" asked Ebony, annoyed that the spell had been broken.

A young girl's voice rang out. "I have your food, and it's nice and hot," she said.

"Stay hard," whispered Ebony, running her tongue up and down his throbbing shaft. "I'll be right back."

Opening the door, she took the food from the young native girl and was about to close the door when she heard a woman scream. "What was that?" she cried as she and Cheyenne hurriedly dressed and rushed outside. Winston was standing outside his hut, a worried look on his face.

"What happened, Winston?" asked Cheyenne. "Is Geigy okay?"

"Yes, he's fine. It's Willie's woman, Taminicka," he said, shaking his head sadly. "I was having something to eat with Simone, remember her, when Taminicka knocked on the door, looking for Willie." He paused and sighed deeply. "I had to tell her that Willie was dead. I'm sorry for upsetting everyone, but what else could I do – I had to tell her."

Cheyenne patted his shoulder. "You had no other choice, Winston, you just told her the truth," he said softly. And they stood in silence for several moments remembering their fallen friend.

Early the next morning, Cheyenne poked his head outside the hut to see torrents of rain pelting the dusty terrain. Eyes widening in surprise, he turned to Ebony who was slowly awaking from a deep, satisfying sleep. "Wow, honey, it's raining cats and dogs out there," he said. "Don't think I've seen rain since I've been here."

"Rain!" exclaimed Ebony, sitting up straight. "That is unusual – it hardly ever rains here."

"Yes, it's lashing down and it looks as if it's going to rain all day." He peered outside again, his eyes scanning the entire village. "And there's not a soul around."

"Well, this might be a good thing. I find the rain to be very romantic and relaxing," she purred.

"Oh, yeah," he said, noticing the huskiness in her voice.

"Yes, come and lay beside me," she beckoned. "Let's finish what we started last night."

In a flash he was by her side, rain forgotten. All he heard for the next hour were Ebony's deep moans and his own as they writhed in ecstasy together. *Let it rain all day and night,* he thought to himself. *There's no place I'd rather be.*

After falling asleep in each other's arms, they woke up several hours later bathed in sunshine. The torrential rain had given way to soft rays of sunshine which streamed through the hut's tiny window. "That sun feels good," said Ebony, rubbing her eyes. "Let's bathe and then have something to eat. I'm famished after that strenuous workout." She batted her eyelids at Cheyenne and nudged him playfully.

"Me, too," said Cheyenne, grinning from ear to ear. "I could eat a horse."

"Then we'll go for a long walk."

"Sounds good to me," said Cheyenne as he suddenly broke into song. Ebony smiled at him.

"It's good to see you smiling, Ebony," said Cheyenne, pulling her close. "I've put you through a lot of very dangerous times. You could have left at any time and gone back to Gabon."

"Do you think that I could ever leave you, Cowboy?" she said, hugging him tightly. "The sea would have to freeze over first or the desert empty of sand."

Tilting her chin upwards, Cheyenne looked deeply into her liquid ebony eyes. "Ebony, am I truly your cowboy?"

"Yes, you're my crazy cowboy, and I love you with all my heart," she said, picking up a wood chip from the floor and hitting him on the legs.

Cheyenne jumped back. "So, that's the way it's going to be," he laughed as he picked up a wood chip to throw back at her. But Ebony was already out of the door.

"Too late," she giggled as she ran across the village, her long dark hair flying in the wind. "Catch me if you can!"

As Cheyenne caught up with her, Ebony grabbed him by the hand and they twirled around in a circle, eyes locked. They were like a couple of teenagers, laughing and giggling, head-over-heels in love. And at this moment in time, it was as if they were the only two people in the world.

"Okay, my crazy, crazy cowboy, let's go and see Goo, we haven't seen him yet."

"Good idea. I expect he'll be with Kia somewhere." Cheyenne patted his sides. "But wait a minute, I forgot to put my guns on. I feel naked without them."

Ebony eyed him saucily. "If you were naked, my love, we wouldn't be standing here chatting."

"You're a wicked wench," he said, laughing. "Now I'm starting to feel horny again."

"Save it for later," she said huskily. "I'm not going anywhere. Just teasing you, that's all." She stroked his thigh, sending a tingling thrill throughout his entire body. "Now, let's go find Goo, and don't worry about your guns, we are very safe here."

"I guess you're right," said Cheyenne, his thigh still on fire after her caressing touch. He looked around at all the villagers basking in the warm sunshine. "The village has come to life again after all the rain."

Arms linked, they walked out of the village, keeping their eyes peeled for Goo. The damp earth felt soft and spongy beneath their feet, and the burgeoning foliage, still dripping from its cleansing bath, looked greener and lusher than ever. A sweet smell of freshness pervaded the air. Two lovers arm in arm, soaking in the sights and smells of this brand new day. They, too, felt renewed, reborn.

Chapter Eighty-Five

"Look, there's Goo, riding on Kia's back," cried Ebony as they approached a wide open field.

"Goo! Goo! it's Cheyenne and Ebony," she shouted, waving her arms.

On hearing his name, Goo turned and looked over his shoulder. His face broke into a broad smile when he saw the two lovers. "Cheyenne, Ebony," he shouted, waving wildly. "Welcome back – it's so good to see you. What a wonderful surprise." He guided Kia toward them. "Come and see some of the new tricks that I've been teaching Kia," he said proudly as he patted Kia's back. "We've been working very hard since you've been gone."

"Go ahead, Goo," said Cheyenne, "we'd love to see them, wouldn't we, Ebony?"

Ebony nodded. "Absolutely."

On Goo's command, Kia knelt down and let the young boy slip off his back. Cheyenne and Ebony looked on in amazement.

"Look what Goo is doing with that stick," said Ebony. "All he has to do is gently touch Kia with it and Kia will raise his leg."

"Now he's raising all four legs," said Cheyenne as Goo touched each of the elephant's legs with the stick.

"I don't believe it," said Ebony. "Did you see that, Cheyenne? Goo just touched Kia on the head and he knelt down to let Goo climb back on his back."

"I know, I know, I'm watching," said Cheyenne.

"Kia loves Goo so much; you can tell by the way he watches Goo's every move."

"Yes, I think the feeling is mutual. Goo has worked wonders with Kia," said Cheyenne as he pointed to a nearby tree. "Let's sit down in that shady spot for a while and watch the show."

"Good idea," said Ebony, taking his arm.

A few moments later, Ho Goo waddled over and plunked himself down beside them.

"I see you are watching my son. He and Kia are inseparable these days."

"We've been watching all the new tricks. It's truly amazing," said Cheyenne.

"Yes, yes, I am very proud of my son," said Ho Goo. "He treats all animals with kindness and respect. But Kia is his favorite." He paused and watched as elephant and boy frolicked in the sunshine. "Talking of elephants, I saw a tusk in the back of your jeep. Where did it come from?"

"That tusk was carried down the mountain by Python," said Cheyenne. "I guess he was trying to put his claim in, that he was the rightful owner."

"Hmm, I see," said Ho Goo.

"Ho Goo, let me assure you, all those tusks in the cave will be sold to protect all the elephants."

"What do you mean, my friend?" asked Ho Goo.

"This is how it will work: we will sell the tusks a little cheaper and flood the market."

Ho Goo shook his head. "I am still not following you. How will this help the elephants?"

"If we flood the market with tusks, there will be a surplus and it will not pay for the poachers to kill elephants just for their tusks." Ho Goo still looked perplexed. "Simply put, if there's a surplus, demand will drop and the poachers will be out of business," said Cheyenne.

The penny had finally dropped. Patting his fat belly, Ho Goo beamed brightly.

"Oh, yes! I see what you mean," chuckled Ho Goo. "That is a great plan. Just let me know when you get this set up, and my people will help you to bring the tusks down the mountain."

"Thank you, Ho Goo," said Cheyenne, reaching over to shake his hand. "Your help is much appreciated."

"As Dr. Gift is fond of saying, 'many hands make light work,' and we have many hands to offer," he said with a smile. "And now, I have to go and check on my cattle," he added, scrambling to his feet, "there will be many births today."

"Thank you again, Chief," said Cheyenne as he and Ebony watched the big man trundle off into the distance.

Cheyenne turned to Ebony and breathed a sigh of relief. "I feel so much better knowing that we will be able to get the tusks down the mountain. I had no idea how we were going to do that."

"Well, the chief is our savior," said Ebony. "With the entire village helping, we'll have the tusks down in no time." She leaned over to kiss him when a sudden sharp noise jolted them apart.

"What the hell was that?" said Cheyenne.

"Sounds like trees snapping and brush breaking. Maybe one of the cattle has broken away from the herd."

Off in the distance, Kia trumpeted loudly and turned abruptly towards the source of the sound. The sudden turn took Goo by surprise. Losing his grip, he plummeted to the ground, hitting his head hard against the ground.

Ebony screamed in terror. "Look, Cheyenne! Look! it's Monsoon!"

The couple looked on in horror as they watched Monsoon charging towards Kia and Goo.

"Oh, no, he's headed straight toward them. We've got to do something, and quick!"

Chapter Eighty-Six

Goo lay motionless in the dirt as the large elephant thundered towards them, his dark eyes filled with hatred, flecks of foam and spit spewing from his mouth. With each thunderous step, he raised his massive trunk and bellowed loudly, as if to say, 'I'm coming for you! I'm coming!'

"We have to get to Goo or Monsoon will crush him," said Cheyenne.

Kia stood up on his back legs and let out a terrifying bellow, sending shivers down Cheyenne's spine. Ebony cowered behind him, covering her ears to deaden the bone-chilling bellow.

Monsoon charged across the open field, closing the distance with every thud of his massive legs. Placing himself protectively between his little friend and the oncoming onslaught, Kia let out another ear-shattering bellow, and charged toward his foe.

The two elephants slammed into each other mid-field. Knocked sideways by the force of the head-on collision, Kia managed to stay on his feet. Although slowed by the crushing hit, Monsoon continued to charge forward, making a beeline for Goo. Cheyenne and Ebony stood paralyzed as they watched the giant elephant stampeding closer…and closer…and closer!

"Oh, my God, I have to get to Goo before Monsoon kills him" cried Cheyenne, shaking off his temporary paralysis and sprinting across the field towards Goo.

From the corner of his eye, Monsoon spotted the dark figure of Cheyenne darting towards Goo. Monsoon's quarry. Stopping mid-stride, he let out a blood-curdling bellow and now focused his attention on another quarry: *Cheyenne.*

But he had reckoned without Kia, who slammed into Monsoon's rear, knocking the huge elephant off balance, and giving Cheyenne the chance to jump out of harm's way. The two elephants locked tusks and rocked back and forth. Two bulls battling for dominance against the vivid backcloth of the vast African plain. Their huge bodies silhouetted in the waning rays of the setting sun.

For Cheyenne, it was an awesome but horrifying sight. He stood transfixed, watching the two animals circle each other, both bleeding from deep wounds inflicted by the other's razor-sharp tusks. He had come to Africa to save the elephants – to save all elephants – and here were two of his beloved creatures locked in a bloody battle to the death. Only one would emerge victorious. Who would it be?

Choking back a deep sigh, Cheyenne shook off his stupor and sprang into action.

"Monsoon has forgotten all about Goo, forgotten all about me. Now is my chance to save Goo."

With one eye on the battling elephants, Cheyenne raced across the field, reaching Goo's side in record time. From a safe distance, Ebony yelled for him to be careful. Semi-conscious and bleeding from his forehead, the injured boy lay moaning in the dirt. "Kia! Kia!" he mouthed deliriously. "Kia! Kia!"

Cheyenne knelt down and gently wiped the boy's bloody brow. The gash was deep but not deadly. "Easy, Goo, easy," he whispered. "It's gonna be okay. You took a nasty fall from Kia's back, but he protected you."

"Kia! Kia!" moaned Goo. "Where is Kia? I want Kia. Where is he?" In his delirium, Goo struggled to raise his head and look for his beloved Kia.

But he had reckoned without Kia, who slammed into Monsoon's rear, knocking the huge elephant off balance, and giving Cheyenne the chance to jump out of harm's way. The two elephants locked tusks and rocked back and forth. Two bulls battling for dominance against the vivid backcloth of the vast African plain. Their huge bodies silhouetted in the waning rays of the setting sun.

For Cheyenne, it was an awesome but horrifying sight. He stood transfixed, watching the two animals circle each other, both bleeding from deep wounds inflicted by the other's razor-sharp tusks. He had come to Africa to save the elephants – to save all elephants – and here were two of his beloved creatures locked in a bloody battle to the death. Only one would emerge victorious. Who would it be?

Choking back a deep sigh, Cheyenne shook off his stupor and sprang into action.

"Monsoon has forgotten all about Goo, forgotten all about me. Now is my chance to save Goo."

With one eye on the battling elephants, Cheyenne raced across the field, reaching Goo's side in record time. From a safe distance, Ebony yelled for him to be careful. Semi-conscious and bleeding from his forehead, the injured boy lay moaning in the dirt. "Kia! Kia!" he mouthed deliriously. "Kia! Kia!"

Cheyenne knelt down and gently wiped the boy's bloody brow. The gash was deep but not deadly. "Easy, Goo, easy," he whispered. "It's gonna be okay. You took a nasty fall from Kia's back, but he protected you."

"Kia! Kia!" moaned Goo. "Where is Kia? I want Kia. Where is he?" In his delirium, Goo struggled to raise his head and look for his beloved Kia.

"Kia's fine," soothed Cheyenne, shielding the boy from the sight of the two elephants still locked in their deadly battle. "He's off getting a drink of water. Now let's get you back to village so that Dr. Gift can take a look at that nasty gash."

"Kia! Kia!" was Goo's only response as he fell back against the ground.

Cheyenne gathered Goo's limp body in his arms and started for the village.

"Okay, now we have to make it past Monsoon and Kia," he whispered to himself.

The two bulls were still fighting – circling and taunting each other like two prize fighters at the main event. Cheyenne could hardly bear to look at them as he raced past to the safety of the village. "Oh, my God, they're gonna to kill each other and this time it isn't the poachers' fault."

Most of the villagers had heard the loud bellows, and were now gathered on the edge of the village watching the battling animals.

"Quickly! Quickly! Make way," cried Cheyenne as he thrust through their midst. "Get Dr. Gift – Goo has been injured."

The shocked crowd parted like the Red Sea and Cheyenne charged forward, heading for Dr. Gift's hut. Hearing all the commotion, Ho Goo emerged from his hut and looked in horror at his injured son. "What has happened to my precious son," he cried, waddling forward as fast as his fat legs would let him. Still delirious, Goo lay back in Cheyenne's arms calling Kia's name.

"Monsoon startled Kia, and Goo fell off his back. But don't worry, Chief," said Cheyenne, "I don't think it's serious. Just a mild concussion. Let's get him to Dr. Gift."

"I'll take him," said Ho Goo, cradling his son in his arms. "You stay here and make sure that no one goes near those two elephants – it's too dangerous." And turning on his heel, he waddled over to Dr. Gift's hut.

"You got it, Chief," Cheyenne called after him.

Meanwhile, the villagers were edging closer and closer to the bloody spectacle, their curiosity getting the best of them. They had never seen two elephants fighting before.

"Don't go out on the field," yelled Cheyenne, stepping in front of the surging crowd. But it was too late. No sooner had the words left his mouth than a small wiry man with a long stick slipped past him and raced towards the elephants.

"What the hell does he think he's doing?" said Cheyenne. "He's gonna get himself killed."

Cheyenne and the villagers looked on in astonishment as the small man stood in front of the mighty elephants brandishing the stick.

"What the hell," cried Cheyenne. "If he thinks he can break up the fight with that little stick he's got another think coming."

Ebony rushed over and grabbed Cheyenne's arm. "What's he doing?" she cried.

"I don't know, but it's suicide," replied Cheyenne. "Get back here!" he yelled at the man.

But his words fell on deaf ears – the little man would not be deterred from his mission. Horrified to see two elephants destroying each other, he was determined to break up the fight, whatever the cost to himself. Edging closer, he prodded the stick in Monsoon's left flank. One prod was all it took…

Chapter Eighty-Seven

Monsoon turned his giant head and locked his beady eyes on the small man. Bellowing loudly, he raised up on his back legs. The man dropped the stick and trembled with fear. He could hardly stand. Only now did he realize the danger, but it was too late.

Monsoon charged. Still shaking, the man started to run, but he could not outrun Monsoon. With one sweep of his powerful trunk, Monsoon lifted the man off his feet and sent him sprawling to the ground. Defenseless, he lay there in the dirt awaiting his fate. He knew it was only matter of time before he was crushed by the giant elephant. A collective gasp went up from the villagers.

Cheyenne rushed forward. "What are you doing?" cried Ebony, grabbing him by the arm. "It's suicide to go out there – are you crazy?"

"I can't just stand here and do nothing," said Cheyenne, shaking off her grasp. "That poor villager has just risked his life to stop those two elephants from killing each other. I may be too late, but I've got to try. I can't just stand here and watch him die." He darted forward.

"Wait, Cheyenne! Wait!" cried Ebony. "Kia is coming to the rescue. Look! Look!"

Monsoon had forgotten all about Kia. Intent on his next victim, he circled around and came in for the kill. As he turned back towards the defenseless man he opened up his left side to Kia. Instinctively, Kia charged forward and plunged his tusks deep into Monsoon's stomach.

Monsoon let out a deafening bellow and crumbled to the ground, falling over on his right side. He lay there exposed and vulnerable to the next assault.

Kia was not finished yet. Rising up on his back legs, he came down on Monsoon with all the force of his body, crushing Monsoon's lungs and ribcage. With his last ounce of strength, Monsoon struggled to fight back, but it was too late. Bellowing in agony, he took his last breath. The mighty Monsoon was dead!

The villagers gasped again, their mouths wide open in shock. Cheyenne and Ebony stood transfixed, looking in horror at the bloody scene. The mighty Monsoon was dead. Not by the hand of man, but by the crushing blows of his fellow elephant. The brave villager who had risked his life could not believe his luck. His leg was broken, but he was alive. Kia had saved his life.

"Kia! Kia!" yelled the villagers as they rushed forward and crowded around the valiant elephant. Gentle Kia had turned into a fighting machine to save two lives.

"We must get him to Dr. Gift as soon as possible," said Cheyenne as he examined Kia's bloody wounds. "He's going to need some stitches to close up these deep cuts."

He and Ebony gently stroked the big elephant whose eyes seemed to be filled with sadness.

"You did good, Kia," said Cheyenne softly. "Thanks to you, your beloved Goo is safe."

Kia nuzzled Cheyenne with his trunk as if to say, 'I did what I had to do.'

Supported by his fellow villagers, the man with the broken leg limped forward.

"I will take him to Dr. Gift," he said, reaching out and stroking Kia. "He saved my life."

As the villagers led Kia away, Cheyenne and Ebony walked over to Monsoon. A crowd had gathered round him, and some of the men were poking him with sticks to make sure he was dead.

"Leave him alone," said Cheyenne sternly. "Although Monsoon may have turned violent, it was not of his own choosing. He was a brave, fearless elephant, fighting for survival in a cruel world. In man's quest for tusks, for their precious ivory, they turned this gentle creature into a killing machine." Wiping away a stray tear, he reached down and stroked the fallen elephant. "Man and man alone is to blame for this poor animal's death. And as men, let us bury him and give him the respect he deserves."

The villagers stepped back and bowed their heads. Cheyenne and Ebony clasped hands. All was silent as they stood together honoring the mighty Monsoon.

Moments later, Winston and Geigy came running up. "What's happening, old chap?" said Winston breathlessly as he and Geigy stared in astonishment at Monsoon's lifeless body.

"Yeah, what's going on?" said Geigy. "We just saw a group of villagers leading Kia to Dr. Gift's hut, and the poor animal was all beaten and bloody. What the hell did we miss?"

Brushing away the tears, Cheyenne turned to his friends. "You just missed the battle of the century," he said simply. "That's all I have to say."

Winston and Geigy looked at Cheyenne's pained expression and knew not to ask any more. Their friend's heart was heavy. An elephant had died today.

EPILOGUE

They buried Monsoon under the shade of a huge Banyan tree. Cheyenne placed his hat on top of the grave and fastened it down with stones. "I guess they take care of their own problems, just like us humans," he said, stepping back to join his friends who were gathered around the grave. "Two lives were saved today, and for that I rejoice." He shook his head sadly and stared at Monsoon's grave. "But one life was lost. I came here to save the elephants. And an elephant died today."

Cheyenne and his friends continued in their quest to save the elephants. They could not wait for the day when the thousands of tusks would flood the market, lowering the demand for ivory, and thus slowing down the poachers' widespread slaughter of innocent elephants.

Cheyenne had honored his father's dying wish. He had come to Africa to save the elephants, and in Africa he would stay. To his dying day, he would continue in his mission to save his beloved elephants. And of all the elephants he encountered, he never forgot the mighty Monsoon.

So beware all poachers, wherever you may be! If you harm an elephant, you will pay the price. Cheyenne and his friends will be out looking for you!
